Match Made in Manhattan

Match Made in Manhattan

A NOVEL

Amanda Stauffer

Skyhorse Publishing

This is a work of fiction. Names, places, characters, and incidents are either the product of the author's imagination or are used fictitiously.

Skyhorse Publishing books may be purchased in bulk at special discounts for sales promotion, corporate gifts, fund-raising, or educational purposes. Special editions can also be created to specifications. For details, contact the Special Sales Department, Skyhorse Publishing, 307 West 36th Street, 11th Floor, New York, NY 10018 or info@skyhorsepublishing.com.

Skyhorse® and Skyhorse Publishing® are registered trademarks of Skyhorse Publishing, Inc.®, a Delaware corporation.

Visit our website at www.skyhorsepublishing.com.
Visit the author's website at amandastauffer.wordpress.com.

10 9 8 7 6 5 4 3 2

Library of Congress Cataloging-in-Publication Data is available on file.

Cover design by Erin Seaward-Hiatt

Print ISBN: 978-1-5107-2809-7
Ebook ISBN: 978-1-5107-2810-3

Printed in the United States of America

To all the men and women
puzzling through the complications of love and attraction,
trying to find their match.

Match Made

in

Manhattan

Dave

"Yes!! Of course I will!!" I squeal.

"I was hoping you would say that."

"Once we're back in the States, we have to talk details! Venue hunting, cake tasting, *dress* shopping!"

"Go, go, go. Get on your flight. I just wanted to ask before you left for vacation. Bon voyage."

"Okay. July in wine country—I love it! Love *you*! Bye!" I slide my cell phone back into my carry-on bag and skip across the gate area. "Catherine just asked me to be her maid of honor," I profess proudly.

"Oh, no way. Fun!" Dave replies.

"I bet their wedding is gonna be ahhh-mazing. They're thinking Napa this time next year. *I'm* thinking maaaybe I'll try to fly out there in the next few months? Help with some of the up-front wedding planning jazz, since she doesn't have a mom to do these things with?"

"I have extra miles you can use. You should totally take a planning trip out there."

"Yay! Oh, that wedding's going to be so fun. We'll stay at a cute bed-and-breakfast, bike through the vineyards . . ."

"Get drizzay in the mo'nin'; suit up for the par-tay; make it rain scrilla in da club." Dave, who happens to be even paler and blonder than I am, has a charming habit of awkwardly stringing together and/ or misusing rap terms. I never correct him because, why deprive myself of these daily injections of humor?

They call our row to board.

"*Et desormais, Mademoiselle Alison,*" Dave says, "*on parle seulement en français.*"

"*Mais bien sûr. On a promis.*"

"*Alors on y va.*"

"This is gonna get old real fast, huh?"

Dave smiles and nods vigorously.

As we bike through Saumur and Bourgueil, stopping and sipping at vineyard after vineyard, what began as a mild wanderlust for the French countryside swells to an enchantment with the Loire Valley. The vintners are magnanimous beyond all expectation and invite us into their homes, where we sit before fireplaces sampling their wines and noshing on local cheese with their families. In one living room with ancient oak ceiling beams, our hosts show us their framed family tree with great pride, and explain that their great-great-great-great-etc. grandparents have been bottling the same wines—from the same vines—for literally hundreds of years . . . *five hundred years* to be exact. As a parting gift they give us two free bottles to "share with [our] parents in the United States." With repeated "*merci beaucoup*"s and big smiles, we try to convey our appreciation for their hospitality and generosity.

Coincidentally, Dave and I each spent the summer of our junior year of high school doing a homestay in France. I helped my French family herd cattle and drive tractors on a farm at the foot of the Jura Mountains to the east; he helped his family pick grapes from their small vineyard in Bordeaux to the west. Needless to say, his knowledge of French wines greatly surpasses mine. Though our French is a bit rusty, the winemakers, shopkeepers, and locals don't speak English and are seemingly charmed by our valiant conversational efforts and our horrific accents.

At one of our stops we're taken to the back room, and the winemaker shows us how he bottles the wine. He proceeds to open fifteen bottles for us to taste—which makes for a very mellow afternoon. As our inebriation escalates, so too does our infatuation with the region.

Seated at a café table on the sidewalk of Sancerre, we feast on the most succulent escargots and the most delicate pastries as we watch the world go by. In the farmers' market we load my straw handbag with jar upon jar of black truffles, sold at such a bargain we can't resist filling the bag to the brim. Our promenade through the gardens at the Château de Chambord, dappled in sunlight, is so exquisite we're no longer strolling but practically skipping with glee. Finding ourselves alone in the grand, arch-filled ballroom of the Château de Chenonceau, Dave grabs my hand and pulls me into a waltz. "One day, this could be ours, babycakes," he whispers in my ear as I hum Strauss's "Blue Danube" waltz (the only waltz I know).

The next morning in Chinon over coffee, croissants, and this creamy caramel yogurt that dreams are made of, we chat with the bed-and-breakfast owner about the history of his picturesque home.

"Seventeenth-century homes," he laments. "They may be beautiful, but they are *work*." He rattles off a list of the modern updates and amenities he has crafted with his own hands. "*Je suis trop vieux. Trop vieux*," he says, mourning his old age. Making up all the beds every day, rising at dawn to bake homemade pastries, this is beginning to take its toll, he explains.

"Will you close the bed-and-breakfast?" I ask, saddened by the idea that others won't have the opportunity to experience this rustic magic.

"Oh, I listed it for sale months ago," he sighs, slowly stirring his coffee.

Dave and I exchange a look.

"If you don't mind my asking, how much did you list it for?" Dave asks politely.

"Seven hundred and fifty thousand euro."

"And you haven't had any offers?" I ask incredulously. The property sits on seven verdant acres, including groves of pear trees, farmed plots of asparagus, and a swimming pool.

"He's totally undervaluing his accommodations, right? We paid eighty euro; those rooms could *easily* go for one forty or one fifty! Also, he doesn't even have a website. We'd create a website!"

"Build up TripAdvisor reviews. Maybe take out an ad or two for Google optimization purposes . . ."

"I could tutor the SAT from our living room via FaceTime!" I suggest. "I know someone who has a bunch of clients she tutors on Face-Time. With the time difference, I'd still be able to do all the day-to-day upkeep chores: check-in, breakfast, laundry. It would definitely help supplement? . . ."

"I think if I worked for another year, or even eight months, in New York until we made the move, I could probably scrape together enough for the down payment."

"Right, but the house still needs some work. We should redo that wonky plaster in the sitting room."

"What's your master's degree good for, if not treating wonky plaster?"

I nod eagerly.

"We could take out a mortgage and then probably pay it off in . . ." Dave punches some numbers into the Excel sheet he has opened on his laptop. "Eight years. If we operate at 70 percent capacity for one third of the year. Anything we make above that is profit."

Again, I nod eagerly.

Unfortunately, tempting though these fantasies are, real life calls and we return on our scheduled flight. As we disembark at JFK Airport, our cell phones emit their telltale buzzes, beeps, and vibrations as a week's worth of emails, texts, and voice mails are downloaded.

With his ear to his phone, Dave announces, "Evan and Hannah got engaged."

With my ear to my phone, I echo the news on my end: "Jess and Phil got engaged. She wants me to be a bridesmaid."

"You're *en fuego*, baby," Dave says. "Miss Popular."

"About to become one of Rent the Runway's top clients." I smile.

As we ride our Uber through the Midtown Tunnel in relative quiet, we each click through and delete the aggregated messages that awaited our return.

* * *

"How was Par-eeeee?" Juan Pablo bellows down the scaffold stairs as I climb up to the ceiling of St. John the Divine on Monday morning. There's something glamorous about restoring the largest Gothic cathedral in the world with my own two hands. There is something decidedly *less* glamorous about having to ascend and descend 232 feet of vertical stairs a dozen times a day.

"We weren't actually *in* Paris," I heave, breathless as I complete the eighteen-story climb to his level. "But yeah, France was awesome. I would like to move there, permanently." I toss my book bag onto the scaffold and kneel down to open it.

"But who would glue all these tiles back together?" Juan Pablo asks. "The ceiling would fall down. The cathedral would crumble."

I pull out my sounding hammer. "But can't you just *picture* me: wearing a beret, cycling over the cobblestone streets on my way home from the butcher's shop, some *saucisson* wrapped in brown paper sticking out of my bicycle basket right beside my baguette?"

"I won't allow it." Juan Pablo shakes his head solemnly. "You can't leave me until the building's complete." He puts his hand to his heart. In addition to sharing the name of one of the more infamous Bachelors on television, he also shares his flirty charm and boyish good looks.

"Which is *never*," I point out. "Because Ralph Adams Cram *never* finished the transept. Or the spires. Or the tower." I fish out my clipboard and a copy of the reflected ceiling plan.

"I'm afraid you can't flee the country until it's done."

"So, like, just another hundred and twenty-five years?" I ask. "Or so?"

"Yep." He reaches over and jostles the top of my hard hat.

"Ow." I stand up. "Is today a good day for me to demonstrate how to readhere the loose Guastavino tiles?"

"As good a day as any. But if so many are failing, why don't we just tear out the ceiling and replace them all?"

"Because these are *original* Guastavino tiles," I say with exaggerated emphasis. "And, anyway, landmarks agencies, preservationists, my bosses at Restoration Associates, they all flip for Guastavino."

Juan Pablo looks dubious. "They kinda . . . look like clay tiles."

"I know. But, in fairness, the more I read about it, the cooler it becomes. It's this whole . . . *system*. You know how Roman arches relied on gravity? Guastavino's arches rely on these interlocking layers of tile." I weave my fingers together to demonstrate. "It was so innovative he actually patented it. There are these awesome black-and-white photographs from the eighteen hundreds that show his crew in the process of constructing them. They're wearing these fancy top hats, just walking on these skinny tile arches, no harness, no guardrails, no structural supports—it's that strong it could bear all their weight!"

"Geeking out again, Alison," he teases. "The ceiling's not much to look at, in my opinion, but if you think of it as—"

"—a structural innovation. Yeah! Totally!"

He pauses. "Are you done?"

I look down, bashful.

"Then it's a bit more awesome, I guess, in light of its strength and composition—"

"See? Who's 'geeking out' *now*? Anyway, can you help me get the grout injection materials up here? They're heavy. And eighteen flights down." I frown.

"Sure." He nods and radios the message to his crew. "'Grout injection.' Sounds complicated."

"Fancy word for 'glue gunning.'" I shrug and remove my safety glasses from the V of my shirt.

"You conservators, always so fancy."

"Ha." I push the neon orange lenses up the bridge of my nose.

* * *

"Soooo, how'd it make you feel?" my roommate, Nicole, asks over a hurried breakfast at our kitchen counter.

"I don't know. The trip was perfect—we traveled so well together. We always do." I squeeze more honey onto my yogurt. "It's a marathon, not a sprint, right? And it's not fair to compare our relationship to Catherine and Andrew's. Or Jess and Phil's . . . or Evan and Hannah's." I sigh.

"Of course. But you can still be frustrated. *Are* you frustrated?" Nicole asks gently.

Two years ago when our third roommate moved to Chicago, my college friend Cassie and I took to Craigslist to find a replacement. The Upper East Side real estate market being what it was, when we held an open house for our spare eighty-square-foot bedroom in a walk-up with a broken buzzer, fifty applicants showed up. After follow-up coffee dates with our favorite few, Cassie and I concluded that there were *many* women in New York City we'd like to befriend. But none more so than Nicole. Though our backgrounds are fairly divergent—I grew up on a leafy street in Scarsdale, she grew up in a double-wide trailer in South Carolina—and our tastes in food, film, and fashion are fairly disparate, it often feels like Nicole and I are of one brain. We share political views, senses of humor, energy levels, and opinions on most things social, romantic, moral, and psychological. Even if I hate it, I often wind up following her advice since, deep down, I know it's the same I would give.

"Remember several years ago, when you were waiting for Dave to say he loved you? And Cassie's ingenious suggestions . . ." Nicole mimics Cassie's always-chipper, this time instructive, tone. "Hand him a bar of soap when you're washing your face before bed and say, 'I Dove you!' Flirtingly push him on the sidewalk: 'I shove you!'"

We both giggle at the memory, particularly at how earnest Cassie was in her suggestions.

"So now I say? . . ."

"Will you carry me?" Nicole asks, brightly.

I chuckle, then groan at the thought, and walk my empty spoon and bowl to the sink.

"Anyway, I think it's like the whole 'I love you' thing. Even when it was patently obvious to the rest of us that he *did* love you, it just took him a little longer to verbalize it. In certain ways, I think he's just a slowpoke."

A mental image of a cartoon snail carrying a heart-shaped balloon comes to mind, and I smile in spite of myself.

I nod and gather my belongings, grab my keys. "I think I was a little . . . I don't know—peeved?—when those voice mails poured in. But," I sigh, "not really anymore. Isn't there some famous saying, 'we get there when we get there?'" I turn to look back at her as I open the front door to leave.

"I think that's from *The Incredibles*." She smirks.

"Well, yeah. That."

* * *

Around noon on a Monday several weeks later, covered in a fine layer of dust, sweat, and grout residue, I speed-walk into my office in Chelsea. I rush to the bathroom to rinse the gray and brown from my face and hands, pull out my ponytail and rearrange it into a messy bun, and hustle into the conference room.

I slide into an open seat next to my officemate, Deepa. "Do you know what the meeting's about?" I whisper.

She shakes her head. "I'm not sure. But Joanne said it's good news, nothing serious."

"Are you sure?" I ask, puzzled.

I love the field I work in. Not many people can say they've walked on the cornice of Grand Central Station or dangled off the side of St. Patrick's Cathedral. But I can't say I love the company. In a creative field, you'd expect the culture to be energizing (or at least, I expected that when I applied to architectural conservation firms after grad school). Yet the culture in our office is so competitive and cold, it feels enervating.

Joanne calls the meeting to order. "So often our meetings focus on areas that need improvement or on continued education. But we, as a firm, have so many accomplishments that go unsung, that I thought for once it might be nice to take a moment to acknowledge some extremely thorough, well-executed work that's been ongoing for several years now. After—how many years has it been, Margo? At St. John the Divine?"

"Four," Margo says.

"After four years of blood, sweat, and tears, we can finally celebrate the project's transition from schematic design into construction."

"One *million* tiles sounded," I write it in the air with my index finger. "Frosted on this huge cake. And Margo says *nothing*. Not a word."

"Bitches be cray," Dave says, shaking his head somberly as he opens the oven door.

"Stop! I'm being serious," I pout. "How could she say *nothing*?"

"I don't know—wouldn't it have been awkward if she undermined Joanne's toast by giving you credit?" He slides our homemade Sicilian pizza out of the oven.

"*I* would have. Isn't that the gracious thing to do? The *right* thing to do?" I fume. "*I* was late to the meeting because *I* was sounding the millionth tile this morning!"

"That's whack." He pulls a pizza cutter from the drawer.

"I *know*, right? A cake? When has Joanne ever done anything nice for anyone? And she calls a staff meeting to give Margo a CAKE? Never mind me coming in, *sounding hammer in hand*. . . . She even talked to me this morning, Joanne, on my cell while I was walking on top of the Guastavino vaults!"

"You got to walk on *top* of the ceiling vaults? We gotta get you a fedora; you're like the Indiana Jones of the building world, baby! Did you find hidden scrolls?"

"No, but I found a few dead pigeons."

"Did you have to carefully balance on the vaults, like on a tightrope?"

"Actually, it was pretty cool. I was in the interstices between the vaults and the roof. It was like spelunking. The slope was so steep, I actually had to sit and scoot down the vaults on my butt, like a giant slide. Getting back to the top was like rock climbing."

Dave takes two dinner plates down from the cabinet above his sink. The injustice unnerves me again. "*She's* the one who approves our timesheets. She knows *exactly* how many hours, weeks, *years* I've spent at St. John's. *Sounding* the ceiling tiles."

Dave hands me a glass of Chianti. "Babycakes, Joanne's *not* a nice person. And she's *not* your biggest fan. This isn't news." He grabs my chin and pulls me in for a consolation kiss. "I'm sorry, but you have no choice but to ignore it. Come on," he commands. "To the couch with you!"

He reaches for his Apple TV remote and relaxes into the corner seat of the brown leather upholstery. I curl up next to him and nuzzle into his shoulder. As the theme song for *The Sopranos* begins, I take a large gulp of wine, and am so very happy that it's Monday, our weekly Italian-cooking-slash-*Sopranos*-watching night.

"How many episodes do you think you have in you tonight?" he asks.

"Eleventy!"

"Three?"

"Three sounds good. I have to be on-site tomorrow at 7:00 a.m."

Basking in the warmth of the late-summer air, Nicole asks, "So Dave's *mom* came up with this recipe?"

I nod vigorously. "She made a batch during my first visit to Seattle a couple years ago. Super delicious, right?" We drink deeply from our margarita glasses, taking in the always-stunning views of the sun setting over the Empire State and Chrysler Buildings. My friend, Ashley, lives in Alphabet City with four roommates who share a private roof-deck that is bigger than my entire apartment. A grill master who crafts her own barbecue sauce and doubles as a party-planning extraordinaire, Ashley significantly ups the fun quotient of my social life. Memorial Day, July Fourth, most three-day weekends, you can count on her to host a spectacular get-together. This evening, the night before Labor Day, is no exception.

Dave circles back to us, blender pitcher in hand. "Refills?"

"Yes, *please*," Cassie trills.

Dave fills her glass to its rim, then takes my half-empty glass and fills it to the top. I look at it, frowning.

"You want me to re-salt the rim?" he asks knowingly. I nod enthusiastically and hand him back my glass. "Be right back."

"Awww, so attentive," Cassie says sweetly. "When am I going to find my lifelong bartender?"

"So what's in this anyway?" Nicole asks.

"Actually, it's *so* laughably easy, you'll probably savor them less once I tell you: one can of frozen limeade, enough tequila to fill the empty limeade can, and a can of beer. And ice."

Nicole laughs. "That's so . . . redneck."

"And so *unexpected* coming from Dave's mother," Cassie points out.

Dave's mother is a tall and beautiful, restrained and exceedingly elegant lady.

"Which is why *this* margarita," I point to Cassie's glass, "was such a great ice breaker."

"Pun intended," Nicole interrupts, and we all giggle.

"I was *so* intimidated," I explain to Nicole, "flying out to spend an entire week with his parents. Things had always been so . . . formal with her the few times I'd met her in New York. But! On the night we flew in, his parents were grilling burgers in the backyard. I don't know if it was just the tequila itself that loosened things up, or the fact that I showed interest in her mixology skills, but I asked for the recipe, and it was like an instant 'in.' She took me inside, we got the blender going together, and ever since then things have been much more . . ."

"Smooth?" Nicole completes the thought.

"Like these margaritas," Cassie jokes, and downs her refill.

* * *

"Hands down, Best. Gift. Ever." And I mean it. This red-and-yellow glass sculpture embedded in a pebble-filled rectangular base is, by far, the best gift I've ever received.

"I was hoping you'd say that. My mom helped me arrange it and she thought—"

"She helped you 'design the composition.'" I hold up finger quotes. "You know, in artist speak," I add, helpfully. With two hands, I carefully rotate the sculpture so I can marvel at it from all angles.

"Yeah. Now you have your very own Dave Chihuly piece," he says proudly.

"Dale Chihuly, you mean. His name's Dale."

"I know. But it's his glass, my design. Dave plus Chihuly. *Dave Chihuly.*"

"SO cool! Sorry I'm a little slow on the uptake right now. I'm just so bowled over by its . . . amazingness. Really." Then I cock my head. "How'd you get pieces of his glass?"

"A couple days before Christmas, I went dumpster diving behind his studio one night."

"So this is black market goods?" I ask, intrigued.

"I mean, it was in their garbage. It's not like I stole."

Glassblowing has long been a passion/hobby (a passionate hobby?) of mine. And as I've continued to rent studio space out in Brooklyn from time to time, Dave has been the lucky recipient of a small collection of brightly colored—if lopsided—glass beer steins and vases. Anyone who blows glass is, by nature, a devout Chihuly fan. His dynamic, undulating forms are so different from traditional, functional glass, they're virtually impossible not to love.

A couple summers ago, the New York Botanical Garden in the Bronx mounted a Chihuly exhibition, and Dave let me drag him there. Twice. Then we watched two documentaries on him, sought out his work in museums from Chicago to Los Angeles, and *my* Chihuly avidity became a shared one. But in my wildest dreams I couldn't have imagined I'd have a piece (or, rather, many broken pieces) of his art all to myself.

I not-so-subtly brush the festively wrapped package I brought to the edge of his dining table. "Can you open yours tomorrow?" Although I bought him exactly what he requested for Christmas—a French cuff shirt and a pair of modern silver cuff links—the Dave Chihuly is an impossible act to follow.

* * *

"I can't believe we're not ringing in the new year *together* this year!" Cassie sulks as she sits on the edge of my bed, watching me fastidiously fold and refold beach attire into my suitcase.

"You'll live." I smile.

"It just won't be the same. You do realize you're breaking a five-year streak?"

Cassie and I met as high school seniors at our college's Admitted Students Day and became fast friends. Freshman year we cochaired the campus winter formal; sophomore year we cochoreographed several pieces for our dance troupe; junior year we moved off campus into a house with five other girls; senior year we coled freshman orientation. We became good at Skyping in the three years after college when she attended law school in North Carolina and I attended architecture school in New York. Once she passed the bar, Cassie accepted a job at a big firm in New York City, took over the lease from my third roommate who was moving (even though on her lawyer's salary, Cassie could have afforded a far more posh apartment of her own), and we've lived together in domestic bliss ever since.

I wrap my wedge sandals in their dust bag and nestle them in among my dresses and bathing suits. "I know. But there will be other years." I turn to face her with an exaggerated pout. "Don't be mad at me. I'm sorry! I promise we'll spend it together next year. Dave just, I don't know. He really wanted to get away. And he had all these expiring hotel points . . ."

"Fine. Have fun." She mopes.

"Wait—*what?*" I bolt upright from my chaise longue.

Stay calm, I coach myself. *Deep breath. Deep breath.*

"I just don't . . ." Dave sighs, sips his margarita, picks up a nacho, and shrugs his shoulders. "I just don't think it's necessary right now."

"'Necessary'? 'Right now'?" I repeat his words back to him, with a little more heat than intended. "We're talking about five *months* from now. We're talking about five months from *now*, three and a half years into a *relationship*." Oops. I didn't intend to whine either.

"I know. But." He stares at the nacho platter. "Why don't we just wait until we're married? I don't think there's any reason we have to do it before we're married."

I sniff quietly, trying to clear my filling tear ducts.

It's New Year's Day, the last night of vacation, and we're having dinner on the beach. Until thirty seconds ago, we'd been planning to move in together when my lease expires in June. *Deep breath.* Until now, except for fleeting thoughts about getting engaged, usually precipitated by the engagement announcements of friends, I'd never felt in any hurry to massage the relationship in any particular direction. It's comfortable, we love each other, and I figured we'd get married someday. The logistics of how or why previously hadn't felt important, and I'd never felt the need to set a timeline, laminate it, and stick it on the fridge. (I actually have a friend whose girlfriend—now wife—did this.)

But this about-face on a move-in plan hatched nearly a year ago feels not only like an insult but also like a giant step backward. I grit my teeth to hold back tears.

Deep breath. Deep breath.

Without intending to, we spent the next week hashing out the reasons to break up and the reasons not to. Dave kept making the case that he loved me! And he loved our relationship! So we should stay together! . . . Just not *live* together. One morning I'd say I needed a night off to think; that afternoon, he'd text me asking if I wanted to grab dinner. And out of force of habit, or a naïve hope that his position would change, I'd find myself in his kitchen after work. And each night, we calmly, amicably, rationally debated the future of our relationship. My eyes would water. His voice would crack. Yet while he pled his case, I found myself tuning him out, psyching myself up to do what I knew needed to be done: *if it's not going to work after three-plus years, it's never going to work.* It was sad and draining. But in a way, that week of romantic purgatory gave me clarity, and all those interior-monologue pep talks gave me confidence: *You can do it! Life will go on.*

Now three weeks later, for the first time, at twenty-seven years old, I am a single New Yorker. When I ultimately allowed my rational side to take over, Dave's broken promises made breaking up with him a fairly cut-and-dried decision. Because there was no deception, no wondering *what if I'd done x, y, or z differently*, and really no regrets—other than having stayed in the relationship for perhaps one year too long (that is if I could have discerned that this wasn't to be The Relationship with a capital R)—there isn't much point in licking my wounds. Instead I need to pull myself together, dust myself off, and ask: What now?

* * *

I've never been on a first date. I didn't pique the interest of many boys in high school, and in college, I was fortunate enough to have my meet-cute on a freshman orientation backpacking trip, which sparked a four-year relationship with a really stellar guy. Throughout college I had a wide circle of kindhearted, intelligent, funny, and attractive guy friends; when my college relationship ended around graduation, some of them, like Dave, naturally morphed into dating prospects. But with friends, before even going on a "date," you've both (hopefully) weighed the pros and cons of dating and decided you're into it, lest you risk damaging the friendship . . . and that means it's really not a first date at all: no first impressions to be made, red flags already flying in the open, minimal high jinks, et cetera.

Until now I haven't had to worry about what kind of signal I'm sending out. I haven't debated which blouse will communicate that I'm classy but casual, nor have I obsessed over how high my heels should be or how much makeup to put on. For the last three years, I showed up at Dave's apartment after work in paint-splattered, chemical-stained jeans and company-emblazoned polos. Before Dave, my college boyfriend Scott lived so close by I sometimes walked over to his apartment in my flannel pajama pants. I've spent countless hours perched on the edge of the bathtub, chatting with Cassie and Nicole as they curled their hair, applied their smoky eyes, and primped for their dates in our tiny tiled bathroom. I suppose it's my turn now to learn how to make a smoky eye? Dave and I, Scott and I, we were pals. They knew what I looked like. And they knew what I *was* like. I didn't have to brainstorm topics of conversation or worry I might say the wrong thing.

So now, in the last third of my twenties—most people's dating prime—I've had two three-plus-year relationships, two or three mini-relationships, and not one blind date, setup, or genuine first date. And I haven't the foggiest clue as to what a typical date looks like. But of paramount importance, it's high time I figure out how to *find* people to date—assuming I want to branch out beyond the alumni population of my college. The world is big and I am small. Where do I begin?

* * *

Nicole swipes at her screen and tosses it to me. I snort with laughter at the profiles before me.

"Come on, I'm way too prudish for Tinder. Can you picture me bringing home random dudes?"

"I haven't brought home *that* many random dudes, have I?"

"Yeah, but, I think there's an expectation there that things will move faster physically than . . . my *slowpoke* pace."

"What about Hinge?"

"Assuming I don't want to date any more college classmates, I should probably cast a wider net, no?"

Nicole reads aloud from *Match.com*'s homepage: "'If you don't find someone special during your initial six-month subscription, we will give you an additional six months at no additional cost to you to continue your search.'"

My cursor hovers over the Subscribe button.

"I think you're really going to like it, Ali," Nicole coaxes.

One hundred and fifty dollars for six months, nay, a potential year of possibilities and new horizons doesn't sound like a bad deal. Right?

"*Please* let me help craft your profile?" she begs. "There is literally nothing I'd rather do with my evening."

With Nicole looking over my shoulder, I begin to type.

In My Own Words:
What can I say that distinguishes me from every other girl on this site?
Let's play a little game called "Two Truths and a Lie:"

1. *I once medaled in the women's lightweight division of the World Championship Wild Hog Catching Contest in Sabinal, TX.*
2. *I have a cameo appearance in not one, but two music videos: one for U2 and one for Bone Thugs-N-Harmony. If you squint, you can see me!*
3. *I have a pet hermit crab named Poseidon.*

My Interests:

I'm an architectural conservator, which means that I spend my days donning latex gloves and wielding scalpels and syringes, attempting to save historic buildings one paint chip at a time. When I'm not working, I like to glassblow, bake cakes, soufflés, and all manner of desserts that require a blowtorch, and/or seek out BYOB restaurants with my friends. I'll never turn down a run along the East River, a walk through Central Park, a mojito, an adventure, or chocolate-covered anything.

About My Date:

I am looking for someone who is intellectually curious, has a big heart, and can make me laugh. Bonus points if you won't protest when I try to drag you to screenings of Italian neorealist cinema or to the barbecue festival in Madison Square Park, even though I fully acknowledge that it is overcrowded and far too touristy (but still, so fun!).

I look at Nicole, who gives me a thumbs-up. "Alright," she says. "Let's publish this thing and let *Match.com* work its magic."

Ready. Set. Post.

cancerdoc10: Matt, the Hands Man

January 16 at 10:42 p.m.

Hey there,

I promise not to protest (too much) when you drag me to Italian neorealist flicks. When I'm not, you know, saving lives and all, I, too, enjoy mojitos and chocolate-covered anything.

You seem familiar. Is it possible I've seen you around the CP Reservoir or at Dorrian's Red Hand?

Matt

After receiving a dozen "winks" and a handful of emails that were alternately raunchy, riddled with egregious spelling and grammatical errors, or just too brief and cursory to give me anything to respond to, Matt's email (in conjunction with his photos, showing a tall, trim, dark-brown-haired guy with green eyes that appear to sparkle) has officially piqued my curiosity.

January 17 at 7:45 a.m.

Hi Matt!

It is possible that you've seen me around the Reservoir. If you noticed someone with a blonde ponytail and gold Asics nearly expiring as she tries to make it to the 90th Street exit, then yes! That was me. Unless you're having flashbacks to five years ago, you probably haven't seen me at Dorrian's, though.

I am deducing that you're an Upper East Sider, too? The "saving lives" part is a bit more mysterious. Are you a firefighter? EMT? Veterinarian?

Cheers,
Alison

After the exchange of a handful of articulate, cute-enough emails about how he has very little time to date but is looking for a relationship like the one his parents have, I'm walking into Uva, a wine bar, to meet Matt. I'm equal parts jittery and excited to get to know this thirty-four-year-old oncologist who, in his photos, sports a childish grin.

I have to do a double take to pick him out sitting at the bar, since he has no hair. Maybe not *no* hair, but significantly less than he has in his photos. My mind is quickly shuffling through the photos I can remember, flip-book style. Doctor's scrubs and a surgeon's cap, a Mets hat in the stands of Citi Field . . .

"Matt?"

"Hey! Nice to meet you!"

"No, no. Don't get up."

He extends a rather firm handshake. "I'm half a glass ahead of you. Don't know how into wine you are, but I can offer a few recommendations."

As I'm perusing the menu, he asks where I grew up, tells me about his apartment, asks about my job. And then:

"So what would you say is your best feature?"

I blink. Twice. "Is this an interview?" I smile, trying to pass my discomfort off as humor.

"No. I'm serious. What's your best feature?"

"What do you mean?"

"You know. Is it your . . . hair, your personality, your butt?"

I breathe in. And stumble through a few uhhhs and ummms. "I guess . . . I *have* a lot of personality? . . . I don't know. . . . Spunk?"

"What does that mean, 'you have a lot of personality?'"

"I don't know. I guess . . . I'm really chatty? I can pretty much talk to a doorknob. And . . . I think that's a not-terrible quality in a lot of situations?" I pause and quickly throw it back at him. "What about you? What's your best feature?"

"My hands," he says matter-of-factly.

Before I can follow up on his cheapskate answer, he's moving on to his next line of questioning. "So what brought you to *Match.com*?"

Friends have told me everyone talks about this on their Match dates, and I've always been mystified as to why. On a non-Match first date, you don't talk about your previous bad dates. Or good dates. . . .

Do you? It's almost as if they're searching for instant kinship or an insider's club just because you've both turned to the Internet for its matchmaking prowess. "Well, I recently got out of a three-year relationship and—"

"Whoa. That's a really long time!"

"Perhaps, but I—"

"Were you living together?"

"No. But—"

"That's, like, a *really* long time! When did you break up?"

"Last month. So then—"

"And are you ready to date yet?"

"Uh. I think so? I *hope* so? Otherwise I wouldn't be here." I shrug.

"Okay. You joined Match then . . ."

"Right. So I recently got out of a three-year relationship," I sound out slowly, waiting to see if he'll jump in again with twenty questions, "and I realized that I don't really have a mechanism for meeting new people. After college, pretty much my entire class moved to New York City, and there's still a rather wide circle of us who are really close." He nods. "It's totally wonderful; we all go out together at night, watch football together . . . but it's also inherently limiting from a dating standpoint. Everyone I've ever dated, I went to college with. And since that hasn't worked out, you know, permanently? I hoped Match would help expand my horizons, or my dating pool at least?"

"So how long have you been on Match?"

"Since last week. How about you?"

"For nine years."

NINE YEARS?! I force myself to smile faintly in encouragement and try to come up with something polite to say. How do you follow that? "Have you been on the whole time? Or did you go on and off, depending on . . . whether you met someone . . . or where your personal life, or work life stood at that time? . . ." I raise my voice at the end trying to form a legitimate question.

He shakes his head. "Yeah, I've just stayed on the whole time."

Then he cracks a smile and says, "Naaah, I'm just kidding." Except when he says he's kidding, he reaches over and puts his hand on my inner thigh. My stomach turns, and I internally panic just a little. How to subtly remove his hand from my leg? I look up, around the room, at the ceiling, all around, trying to feign thinking, hoping he'll get the hint that I'm not quite digging this whole touching thing.

"Uhh, cool." I stumble, "So . . . which part . . . are you kidding about?" I pick up the menu and lean in to get the bartender's attention so I can order. His hand is still there.

"The never-going-off part. I *have* been on for nine years. I have *also* deactivated my account every now and then." This isn't totally reassuring.

"That's when you reactivate your Tinder app, right?" I smile, joking.

"Oh, you don't need to deactivate Tinder. You just don't log on that day. Or week. . . . I take it you're not on Tinder?"

I shake my head. "I'm new to this whole meet-strangers-on-the-Internet thing, so I thought I should wade into the shallow end slowly." He doesn't respond, so I continue. "Not that I'm an expert—well, obviously—but I get the sense that the apps all move forward way faster, and I kind of *like* the idea of exchanging getting-to-know-you emails and having some lead up before you meet in person."

"Maybe. It's just not as *efficient* as Tinder . . . or Hinge or Happn."

Interesting word choice. "Have you tried all of those?"

"Yeah, I'm on all of those. Everyone is. You probably should be, too. Don't you feel like you're doing yourself a disservice by only using one?"

It's a legitimate question. "I guess I just need to take baby steps for now. For me, the Match profiles and messaging system offer, I don't know, a mini vetting process, which doesn't happen with the others? It somehow feels a little less superficial than 'swipe right on the hot people, swipe left on the . . . not-so-hot people.'"

"People text before meeting on Tinder, too."

"Yeah, but, can you get a real sense of someone's personality through a quick text? Match profiles and emails divulge a lot more. I kind of want to know the person I'm committing an evening to. . . ."

"So what are you looking for on Match?"

"We are just *full* of direct questions today, aren't we?" I joke. Except not.

"Well?"

"I guess . . . someone to have adventures with? To cook with, to travel with? To laugh with? Who can maybe be what my sister and I have dubbed the 'porch swing candidate?'"

"And that is?"

"The person you want to grow old and gray with . . . and share your porch swing with?" I shrug.

"So you're looking for 'The One?'"

"I don't know that I think there *is* only one porch swing candidate for each of us." I hedge, "I think there can be several, but timing can obviously impact candidacy. And then out of the many candidates, there becomes one. Does that make sense?"

"Not really." We both laugh. "Well, do you have 'a type'?"

"I don't know." I slowly chew over Matt's question. "My last two boyfriends were outwardly quite similar—six-foot-two, six-foot-three, blond-haired, blue-eyed rowers—though inwardly quite different. And both complemented me really well. . . . I guess I don't want to, just, tick a lot of boxes, but maybe be a bit more open-minded, assume the next guy doesn't have to fit their specific mold?"

"Okay, so, who would be your ideal date?"

I pause to formulate an answer . . . except I can't. I actually *don't know*. "I guess I want to see what's out there. What about you? What are you looking for?"

"Well, I'm thirty-four and I'd like to be married yesterday." So the Match rumors I've heard are true! But why do people think this makes for good first date conversation? "What's the worst Match date you've ever had?"

"You're my *first* Match date."

"Wait, *really?*"

"Mmmhmm. So . . . I guess this one?" I raise my eyebrows. This, though true, is a bit harsh. So I add, "But in fairness, by default it is also the *best* Match date I've ever had." Crud! Now I sound like I'm interested. So I clarify, "You know, since it's the only one I've had."

"Do you want to hear about my worst Match date?"

No. But I also don't want to be rude. "I guess . . . if you want to tell me about it? I also don't feel a need to swap battle stories if you don't want to."

"No, it's a great story!"

The bartender arrives with my glass of wine, and I thankfully have a reason to reach for my purse, thereby, at long last, setting free my thigh from his grip.

"Oh, please. Put away your wallet," he urges. "My treat. And let's cheers to your first Match date." But then he replaces his hand on my knee. "So I was at Marquee. Have you been there? That place is incredible on Wednesdays . . ." He drones on, name-dropping and regaling me with a long-winded description of his evenings filled with "you know, models and bottles." I'm half-listening, half-staring at his hand on my knee. Without saying anything, I carefully pick up his hand, move it four inches to the right, and drop it so it falls to his side. He looks down at his hand, seems unfazed, and continues, "So this woman, who's a *cop* and a single *mom*," as if both are crazy, far-fetched occupations, "is giving me a lap dance and—"

"Wait. This is a Match date?"

"Yeah, and—" Now it's me cutting him off.

"You had a Match date at Marquee on a Wednesday?"

"Well I was out with friends, we'd never met, and I texted her to come out. So anyway, she's giving me a lap dance and . . ." He cuts himself off, noticing his empty glass, "Do you want another round?"

"No!" I blurt out a little too eagerly. "Uhh, I mean, I'm cool, thanks. I've . . . gotta get up . . . this thing . . . early tomorrow." Smooth!

"Okay. Anyway, so she's giving me a lap dance at Marquee and my friend is just, he's just snapping photos on his phone and . . ."

I'm walking home from the subway when my phone vibrates.

January 19 at 10:06 p.m.

MATT: HOPE YOU WEREN'T SCARED OFF BY THE WHOLE NINE YEAR THING. THAT WAS FUN - WANNA DO IT AGAIN?

I respond with two truths and a lie.

ALISON: THANKS. I REALLY ENJOYED MEETING YOU TONIGHT, BUT I'M NOT SURE WE'RE A GOOD MATCH. HOPE IT WORKS OUT FOR YOU SOON - GOOD LUCK!

bmorecrabcake: Breakup Brendan

Hey there,

So this site tells me we're pretty compatible. In fact, it tells me you are among the top 5 women with whom I am most compatible on this site. I dig chicks who can rassle hogs, and I would like to think I'm probably smart enough to figure out how to make you laugh, too.

There are a couple things I would like to know first, though. If you were a fruit, what fruit would you be? Also, if you could peruse my photos and profile, what fruit do you think I would be? Warning: I will weigh your answers seriously, so please do not make light of these questions.

Talk soon,
Brendan

If a bit eccentric, at least he read my profile? Also, he's a whopping six-foot-six and went to a good East Coast college.

January 19 at 8:07 a.m.

Hi Brendan,

Your questions indeed carry much gravitas. After great consideration, I have come to the following conclusions:

If I were a fruit, I'd be an orange. Like me, an orange has thick skin, promotes energy, and flourishes in sunny environments. I live in what is currently a snowy and gray metropolis, as opposed to a sun-rich orchard in Florida, but I think that last quality correlates with my sunny disposition. Maybe?

Because this is a very probing question and we've never met, I don't presume to understand your character well enough to ascribe it a fruity relative. But just so you don't think I'm copping out, I am going to guess you are a stone fruit – let's say a plum? This is based on the fact that plums have a hard pit and you seem like a tough nut to crack. How'd I do?

Cheers,
Alison

January 19 at 11:03 p.m.

Hi Alison,

You're right. That was a presumptuous question on my part. It's a shame you don't know me well enough to know that I am actually a kiwi. Shall we meet face-to-face and rectify that problem?

Don't feel badly about having gotten that wrong. It was a really tough question. I should have waited to ask it until our third date.

Wednesday or Thursday night at La Lanterna di Vittorio in the West Village?

Ci sarà perfetto?

Brendan

He's already seated at a corner table, and he looks up when I walk in. I wave and walk toward him. His dimpled smile is engaging, and this date I can pick out based on his photos. A better start.

"*Allora! Dobbiamo condurre la data tutto in Italiano perché siamo in un caffè Italiano?*"

I can feel my face flushing, partly in terror because my Italian skills are so rusty, partly in terror because this level of "wit" (read: eccentricity) is a bit more than I had anticipated. "Umm." I swallow and squint at the ceiling, trying to translate in my head. "*Se vuole . . . ma . . . non preferisco farlo.*"

He looks at me blankly, pauses, and punches me on the shoulder as he starts to smile. "I have no idea what you said. But hey, look who speaks Italian! What other fancy skills do you have?"

I am bewildered, and my cheeks must be so pink right now. "But you just . . ."

He shrugs. "I just looked it up on my phone two minutes ago. I figured, you know, when in Rome . . ." He gestures to the ivy-draped ceiling and villa-like ambience. "But man, you totally kept your cool!"

I smile, take off my coat, and try to remember how to relax.

"So. Since you failed the fruit test, but you're evidently an Italian connoisseur, can you educate me on something fruit-related . . . about Italy?"

"Uhhhh . . ." I trail off, scratching the side of my neck in discomfort. But then, "Wait! I actually *do* have a story about fruit! In Italy!" I exclaim brightly, proud that I actually have something to contribute to this zany line of questioning.

"Alright, orange peel, let's hear it." He lifts his coffee mug toward mine in a gesture of cheers.

"So!" I clap my hands in spite of myself, pleased that I might not be bombing this awkward exchange after all. "One summer back in college I was working in Florence for a magazine . . . though I guess that's . . . not the point of this story." I pause to gather my thoughts. *How am I going to explain this?*

"Anyway, we didn't have Internet, and our television was an old-fashioned box, so the pickings were slim." I pause. "Have you ever seen Italian game shows?"

He shakes his head.

"Well there was this one show—I forget the title, but—they had two contestants compete over trivia questions. And there was this panel of women all dressed up as fruits. Whenever a contestant answered a certain number of questions correctly, he could choose a fruit, music would come on, and the fruit would trot out and perform a striptease." Brendan laughs audibly.

I wave my hand. "I'm not done though! The best was when you had a male and female contestant going head-to-head: Every time the man answered a question right, he'd get super stoked. He was *ready*, he knew *exactly* which fruit he was picking. He'd cry out, '*L'ananas! L'ananas!*' and this salsa-y music would come on, and the pineapple would do its striptease." I mime peeling layers off my shoulders. "And he'd be the happiest man on earth. But when the *female* contestant won, it was like she wanted to be anywhere but on that platform. She'd shake her head sullenly before saying in an exasperated tone, '*Non mi interessa . . . la banana?*' It was," I pause for effect, "nothing short of amazing."

"That. Is . . ." Brendan nods emphatically, "a *way* better story than I was expecting. Nicely done!"

"Thank you," I accept. "Now it's your turn to tell me a story. About . . . produce? Or strippers?" Remembering my date with Matt, I quickly add, "But please not strippers."

* * *

"How was the kiwi?" my college friend, Jason, asks over happy hour wings and drinks at The Liberty in Midtown. "He's not actually from New Zealand, is he?"

"Nope. It was fun."

"Is he as charming or *hil-a-rious* as his emails?" he asks, throwing a New Zealand accent on "hilarious."

"Kind of?"

"What'd you guys talk about on your date?"

"Mmm," I add another chicken bone to the slowly amassing pile. "He asked me to tell him about something fruit-related in Italy? It was a really weird question."

"You tell him about the stripper fruits?"

"Yes!" I inadvertently slam my copper mug on the table. "*How* do you remember that? Gosh, it was so long ago."

Jason shrugs. "Did you act it out? Pretend to shed your banana peel?"

"Oh no!" I bite my lip. "Am I that predictable?"

"No. Just, you know how you sometimes have a mental snapshot of someone? I have this vague recollection—"

"—Or *not* so vague recollection."

"—Of you animatedly describing that show to me when you came back from Florence. I don't know. It was kind of cute," Jason says. "You should probably consider reenacting stripper fruits on all your dates."

I ignore his comment.

Jason and I met on the rugby field freshman year when the girls' team scrimmaged the guys'. Something of a closeted brainiac, you'd never guess he has a biomedical engineering PhD under his belt. Outwardly he projects a jockish, fratty bro who is always, *always* happy. It took several years for me to warm up to him (because of the whole jockish-fratty-bro persona), and for my boyfriends—first Scott, then Dave—to warm up to him, too (same reason). But ultimately, Jason's so fun, and over-the-top considerate, that everyone winds up wanting to be around him. And when it comes to dating advice, he's probably my most valuable confidante, given that he thinks like a typical dude.

"On second thought, you should try to tone it down. Talk about getting-to-know-you things." Jason reaches for a napkin. "Don't want a repeat of the cancer doctor. Wanna order another dozen?"

* * *

Sunday afternoon a week later, Brendan and I are meeting outside the 86th Street subway stop, close to my apartment. (*A true gentleman,* Brendan had informed me over email, *calls on the lady and doth not make the lady travel to him.*) I'm reading my cell phone, trying not to appear eager or anxious or . . . solitary? When did I become so insecure about totally normal occurrences like waiting for someone on the sidewalk?

He taps me on the shoulder, and I turn and look up. He's practically a giant. "Hey!"

I crane my neck to make eye contact.

We order coffee to go, and we stroll over to, around, and through the Great Lawn in Central Park. We talk about everything and yet nothing at the same time. He describes growing up in Baltimore, and I interrupt with: "All in the game, yo. All in the game."

Brendan hesitates.

"It's a not-super-witty *Wire* reference." I clarify quickly, "Omar. You know."

"You come at the king, you best not miss," Brendan says without missing a beat.

"Omar don't scare," I respond with bravado. "Sorry, that was bad. I'm out of Omar lines!"

He laughs, and it's a real laugh, not just a polite chuckle. He makes dumb blonde jokes at my expense. We talk about our dream cities (his: Galway, Ireland; mine: Vicenza, Italy), joke about our roommates' dating dramas, and play a lot of "would you rather."

"Would you rather lose your sense of taste or your sense of touch?" he asks.

"Ooh, that's *really* hard. I guess touch? I tend to live through my stomach, so giving up the pleasures I derive from food would be sad. Would you rather be a cat or a dragonfly?"

"Dragonfly. That's easy. Would you rather have four legs or four arms?"

"Can I have both?"

We learn remarkably little about each other on the second date, but it's fun and our walk lasts nearly four hours. The wheels in his head spin really quickly, and he's definitely cute enough. We keep up with each other pace-wise conversationally, and when he makes eye contact, it seems intent and a bit sparkly . . . so there's that. I *think* we have chemistry, because otherwise how could we have talked for four hours? For the first time since Dave, I feel a glimmer of romantic possibility.

I'm on the couch watching *Orange Is the New Black* with Nicole. As she bemoans how painfully self-centered Piper can be, my phone rings, and BRENDAN flashes on the screen. "It's . . . Brendan?" I remark, surprised. "I'm . . . gonna take this." I hustle into my bedroom, closing the door behind me.

"Couldn't wait to talk to me again?" I ask. It's only been two hours since our date ended.

He chuckles. "Something like that."

Hmm.

He continues, "Before this goes any further, I thought we should talk."

Hmm again. Then silence.

A bit perplexed, I try to muster a tone of open-minded understanding. "Okay."

Silence. So I add, "You called me, right?"

Still silence, so I prod, "What do you want to talk about?"

After an intake of breath, he starts, "I think this is moving a little fast for me, and I think we want different things."

In my head, a record scratches to a halt. Am I being dumped?

He doesn't continue, so I follow up, "How so?"

"Well, I just, I just think you might be more into this relationship than I am."

"Are we *in* a relationship?" I ask.

"Well, no, but I mean, well . . . I kind of think you think we are."

"Really?" Admittedly, up until my phone just rang, I was starting to entertain the notion of dating Brendan. Not the notion that we *were* dating, but the notion that doing so could be . . . nice? But with this insinuation that I am . . . needy? More into him than he is into me? . . . that preconceived notion starts to flutter away.

"Because . . ." I continue and trail off. "Look, you're a nice guy. We had two nice cups of coffee. And maybe there was some potential for us to . . . I don't know, date? But we haven't shared a meal. We haven't even shared drinks. And we certainly haven't shared a make-out session or anything remotely resembling a 'relationship.'"

He's quiet for a beat and then explains, "Those aren't the only symbols of a relationship, Alison."

"I know, Brendan. If you're asking if I *wanted* to go on a third date with you . . . I guess . . ." I pause. "Yes. But if you're asking if I was doodling our names in hearts all over my binders or practicing monogramming our initials together in cursive? I wasn't."

He sighs, annoyed. "I guess I'm just saying things are moving too quickly for me. And I either want to slow things down, or be friends. You know, I think maybe be friends."

After some awkward attempts at politesse, we get off the phone. I walk back into the living room, puzzled.

"What did *Brendan* have to say?" Nicole asks teasingly, as if on the brink of breaking into song about us sitting in a tree. Though Nicole hasn't had a serious boyfriend since I've known her, she's had no shortage of suitors. Petite, tan, outgoing, and bubbly, Nicole is (not surprisingly) extremely successful as a medical-device sales rep. She waltzes into the offices of Manhattan's top spinal surgeons bearing homemade chocolate chip cookies, and she walks out with hefty contracts and commissions. Between the pedigreed doctors, handsome nurses, and hard-partying male sales reps she meets in hospital hallways, Nicole rarely has to work very hard to find herself a date. Accordingly, it is most exciting for her and Cassie to witness my newfound attempt at dating and all the foibles that go hand-in-hand with it.

"He broke up with me?" I say, as if it's a question. "Two coffee dates and a non-relationship later, and he dumped me?"

"*What!*" Nicole exclaims. "You have *got* to be kidding me."

"Yeah . . . no, that really happened. I think?" I shake my head, brow furrowed and yet smiling at the same time. "I think my nerves can't decide if I should laugh or cry right now. Am I that pathetic that men want to break up with me when we're not even dating?"

"*No!* That is *crazy. He* is *crazy.* Where do you *find* these people?" she says, starting to laugh.

"The Internet, remember? But . . . it gets better, right?" I ask hopefully. "Tell me it gets better," I plead.

"Ohhhh," she sympathizes. "But then I'd be lying," she says, through laughter.

"So what you're saying is: This is what I've been missing out on all these years when I kept saying I wanted to live vicariously through you and Cassie?"

"Yep."

"And this is what I have to look forward to?"

"Precisely."

Jsa82: Secret Agent Man (a.k.a. John)

January 20 at 6:51 p.m.

Hi,

Your job sounds fascinating. I grew up in an 1812 farmhouse, so I can see the allure of working (and living) in old buildings. There aren't many farmhouses in Manhattan though, so what kinds of projects do you work on? If it makes for an easier question, what are your one or two favorite projects to date?

I consider us among the luckier people I know (or hope to know soon). Not many people love their jobs like we do. Every now and then I complain about my long hours and endless travel and fantasize about retirement, but when your location, projects, and tasks change every week (and it sounds like yours must as well), it certainly keeps life exciting. I feel like I'm learning something new with each day, constantly on a treasure or scavenger hunt.

Are you an Upper East Sider, too? Your profile makes me think you are. Perhaps we're neighbors?

John

January 21 at 9:15 a.m.

Ooh. The secrecy with which you talk about your job (don't talk about your job?) is oddly intriguing, particularly given that you neglected to fill out the job section in your profile. Can we play 20 questions? OK, I'll start:

1. Do you wear a uniform (other than a business suit)?

2. Do you speak Arabic?

In terms of my work, I'd say two of the projects I'm on right now are by far the most interesting. But then again, I pretty much say that about every project I'm on when I'm on it. At any rate, one is the treatment of a 17th century antique Italian ceiling that was imported by the Vanderbilts to their mansion in the 1890s. The other is the Seventh Regiment Armory on Park Avenue – maybe you've seen it? Its relatively boring brick façade belies the crazy over-the-top interior spaces in which hand-painted wallpaper, decorative plaster-work, and Tiffany glass abound. . . . Goodness, I do sound geeky.

Your childhood home was built in 1812? That is super cool! Houses like yours are the reason I went into architecture to begin with. Was it retrofitted with modern appliances or were there log cabin-y aspects to it? So. Can I restore it? It never occurred to me to seek out potential clients through Match.com, but . . . :) Kidding. Kind of.

Cheers,
Alison

January 22 at 9:48 p.m.

Hey Alison,

The answers to your questions are "no" and "no." But mum's the word on my job. I can explain it a little better in person, but I probably shouldn't transmit information about it over the Internet or in writing. I just reread that, and I sound pretty badass. Don't get your hopes up too much.

You, however, did not answer my question about where you live. Is that information you don't want to transmit over the Internet? I'm trying to come up with a location to suggest for our first meeting. I want it to be convenient for you, except I don't know how to plan for that when you're secretive about your whereabouts. My turn for questions:

1. Do you live on the Upper East Side?
2. Do you live on E. 91st Street?

John

January 23 at 7:14 a.m.

Hi John,

International Man of Mystery, huh? I can't wait to hear what you do for a living. I'll hold my questions for our in-person rendezvous but will answer yours:

1. *Yes.*
2. *No. (Thank goodness! You seem nice and all, but I would have been super creeped out if you knew my address. Though I guess that's just how FBI agents like yourself roll.)*

When's good for you? I'm staying up in Hyde Park for work this week, but I'll be back in town on the weekend.

Cheers,
Alison

Over the course of a few more planning emails that transition to planning texts, John offers to meet at my place and walk over to the restaurant together. Not wanting him to know where I live (*what if he's a serial killer?*), I suggest we just meet at the restaurant.

I arrive first, so I stand outside reading the menu. It's a *really* nice, pretty pricey spot. Long ago, Dave had informed me that all his friends subscribed to a strict dating formula: first date = drinks at a low-key bar; second date = drinks at a swanky bar; third date = moderate to expensive dinner; fourth date = cheap dinner, to "make sure a girl doesn't get too used to fancy dinners, and to confirm that she's not using you for your money." Accordingly, I'm surprised John picked this as our first date spot. Maybe he's a jetsetting millionaire? Maybe he's never dated before? Or maybe he thinks my emails demonstrated a lot of promise? (The latter being the least likely.)

Over appetizers, I finally learn what John does for a living. And it is *insanely* cool.

"So, you can't . . ." he clears his throat, "tell anyone, or post a picture of me with my last name anywhere on the Internet." I lean in across the table, as if I'm about to be complicit in a top-secret exchange of classified information. Which I guess, in a way, I am. "It's hard to explain, but basically I track illegal natural and animal products. And about-to-be-imported illegal natural and animal products."

"Like . . . ivory tusks and teak?"

"Exactly. The tusks and teak as raw materials, but also any items that are carved from them: works of art, musical instruments, jewelry."

"How?"

"All kinds of ways. For instance, we have undercover agents who sign up for trophy hunting trips throughout the Southwest. They will camp and eat and explore with these high-end tourism expeditions, and then right before the leader goes in for a kill, they'll make the arrest."

"No way! But those trips are illegal, right? Have you gone on one?"

"Yes, they *are* illegal, and no, not personally. But I have provided backup for the guys who are undercover."

"How do you 'back' someone up when they're in the middle of the wilderness?"

"We do stakeouts."

"In the desert? Or does this not happen in the desert? Am I picturing the wrong . . . ecosphere?"

He nods. "It does happen in the desert, but also in the marshlands and swamplands, et cetera. We also do stakeouts for trading of illegal imported goods. I have to travel for those most often. But we'll spend months or years tracking a ring of importers and dealers, and then before the arrest, we have to stake out on their property or on the periphery to closely monitor all of their contact and activities."

"Just like on *The Sopranos*!" I marvel.

"Yeah. It's actually a lot like that."

"How long do you have to camp out—stake out?—for at a time?"

"It can be two or three days per shift."

"Do you get to sleep?"

"We take turns."

"Do you have to wear camo?"

He laughs. "Not usually."

"But sometimes?"

"Ehh." He hesitates. "Sure. Sometimes."

"So let's say you make a big arrest and bring down the . . . international teak trade ring. What do you do with all the artwork you find? Does it go to museums? Can you get me a bejeweled teak tiara?"

He laughs. "We have a giant warehouse in Colorado—like, giant. Like the size of four city blocks."

"Do you work for the EPA?" I ask.

"US Fish and Wildlife, actually."

I nod. "And they have a single facility for all this? And it all just gets stashed there?"

"Yeah, it's crazy. Aisles and aisles and aisles of boxes stacked ceiling-high, filled with illegal artifacts."

"But that's so sad! Can't you catalog it and . . . transform the darker, illicit nature of the products into something that benefits humanity? Like public education, art, or . . . I don't know. It's like you save it, only to jettison it?"

"I sort of agree. But there *are* times when you *can't* send the spoils to our warehouse."

"Like? . . ."

He leans in again, as if divulging clandestine information. "So last year, I got a call in the middle of the night from the security at JFK Airport. They told me I had to come in and pick up a shipment that they couldn't store overnight. Before telling me what it was, they rattled off all the logistics of access codes to punch in and directions, and I was wondering what it could possibly—"

"What was it?!?" I am quite literally on the edge of my seat.

"It was a polar bear."

"A *polar* bear? Like from Antarctica? Or the North Pole? Or wherever polar bears come from?"

"Yep. A polar bear."

"It was alive?"

"Yep."

"Was it in a cage? Or on a leash?"

"It was in a cage. How do you think they put it on a plane if it wasn't in a cage?"

"I think the better question here is: How do they put it on a plane in the first place, cage or no cage?"

"Okay, touché."

"What did you *do* with it?"

"I brought it home."

"No, seriously. What did you *do* with it?"

"Seriously. I brought it home." He shrugs. Without meaning to be quite so dramatic, I realize I have actually clapped my hand over my agape mouth.

He starts to laugh. "Okay. *First*, I called around to all my contacts. We have a small network for these sorts of incidents. So mostly I called a bunch of zoos. I couldn't get anyone to take it off my hands right away, and the airport's policy is that they can't keep it overnight. So I took it to my place, spent all night trying to find a proper home for it, and in the morning was able to ship it over to a zoo in California for temporary holding."

"Did you take video? Of it in your apartment? Why isn't there a photo of you and the polar bear watching football on your Match profile?"

"Because then someone might be able to figure out what I do or who I work for. And it's top secret."

"Yeah, you've mentioned that," I tease. "But . . . how top secret are we talking? Like, if I knew your last name, could I find you on the Internet?"

"My name, yes; you could find things from college or road races I've run or whatever, but my name is never anywhere associated with my address or my photo or my job."

"I challenge."

"Sure, give it a try."

"Homework for tonight. So, if you're a federal agent, does that mean you own a gun?"

"Yes."

My biggest fear in life is guns. My heart picks up its pace. "Are you carrying it now?"

"No. Are you crazy?" He smiles.

"I don't—I don't know. I don't *know* anyone who works for the FBI, or CIA, or . . . *Fish and Wildlife.* I don't *know* if you have to carry it on you at all times."

"Ah. Well, I do own a few, but as a general rule, I don't pack heat on dates."

"But they're in your apartment?"

"You seem oddly fascinated by my guns."

"No, not fascinated. Terrified. But anyway, continue."

"You have a thing against guns?"

"Sort of. Actually, it's funny. My father grew up in a tiny town in Ohio that's not even really on maps, and with all that farmland and nothing to do . . . he was an avid trap shooter. Actually, our family claim to fame is that he was a National Trapshooting Champion. The NRA somehow got ahold of my dad's name through trapshooting record books or something, and every few years they send him a complimentary membership card. . . . It's pretty funny, since he's pretty liberal and just tears them up on arrival. . . . But . . . where was I going with this? Oh yeah, guns. Scary . . . not that I'm judging."

"No no, that doesn't sound very judgy at all," he teases. "But . . . you're allowed to hate guns. I try not to use mine."

"So how do you fly with your gun when you travel for work?"

"All federal agents do."

"How do you skirt security discreetly? Do you walk through with the cabin crew?"

"They actually have us all meet before the flight, exchange business cards, et cetera, so we know who else is flying with a concealed weapon. That way, if someone gets up to go to the bathroom and you see the bulge of the weapon, you don't tackle him to the ground thinking he's a terrorist."

"Is it really *that* easy to tell if someone's carrying a gun under their clothing? I don't think I could tell."

"Yeah, if you have to conceal it yourself every day, it becomes easy to spot on others."

"And how many times have you actually flown with other federal agents, though?"

"Every time."

"What do you mean '*every time*'? Aren't you flying to really random locations in, like, the American Southwest?"

"Yeah. I've actually *never* been the only federal agent on a flight. It might be a change post-9/11, but I wasn't working before then, so I don't really know. But in my experience there are always at least three federal agents on every flight."

"And they all fly undercover?"

He nods.

"That kind of makes me feel really safe, knowing there are people to protect me on every flight. But also *not* safe in that there are people with guns on every flight?"

"No, you *should* feel safer knowing that."

"So how can I pick them out? What do I look for—where do you hide your gun?"

"It's really easy on overnight or red-eye flights. We're not allowed to sleep on planes, so look for those lonely souls in coach who have the overhead light on at all times and are downing round after round of coffee from the stewardesses."

"Do they know you? The stewardesses? Or flight attendants . . ."

"Yeah. That's why we get special attention in the form of a steady stream of caffeine."

"Wow. Your job is *so* cool. I'm sure you get that all the time, but really. It sounds *super* interesting."

"Well that's good." He half smiles. "Because I think *your* job is super interesting. I was thinking about this on the walk over: we should start a reality show that trails us on our day jobs. I would totally watch the episodes that follow your discovery process of murals that have been forgotten and buried from view for centuries."

"And who wouldn't watch you take a polar bear home with you for the night? You'd get the *CSI/Law and Order* crowd and also those people who are addicted to cat videos on YouTube!"

Later that night, Nicole, my older brother Ben, and I are collecting our drinks from the bar and moving toward the main floor of Rockwood Music Hall on the Lower East Side, where Ben's friend is performing.

"How was the date?" Ben asks.

"It was great."

"You get drinks?"

"Actually we got dinner."

Ben looks surprised. "On a first date?"

"I know, I was surprised, too. But it was really nice. Food was really good. And he was really nice!"

"Was it pricey?" Nicole asks.

"I . . . assume so? The prices on the menu were not cheap, and he ordered a bottle of wine. But he didn't let me look at the bill. . . ."

"That's a *serious* date," Ben says.

"I mean, not really. It's . . . a first date. But yeah, it was nice."

"Is he cute?" Nicole asks.

"He looks like his photos. He's half-white, half-something else. Maybe Japanese? Really attractive."

"Tall? How old?"

"Yeah, six-one maybe. Thirty-three? I think?"

"So how'd you ditch him after a dinner like that to come down here?" Ben asks.

"I . . . said thanks and goodbye? . . . I mean, it was a first date! Just 'cause he bought me dinner doesn't mean we need to make a whole night of it or anything." Ben looks skeptical. "It was a first date!" I insist.

"Oh-kaaay." Ben rolls his eyes. "Well, how'd you say goodbye?"

"What do you mean, 'how did I say goodbye?' I said, 'Awww, thanks so much for this delicious dinner! I have to go meet my brother downtown now.'"

"Did you . . . kiss him?" I must look taken aback, because Ben adds belatedly, "On the cheek?"

"What? On a first date? Do you know me at all?"

Ben and Nicole are laughing heartily at my expense. Ben asks, "Well, did you shake his hand? Give him a hug? You have to have exited *somehow*."

"We . . . walked two blocks to the subway. I said, 'Aww, thanks so much for this delicious dinner!' and then I waved and ran down the stairs before it could get awkward."

"You waved? You *waved* goodbye? Was it, like, a beauty queen wave, did you blow him a kiss, or was this a Paul-Pfeiffer-from-*The-Wonder-Years* enthusiastic wave?"

"It was . . . a Paul Pfeiffer kind of wave," I admit sheepishly. "But that's the only kind of wave I know how to do!" I protest, to peals of laughter from my peanut gallery.

"But you had fun?" Ben confirms.

"Yes, I already told you that!"

"Good god, Ali, you are *never* going to date again."

"But . . . *But* . . . But I already sent him a text message when I got off the subway that said thanks and that I had fun. So he knows I'm at least *somewhat* interested . . . or else why would I have bothered to text him to say I had fun?"

Ben shakes his head. "You *waved* goodbye. I mean, couldn't you have at least *hugged* the guy?"

"But . . ." I start to fret. "But if I *hug* him, then our faces are in prox*imity*, and he might . . . I don't know . . . get the wrong message and try to kiss me? And that would be *way* more awkward!"

"Seriously? Are you twelve? You could at least—"

"Be nice to your sister!" Nicole chastises, though she's laughing with him, at me, too. "Besides, isn't it better for her to *wave* than to scare him off on date one with the Pants Speech?"

* * *

It's the following weekend, and I'm sitting at a table by the window inside Corner Café and Bakery waiting for my second date with John. He walks in, smiles, and reaches out and massages my left shoulder as he says hello. The only sense I can make of this is that while Ben was 90 percent wrong in that John *did* call again, Ben was 10 percent right in that I thoroughly scared him off from ever trying to touch me. Beyond a one-handed, one-shoulder massage.

"Ah, this place is so awesome. I was drooling on the walk over. I can't believe you've never been here before."

"You can now take credit for introducing me to *two* cool neighborhood joints. What's good?" I ask.

"The mozzarella-pesto-red-pepper omelet. The best omelet I've ever had."

"Hmmm. I *do* have a weakness for pesto, but I *also* have a weakness for grits and was kind of tempted by the shrimp and grits."

"Wanna split?"

"Man after my own heart! You pass and share? Even on a second date?"

"There's . . . a lot you don't know about me," he says mischievously, smiling behind the menu.

Brunch food is as tasty as billed, and after we're done, John asks, somewhat timidly, "Do you want to keep hanging out? Or do you need to . . . go home?"

"I can keep hanging out," I offer. I'm curious to see if the conversation can continue to be so comfortable and effortless.

"How do you feel about ice skating?"

"Good, I think?"

We place our shoes in the lockers of Wollman Rink and sit on the wood bench to lace up our skates.

"I used to be really good at skating, but I haven't done it in probably a decade," he says.

"Well, I won an Easter skate competition when I was four."

"Wait, really?"

"Yes, really. The competition was fierce. But the award was actually for the best Easter hat. Worn by an ice skater."

"Your family goes all out for Easter outfits? I thought you said you were half-Jewish."

"You had to make your own Easter hat, so it was kind of a fun arts-and-crafts project my mom had me and my brother and sister do. I actually still remember sitting around the kitchen table gluing the plastic bluebird onto the rim of my hat."

"So by 'ice skating trophy' you mean 'arts-and-crafts trophy.'"

"I never said 'trophy' at all. I just said I won an Easter skate competition. Which I did. You had to skate out and show off your hat."

"But you could skate."

"Hey now, I still *can* skate. My parents' vacation house has a lake, and when it freezes over every winter, we pull out our skates and make up some really fabulous routines."

"To music?"

"We don't have a sound system, but to music we sing aloud, yes."

"Like?"

"I dunno."

"Come on."

"Like 'Everybody Dance Now,' . . . you know, and other classic late eighties, early nineties hits."

"So you're going to reenact your award-winning routine for me now, right?"

"Nice try," I say wryly.

Caught up in the counterclockwise flow of our fellow skaters, we reminisce about our first memories of New York City and critique the pros and cons of living in a concrete jungle.

"I'm getting cold," I say shyly. "Is it okay if we head back now?"

"What? We've only been skating for"—he glances at his watch—"two hours. You *don't* want to stay out until sunset?"

"No, I just—"

"I'm teasing. It's okay."

We walk east down 90th Street. "Do you want to come over to my place?" he asks, keeping his eyes on the pavement.

He has a gun. In his apartment. And there is a nonzero chance that he also could be psychotic, even though my assessment based on the cumulative seven or eight hours I've spent with him is that chances of that are slim. But really, how do you ever *know*? "No, thanks. I'm . . . uhh . . . I have dinner plans tonight with some friends, so I should probably get home and . . . change. . . . Rain check?" I ask, biting my lip.

"Sure."

We reach Lexington Avenue. "I turn right here," I say, halting abruptly at the corner.

"Can I walk you home?" he asks.

Such a gentleman! But a gentleman who owns a gun. So I'd rather he not know where I live. "No no." I shake my head. "It's really close, and you're turning left. No need to go out of your way."

"Okay." He shrugs and smiles. He reaches over and gives me another one-handed, one-shoulder massage. "This was fun. Let's hang out again soon?"

"Sure." I smile, back away, wave like Paul Pfeiffer, and cross the street.

"Sooooo'd you wave?" Nicole asks from the couch before I've even crossed the threshold into the apartment. Cassie giggles beside her.

I open my mouth to speak, then shut it. "Kind of?" I pause. "Okay, yes." Then I add quickly, "Don't make fun of me!"

"I won't. But did you also hug him?"

"No."

"Did he try to hold your hand?"

"No. But he did quasi-massage one of my shoulders. Twice!"

"Ohhh, that's like, the new second base for women in their twenties, I hear," Nicole teases.

"Ha ha. Very funny," I say flatly.

"Do you think you'll see him again?" Cassie asks, sounding hopeful.

"I don't know. It's weird. Dating is weird. He is *super* interesting, and he's really nice, and smart, and cute, yadda yadda. But I feel like when I'm on these dates, not just with him, I find myself sort of . . . zoning in and out. Like I'm listening 80 percent of the time, and assessing if I'm interested 20 percent of the time. Is that weird?"

"But don't you know, like within the first five or ten minutes, if you're attracted to him?" Cassie asks. "If you'll want to see him again?"

I feel insanely lucky to have Cassie as my friend. She is the textbook definition of *supportive*. When a key writer for the campus publication I edited quit, Cassie—with no interest in journalism whatsoever—joined the staff and took over his workload. When I broke my foot in an intramural game and couldn't descend the stairs to our basement, Cassie did all my laundry—every week. She even ironed my jeans, which I'd never done before. When I broke up with Scott on a Tuesday night of senior year, Cassie approached her history professor on Wednesday morning and explained that her best friend was going through an emotional rough patch, and she requested to be excused from class—weirder still is the fact that her professor complied. So Cassie and I spent Wednesday afternoon drinking hot chocolate, strolling across campus, and ruminating on life and love. And yet, we are essentially opposites in every which emotional way. She's a Republican, I'm a Democrat. She wants *everyone* to like her and is a self-professed pushover, whereas I don't especially care what people think of me. She wears her heart on her sleeve where I . . . don't. Consequently, she falls for men instantly, often, and hard, where I, again, don't.

"No? I mean, sometimes yes. But only when I know I *don't* want to see them again. When I'm tuned in and . . . not turned off? . . . I feel the wheels in my head turning to figure out if I want to see them again."

"So what'd you conclude about Secret Agent Man?" Nicole asks.

"I guess . . ." I sigh. "I guess I won't?"

"But you said he's really interesting! And cute! And he likes good food?" Cassie would greatly prefer it if I were a romantic, too.

"Yeah." I nod. "These are all true things."

"But?"

I shrug. "I don't know. It just doesn't feel . . . spark-y? Sparkly?"

"But did it feel 'sparkly' with Scott and Dave right off the bat?" Nicole asks.

"With Scott it *definitely* did," Cassie answers for me. "Their eyes practically locked across the quad on the first day of college."

"It's true," I sigh wistfully. "I felt so . . . lucky that he would talk to me at all. He was so gorgeous, and he laughed at everything I said, this great, belly-filled, totally unforced laugh. When we met, it was kind of a take-your-breath-away moment, so sweet and innocent, so . . . you know, *sparkly*. I couldn't believe my good fortune when he asked me to sit next to him on the bus that day. I was on cloud nine the whole ride. The whole weeklong orientation, actually. All of freshman year, in fact."

"What happened after freshman year?" Nicole asks.

"Nothing. I mean, we stayed together. I guess I just got used to the fact that he was my boyfriend, so it wasn't quite so . . ."

"Sparkly?" Nicole raises an eyebrow.

"Probably."

"So if the 'sparkle' doesn't even last beyond a year, does it have to be there from the outset? Does it matter?"

"I mean, kind of. Doesn't it?" I look to Cassie for affirmation.

"Do you even need to ask?" Cassie rolls her eyes.

While I was living out one great love in our college years, Cassie lived out approximately seventy. Or eighty.

"I broke up with Scott because—despite him being my favorite guy on earth—that spark had sort of petered out. Sometimes I wonder if maybe I was just too young and immature to realize that if it's a good relationship and you love each other, you can work to restore that zesty, passionate part. *But* if it had never been there at all, how could I have been interested in . . . kissing him? Or sleeping with him?"

"Whoa, whoa, whoa." Cassie feigns backing up. "Let's not get carried away here. You can hook up without it needing to be sparkly."

"Yes, we know you're a little passion pit," Nicole teases, "but what if it can be more like a slow burn? It feels like that for me sometimes."

"I think it *might* have been like that with Dave, the slow burn? But there was this quality of levity or amusement from the beginning that translated into instant ease. And that in and of itself was kind of sparkly. Like, the first time Dave took off his shirt in front of me, he burst into that Rod Stewart song, '*If you want my body and you think I'm sexy, come on, Sugar . . .*'"

"I can *totally* see Dave doing that," Nicole muses.

"He sang in this silly falsetto, and it immediately diffused the awkwardness of disrobing for the first time; he made me laugh so hard, which just made me more attracted to him. I don't know, maybe I just need that levity or humor to minimize the awkwardness of dating in general."

"But it's always going to be awkward in the beginning," Nicole says.

"But it *wasn't* with Scott. And it *wasn't* with Dave. Those first years, they were . . . kinda sparkly."

"But that sparkliness *died*!" Nicole protests. "How do we know it isn't always going to die after three years? Maybe that's the sparkly threshold, and then it segues into a different kind of love?"

"Or *maybe* the whole point is that you just keep chasing that sparkle until you find the one where it sticks forever?" I wonder aloud. "Or you never find it?"

"Nope. You find it," Cassie says.

Nicole looks skeptical. "I don't think you can expect that sizzle or intensity to remain forever. It's got to evolve into a different, deeper kind of love at some point, right?"

John calls a few days later, and I let it go to voice mail. I decide to text him and spare him an awkward conversation.

> February 6 at 9:07 p.m.
>
> ALISON: THANKSFORTHEVOICEMAIL.IREALLYTHINKYOU'REFABULOUS.TRULY. BUT I'M NOT SURE I SEE A FUTURE. SO . . . FRIENDS?

A few weeks later I receive the following text from him:

> February 27 at 10:11 p.m.
>
> JOHN: WHICH BLIND PIG ARE YOU AT?

Followed by:

> JOHN: OOPS, SORRY THAT WASN'T MEANT FOR YOU. HOW ARE THINGS?

I never understood the logic behind the random late-night mis-texts. Is the assumption that, although I wasn't interested before, a random "hello" faux-intended for someone else will make me realize how much I miss him? That it will rekindle a flame that wasn't really there before? Or make me jealous and spur me to write back, "OH, HA! NO WORRIES. SO . . . DO YOU WANT TO MEET UP AT THE BLIND PIG? THE ONE, THE ONLY ONE, NEAR UNION SQUARE?" Men are strange.

The Evolution of the Pants Speech: Tom

The first person I dated after my college relationship ended was Tom. Tom had politely but doggedly courted me for years. Throughout the duration of the courtship, we managed to remain friends. We sat next to each other in history classes, studied together occasionally, and cooked dinners together two or three times per semester. And without fail, every September, the first week back on campus, Tom would phone me and ask how my summer was. How was my internship? Did I get to fit in any travels? Was I still dating my college boyfriend? And every September when I'd say that I was, he'd make some weak but kind attempt at a joke about how you can't blame a guy for trying and how we should meet up for dinner once class schedules were finalized and we were settled in.

So when I was suddenly single at the end of senior year, I suspected Tom wouldn't wait too long to call. My phone rang within the week. We cooked another dinner, met up for drinks at a local bar, jogged through East Rock Park on a Sunday morning, suffered through *A History of Violence*'s painfully long sex scenes while holding hands on his couch, and generally enjoyed each other's company as more than just friends. After a campus party one night, we wound up back in my house, making out.

"So. I don't want to . . . make you uncomfortable or anything, but . . . are we going to have sex tonight?" Tom asked.

I laughed out loud. And then I realized he was serious. I pointed to my shirt (fully buttoned) and my pants (fully zipped). "Does it *look* like we're going to have sex tonight?" I asked, hoping to make light of the awkward question.

"Well. I just . . . If not tonight, when?"

I paused to envisage the timeline. "We're graduating. Soon-ish. Like in a month. And then you're moving to London and I'm moving to . . .

somewhere. Probably New York. But not London . . ." my voice trailed off. But since he said nothing, I pressed on. "So, I like you. I do. But I don't think we have enough time for this to get serious enough for me to . . ." He waited for me to finish my sentence, though I was kind of hoping he'd jump in with some understanding to spare me of this awkward dance. "Sleep with you."

"Ever?"

"Well, not in the near future?"

"So. You're never going to sleep with me."

"I mean. Not *never*? But not between now and . . . when you move to London?"

"So never."

I furrowed my eyebrows.

"I'm sorry. I like you. But if this isn't going to lead to . . . that kind of relationship . . . then I don't really see the point in continuing."

I furrowed my eyebrows further.

"What are you thinking?" he asked.

"I'm thinking I want to elbow you in the rib cage. Really hard."

He chuckled awkwardly. And we sat in silence.

And then I wondered aloud, "I'm sorry if what I'm about to say comes off as . . . heady or arrogant . . . but . . . you pursued me for . . . *years*. And now that we're finally . . . dating, or whatever . . . you're going to throw it away just because I won't sleep with you? When we've only been seeing each other for one or two weeks?"

"Well," he sighed. "I just think that . . . to me, sleeping together is an essential part of a relationship. And if you're not ready for that, then . . . yeah, I guess I don't want to pursue this any further."

"All those *years*," I sulked. "Just for a quick lay?" I punched him in the bicep. Then I pouted. "You're a jerk."

If I learned one lesson from Tom, it was that no matter what signal you *think* you're sending out, it can, and probably will, get misinterpreted by the male species. People see what they want to see, and hear what they want to hear. It wasn't that I was *afraid* of the physical aspects of relationships; Scott and I had shared a bed for years—three and a half years to be exact. It was just that unlike some of my college friends, whose "numbers" were well into the double digits—one housemate even broke one hundred, which she proudly declared made her a member of "the union"—I didn't want to be intimate with someone unless we were actually in a relationship. I didn't share my intimate thoughts and secrets with everyone—those were reserved for the Cassies in my life; similarly, I wasn't going to engage in the most intimate aspects of a physical relationship unless the relationship was a committed one.

However, this line of thinking tends to be a buzzkill for men. So after the Tom debacle, I decided best practice was to be as direct as possible, and to avoid any awkward conversations in the bedroom. Hence, the Pants Speech:

If ever I enter an apartment under romantic pretenses or invite someone into mine, I always pause at the front door and make a point of stating, "I like spending time with you, and I'd like to continue hanging out tonight, but before we go inside, I need you to know that you're not getting in my pants tonight."

If a long pause ensues, I might follow up with, "If you want to go home, or if you want me to go home, that's cool. No hard feelings. But . . . no pants tonight."

I never thought this conversation was a big deal. I still don't think it's a big deal. And I've never had anyone since Tom say they'd rather go home.

My friends, however, think this speech is utterly hilarious. Once, Jason had a group of his coworkers over at his apartment. One of them was asking me about my dating life, in a friendly, platonic way. We got to chatting, and you could see the *Eureka!* moment cross his face as he exclaimed, "You're the Pants Speech Girl!" At first I was baffled because I'd never heard it referred to that way before. But then I realized what he meant and admitted that yes, I am the Pants Speech Girl. And thus my doorstep dating ritual acquired its formal title.

COboarderPN: Pantsless Paul

February 2 at 3:27 a.m.

Hi,

This website tells me that we live half a mile apart. I just moved to the Upper East Side four months ago and, thanks to work, I haven't had a moment to explore it beyond Central Park. Not that I'm knocking Central Park. But there's this annoying trade-off that comes with trying to keep your job to pay off loans – you don't actually get to experience the city you're paying sky-high rent to live in. So, all the excitement of my life aside, what pointers can you give me? Top running routes in our 'hood? You seem like the right person to ask this of.

Also, doesn't the city designate dozens of landmarks every year – I would think the steady stream of new designations must mean you're never short on work?

Talk soon,
Paul

P.S. That's a pretty rad yellow harness you've got.

I can't decide if he's attractive or not. A fine-enough introductory email, and his profile says he has post-college education, which is a plus. But he just doesn't look cute to me. His eyes look a little on the small side. And he's short.

"Five-foot-nine is not that short!" my mom argues.

"No, but, it's short to *me*."

"You're not an Amazon yourself, you know. Dad's five-nine."

"I know, but *maybe* if he were cute I could overlook the height thing. But that, and his face . . . it's just . . . I don't think so."

"Can I see his pictures? Show me his pictures."

Over the phone, I walk my mom through the log-in process. She signs in as me, and I can hear her typing as she enters his username into the search box.

"Wait. You're kidding, right?" she asks. "Ali, he is *really* attractive."

"No . . . I don't think so."

"COboarderPN? No, he is. Look at the cell phone photo of him in the bathroom mirror."

"That's *exactly* the photo that made me think he wasn't cute in the first place!"

"No," she insists. "I promise you, he's very attractive."

"Well . . . not to me."

"No, he is objectively attractive."

"There is no such thing. And also, I really don't think so."

"I've never told you that you should or should not go out with someone—"

"What are you talking about? You tell me *all* the *time* that I shouldn't bother going out with certain guys. Or that I should break up with Dave. Or—"

"We're getting off topic. Fine. I've never told you you *should* go out with someone. But you should go out with him."

"Why?"

"Because he has an advanced degree, and he sounds thoughtful and sincere in his profile, and he's the right age," (the right age in this case being thirty-two) "and he's totally adorable."

"Adorable to you."

"Which means he'll be adorable to you."

"Ha!"

"We never disagree. You almost always agree with me on who's cute—celebrities, contestants on *The Bachelor*, men from your college class . . ."

"Fine, fine, fine. Yes, we almost always agree. Except this time, you're wrong."

"Give me the benefit of the doubt. One date. Just go on one date."

"If he even asks me. Just because I write back doesn't mean we're actually going to meet up."

"Okay. One date."

* * *

I'm sitting on a bar stool at Café d'Alsace, scanning the wine list slowly, the only person in the restaurant. Out of the corner of my eye I see the door open, and instinctively I turn my head. It's him, but he looks . . . different. Or, different than his photos. Kind of . . . shockingly handsome, so much so (and so surprisingly so, given what I'd expected based on that bathroom cell phone picture) that my head jerks back in surprise, a kind of quasi-double take. Dark brown hair with sparkling James Marsden-y eyes. Mom was right!

My mind swims with ringing melodies and visions of clouds parting and—well, it's not quite that dramatic, but . . . is this what the French mean when they refer to a *coup de foudre*?

But it's not just me. Paul's still standing in front of the door, semi-frozen in place. Our eyes are locked, but not totally in a steamy, sexy, come-hither way, more like a deer-in-headlights kind of way.

I cock my head and give a half smile, trying to wordlessly communicate, *Hi. Are you my date?*

Finally, after what feels like a prolonged awkward freeze frame, but probably lasted fractions of seconds, he walks toward me.

"Alison?"

"Yep." I smile and nod.

"Hey! . . . Sorry, I—you look different. Than I expected."

I grimace.

"I mean, prettier. Way prettier. Your photos are pretty . . ." he trails off. "But you're even prettier in person."

"Thanks. I think?" I bite my lip unconsciously. "But I actually thought—"

"Yeah, it's . . . it's a compliment."

"—the same thing when you walked in."

We both smile during the pause that ensues. Then he starts:

"So, have you been here before?"

"Nope. I actually live right up the street, two blocks due west, but I haven't been here. I've been meaning to, but . . . no. You?"

"No. I really haven't been anywhere in the neighborhood, but I've heard they have an extensive wine list—"

"They do," I interrupt, brandishing the binder of wines by the glass and bottle.

"—and apparently good bar eats, too. I don't know if you're hungry. I guess normal people usually eat dinner by now."

"No, I actually haven't eaten yet. Long story, but I tutor sometimes, and I didn't have time to go home in between leaving the student's apartment and coming here."

"Huh. What do you tutor?" he asks.

"Math. English. And the SAT."

"For . . . like, community service?"

"No, for money. I'm not that good of a person."

"How often do you do it?"

"Umm." I pause to think. "It changes seasonally, but right now I tutor one to two hours Sunday through Thursday."

"After work?"

"Yeah, after work on weeknights. Midafternoon on Sundays."

"So when you say you tutor 'sometimes,' you mean 'all the time.'"

"Yeah, I guess." I smile.

"Does it pay well?"

"I mean, not like, lawyer money. But way better than conservator money . . . I basically make as much from tutoring each week as I do from my full-time job."

"And it's year-round?"

"Not in summers. Or over holiday weeks, Christmas, New Year's, you know."

"That sounds like a sweet gig."

"I mean it's really good money, and I actually like teaching the math stuff. But it's hard to say it's 'sweet,'" I hold up finger quotes, "when you need a part-time job to supplement your full-time job."

"Yeah. I get that." He picks up the menu. "So if you haven't eaten, should we eat?" He scans the menu. "Olives? Cheese? Charcuterie?"

"Yes."

"To everything?"

"To anything." I shrug.

"What kind of wine do you want?"

I shrug again.

"Everything and anything?" he asks, an eyebrow raised as he looks into my eyes. Our eyes lock again, and my heart feels like it's hiccuping, which is vaguely irritating. I *hope hope hope* I'm not blushing crimson.

"Pretty much. But if you need me to be decisive, something Cabernet-y, or Cab Franc-y. Or from Bordeaux."

"Cool. I have no idea what that means, but there's only one Bordeaux by the glass, so that makes it easy." He leans into the bar and gets the bartender's attention.

"Did you grow up here? In the city?"

"No, I grew up in the suburbs. My whole family's actually here now, but despite that I like to maintain that I'm not a true 'New Yorker' at heart."

"What's so bad about being a New Yorker?"

"Nothing. My parents and siblings consider themselves New Yorkers, but I . . . like green grass and open plains and smaller-scale buildings."

"Do they all live in Manhattan?"

"Yeah. I'm the youngest of three, and when I went to college my parents did that whole 'reverse-migration' thing and moved out of the suburbs and back into the big city. My sister was already here since she'd graduated college. She's married now with a toddler. My brother followed shortly after. Then me."

"Do you all live near each other?" he asks.

"Embarrassingly, yes. I live within two blocks of my sister and her family, and two blocks from my parents in the opposite direction. My brother lives downtown, so we like to pretend he's the black sheep of the family, but he's still on the 6 train, so that's . . . not far by most peoples' standards."

"Yeah, I'd say that's close."

"What about you?" I ask, at the same time he says, "What's your family like?"

We both smile, then repeat our questions, again at the same time.

"You first," Paul commands.

"That's a good question, but I don't know. They're really nice? And we all love each other a lot? I have nothing to compare it to."

"Did you guys, like, have dinner together every night in the dining room? Or did you have TV dinners on your lap in the den?"

"Oh. That kind of stuff? We definitely grew up in the 1950s, not the 1980s. My sister used to call my mom 'Donna Reed with a brain.' It would have been *unheard* of for one of us to eat dinner alone. We often got up extra early to have breakfast together before my dad left for work."

"Whoa. Intense."

I laugh. "I know. But my mom's an awesome cook, and she focused pretty much all of her energy on us. We had limited TV time, and usually it was for shows that we'd all sit and watch together, like *Star Trek* or *The Wonder Years*. No Nintendo, no Sega—"

"Man, that sucks."

"I know, right? Except this one summer, when we all piled into a rented RV and drove cross-country for four weeks to all the National Parks, *then* we were allowed to play Sega Genesis . . . mostly because the RV came with one."

"It must have been like crack for you guys, if you'd never played it before."

"Oh, we always played at our friends' houses. But, yeah. I think my mom was actually pretty disappointed. Here the whole point of the trip was to stare out the window and take in nature's beauteous bounty . . . and we couldn't take our eyes off Mortal Kombat and Sonic the Hedgehog."

Paul smiles. "I don't think I knew any families like yours growing up."

I can't tell if this is a good thing or a bad thing. "Okay! Your turn."

"Well, I grew up in Lancaster, Ohio and—"

"—I just finished working on a preservation plan for your arts center!"

"Really?"

"Yeah. I never actually went there, but I had to work on a historic structures report for it to help them secure state funding for the restoration."

"Random. You probably know more about the history of my city than I do, in that case."

"Yeah, that's probably true. Let me know if you want to read my history report. Sorry! You were saying?"

"My parents still live in Lancaster. I went to college out in Colorado, and after, I just kind of stayed for a long time."

"What'd you do?"

"I was a ski bum."

"Really," I say, more matter-of-factly than as a question.

"Yeah." He nods.

"For how long?"

"Five years."

"Five years? That's a long time!"

"Yeah. I guess."

"You must be a *really* good skier!"

He nods. "I snowboard, too."

"How'd you . . . make money? As a ski bum?"

"I waited tables."

"Did you have friends out there doing the same thing?"

"Yeah, a bunch of my college friends stuck around there, too, when we graduated. Ski bumming and working odd jobs."

"So how'd you transition into being a fancy lawyer?"

"Ha. I'm hardly 'fancy,' if a lawyer." He takes a swig from his wine glass.

"But . . ."

"Right. But just when I was kind of at the apogee of my skiing career"—*he said* apogee. *Impressive vocabulary for bar small talk*—"I had a bad fall and broke a few ribs. It took me out for the rest of the ski season, and I decided it was time to figure out what I was doing with my life."

"So how'd you settle on law school?"

"This sounds stupid, and shallow, but I kind of just wanted to make money and have a steady job. I was tired of being broke all the time. And that seemed like the easiest way."

"Well, not *really* the easiest way," I point out. "It does involve three years of graduate school. You could have gone into . . . I don't know . . . finance. Or real estate. Or . . ." I trail off.

"True, but I also kind of wanted to do something that helps people."

"So do you do civil law? Or . . ."

"No, I work in corporate finance. I know, it's lame—"

"That's not lame. My roommate Cassie is a corporate finance lawyer."

"Oh really? Huh. Cool. Anyway, I figured I'd do this for a while until I paid off all the law school debts. And then try to move over to an area that's got a bit more . . ."

"Heart," I say.

"Soul," he says at the same time. We both chuckle.

"Heart and soul?" I volunteer.

"I try to do pro bono work, and I'm staffed on a pro bono case right now, but it's not actually working out so well."

"For you? Or for the client?"

He smirks. "Both, actually. Though I hadn't thought of it that way. What they don't tell you when you take on pro bono work is that you're still expected to log just as many hours in your day-to-day case work, and the time you spend on pro bono cases is more or less discounted."

"So you've got, like, two cases' worth of work?"

"Yeah."

"Given all that, I'm actually impressed you could make it to drinks at all on a school night."

"School night. I like that. Yeah, it's not typical, but my boss is away today and tomorrow, so I seized the moment."

"You work weekends?"

"Yeah." Then again, almost to himself, "Yeah . . . it sucks." Then he looks up. "But, my job's really boring, so let's talk about something else."

"So your family's in Lancaster?"

"My parents are. My brother is married and lives in Pittsburgh."

"Do your parents work?"

"Yeah. My mom is a schoolteacher and my dad is an undertaker."

"Like, a morgue undertaker? Or . . . mortician? Sorry, I don't know the lingo."

"Yeah. He owns a funeral parlor."

"I'm picturing *My Girl*. Is the funeral parlor attached to your house?"

He laughs. "Not quite like *My Girl*, but it's close by."

"How did he get into that business?"

"It was a family business." He nods. "My grandfather ran it before him, he inherited it."

"Was he disappointed that you didn't want to take it over? Or that your brother didn't want to?"

"I think a little, but not enough to pressure us into doing it."

"Did you grow up then . . . around . . . dead people?"

He laughs again. "Not really 'around dead people,' but I did work for him during high school and then again during my summers in college."

"What'd you do?"

"Bookkeeping. And I drove the hearse."

"No. Way," I exclaim, wide-eyed. "You drove the hearse? Now it's like you're Lurch from *The Addams Family*." I quickly add, "Except slightly less creepy."

"No, it was a pretty creepy part of the job. This one time . . ." He regales me with a hilarious—and decidedly creepy—story about the time when he got into a car accident at an intersection, and the back door to the hearse opened, and the coffin he was chauffeuring slid out the back and onto the street to the horror of every driver and bystander.

"Come on, you don't have to look *that* horrified," he chides. "It only happened once."

"I think 'mortified' would be the word you were looking for," I tease.

"Very punny."

We talk for three hours until the bartender informs us they're closing.

"Wow, we're the last people here," he observes.

"I think we were the *only* people here."

"I've never closed out a bar before on . . . a 'school night.'" He smiles.

"Then you haven't *lived*," I say mock-incredulously.

"I get that every now and then," he says as we turn to walk up the street.

"I don't know about that. Ski bumming for five years before going to law school sounds to *me* like a ripe way to live out your twenties."

"I guess." His hands are in his pockets. "So." He looks first at the ground, then up at me. And we lock eyes again, and my heart hiccups again. "I had a really good time hanging out with you tonight. Do you want to do this again sometime soon?"

"Yeah, sure!"

"I've got a friend in town this weekend—maybe we could all meet up Friday night?"

"I've got an alumni reunion-y party on Friday night." I chew my lip. "But after? I'll have friends with me, but . . . that could work well if you've got friends in tow, too?"

"Yeah. Let's do that. I'll shoot you an email or text to confirm."

"Cool. See you soon, and thanks for tonight." I wave goodbye.

* * *

"I think he just got tied up with work. It sounds like he's pretty busy, or stressed, rather, about his job," my mom says.

"Yeah, but *if* someone's interested, he'll find a way to make time. Even just a two-line text."

"But I don't think he would have been so specific. 'Friday night.' When a friend was *already* coming in to visit. If he didn't want to see you, he would have just said, 'I've got friends in town this weekend and work is tough, so I'll call you in the future.' Or have said nothing at all."

I sigh. "So what should I do?"

"Email him. Short and sweet, just say you hoped he was hanging in there since it sounded like he had a rough workweek ahead."

February 10 at 12:20 p.m.

Hey Paul!

I know you said you had a lot on your plate this week, so I just wanted to say hi & that I hope you're hanging in there. Have fun with your friends this weekend!

Cheers,
Alison

It felt surprisingly good to send that. Kind of like mini-closure, though it's not exactly as if one should require closure after a single date. Unless you're Brendan.

February 10 at 12:27 p.m.

Hey Alison,

Good to hear from you. This email is making me wonder: did you not receive my text? Hang on.

OK. So I sent you a text yesterday about meeting up tonight, and it's there, in my Sent Messages. But when I click on it, there's a red X that says "Error. Message not Delivered."

Work sucks, thanks for checking in. Are you still up for hanging out tonight after your alumni thing?

Paul

February 10 at 12:39 p.m.

Weird. I thought the failed missive was just something girls dreamed up to justify why they haven't heard back from guys they're crushing on. I didn't know those actually existed. . . .

Meeting up tonight post-alumni shindig still works. What time? And where? We'll be coming from Midtown.

Cheers,
Alison

February 10 at 12:45 p.m.

10:30? Have you been to The Penrose?

Paul

February 10 at 12:49 p.m.

I love The Penrose! 10:30 could be a bit tight, though. Can we push it back to 11 or 11:30? I hope I don't sound totally sketchy wanting to meet up late-night, but tonight's party is a

costume party, themed "Dirty Dancing: Havana Nights" (yes,
we Yalies really know how to get down) and I kind of really,
really don't want to meet up with you in costume.

February 10 at 12:57 p.m.
Oh. No, now we must meet at 10:30. And you must come in
costume.
Kidding. 11 or 11:30 is fine. Why don't you text (and if
I don't respond, call, since maybe our phones are jinxed)
when you're out. But please don't go home and change first.
What is your costume? I hope it involves coconuts.

"Ugggggh, no. Are you *really* going to make me do this?" I wail to
Cassie as we climb the steps from the subway.

"It's already eleven-fifteen! If we go home to change, we won't be
able to get there until eleven-forty-five or later."

"But I look like a tramp." I pout. "And you do, too."

She turns to face me. "You look amazing. And maybe a little tramp-
ish. But if we meet up with them at midnight, isn't that just as bad?
You're totally booty calling him without meaning to at that hour."

"I think *this*," I point my hands to my chest and wave them up and
down my body, at my coral-pink, mostly Lycra tanked dress, "is more
of a direct booty call."

"Call him and ask. They're probably just waiting around for us, so
I'm *sure* he'd rather see you in your strappy silver shoes and *Dancing
with the Stars* dress now than in jeans and furry boots in an hour."

"This wasn't about what *he* wanted," I retort. But I pull out my cell
phone and call him.

"Oh my God, you weren't kidding." He smiles as he taps my shoulder
from behind. Cassie, Ashley, and I spin around from our bar stools to
face him and his friend, also attractive.

"Stop making fun of me!" I complain, eyebrows furrowed. "It was
a *theme* party!"

"We take theme parties very seriously," Ashley explains.

"No, you look *good*. Really good. Just, not like a New Yorker in
the middle of winter."

"Well, in fairness, when I stepped outside earlier tonight, I was struck by this . . . impending sense of doom that I was about to keel over from frostbite or cold-induced cardiac arrest. Besides, I told you I'm not a New Yorker," I tease. "*Also*, it's a really long story, but I kind of needed an excuse to exercise my wardrobe."

"Oh yeah? What does that mean exactly?" Paul smiles.

"Well. So this dress was an amazing, super-luxe designer, at 90 percent off." I feel myself speeding through this like the Micro Machines commercial spokesman from the early nineties, fairly certain that men hear "dress" and "shopping" and instantly tune out. "And I found-it-on-the-floor-of-T. J. Maxx, it was the only one. My size. Yadda yadda," I gesture and-so-on-and-so-forth with my hands, "and I had to buy it. This was four years ago. But then I never had an opportunity to wear it. . . . Then we got the invite to this 'Dirty Dancing: Havana Nights' party . . . it was like kismet . . . but now I'm evidently never wearing it again." I sigh.

"Wait, why not?" his friend, whose name I still don't know, asks.

"Because of your—plural—reactions!"

"No, you should wear it every day. Even in winter," Paul says.

"It does . . ." his friend nods, "leave nothing to the imagination."

"STOP!" I scold through gritted teeth. Then I turn to Paul and whine, "See I *told* you it would be better if I could go home and change first. You too!" I turn and scold Cassie.

"Really, though." Paul nods. "You should wear it every day."

"Ohhhkay." I sigh. "Can we talk about something else?"

"Tell us about the party," his friend says.

"Oh, but first! Cassie, and Ashley," I point to each in turn as I say their names, "this is Paul and . . ." I raise my eyebrows.

"Brian." Brian smiles and extends his hand to shake first mine, then Cassie's and Ashley's. "Nice to meet yous" are mumbled in chorus.

"So, the party is kind of a long story, but back in college, there was this thing called 'Feb Club.' The idea was that to combat the winter doldrums, fraternities, dorms, et cetera would rotate throwing parties each night so that every night for the entire month, there was a big fun party to go to."

Brian asks, "And you guys went to *Yale*, Paul said?"

"Yeah. Nerds can be fun, too," I say. "The alumni, maybe fifteen years ago, initiated 'Feb Club for Old People.' It's not like there's a party *every* night in New York, but there's an alumni Feb Club party *somewhere* in the world every night in February. And because there are so many people living in the city, we get maybe ten or eleven in New York this year."

"That's cool," Paul says.

"Have you gone to all of them?" Brian asks.

At once, we each give our different answers. "Most," "Some," "Yeah."

"Tonight's," I explain, "was the biggest . . . the one that was actually thrown at the Yale Club proper, whereas most of the others are at random bars or people's apartments."

"Well, Colorado kids know how to party, too," Brian says flirtatiously.

After two rounds of martinis, I beg to go home and change before we relocate to a new venue. The five of us walk back to our apartment, and Paul, Brian, and Ashley wait on the stoop while Cassie and I run up to change.

"Paul's *adorable*," Cassie says as we turn the key into our apartment.

"Brian's not so bad either."

"Wanna trade?"

"No, I'm cool, thanks." I smile.

As we step back onto the stoop, Paul says to Brian, "See? I told you she doesn't always dress like that."

I feign looking offended, and Paul says, "Awwww," kind of like I'm a wounded puppy, and he reaches over and takes my hand in his. Surprised, my head jerks to see my hand, then embarrassed by my surprise, I look up at him and smile. Those sparkling blue eyes again. My heart hiccups, and I feel myself blushing again. Luckily it's ten degrees outside so I probably just look cold. Or so I tell myself to quell the heart hiccups.

I look at Cassie, who makes her eyes wide, raises her eyebrows, and smiles, clearly saying, "Yes, *I* noticed he's holding your hand, too. Cute!"

Ashley announces she's heading home, and when she and I hug goodbye, she whispers in my ear, "You got this. I want details tomorrow."

The four of us walk over to a dive bar full of darts and pool. Cassie, a lover of darts, challenges Brian to a round, wagering a beer for the winner. Paul and I are hovering over the jukebox, trying to decide which songs to invest our quarters in.

"How do you feel about Creedence Clearwater Revival?" he asks.

"Good. *Very* good. But . . ." I press the arrow button, flipping through several more pages of song options. "*Not* as good as I feel about 'Bleeding Love' by Leona Lewis."

"I can't tell if you're kidding."

"I kind of am. And kind of not. It's Cassie's favorite song."

"Really? Favorite? Isn't it kind of depressing?"

"Yeah, well, by 'favorite,' I mean it's her most recent breakup ballad. When her last Tinder romance ended a few months ago, the song was on loop for about three straight weeks, seeping into the living room from beneath her door at all hours of the day. And night." I take the quarters out of Paul's hand and slide them into the machine.

"Isn't that, like, torturing your friend?"

"No, she'll think it's funny." He looks at me suspiciously. "I *promise*. It's been long enough that I'm pretty sure she sees the humor in the situation. Or, you know, she'll break down into tears in front of the dartboard. But let's hope for the former."

The first notes of the sad, slow song emanate from the speakers, and Cassie immediately looks over to us in front of the jukebox. "I LOVE THIS SONG!" she exclaims, and she starts to jump up and down, darts in hand, with glee.

"See? Told you."

"Girls are weird."

"We always say the same thing about men."

"Do you have that? A breakup ballad?"

"Would you believe me if I said no?"

He smiles.

Cassie, from across the room, lip-synchs along, "*But something happened for the very first time with you . . .*"

"Do you want a drink?" Paul asks.

"Sure. I'll have a cider."

Paul moves toward the bar, so I join Cassie in lip-synching passionately across the room, "*But I don't care what they say . . . I'm in love with you.*"

"So." Paul comes back with bottles in hand and hands me a cider.

"Thanks."

"Do you think they're gonna hit it off?"

"Cassie and Brian?"

"Yeah."

"I don't know." I shrug.

"Well, is she interested?" he asks.

"I don't know."

"Really," he says. "So you *didn't* ask her when you were upstairs changing? Or when we went to the bathroom earlier. Or . . ."

"I don't know," I say, a bit more mischievously this time. I look over and Cassie is still lip-synching at me.

"So. How can I get you to tell me?" Paul asks.

"I . . . that would be impossible," I say. "Scout's honor, pinky swears, you know, girl-code stuff . . ."

"What if I . . ." He puts his beer down on top of the jukebox. *Uh-oh.* My heart hiccups. "Tickle it out of you?" he asks, placing his hands on my sides and starting to tickle my stomach.

"NO, no, no, no, no, no, no, no! Please, no!" I say through uncontrollable laughter, because it actually *does* tickle. "Please no! Stop! Stop!" I'm having trouble catching my breath. "I'm so, so, so ticklish! Let me—"

"—Yes, I can see that."

"—at least—" He keeps tickling me as I gasp for air. "Let me at least put my bottle down!" I manage to blurt out quickly.

"So. I take it," he says slowly, "that you're really ticklish."

"You think?"

"So are you going to tell me now?"

"Now that you've tortured me? No thanks."

"How about if I . . ." my heart flutters again. Harder, once he looks straight into my eyes. Our eyes search each other's, and my heart races. "Kiss you?" I feel like I've had the wind knocked out of me. I pull my eyes away and look around awkwardly, focusing on nothing in particular.

"Uhh." I search for words. Or composure. Or both. Well, I killed that moment. "Nope. *I'll* never tell."

"I'm gonna do it anyway," he whispers as he leans in and kisses me deeply. It feels nice, and exciting, and it lasts for what feels like a very long time. Leona croons, *"Yet I know that the goal is to keep me from falling . . ."*

"Oww oww!" Brian catcalls from across the room. I put my hands on Paul's chest and push him away, then scratch at my neck, embarrassed, and look over at Brian and Cassie. "Get a room!" Brian shouts, grinning.

Paul gently places his hand on my cheek and redirects my face toward his again. "Let's ignore them." And with his other hand on my lower back, he pulls me in and kisses me again.

"Okay, so you put infants in this," Cassie says, reading her Taboo card as she stands beside our living room couch.

"Stroller!" Brian guesses.

"No, more like, when you're at home. It doesn't move, it's got mesh siding, you put it on the floor."

"Baby cage!" Brian guesses again. Paul and I exchange a look of confusion.

"*Baby cage?*" I ask. "Who . . . puts their baby in a *baby cage?*"

"I think someone's had a bit too much to drink," Cassie says sweetly. "But keep going! We're being timed!"

"Rugrat . . . cradle . . . a little help here?" Brian asks.

"No, you were closer with 'baby cage,' go back to that idea."

"Aaaaaaaand time," Paul says, turning over the plastic hourglass.

"*Really?*" Cassie asks. "Really? Baby cage?"

"I plead fatigue," Brian says. "It's . . ." he glances at his watch, "four thirty a.m." He stands up and starts walking down the hall. Cassie, still standing near the couch, looks from me to Paul, a little confused.

"Well, are you coming or not?" Brian calls out.

She glances again from me to Paul. "Who are you talking to?" she calls out.

"You," he says, without turning back.

"Wait—where are we going?" Cassie asks.

"You live here, don't you? Isn't this the way to your bedroom?"

Cassie looks back and forth between me and Paul again, eyes wide, then smiles and trots off down the hallway behind him.

"Well that was—"

"—unexpected," Paul says.

"—smooth," I say at the same time. We laugh, looking at each other.

"So . . . do I get to stay, too?" Paul asks, leaning in and kissing me again. We kiss for maybe a minute, all the while I'm trying to formulate what to say. I pull back. "So, umm. Normally . . ." We kiss a little longer. "I would have laid this out before letting you come upstairs." I lean in to kiss him again. "But since we had . . . company, I didn't really get the chance." He keeps kissing me.

"Oh yeah?" Kiss again. "What was it about?" More kissing.

I sigh, then start. "Well, I *would* have said, 'you're welcome to come upstairs,'" I lean back in to kiss him. This is probably the least direct version of the Pants Speech ever given in the history of the world. "'But I need you to know you're not getting in my pants tonight.'"

"Oh." He kisses me again. "Is that so?" he whispers.

"No, I'm being utterly and totally serious," I say, still kissing him. Then I pull back. "I am, actually, being kind of totally serious," I say, more seriously.

"Do you want me to go home?" he asks.

"No." I shake my head. "I mean you can, if you want to. But this is nice." We kiss again.

I wake up to faint knocking on my bedroom door. I poke Paul in the ribs. His eyelids flutter open. He smiles and pecks me on the lips. "Good morning."

"Someone's knocking," I whisper and point to the door. "Should I tell them to come in?" There's another set of four faint knocks in succession.

"Uhhh, sure." Paul groans and rubs his eyes.

"Yes?" I call out. "Come in?" The door inches open, and Brian pokes his head in.

"Sorry, I didn't mean to wake you guys up." He looks at us. "Oh. I *did* wake you guys up."

"Yes. Yes, you did," Paul says. "What do you want?"

"Well, first, uh . . . oops. Sorry. Well, I'm going to get going now. Except . . . I don't know where to go since all my stuff is at your place," he says to Paul.

"Do you want my keys?" Paul asks.

"Sure." Brian pauses. "Where is your apartment, again?"

Paul sighs. "Okay. Can you give me a few minutes?"

"Sure thing," Brian says. "I'll just be in the living room."

Paul rolls over to face me and says, "That was . . ." His eyes look away, as if he's trying to remember something. He smiles. ". . . really, really fun last night."

I smile. "Yeah. I had fun, too. . . . And who knew? Brian and Cassie? Kinda random, huh?"

"Yeah, I guess so. You and Cassie seem pretty different. I'm not sure I would have pegged you as best friends."

"Is that code for she's more fun than me?" I pout.

He kisses me for a few seconds then brushes my hair behind my ear. "That's not what I meant. I just mean she's more . . ."

"*Wild*?" I suggest. "Yeah, we know. Cassie and I are different animals. In college we'd start our Saturday nights together, go to the same parties, same bars, but wind up rehashing two *totally* different evenings over brunch the next morning. By the end of the night, she'd be blackout drunk and have lost her coat and her purse, and then she'd stumble home—sometimes barefoot because she'd lost her shoes."

Paul laughs. "Yeah. I can't quite picture you doing that."

"Me?" I point at myself. "Yeah, not quite. I . . . tend to be what *Match.com* would categorize as a 'social drinker.' I've never gotten sick from drinking; never blacked out . . ."

"Then you haven't *lived*." Paul smiles, and at the sight of his dimples, that giddy feeling in my gut returns.

"So how long is Brian staying for?"

"He leaves tomorrow." As he talks, he climbs out of bed and starts gathering his socks and shirt. I sit in bed, watching him get dressed, half-wondering what happened to Cassie, half-wondering if I'll see Paul again. It would have been pointless for him to leave at four-thirty in the morning even after the Pants Speech, because who wants to walk home in the cold at that hour?

"What are you up to for the rest of the weekend?" he asks.

"You're lookin' at it," I say. "I plan to sleep, maybe run, go to another Feb Club party tonight . . ." This is a lie, I have a date tonight. "Watch the Oscars tomorrow night. . . . I don't know. Typical weekend stuff. You? Are you working?"

"Yeah, I have to go into the office today. And then hopefully get out in time to hang out with Brian and some of our friends tonight."

I nod.

"Do you want to watch the Oscars together tomorrow night?" he asks, then adds quickly, "Or did you already have plans for that?"

"No. I mean, yes." That didn't come out right. I shake my head, then self-correct: "No, I don't have plans to watch. Yes, let's watch together."

"Great." He smiles. He finishes buttoning his shirt then says, "Sorry I have to run off like this. I don't want Brian to—"

"—Say no more. It's fine. I don't want Brian to hang out in our living room all day either." I smile.

"Well." He breathes in. "I'll see you tomorrow night. What time do those things start anyway?"

"I don't know. Maybe seven? Eight?"

"Why don't we say seven. Do you eat sushi?"

"I do."

"Excellent. I'll text you my address."

"Cool. I'll text *you* if I don't receive it."

He kisses me quickly and then leaves, closing the door behind him.

After washing my face and brushing my teeth, I walk into the living room.

"Hey, sleepyhead," Cassie says.

"It's ten o'clock! *I* only got five hours of sleep. How on earth are *you* up? And functioning?"

"Functioning is a relative term," Nicole says, a commentary on the fact that they're both settled into the couch, still in pajamas, watching TV.

"So why did Brian get up and leave?"

"He said he needed to get up, that he's not a fan of lying around in bed once he's awake."

"Isn't that every man?" Nicole asks. And then, turning to me, "And more importantly, Hi! You had a boy sleep over last night? How was *that*?"

"It was . . . good? He didn't really have much of a choice, I think, since we didn't finish playing Taboo until close to five."

"Did you . . . sleep with him?" Nicole asks.

"God, no! Do you know me at all?"

"Well, I didn't hear the Pants Speech on our doorstep last night," Cassie says.

"Because you were standing right there! With Brian! I gave it to him on the couch, after you guys went to sleep. Or to bed, rather."

"Was that awkward?"

"What?"

"Giving him the Pants Speech right after your friends sneak off to go bang? Your friends who only met that night, through you?"

I shrug. "I don't think so. But speaking of which . . . how was it?"

"Let's just say I'm glad you met Paul," Cassie says, smiling.

* * *

"You don't know who Hugh Jackman is?" I exclaim.

"No?"

"First of all, Wolverine? From *X-Men*? Jean Valjean from *Les Mis*? Aussie actor—obviously, as you can tell from the accent—kind of a triple threat singer-actor-dancer?" I search his face for a hint of recognition. "Nothing?"

"Sorry."

"He was in one of those magician movies?"

"Yes! Uhh, *The Illusionist*! Is he in that?"

"No, the other one. But you know the title of *The Illusionist* and you don't know who Hugh Jackman is? I mean, his physique alone is famous. . . . Fine. Can you pass the soy sauce?" I ask. "I still can't believe you don't know who Hugh Jackman is," I mutter under my breath.

"I still can't believe you watch lame musical movies," he mutters back.

"So if you're not into film . . . and you don't ski so much anymore . . . what other kinds of things do you do?"

"Apart from being a lawyer for a hundred hours every week?"

"Yeah. You know, in your copious amount of free time?"

"I like music. I play music, occasionally."

"Guitar?"

"Yeah. How'd you know?"

"Every guy on Match plays guitar."

"Really?" he asks, seemingly genuinely curious about this fact.

"Yeah. They all play guitar, and they either ski, snowboard, or surf. Or all three."

"I feel so unoriginal." Then he perks up. "But how many of them are lawyers?"

"I don't know. Half?"

"Seriously?"

I shrug. "I haven't run the statistical analysis, but I'd say that's a safe bet."

"How many of them have tattoos?"

"A lot. Sixty-three percent? Wait—do you have a tattoo?"

"No. . . ." He laughs. "But so what makes me original?"

"I don't know, you tell me."

"Well, why did you decide to go on a date with me?"

"Because you asked."

"So do you go on a date with everyone who asks?"

"*No.*" I shake my head, smiling. "Not even close."

"Because you're so desirable, it's hard work driving off the hordes of men flocking to you on *Match.com*, huh?"

"Hey, be nice. *No.* Because there are a lot of crazy people on Match. And in the world. And generally a whole lot of people I'm not interested in, for one reason or another."

"So do you have many suitors?"

"I have no idea."

"So why me?"

"I already told you: because you asked."

"But why did you say yes?"

"Ohhhh, *I* see how it is. This is the point when you want me to stroke your ego. Well, let's see. . . ." I count off on my hands, one trait at a time. "You seemed very articulate, both in your emails and profile. You have a job. You live in the same state as me. And your pictures were kind of okay. But you're actually cuter in person. . . ." I smile teasingly. "Your turn! Why me?"

"Because you lived within half a mile, and I don't have time to date someone I need to take a subway to." He smiles as he puts his chopsticks down, then leans over and kisses me.

"Well, I guess that's as good a reason as any?"

"But also, you're not like the girls I usually date."

"What does that mean?"

"I don't know. You're just not." He shrugs.

"Well, you must have meant *something* by it."

"I don't know. You're . . . different. Maybe classier?"

"Are you about to make fun of my dress from Friday night again?"

He laughs. "No. I'm serious. You just . . . you're different. It's a good thing."

"So I take it you haven't dated many architectural conservators before."

"Fine, fine. Make a joke about it. I was *trying* to be nice."

"You didn't *say* anything!"

"I just wonder if you would have dated me six years ago."

"When you were a ski bum?"

"A ski bum, with a ponytail, and no—"

"You had a ponytail!" I exclaim, laughter bubbling up.

"Yeah, is that so hard to believe?"

"Yes. As a matter of fact, it is. . . . I really . . . can't picture you with a ponytail. Do you have photos?"

"Seriously?"

"Oh yes. Please show me pictures! I want to see your *ponytail*! Was it as long as mine?"

"Here, I have photos somewhere." He gets up and walks to his bookshelves. He pulls off a photo album and starts flipping through the pages. "Here are a few. Oh, and Brian's in that one, too." I study the photos. The truth is, I *wouldn't* have dated him then. A ski bum with a ponytail, no big plans, (seemingly) no aspirations. I wouldn't have responded to a Match message from him.

"Well, you were still kind of cute. So maybe I would have dated you," I lie.

"I . . . kind of doubt that," he says.

"Well, *maybe* you're right." I say, trying to spin my response as if in jest. But it's true. It's funny how life works: cut off your ponytail, get a different job; you're still the same person underneath the glossier sheen. So why does that stuff matter? Am I really that superficial? "But you know what? You probably wouldn't have dated me then either," I suggest.

"Oh, yeah, there's no question. I definitely wouldn't have dated you then."

"Wait—why not?" I demand.

"I don't know. You seem . . . mainstream."

"Like, vanilla? Boring?"

"No. I just used to go for edgier chicks."

"I'm edgy!"

He laughs.

"I *am*!"

"No, it's true." He nods. "You are. You're a girl who wears a hard hat . . . and wrestles pigs . . . and wears Lycra dresses on Friday nights . . ."

"I *am* edgy," I protest.

"And *I'm* being serious," he says. "My ex-girlfriend was kind of a hard core snowboarder type." My mind wanders. Does this mean he hasn't dated anyone since he lived in Colorado? "You're not as edgy as *she* is, but you're not totally mainstream and boring either. You're like an amalgam, a crossbreed."

"Thanks? I guess?"

"It's a compliment. I promise."

"So why do you . . . date 'mainstream' girls now? What changed in *you*?"

"I dunno. Priorities, I guess?" He kisses me again, but midway through I push back to get up and go to the bathroom.

When I come back from the bathroom, his T-shirt and jeans are balled up on the floor, but he's not watching me. He's reclined on the couch, watching Matthew McConaughey approach the lectern, like this is totally normal. Startled, I begin with "Umm . . ." and my mouth (and brain) stops there. I feel frozen again—an increasingly familiar feeling around Paul. Then, trying to salvage the moment with humor, I finally say with mock incredulousness, "What part of my Pants Speech did you not understand?"

He looks up. "Oh!" Then more softly, "But that was . . . on our last date. . . . And this is our . . . third date?"

I sit down, awkwardly, at his feet and toss the nearest blanket at him. "Ummm . . ." I blink, look away, and breathe. "I'm sorry." He doesn't say anything, and uncomfortable with the silence, I add, "I don't . . . I guess I didn't make it clear, but I don't really abide by the 'third date' rule."

"Oh."

Silence ensues again. And to break it again, I follow up nervously, "I like you. And I really like spending time with you. . . . And I hope we can continue to spend more time with each other."

Silence.

"But I," I furrow my brow, "I just." I breathe in again. "I just move much more slowly than a lot of girls." I bite my lip. "And I'm happy to talk about it, though I don't know that there's a whole lot more to say. And it's fine if you want to make fun of me for being a prude. But," I stumble, "I need to be . . . *there* needs to be more of a . . ." I hunt for the right word, then settle on, "relationship . . . there before I move forward . . . under the sheets."

He says nothing. So I raise my eyes from my lap and study his face, trying to read his expression, trying to get him to look me in the eyes. "Is that okay?"

He pauses and speaks slowly. "Yeah, I guess."

"I'm *not* trying to rebuff you, in fact I—"

"No," he interrupts. "It's fine." He rolls onto his side, then sits up. "I'm . . . totally not used to moving at your pace either . . . but it's fine." He nods. He reaches for his jeans, slides them on one leg at a time, then he turns his body and faces the television, returning his attention to the Oscars, which until now, he'd hardly watched for ten seconds.

"Are we? . . ." I reach out and touch his hand. He moves his hand away abruptly.

"No, Alison, I'm fine," he says somewhat adamantly.

I chew my lip, then echo his body language and face the awards show, too. Am I supposed to get up and leave now? But that would be a terrible way to exit, a surefire way to never see him again. And I *want* to see him again.

After the award for Best Picture is announced, I pull on my boots and coat, and he offers to walk me home. Hoping this will help return us to good footing, I accept the offer. But we've walked four blocks in complete silence.

I start, "You mentioned you have a busy week ahead. What's going on at work?" This tactic seems to work, and he talks at length about how the pro bono case he's working on should move to trial the week after next. This conversation brings us to my doorstep, and my heart starts racing, unsure of whether we're going to end this with a high five or a handshake or . . . hopefully more?

We stand there, quietly fumbling. I take a deep breath: "Look, I'm . . ." I stumble over my words, and then my mouth starts moving before my brain can catch up, "really shitty at talking about this kind of stuff, but, like, remember how we talked about Cassie's version of a Saturday night? Mine's always been more like the one of a designated driver. In fact, I *was* the designated driver for my friends all through high school. It's not that I don't want to have fun, or, *ever* have sex . . . it's just that I enjoy *being* at the party without needing to get hammered. I like *kissing* and . . . *other* stuff." I cringe at how awkward this is. Do I actually need to finish this thought? Would it be weird if I just stopped talking right now? "But I just need to, I don't know, 'round the bases' a bit more slowly. I want to . . . kind of . . . have a foundation to a relationship before I . . . go all in. Physically. Does that—"

"—It's okay." He puts his hands on either side of my coat hood and brings my face to his. "Sorry about before," he says, uncomfortably. "I don't want"—then he kisses me. *Don't want what? Where were you going with that? Can you please finish your sentence?* We're still kissing, but I can't help but try to fill in the blanks. *Don't want to see me again? Don't want that to ruin our potential? These are very different things!* So I pull my head back and demand, through a smile, "Don't want what?"

He smiles flirtatiously, urges "*Stop,*" and pulls me back in again.

* * *

Monday morning, Deepa tells me that Joanne was looking for me.

"You can close the door." Joanne looks up from her desk.

I do and I take a seat across from her. "You wanted to see me?"

"I wanted to talk about your analysis of the oxidation on the copper paint at the Armory."

"Oh?"

"I feel that you're a bit too," she searches for a word and settles on, "*complacent* in your research and investigative techniques. Restoration Associates has obviously invested a great amount of time and resources in your training, with the goal of seeing you advance within the company. But if you look around at your colleagues, they all seem to show a bit more *initiative* than you."

My stomach sinks. "I'm sorry, I don't . . . really understand. We wound up *specifying* the treatment I devised for the oxidation removal. I did all the testing; the rusty appearance, the blue streaks—they're gone. The paint looks . . ." I say slowly, waiting for her to criticize, "like shiny copper again."

"You arrived at the correct result, it's the way you got there that frustrates me."

I look perplexed but say nothing.

"You asked too many questions. We have a rich in-house research library; you need to develop your own expertise. Look at Margo. She has never done paint analysis before, and she devised the restoration color palette for the column capitals at St. John's—"

"—wait, but *I* did that analy—"

"You helped her get started, but she matched nearly thirty samples, expanding her skill set and billable tasks."

"But I . . ." I stumble. Last week, Margo said she needed to give the color matches to the contractor by Friday morning. I spent a day and a half holed up in the lab, sanding, mounting, and analyzing three dozen samples under the microscope. Then I emailed her an Excel sheet of my results with a paragraph or two of interpretation. *She sent it to Joanne? And didn't mention the findings were mine?*

But Margo is the golden child of RA. Pointing out that "her" results were actually mine won't get me anywhere. Will it? I stumble through a few "buts," "umms," and fragmented "I thinks" as I try to gather my thoughts.

Joanne studies me but says nothing.

"I mean, I really love working on all the paint stuff. Metallic finishes and gilding, too. But . . ." My brain is rushing to piece together a calm but forceful defense. I sputter, "I *do* think of myself as driven, but . . . I also have to learn it from somewhere. And I thought asking you would be a good starting point? Like, knowledge sharing?" I hope that didn't come off as condescending but fear it did.

Joanne clasps her hands on her desk. "I'm glad you mention the word 'driven,' because that was something else I wanted to discuss: Every day, you're the first to leave the office. If you *were* really 'driven,'" she hits the word hard, "I would think you'd work longer hours. Your coworkers stay late each evening to meet deadlines or to catch up on the latest journals and scholarship. As it is now, you're depriving yourself of that same opportunity."

My stomach sinks further, now down to the floor. "I'm *always* on time to work, if not early. The days I'm on-site, I get there by seven, come back to the office after, and still don't leave until five-thirty." I take a deep breath to calm myself. "You are right that I'm out the door at five-thirty most days. I work another—"

"Oh?" Joanne glares at me sharply.

"I'm not moonlighting," I assure her quickly. "I tutor. I just . . ." I glance up from my hands to gauge if this has softened her reaction. It hasn't. "I can't support myself on my RA salary. I'm not complaining, or asking for a raise. But . . . everyone else in the office is married or lives with a partner. I don't have a joint income to rely on, and I can't afford rent if I don't work evenings, too." My eyes are getting watery, and I try to compose myself.

"This is news," Joanne says matter-of-factly.

"Tutoring is how I supported myself through grad school. But I *don't* let it interfere with my conservation work. I get that everybody else stays later than I do. But I also work through every single lunch break and eat at my desk. I actually just . . . try to be extremely efficient so I don't *have* to stay late. And none of my clients, or the project managers at RA, have ever expressed disappointment in the quality of my work before, or in my efficiency." I wish this sounded more like a statement, but I'm so disconcerted I know it sounds more like a whine.

"This is all interesting to note," Joanne says. "Moving forward, you need to work on being more of a self-starter. As you know, our employee manual lays out the criteria and skill sets required at each level for professional advancement. I encourage you to consult it and see which areas need further development and attention before you go up for promotion this summer."

"Yes. Of course. I will. Thank you." I try to swallow, but my mouth is so dry I can't.

As I head to the subway after work I receive the following email:

February 13 at 6:14 p.m.

Dear Alison,

I hope your day's going well. Mine's been busy and annoying, as expected.

I wanted to tell you that you're a great girl. And I'm more attracted to you than I've ever been to anyone. But we're just too different, and I don't see this working out.

Good luck,
Paul

That night, I'm cooking dinner at home with Cassie and Nicole. "Oh, hey," I say, as if just remembering, "I have this email I want to show you guys." I walk over from the kitchen to the living room and click open my laptop. I pull up my inbox and walk back to the stove, leaving the screen up for them to read, trying to mask my emotion, specifically the eagerness with which I await their collective response. And their sympathy.

"What *happened*?" Nicole asks, with concern wrapped in melodrama that I so appreciate at this very moment. I recount the story about his Sunday night pants-shedding charade and our walk home, and our embrace on the front stoop.

"You would *think* that kiss meant that he was going to get over it," Nicole points out.

"I know." I sigh, stirring the spaghetti. "I wasn't sure what to make of it, but that's what I hoped it meant."

"Umm," Cassie begins, "I have a theory?" We both look to her. She looks embarrassed. "Do you think I ruined it for you . . . by sleeping with Brian on Friday?"

"Ha!" I laugh out loud. "I hope you don't take this the wrong way, but I wondered that, too."

"No, really," Cassie persists. "Do you think that I somehow gave Paul expectations of what would come next?"

"'Next,' as in 'the very next night'? Maybe? I don't know."

She bites her lip and appears pained, "If that's true. I am *so sorry.*"

"No. Don't be sorry. It seems . . . from his email . . . like this was bound to happen with him sooner or later, right?"

"But maybe it would have happened on a more acceptable timeline?" she asks. Nicole is looking back and forth between us, following the conversation, completely amused.

"Well, if you want my opinion," Nicole says, "that definitely could have done it."

"Stop it!" I chastise her for making Cassie feel guilty, even though secretly I *do* think she had a hand in my receipt of this depressing email. "At least," I counter optimistically, "*one* of us had fun this weekend?" Everyone laughs.

"Are you upset?" Cassie asks, sympathetically.

"Yes." I pause to think about this. "You know, I'm not sure if I liked him for quote 'the right reasons.' I didn't even really know him very well. But there was this, like, electrostatic spark the minute he walked into Café d'Alsace. I think I'm just really attracted to him . . . but, like, to his face. Not necessarily his personality." I wonder if Mom will practically run a victory lap around her apartment when I tell her this, given that she had to convince me he was "cute enough" in the first place.

"Do you feel regret?" Cassie, ever the emotion-seeker, asks.

"No." I stir the spaghetti slowly as I contemplate this a bit further. "You know, I *did* like him, but I don't know how I could have really played this any differently, without landing in the exact same spot." Cassie puts her hand on my back and rubs it gently. I grimace. "You know what's bothering me the most though?"

"What?" Nicole asks.

"That I am so, utterly, screwed." I shake my head.

"Noooo," Cassie tries to reassure me, then asks, "What do you mean?"

"Just . . . that this is going to happen to me on *every* third date. With *every* guy. I am *never* going to make it to a fourth date. *Ever.* I am . . . just . . . totally screwed!"

"Well, technically," Nicole points out, "you're the opposite."

poplockandroll03: Doppelgänger Greg

January 30 at 9:51 p.m.

Dear Alison,

Fancy finding you on this site. Do you remember our romantic weekend last summer in Montauk? I still can't stop thinking about it.

Fondly,
Greg

P.S. What'd you do with the guy who brought you?

January 31 at 8:09 a.m.

Dear Greg,

I do! I think about it all the time. You, me, 6 other dudes, pouring rain, and really loud Top 40 hits. Oh, and I had the flu the whole time. . . .

If that doesn't spell romance, I don't know what does.

Fondly,
Alison

P.S. He and I had our differences. It was nice while it lasted.

February 1 at 11:01 p.m.

Dear Alison,

Since we've already shared so much together, what do you say we take this conversation off Match and to the next level: cell phones?!

Fondly,
Greg

                                    February 2 at 8:07 a.m.

Dear Greg,
    You certainly don't beat around the bush, do you? ;)

Fondly,
Alison

Cell number below.

February 4 at 11:56 p.m.
347-466-1221: I'M IN SO MUCH TROUBLE.

ALISON: IS THIS GREG? WHY ARE YOU IN TROUBLE?

347-466-1221: YES. GOOD MEMORY. I VIOLATED BAND OF BROTHERS. EXILED.

ALISON: WHAT?

347-466-1221: OUT WITH PETERSEN BROTHERS. TOLD THEM ABOUT OUR BLOSSOMING ROMANCE. OUSTED.

Dave's best friend is Evan Petersen. Evan's brother, Joe Petersen, is Greg's best friend.

ALISON: BROS BEFORE HOS?

February 5 at 3:21 a.m.
347-466-1221: WERE YOU EAVESDROPPING, ALISON? DID YOU BUG MY PHONE?!?

February 5 at 8:14 a.m.

347-466-1221: UH BOY, LOOKS LIKE YOU WERE A VICTIM OF SOME LATE-NIGHT TXT BLATHERING. YOU'RE A GOOD SPORT FOR TRYING TO MAKE SENSE OF IT.

347-466-1221: THINK I WATCHED ONE TOO MANY *GOSSIP GIRL* RERUNS YESTERDAY . . .

February 5 at 9:21 a.m.
ALISON: YOU'RE A GG FAN, EH?

347-466-1221: HMM . . . MUST BE MORE CAREFUL WHEN USING CLEVER METAPHORS . . . BUT YES, I'VE SEEN THE SHOW "A FEW TIMES." LIKE THE AVALON, SPENDING TOO MUCH TIME W/ O-TWINS HAS LINGERING SIDE EFFECTS.

The mention of the Avalon makes me laugh. It was the flea-infested motel Dave and I shared in Montauk with the Petersen brothers and their friends, Greg among them. At the time, Greg was dating the personal assistant of the Olsen Twins.

* * *

Cassie, Nicole, and I had debated spending Valentine's Day watching *The Notebook* and going to town on some quarts of Edy's Slow Churned Caramel Delight, with me in my ex-boyfriend pajamas—a gift from my sister when I broke up with Scott, they display cartoon photos of couples, torn in two, with the word "EX-BOYFRIEND" emblazoned every three or four inches. Alternatively, Cassie suggested we could negotiate drink specials at a bar and host a single mingle. We collectively opted for the latter, so I text Greg the following:

February 14 at 11:51 a.m.
ALISON: ALRIGHT, IF OUR ROMANCE FAILED TO LAUNCH, WHY DON'T YOU COME TO A VALENTINE'S DAY SINGLE MINGLE TONIGHT? I HAVE LOTS OF LOVELY LADIES WHO AREN'T FAMILIAR WITH THE PETERSEN BROS.

ALISON: KEYBAR. 9 P.M. ON. BRING ELIGIBLE SINGLE FRIENDS!

I then copy and send that exact text (minus the line about the Petersen Bros.) to Secret Agent Man, since one woman's loss . . . or so the saying goes.

* * *

Greg shows up at the party, John does not. When I'm not circling the room trying to play matchmaker, my dream job, I wind up always coming back to Greg. It's not that I specifically want to or try to, it's actually that he seems completely uninterested in meeting anyone new. And since he's quite an engaging conversationalist, and I haven't met any true dating prospects at the party, talking to him makes for a fun evening, if one that is only slightly more romantic than watching *The Notebook* with Cassie and Nicole.

On the bright side, Ben finally buys a drink for a college friend I'd been trying to push him toward for nearly six months—their shared drinks are the official highlight of my Valentine's Day.

* * *

A month later I'm at a bachelorette party on Long Island.

"Why don't you go say hi?" Nicole asks.

"I—I really can't tell if it's him or not? I haven't seen him in forever, so I just don't know."

"Would he be here?"

"I have no idea. Maybe? He's a banker, so . . . it's within reason that it could be him?"

"Go say hi!"

"But if it's not him, I don't want to get stuck in a conversation with some random dude who thinks I'm hitting on him."

"There are worse things."

"Ehh, I'll text him. If I see him take his phone out of his pocket after I hit 'send,' I'll go say hi."

March 18 at 11:33 p.m.

ALISON: RANDOM, BUT I THINK I SEE YOU OR YOUR DOPPELGÄNGER. ARE YOU AT THE BLUE PARROT RIGHT NOW? IF YES, I'LL COME SAY HI!

The next morning, I wake up to the following slew of texts from Greg:

March 19 at 2:13 a.m.

GREG: RANDOM BUT I THINK I SEE YOU OR YOUR DOPPELGÄNGER. ARE YOU IN STATEN ISLAND RIGHT NOW?

GREG: DID YOU JUST DO A BODY SHOT OFF YOURSELF? AMAZING.

GREG: I OWE D U FOR THINKING THAT I MIGHT BE HANGING OUT ON THE UPPER EAST LAST NIGHT....... PUHLEESE... I DON'T THINK THEY WOULD EVEN ALLOW ME THERE ANYMORE. TOO OLD.

To which I respond:

March 19 at 10:18 a.m.

ALISON: BLUE PARROT? ON THE UPPER EAST? I THINK YOU MADE THAT UP - I WAS IN THE HAMPTONS FOR A BACHELORETTE PARTY AND THOUGHT IT WASN'T BEYOND THE REALM OF POSSIBILITY THAT YOU WERE OUT THERE, TOO. PUHLEESE.

March 19 at 10:50 a.m.

GREG: OH. RIGHT. THAT BLUE PARROT. APOLOGY ACCEPTED THEN. BE MORE CAREFUL NEXT TIME. GEEZE, LADY.

The following Saturday morning, I wake to find the following, from Greg:

March 25 at 3:43 a.m.

GREG: RANDOM BUT I THINK I SEE YOU OR YOUR DOPPELGÄNGER. ARE YOU AT A BOWLING ALLEY IN NEWARK?

GREG: DID YOU JUST GET A TURKEY? AMAZING!

GREG: I KNEW YOU WERE A FUN GIRL. KNEW IT.

ForrestForTheTrees202:
Rain Forrest Guy

"So, what did you have, like, three dates today?" Jason asks as we stroll through Richard Serra's giant metal masses in a Chelsea gallery.

"No, just two. And so far only one. The other's tonight."

"You're a veritable dating mach*ine*. Don't you ever get tired? You used to be such a . . . whatever the inverse of 'one-woman guy' is."

"Sometimes it's tiring, just from a scheduling standpoint. But sometimes not." I shrug. "Like not today."

"Two-a-days take me back to rugby training season."

"Yeah, the girls' team never had to do those. I guess that's why we weren't very good. But anyway, I've gotta make the most of the hundred and fifty bucks Match is making off me, right?"

"I think you've already earned that back hand over fist in drinks tabs from your dates."

"Probably," I muse.

"But seriously. Are you finding it tiring?" he asks earnestly. "Keeping them all straight?"

"Ha ha," I say flatly. "It's not like I'm dating a hundred people. And besides, don't you know I have the memory of an elephant? I'm dating two or three guys, max, at the same time. And most of the time they're not going to lead to second or third dates, so it's really just like having coffee . . . or *wandering an art space . . .*" I elbow Jason, "with a friend. What else would I be doing with my Saturdays anyway?"

"Enriching your mind. Sleeping. Working out."

"I ran this morning. And I enriched my mind learning about the transfer of energy cycles in tropical rain forests this afternoon. And I'm enriching my mind *now*. And I'll sleep tonight."

"And they say women can't have it all."

"Did you just wink at me? Ah! Is that how you hit on girls? Jason! That's, like, what our *dads* did when they were courting our moms forty years ago. You've gotta up your game."

"I'm *Korean*, Alison. It *always* looks like I'm winking!"

"You *totally* winked. Admit it!" I tease.

"Don't you need to go home and get ready?"

"For my next date? Why?" And then, "Oh wait. Why? Do I look like I need to change?"

"Well, you don't look like you're ready for a night on the town. I mean, you look nice, but you could . . . you know, put on high heels, or tighter pants, or something shorter. Like 'sexier?'" He holds up finger quotes.

"First, shut up. Second, we're not going to 'da *club*' or anything. We're going to get Mexican food. Besides, I try not to primp too much for my dates."

"Keep their expectations low?" Jason raises his eyebrows.

"No, not seem like I'm trying too hard. Or, rather, *actually* not try too hard. I feel like if you spend all this time primping, you get nervous. If you *don't* spend time primping, then you're being you . . . rather than sizing someone up and being sized up."

"Whatever. You can keep telling yourself that, but you *know* you're being judged. Because you're judging, too!" he accuses.

I laugh. "I know. But it makes *me* feel better thinking I'm not trying too hard. Soooo, I'm gonna stick with that. And go straight from here to dinner."

"So you, of all people, don't feel a little strange dating multiple guys at once?"

"It's not like I'm sleeping with any of them. And besides, you *know* they're all doing the exact same thing."

"Not necessarily."

"*Yes*, necessarily."

"I don't knoooow," Jason singsongs.

"*All* our guy friends would be doing the same. They *do* do the same!"

"Yeah, but you would never date most of them. And they would never date you. Especially not if you showed up looking like that." He rolls his eyes and points at my furry brown boots.

I roll my eyes, too.

"So tell me about your dates."

"Which ones?"

"Today's. Rain Forest Guy."

"Well, his name actually *is* Forrest. But you can call him Rain Forrest Guy. He's a real estate investor; currently lives in Boston but spends most of his time in New York and is moving here soon. In his spare time he's a singer-songwriter—he kept emailing me MP3 files before we met. He's good."

"He sent you love songs before you ever met him?"

"They're not *love songs*, they're songs from an album he's working on. But he's not bad."

"So what'd you do on your date?"

"Not a whole lot, actually. He was in town staying at the Standard in the East Village. I was having brunch in the vicinity with high school friends, so we met in the lobby after."

"And?"

"And nothing. We just sat on the couches and talked. I guess it's kind of strange that we just hung out in a hotel lobby without getting coffee or drinks or anything, but . . . it didn't feel weird at the time."

"What'd you talk about?"

"Life. Music. Forested areas his company is investing in for eco-tourism resorts—I think it might be his pet project. Or something."

"And? Sparks? Chemistry? Smooching?"

"Are you twelve? Who says 'smooching?' And no."

"No smooching, or no chemistry?"

"No smooching, the jury's still out on the chemistry."

"You'll see him again? Assuming you don't fall in love with tonight's date?"

"Yeah. He's smart, cute, and really pensive-thoughtful . . . so check, check, check, I guess?"

February 20 at 3:46 p.m.

Alison,

I really enjoyed meeting you Saturday afternoon. It sounded like you had quite the packed day, and I appreciate that you carved time out to meet me. I think you said you were in town next weekend. . . . If so, I'll be back down here again. Do you want to meet up? I was hoping you might give me the behind-the-scenes tour of St. John the Divine. I loved watching you light up as you described the history of the building and all the work you put into its restoration.

As promised, my cover of The Civil Wars & Taylor Swift's "Safe & Sound" is attached for your listening pleasure. Let me know what you think.

Forrest

* * *

Juan Pablo and I are crouched on the uppermost level of the scaffold—only three or four feet below the ceiling—straining our necks to repair the Guastavino tiles overhead. While he holds two halves of a cracked tile in place, I secure them with a micro-pin.

"So," I begin tentatively, removing another micro-pin from the bag. "Do you . . . think it would be okay if I brought someone to the job site this weekend? Like, for a behind-the-scenes tour of the restoration?"

"You trying to make me jealous, Alison?"

"Right. So I was hoping to swing by—"

"Who's the new guy?"

"—not for a long time, maybe twenty minutes, on Sunday to show a *friend*," I say with added emphasis, "you know, what I've been doing with the last three years of my life?"

"That's all you're gonna give me? A *friend*?"

I smile, a bit teasingly, and shrug.

Juan Pablo smiles, too, and his voice shifts into a slightly more serious register. "I think it's fine. You can bring your . . . *friend*. Just make sure to grab hard hats if you cross the construction barrier. Wouldn't want us getting in trouble with OSHA."

I nod obediently. "Of course. Thanks."

"So when do I get you next week?" he asks. "Are you still at the Armory?"

"I'll be here . . ." I try to picture my planner. "Monday and Thursday mornings. The rest of the time I'm at the Armory. I think."

"Are you ever going to offer *me* a behind-the-scenes tour of the restoration there?" he asks flirtatiously.

I consult my reflected ceiling plan and cross out the tile we just stabilized. "If you ask nicely, I will," I say without looking up.

I crawl across the steel plank to reposition myself beneath the next tile that requires pinning. Juan Pablo follows.

* * *

February 21 at 8:01 a.m.

Hi Forrest,

It was great to meet you, too. Yes, I am in town this weekend. Would Sunday afternoon work? Meet in front of St. John the Divine and take it from there? I'm definitely going to dork out if you want the full insider's tour of the restoration. I love that church so much it makes my heart hurt.

I gave your cover a listen as I was getting ready for work this morning. It sounded familiar - it's the one from The Hunger Games movie, yes? I think you improved on it!

Let me know what time works on Sunday.

Cheers,
Alison

February 28 at 7:16 p.m.

Alison,

I enjoyed seeing you Sunday. The fortuitously timed evensong practice was great background music for exploring the different chapels and viewing the restoration. I added "go to a concert at St. John's" to my To Do list. I was pleasantly surprised when you told me that you're not dead set on living in NYC forever. Sometimes I imagine living in the middle of nowhere, either in a log cabin or interesting prefab modern structure. My desire for a remote location probably has something to do with a global theme

of simplicity that I'm drawn to. You should check this com-
pany out: http://www.rocioromero.com/LVSeries.html

Forrest

> *March 1 at 9:11 a.m.*

Hi Forrest!
    What else is on your "To Do" list? I'm intrigued. . . . Back
when I turned twenty, I formulated my own mental "mini-
to-do list in life." It included a slew of places to go (Greece,
Morocco) and skills/hobbies to acquire (learn to surf, learn
to knit, run a marathon, etc.). I guess I was a little overeager
in that I rather quickly worked through the bulk of the items
on the list - consequently I now feel like I have very little
ambition. Haha, oops.
    Did you see the prefab housing exhibit at MoMA years
and years ago? I used to think I wanted to grow up and live
in a Lustron house, until I was able to walk through one at
this exhibit and realized all the walls looked and felt like cold
metal hospital tables. The one you sent looks way cooler. In
reality, though, I think I'm more of a log cabin type of girl.
    OK, now I really must get down to work.

Cheers,
Alison

"Hey!" I open the car door and climb into the passenger's seat.

"Hey, how's it going?" Forrest leans in and kisses me on the cheek.

I blink, a bit flustered since it's the first time we've had even grazing physical contact. "Good, good. So . . . *now* are you going to tell me what's on tap for today?"

"Man, you really don't like surprises, huh?"

"*Nooo*," I say emphatically, "I just . . . am curious to know where you're taking me."

He laughs to himself, keeping his eyes on the road. "Yeah, I enjoyed that bit where you asked me if I was a serial killer." He turns his head quickly to glance at me. "You know, serial killers probably don't just come out and admit to being serial killers."

"I know. But I thought *maybe* if I asked you over the phone, I could detect a note of panic or hesitation in your voice."

"Did I act especially serial killer-ish the last two times you saw me?"

"No, but it's not every day a girl receives an invitation that's so . . . clandestine-seeming . . . 'Wear clothes you don't mind getting dirty,'" I say in a mock deep voice. "'Maybe bring a bottle of water . . . I insist on picking you up *in my car.*'"

"Ahh, I see. So all drivers are potential serial killers."

"When you live in New York City, yes. Normal people don't *have* cars. And if second grade taught me anything, it was 'don't get in cars with strangers.'"

He laughs aloud at this. "Oh, I see. So I'm a stranger now."

I groan faintly. "I didn't mean it that way. But . . . wouldn't you think it was weird if *I* said, 'Oh hey. Let's go on a date! But first! I am going to blindfold you, and put a bag over your head, and take you in my white van out to the woods?'"

"How did you know the plan for today? Did you hack my email?" He laughs. "You know, you can still get out of the car. Before I have time to dig out the blindfold and the paper bag."

"Well, I decided that I'm not young enough to be jailbait, and that you seemed kind of okay the last two times. Also, I gave my roommates your name and phone number and told them to report me missing if I wasn't home by midnight."

"Did you text them my license plate, too?"

"Gah! I can't believe *I* didn't think of that! Do you mind pulling over for a second so I can jot it down?" I smile.

"Loading docks on the Brooklyn waterfront?" I scan the somewhat deserted vista before me, which includes rocky banks of what I think is the East River.

"Nope, over here." He locks his car and walks ahead of me to a nondescript one-story building, the siding of which is corrugated sheet metal. A lobster shack?

He tugs on the metal door and cautiously steps inside. "Hello?"

"Back here!" A woman's voice carries from the rear of the building. Just then she emerges, her gray-streaked brown hair piled high in a giant bun, goggles protecting her eyes, and a dark leather apron on which she's drying her hands. "Nice to meet you . . . Forrest, I assume?"

She extends her hand to shake his and turns to me. "And you must be Alison?"

I smile and introduce myself.

"I still haven't told her where we are or what we're doing," Forrest says.

"Oh! How lovely!" Then she looks embarrassed. "I guess I kind of ruined the surprise coming out like this." I look at her askance.

"Nope." I shake my head. "Still no idea."

Forrest turns to me. "Today, we're going to learn how to metal weld."

"Wait, *what*? That's *so cool*! But how did you . . . organize this? How did you *find* this?"

"Google." He shrugs, his hands in his pockets. "When we were at St. John the Divine, I talked about how I always wanted to turn wood on a lathe. You said you'd done that but had always wanted to metal weld. I did some searching, and Marina offers private tutorials. So . . . here we are."

"Here we are indeed. *So*. Cool!" I shake my head in disbelief.

"Alright, should we get you guys fitted up in aprons and face shields?"

As I'm tack-welding the veins onto my leaf-shaped belt buckle, Marina stands beside me.

"Your boyfriend's pretty romantic, huh?"

Keeping my eyes focused on the task at hand, I bite my lip and reply, "Umm, yeah. Don't know how he'd ever top this. But . . . he's, actually, not my boyfriend. This is only our third date."

"He did this for your *third* date? Does he have any single brothers?"

"What an afternoon!" I beam. "Torches and welders and flux, oh my!"

We shed our aprons and gloves and walk toward the car.

"So I know we're kind of dirty," Forrest says, "but I read about a few things to do around here. Mostly eating and drinking. You hungry?"

"Aren't we having dinner in a few hours?" Forrest had asked me to clear my Saturday; he'd said we'd have a daytime activity, then each head home to shower and change, followed by dinner in Midtown.

"Yeah. But it's three o'clock. Dinner's not until eight," he says.

"Okay. I can always eat. And drink."

"I read about a great hole-in-the-wall tea room not too far from here that serves famous petit fours and half-priced champagne on Saturday afternoons. You game?"

"This day can't *get* any more perfect!" I say, wide-eyed.

"I was hoping you'd say that." He grins.

Fifteen minutes later, we're sitting on a banquette beneath an adorable pressed metal ceiling, with adorable gold-flecked champagne flutes in hand. "Cheers to an amazing day," I say, raising my glass. "And cheers to *you* for making all of this happen. It's been incredible!" I look him in the eye and nod, for emphasis, "Thank you. That was . . . insanely considerate . . . and generous . . . and Prince Charming-y. I totally don't deserve all this, but I hope you know I really appreciate it."

"No, you *do* deserve it. We had all these unconventional first dates, where we just met and walked and talked." I squint and study his face. Am I attracted to him? I can't decide if I'm attracted to him. "It was pretty easy to tell you don't . . . expect . . . these kinds of things. Which makes it all the more fun to plan them for you." He smiles.

"Ahhh, I see." I smile back. "You were *testing* me. Taking me on these dates that left me thirsty and hungry to see if I would complain. Or turn you down for the next date."

"No, not like that."

"Yes! *Exactly* like that!"

"Stop trying to deflect my compliments. Let's just say, 'it's fun to do nice things for you,' and leave it at that. Okay?"

"Don't you have a date tonight?" Nicole asks from the kitchen when I enter the apartment.

"Yes! Longest. Date. Ever."

"Uh-oh. You wanna bail?"

"No. It's just . . . it's just been an interesting day."

"But you didn't get kidnapped, so that's a plus. Where'd he take you after all?"

"Swoon! He took me *metal welding*," I say, flourishing my fancy new belt buckle.

"He did what?"

"*Metal* welding," I announce. "Best. Date. *Ever*."

"You just said, 'Longest. Date. Ever.' Which was it?"

"Well, that, too. It's still ongoing. I have to shower and meet him for dinner. But yeah, he took me metal welding. I got to wear a leather apron, and giant leather gloves four sizes too big, and a *face shield*. Nothing says 'sexy' like a face shield on date three."

"So where are you off to next?"

"The Plaza. He's staying there for work this weekend."

"Are you having dinner at the Plaza?"

"Dunno. Didn't ask. He told me to dress nice-ish."

"Well, this should be an interesting night. Keep me posted."

"You know I will!" I sing as I head to my bedroom.

I walk into the lobby of the Plaza Hotel, and Forrest is standing there in a sports coat, smiling, hands clasped at his waist, ready and waiting as if in a scene lifted from *Some Kind of Wonderful* or *Sixteen Candles* or any other John Hughes movie from the eighties.

"Hey, way to clean up!" I say teasingly.

"Way to clean up, you."

"So . . ."

"So . . . dinner's in thirty minutes, it will take us ten minutes to walk over there. If you don't mind walking, that is."

"Of course, don't be silly."

"So we've got ten minutes to kill. Do you want to come up and see my room?"

I freeze. "Uhh . . . you mean, like, now?" I ask timidly.

"Yeah, now. The elevator bank's right here. They upgraded me to a suite. It's . . . kind of *amazing*. Have you ever stayed here before?"

"No. Uhhh," I scratch at the left side of my neck. "I . . . uh . . ."

"You made it through a whole day with me. In *Brooklyn*. And look, you're still alive." He smiles. "If I had anything deviant planned, I kind of missed my opportunity this afternoon, right?"

"Uhh, right?" I smile. Wordlessly, I follow him to the elevator. He's talking about the plaster moldings, "which I know you're going to love," and I'm internally panicking. It's *not* that I don't trust him. It's *not* that I don't trust myself. I just still haven't figured out if I want to kiss him or not. And if I *don't* want to, it's going to be a lot more difficult to wave like Paul Pfeiffer and gracefully exit a hotel room. At *the Plaza*.

We walk in, and it's as if we're swimming in decadence. Marble pilasters, marble columns. I can see into the marble bathroom, with its gilded claw-foot bathtub. A canopy over the headboard and two plush robes hanging on the door. And there, in the corner, an ice bucket with Veuve Clicquot's easily recognizable yellow label. Crap.

Forrest follows my eyes, which are fixed on the champagne. "Soooo. As you can *see*, I took the liberty of ordering a bottle of champagne up to the room. I figure we can have it after dinner. . . ." I can't answer, because my vocal chords, along with the rest of me, are stunned.

* * *

"We split what I think was a really delicious porterhouse at Smith & Wollensky, but I just couldn't get my mind off those robes and that bottle of Veuve."

"So what'd you talk about at dinner?" Nicole asks.

"I have no idea. I spent the whole time in hyperoverdrive-panic mode trying to figure out how I'd handle post-dinner activities. First I tried to plot an exit strategy. Then I tried to assess if I could step up and wear my 'big kid jeans' as you'd say"—I point to Cassie—"and go home with him without knowing if I'd be attracted to him."

Cassie looks at me hopefully.

"I couldn't."

Cassie frowns.

"Uh-oh. What'd you do?" Nicole asks.

"I panicked. I tried to give myself a decompressing pep talk in the bathroom at the restaurant. That failed, so I went back to the table, popped a Nyquil in front of him, and said I'd been battling a cold all week and was feeling wiped from our tremendously fun, activity-packed day."

"You actually took a Nyquil?"

"I *clearly* was not thinking straight. I think I said something like, 'I'll be knocked out in, like, twenty minutes flat, but hopefully-I-can-make-it-off-the-subway-and-face-plant-onto-my-bed in that time.'"

"Smooth." Nicole laughs.

"I just . . ." I throw my hands up in despair. "He's *so* nice. And I felt like when I bailed on the hotel thing, I just watched him, crest falling, become, finally, crestfallen. UHHH," I groan at the memory. "It was *terrible*."

"How'd he handle it?" Cassie asks. "I mean, your reaction totally makes sense."

"A little passive aggressive, but, I guess, better than it could have been? I mean, he was totally gentlemanly and whatever."

"How'd you say goodbye?" Nicole asks.

"He walked me to the subway in this drawn-out, anger-tinged silence. I tried to hug him . . . but he dodged it."

Cassie sighs. "More wine?"

* * *

"Hey Alison. It's Forrest. Sorry I took awhile to call. Also, more importantly . . . I just want to say," he breathes in deeply, *"that I thought about it, and I totally get where things went wrong on Saturday. I guess . . . you took the champagne and the room to . . . mean something more . . . and I think I did mean it to . . . mean something more . . . but I wasn't trying to rush things. I was just trying to make the night . . . perfect. And if you had just wanted to watch a movie and hang out with champagne, that would have been fine with me. The last thing I would have wanted to do was put pressure on you. And . . . I just wanted to get that out there. . . . Annnd, this is officially the longest voice mail ever. So, yeah. Okay. Bye."*

"Ooh! Can I listen to it?" Nicole asks.

I hesitate. "Can I just summarize it for you?"

"Yeah, but why don't you want me to listen to it?" She cocks her head, confused.

"It's not . . . that I *don't* want you to listen to it. It's that I'll feel like a triply shitty person if I play it for you and then we sit around analyzing it. I was shitty enough to him already!"

"First of all, aren't we going to analyze it anyway? Second of all, you *weren't* shitty to him. You didn't take him for granted. Or blow him off—"

"I *did* blow him off."

"But not in a way that's flitty or bitchy. You blew him off at the end of the night because you felt un*com*fortable. It's not like just because he bought you champagne, you owe him anything. Certainly not a sleepover."

"I know," I say softly. "But I feel like everything he did came from this deep well of amazingness: generosity, thoughtfulness . . . and I couldn't . . . reciprocate in any meaningful way other than to stammer through a lot of 'thank-yous.'" I chew on the inside of my cheek. "And I hurt him in the process."

"But that's not your fault."

"But it can still suck. And make me feel bad."

Nicole nods. "If you could go back and relive Saturday all over again, what would you do differently?"

"Nothing. That's what's bothering me. I don't want to call him back because I don't know what I *could* have done differently, and I don't know how to move forward from here. . . . But I also feel like ghosting him at this point is the ultimate bitch move."

"So call him back."

"But then I'm, like, kicking a wounded puppy. I'd be all, 'Hey Forrest. I think you're *won*derful. Like, *really*, wonderful. And I have a lot of fun with you, and you shower me with every kindness. . . . But when you pressurized the situation on Saturday night, I freaked out . . . and thought that I might be physically repulsed if you kissed me.' I mean, what the hell am I supposed to say?" I whine.

"Well don't say *that*." Nicole laughs. "And really? Repulsed? I thought you said he was cute."

"He *is* cute. But if you're not *ready*, or, mentally stoked to be . . . physical with someone, then doesn't it just feel gross when he kisses you good night? Like you're just pretending to be into it but you actually feel like throwing up?"

"Do you think Cassie has *really* found someone she's deeply attracted to every single Saturday night? Or Ben has? Doubtful. Sometimes you just do it because you're horny and it'll be fun."

"Well, I don't think *I* can force those feelings. Or fake them."

"Well. People can. And sometimes if you like someone's personality, you *do* force it, and hope the attraction part develops later. But regardless of other people, he totally misread *you* and misread the situation."

"He's trying, though. Right? He's trying *so hard*, which is part of the problem. I don't want to ignore his voice mail, because he's being sweet. And trying to right the . . . awkward wrong. But I don't want to call, because I have no idea what to say."

"Do you think if you saw him again, you could be . . . not completely awkward?"

"No." I massage my temples. "I feel like I'm viscerally so rattled by the Plaza and the Veuve, I doubt I could be normal or myself if I saw him again."

"You still have the voice mail?"

I nod.

"Then do that thing where you direct-dial into his voice mail and leave a message. Short and sweet."

"Hey, Forrest. Thanks for your message. That was thoughtful of you and . . . I appreciate it. I'm about to start a really busy period of work and work-travel, so I don't know that I'll get to see you again for a while. But I just wanted to say thanks. You're really sweet."

WorldTraveler619: Kevin the Bowerbird

February 16 at 9:35 p.m.

So, I do not run (outside) and I'm a wimp in inclement weather. Is this gonna be a deal breaker? Anyways, we can meet friends on this site, right, even if we're clearly not meant to be? Because either way, Time Out New York's cover article is about the 100 dishes you must try in NYC and I'm going to need company.

But I did read your profile and I find you very interesting . . . and we have an alma mater in common, so there's that (did my PhD at Columbia). ;)

The last really stupid thing I said in front of people was "My opinion on the matter is split 60/30." My faulty addition had to be pointed out to me. FML. I don't know why I told you that, but I thought it might break the ice. You know, self-deprecation is good for that.

Talk later,
Kevin

February 17 at 6:55 a.m.

Hi Kevin!

I don't know if you were kidding about the friend comment, but it's probably only fair that I alert you that I actually have honed quite a skill for amassing friends via Match. My girlfriends keep telling me I'm going about this all wrong, since at the last party I threw, my guest list had two friends I made from Match, but zero dudes I was interested in dating. Oops.

Man after my own heart, though, you're into adventur-ous/inquisitive eating, too? I'm game to keep you company in your endeavor to sample those 100 dishes. In fact, I think that's an excellent goal to put on the life to-do list. Apropos of that, what's the best meal you've had in New York City? Weirdest?

Cheers,
Alison

Our email topics run the gamut from his job ("I'm a scientist for a chemical research company") to his dream vacation ("how cool to lasso cattle on a dude ranch!") to questions—and responses—about the specific emulsifying agents I use to clean the murals at the Armory ("Get out! I use Pemulen TR-2 in my lab, too!"). And still, no date. But, we *do* have a phone date set up for the coming Sunday night. I feel transported back to middle school, looking forward to a phone call.

"So what ever happened with your snowboarding lawyer?" Ben asks.

"Ugh. I don't want to talk about it."

"Ohhh," he says gently, "that bad, eh?"

"No, I'm just bummed about it." I stroke my paddle through the brackish water of the lake behind my parents' house in the Catskills. "He wasn't a big fan of the Pants Speech, I guess. . . . A story as old as time."

"Huh," Ben says. "That won't be everyone, though."

"I know. I think I'm just not cut out for modern adult dating."

We row silently toward the edge of the lake.

"How are you in general? Dating now, post-Dave?"

"Okay, I guess. The snowboarding lawyer was kind of a . . . low point, but other than that it's been fun? I like meeting new people, see-ing new places."

"So who's on your dating roster at the moment?"

"A couple people. A banker who kind of looks like Dave . . . I've seen him a few times already. And I've been having a really long email exchange with a scientist who got his PhD from Columbia." I continue rowing, then pause. "It's kind of annoying, actually. It's been over a month and is starting to feel like a time sink with no upside."

"Has he suggested specific dates yet and they just haven't worked out?"

"Nope. Just keeps writing cute, smart-sounding emails and never proposes anything concrete. We're *supposed* to have a phone call on Sunday. In theory." I stroke my oar through the water again.

"Ah! Don't do it!"

"Wait. Why?" I ponder this for a moment. "Wouldn't it be better to get all our thoughts out there in thirty minutes, in one fell swoop, rather than keep wasting precious hours at our computer screens, editing and reediting our emails?"

"Meet in person. The Match phone call is like the kiss of death."

"That makes no sense."

"No, it just is. Every time a girl wants to talk on the phone *before* meeting, we never actually wind up meeting afterward."

"Talk about time sink. But maybe they can just tell there's no chemistry on the phone? So this way you both saved commute time, and *you* save drinks money?"

"Yeah, but some of the conversations are good. Most of them are." We row again, both contemplating this.

"When *you* hang up the phone, do *you* still want to meet them?" I ask.

"Yes. Otherwise why would I waste time on the phone with them?"

"Right, so then . . . why do *they* stay on the phone with *you*?"

"Preaching to the choir, Ali."

I put my oar in my lap and crane my neck so I can face him. "Why are people so weird?"

"Hey! Alison? It's Kevin."

"Kevin! Nice to finally put a . . . voice . . . to your name. And typeface."

"Is this a good time? How was your weekend in the Catskills?"

"Yeah, now's a good time. Catskills was fun! My brother and I canoed around mini ice floes in our winter coats for about half an hour, but then I got too cold and we had to come inside."

"Aww, bummer. Sorry."

Kevin tells me that after sticking around Morningside Heights for a few years after graduation, he just moved to Long Island City.

"Long Island City's the best!" I exclaim. "Are you in one of the modern-y high rises?"

"So you know it! That's us. Or at least a building a lot like ours."

"'Us, ours' . . . so you've got roommates?"

"Yeah, one." *Is it wrong for me to judge a thirty-three-year-old for having roommates? Probably.* "But this place, it's a dream. The roof will be tons of fun as soon as it warms up a bit! We've got a *fireplace*—"

"Okay, now I feel like you're lying. Who gets *both* a roof-deck *and* a fireplace in New York?"

"I know. I feel like we won the real-estate jackpot. At the risk of sounding deviant, I'd love to have you over for wine, s'mores, and some serious foot warming by the fire."

"Sure." I wait. No invitation follows.

He continues, "The place is super cozy, and decked out with a million and one souvenirs from my travels. I never had room for any of that stuff in my old place. All these relics just sat in boxes. Now it feels like my own mini-museum!"

"What kinds of 'relics' have you amassed from your travels?"

"Oh, random stuff. Masks from Papua New Guinea, a flat-weave rug from Jaipur, alabaster trinkets from Volterra. I'm your average bowerbird."

"Average what bird?"

"Bowerbird. Didn't you learn about these guys in high school biology?"

"I might as well come clean now: I suck at science."

"But you play with chemicals all day!"

"True. I have no idea why they trust me. . . . Buuuuut, bowerbirds?"

"Right, so bowerbirds have these very funny mating rituals. To woo a ladybird he's courting, a male bowerbird will go around accumulating tons of . . . schlock. Anything he can find. Buttons. Ribbons."

"Twigs and leaves?"

"No, usually brighter, shinier, often man-made goods. Then he makes a nest out of them and presents it to the ladybird he's macking on. Like, 'Come with me, and this can all be yours.'"

"And it works? This materialistic dating . . . mating ritual?"

"Yeah. That's why they're famous. Bowerbirds. You should Google it."

"So . . . you're festooning your apartment with relics, ribbons, and bells for the love of your life? When you find her?"

"When I find her, yes. Speaking of relics, the Match photos of you on your job sites look terrific. Makes me think that every day on your job must be so much fun! What have you been up to lately, work-wise?" he inquires.

We talk for two hours. *Two hours.*

"So. Apparently I could talk to you forever," I say, "but I've gotta get going. Laundry, cleaning, big Sunday night plans ahead."

"Cool. Yeah, I should get going, too. But it was great talking to you, Alison. Have a good week."

Wait. That's it? *"Have a good week?" "Great talking to you?"* Ben was right! The *Match.com* telephone curse is an actual thing! What an infernal waste of time.

GolfersTan0506: James Takes the Stairs

"Promise you won't get mad . . ." my mom's voice trails off.

"What did you do?" I groan as I mount the steps to the Armory Monday morning.

"Well . . ."

"Did you Facebook stalk him?" I made the mistake of showing my mom the profile of tonight's date.

"No, I Googled."

"And? . . . Is he a serial killer?" I drown the dregs of my takeout coffee before tossing it in the nearest trash can.

"No. I think he's impressive but humble."

"Google told you this."

"Kind of. This story ran in the *San Francisco Chronicle* about him when he was in college. Apparently he played baseball at Stanford."

"Okay."

"Well, it seems he was a benchwarmer for his first three years. But then San Francisco had this semicentennial celebration, or something, and some of the Stanford players were asked to dress up in old-timey Giants uniforms from the nineteen-fifties and stage a game in AT&T Stadium. Apparently James bears a striking resemblance to the team pitcher from that era, so the city had him suit up and pretend to be him. And . . . during this memorial game, James pitched a terrific game. The Stanford coach was really startled since he'd never played him before. So then he started James as pitcher in Stanford's next game, and James led them to a winning season."

"That's funny."

"Right, so the team captain commented that James is very modest, so he'd never challenge a coach's decision to bench him, but being able to show off in this kind of forum . . . well, you get the idea. Should I send it to you?"

"No. I don't want to stalk him before I've met him—" Then I catch myself, "I mean, stalk him any more than *you* already have . . . before I've met him."

"So you're pretty hard to pin down, huh?" James smiles across the table.

"Nah, it's just February's a really big month for Yalies. The other eleven months are considerably less booked up." I wink. *Oh gosh, I flirt like Jason. And our dads.*

"Why February?"

"Well, as undergrads we 'celebrated,'" I hold up finger quotes, "the fifty-plus-year-old tradition of Feb Club, for which you combat winter doldrums by drinking at themed parties for twenty-eight consecutive days. Twenty-nine on leap year."

The more often you go on dates, the more you start to feel like you're dating yourself. At this point, I've perfected my description of Feb Club without really giving it any thought. Same goes for why I went to grad school, why I love the Armory, where my family lives . . . I'm starting to bore *myself* with these scripts that I memorized without really meaning to. "As alumni, we carry the tradition forward with the aptly named 'Feb Club for Old People.'"

"So you drink every night?"

"Well, no. But, when there are events, yes. But sadly, my liver isn't getting any younger, and I don't think it likes me very much right now." I know I've said *that* one before, too. They kind of just start rolling off your tongue. "But enough about stodgy old Yale traditions. You said you're going to Florida this weekend? What for?"

"I'm a big golfer. And my family has a place there. So I try to get to Florida as much as possible to hit the links." I've written "hit the links" in emails, but who says that out loud?

"And how often is 'as much as possible?'"

"Once a month in winter. Two or three times per month during the spring."

"Whoa. That's . . . a lot," I say, trying to quickly calculate how much that means he spends on golf each month.

"Yeah, but it . . . makes me ha-ppy," he says in the singsong voice of a cartoon bear, drawing a heart in the air with his index fingers.

I laugh. That was cute, in a dopey kind of way.

"What about you? Do you golf?"

I nod. "I'm not that *good*, but I really enjoy it."

"Do you play other sports?" His voice is really loud. I glance around to see if any of the other patrons are giving us the evil eye.

"I spent a few seasons playing intramural soccer. But I got one too many injuries, so now I stick to running. And very occasional surfing. What about you?"

"We should run together!" he exclaims loudly. "That'd be fun, right?" He takes a sip of his Suntory. "So did you play sports in college?" he asks.

"Rugby."

"Aren't you small to be playing rugby?"

"I was the last line of defense, so I'd be small for the scrum, but they just had me run laps up and down the field, chasing all the girls on the opposing team. Whenever anyone passed me the ball, and I'd see the defenders of the other team running at me, I'd panic and basically hand them the ball so they wouldn't tackle me." I mime handing a rugby ball out like a platter for the taking, a look of panic frozen on my face.

"Wow, you sound like you were bound for the Rugby World Cup. It's a shame you gave it up."

I smile. "Quitting was the greatest relief I think I've ever experienced. What about you?"

"I played baseball in college."

"What position?" *Let us pretend for a minute that my overinvolved Jewish mother did not stalk you online.*

"Benchwarmer, then pitcher. It's a funny story, actually. Well, frustrating for several years, then validating, now funny." I nearly choke on my saketini as I try to stifle my smirking. Nod slowly. Look engaged.

". . . anniversary game, so the *San Francisco Chronicle* . . ."

Nod again. Raise an eyebrow, as if this is new information, as if saying *Go on! I want to hear more.*

". . . everyone said I looked a lot like . . ."

I rest my chin on my hand, nod wide-eyed, nod some more. No way! That's really how it happened? What a funny story! Given that I have the worst poker face in the history of mankind, I am never going to forgive my mother for her aggressive sleuthing.

"Nowadays I row for a club in Connecticut and play some squash."
I laugh aloud at this, not intending to.

"Why is that funny?" he asks.

I blush. "No . . . it's not. Sorry."

"Do you have a thing against rowers?"

"No, actually, all my serious boyfriends have been rowers, or ex-rowers. I was laughing because . . . take this with a grain of salt since I *just* said all my ex-boyfriends were rowers, but it's like you're a superstar in the blue-blood Olympics."

"What?" He smiles gently.

"Sorry, that came out wrong. But it's like: *golf* and *rowing* and *squash*. Sports I refer to as 'blue-blood' sports."

He shrugs. "I guess I am pretty blue-blooded. I never thought of it that way." He chuckles to himself, and I smile, partly because it *is* funny how upper-crust he seems, partly because I'm relieved that I didn't offend him.

"But, you think that's pretty funny, right?" he counters. "This, coming from someone who just got over telling me about her nightly ritual of drinking with *Yalies*," he pronounces the last word in a put-on British accent.

"So *where* do you live again? I feel like it was complicated," I ask.

"Not super complicated, but not straightforward either. I have a house in Westport, Connecticut. You know where that is?"

I nod. "Of course. It's on the New Haven line."

"Oh, right. Duh." He smacks his forehead as he utters the 'duh,' eliciting laughter from me. This guy's kind of a goofball. "So, yeah. My house is in Westport. It's in the country, effectively. It's an old farmhouse, you'd love it, based on your job and all. And my office is just a fifteen- or twenty-minute drive from there, so I stay most weeknights up there. But then I also have a small place in Manhattan."

"Pied-à-terre?" I tease.

"Kind of." He shrugs. "When my ex and I broke up, I wanted to move back into the dating scene in New York City. Not too much under-forty action in Westport. So I rented a place here, near Grand Central, so I could be a bit more social, and also not be too far from the train that takes me home home." *Home home*—that's something I would say to distinguish the two as well. I smile to myself.

"How long did you live together for? You and your ex-girlfriend?"

"Oh. Not long. Actually less than a week." I raise an eyebrow. "She'd basically been staying at my place for a while, but when she officially moved in—you know, with boxes and everything—I knew almost right away that it wasn't the right thing."

"You knew that in less than a week?"

"Yeah. She just took herself so seriously. She's a runner, too, but more of a compulsive marathoner type. When she moved in, it became clear to me she was . . . I don't know . . . too finicky about it, or too regimented, so I asked her to move out because I knew that we weren't compatible in the long term."

"After *how* much time?"

"Three days."

"And how much time of dating?"

"Maybe two and a half years?"

"But then weren't there signs before? Like, while she was effectively living with you?"

He shrugs. "I don't know."

I puzzle this over but decide it's better not to cross-examine someone on a first date. "So what's your 'pied-à-terre' like?"

"It's not anything fancy. Just a studio. I don't even have a full kitchen. And just a mini-fridge. But I like it."

"Had you spent much time in Manhattan before?"

"Me? Yeah. I lived here after college for *pfriseveight*," he mumbles the number into his hand, "years. That many. Then I moved to my house in Connecticut, and I was there . . . ehhhhhhh," he makes a screeching noise as he ponders the timeline, kind of a cross between a siren and a school boys' choir, "for two years maybe? And then I got my apartment last year."

"So was New York different than you remembered? Was it like exploring a new city?"

"Kind of." He nods. "I like that idea. 'Exploring.' It *is* kind of nice to see the city from a new neighborhood, a new vantage point. And it's different, being in your thirties, than being in your twenties. But *you*," he flashes raised eyebrows, "you wouldn't know about that. You're just a young'un."

"Nah, I've been here a long time. I've gone through phases in New York. You know: my street-fair phase, my hookah-bar phase, roof-top-bar phase . . ."

"What phase are you in now?"

"My BYOB-restaurant phase."

"Wow, you didn't miss a beat on that one."

"Yeah, that was funny." I shake my head. "Usually you recognize your phases in hindsight. But when I was telling you about my *past* phases, it sort of dawned on me that I must currently *be* in a phase. And then it was easy to figure out."

He stares at me blankly. I feel myself blushing, shrug, and look away.

"Your mind works fast. You're *smart*," he coos.

"Yeah, right. Anyway . . . what phase are you in?"

"I don't think I have phases. Or if I do, I'm not aware of them. I'm always attracted to the same kinds of bars, kinds of cuisines, kinds of girls . . ."

I laugh at this, amused that he wants to tell me about the kinds of girls he's attracted to. "And what kinds . . . are those?"

He cocks his head in curiosity. "Which? The bars, cuisines, or girls?"

"Uhhh, whichever you want to tell me about?"

"Okay. Bars—ones that have good cocktails. But, like, the *manly* kind," he pumps his arms up and down, as if marching to the word "manly." "And ones that have neat décor. Like this one!" He brightens up and looks around Le Colonial's Asian-chic atmosphere. "Except those stairs are weird, huh? What do you think those stairs are for?" He rises from his seat and walks two paces back, near a stepped display shelf that ascends from the floor and has a burning votive on each stair. He's right, they *are* weird. They look like stairs to nowhere. But as he mimes mounting them one step at a time, I can only look around the room hoping nobody is watching him. Or us.

He sits back down and continues, "Cuisines—Mexican and Italian. Girls—smart ones, usually with blonde hair and blue eyes. Who run." I blush and look away, and he notices. "Oh, I didn't mean you. . . . Well,

I mean, maybe I mean you. I don't know you well enough to say. But yes, I guess you fit all those descriptors."

Now it's me cocking my head, looking a little confused.

"Who was your date with last night?" Cassie asks as we run side by side on the treadmills at the gym.

"A guy named James."

"*And?* What's he *like*?"

"I . . ." I breathe, "I don't know."

"What does that mean?"

"Well. Okay. Blond hair, tall, *very* handsome. Kind of looks like Dave, but maybe more attractive even? Kind of a blue-blooded, über-preppy banker."

"How old?"

"Thirty-three."

"Good age."

"Yeah."

"Boring?"

"No. Not boring. Kind of . . . different?"

"Different how?"

"Uhhh. Good question! I *think* he has a crap ton of money. He owns a house in Connecticut and rents a bachelor pad in Midtown. But he seems kind of grounded. He's not, like, snotty about his money. Assuming I'm right about that assessment." I grab for my towel and dry my face and neck.

"He seems nice? Smart?"

"Yeah, both. He went to Stanford." I shrug. "And he seems, kind of, I don't know what the word is. Pensive? Like he's thinking over the things I say. Processing before he responds. It's . . . interesting to watch. And," I quickly add, "the opposite of me, who leads with my mouth and follows with my brain."

"So. Second date?"

"You know, I don't *know*?"

"He sounds pretty great. What's off?"

"That's EXACTLY it. Something's . . . *off*. Like . . ." my eyes go to the ceiling as I try to put my finger on what, exactly, that is. I settle on ". . . *quirky*."

"Quirky's not always bad. Quirky how?"

"Quirky, like . . . he makes this weird siren-y noise when he's thinking, or approximating. 'EEhhhhhhhhh.'" I do my best to imitate it. "But. You know, weirder than I just made it sound."

Cassie chokes out a laugh. "That was pretty weird," she affirms.

"And! He makes these sad, pouty faces. Like, 'Awwwww,'" I jut out my lower lip and turn my head so Cassie can see, "that kind of make me feel like I'm talking to a child. Oh! And there were these, weird, shelflike stairs in the bar, and he was super excited to pretend he was climbing them."

"Okay. That sounds quirky." Cassie nods vehemently.

"I was just hoping I didn't *know* anybody in the bar!"

"I can see that." Cassie nods. "But maybe he just had first date jitters so he was extra weird. Maybe he'll normal out on a second date?"

"One can hope, I guess?"

* * *

"Just so you *know*," James says as our cab approaches my corner, "you're not getting off without kissing me tonight."

"Uhhh—"

He leans over and stifles my nonsentence by kissing me. We're not perfectly positioned, so it's a little bit sloppy and a bit more drooly than I would have liked, but it's deep. And *manly*, as James would say. And I kiss him back.

"You totally did this funny wave-half-hug thing at Le Colonial after our first date. I didn't want to let you escape with that again. Otherwise, on our third date, it would be like we're just buddies." And he's *right*! My heart hiccups and my stomach churns whenever someone tries to kiss me for the first time, including just now, but he's right: if you're not careful, you fall into the "friend zone"—even if you *did* meet on an Internet dating site. See: Secret Agent Man; Rain Forrest Guy.

"So, now you know. We're not friends," he says nonchalantly, and I laugh.

"Annnywaaay, this is me!" I say as the cab pulls to a halt. "Thanks again for dinner. And for drinks after! Good choices, both." I nod.

"You're welcome. Are you around this week?"

"Yeah."

"Would you . . ." he searches my eyes, "want to get together?"

"Yeah." I smile. "Why do you say it like that?"

"Oh, I don't know. You just like playing games. Like I ask, 'Are you free?' and you say, 'Yes,' and then you wait for me to ask, 'Would you like to hang out with me?' But you could, you know, take a little initiative. Not make me work for it. With your . . . *silly* games." He says silly with a British accent that conjures the Monty Python sketch "The Ministry of Silly Walks."

"No games involved. I promise." I cross my heart with my finger. "I'm just happy to let you call the shots on the where-when."

"Oh! And one more thing," he says as I'm one foot out of the car. "There's this thing. It's called *'email,'* and I think you should try it." He reaches around and slides his business card into my pocket. "I don't feel a pressing need to be checking my Match account every day to see if I've heard from you." I smile and shake my head, then close the car door and walk inside.

* * *

It's Tuesday morning and I'm back up on the scaffold at St. John's.

March 7 at 10:55 a.m.

JAMES: GREETINGS FROM SUNNY FLA! HOW IS EVERYTHING IN THE BIG APPLE? . . . JAMES

"Texty McTexterson," Juan Pablo teases when my phone vibrates again. I quickly slide my cell into my back pocket without typing a reply.

I pretend to ignore his comment. "It's freezing up here today."

"Who's the lucky dude?"

"Have you seen the burnt umber pigment?"

"Oh, come on, Alison."

"You know, I could have sworn I brought it up with me . . ." The replacement Guastavino tiles arrived last week; unfortunately, only *after* Juan Pablo's crew installed them were Margo and I able to view them, only to discover that they were not perfect color matches with the original tiles. In the interest of saving time and money, I suggested that I could tint the new tiles by hand to match the adjacent historic ones. Joanne approved this treatment plan.

So now, I'm mixing mineral paints on the top level of the scaffold, effectively repainting (sections of) the ceiling of the largest religious structure on the continent, while Juan Pablo follows directly behind me and applies a sealant coating to each color-corrected tile.

My phone vibrates again.

"That's a lot of texting. New boyfriend?" he ribs.

I continue painting.

"You're not giving me a lot to work with here, Alison. Do you *want* me to break into song? 'Kiss the Girl'? . . . 'Can You Feel the Love Tonight?' . . . 'Love Is an Open Door'? I'll take requests."

"That would be lovely!" I say with false sincerity. "Though I wouldn't have taken you for a Disney-soundtrack-loving kinda guy. I guess you're just full of surprises, huh?"

Juan Pablo shrugs. "I got kids. What else do you sing with them?"

"Wait—you have *kids*?" I turn my attention from the ceiling overhead to look at him.

"Yeah. One son, one daughter."

"You have *two* kids?"

"Yeah. Why is that so surprising?"

For three years I've been working in St. John the Divine; for three years I've seen Juan Pablo on a weekly—sometimes daily—basis. We get along swimmingly, and though we haven't ever had "deep" conversations, we make a lot of chitchat: about our weekends, about TV shows, about Monday-night football, about buildings we've worked on or in.

I generally like all the contractors I work with. By nature, they tend to be easygoing, funny, life-loving types. But they're not always smart. Which is fine. But Juan Pablo, and most of the guys on his crew, are more interesting, more curious. They don't just want to know which treatment to perform, they want to know *why* we recommend it. They want to know where we've used it before. Also, most of them went to college.

"You've just, never mentioned having kids. Are you married?"

"Pssssh, me? Don't you think I'd have mentioned if I were *married*?"

"I don't know. You didn't mention you have *kids*. Is their mother your girlfriend?"

"Nope. No girlfriend. Don't you think I'd have mentioned that, too? I wouldn't two-time you."

I roll my eyes at his come-on.

"I've got baby mamas," he says nonchalantly.

Go figure. The only smart, playful, attractive guy I've ever met through work has a baby mama. Two baby mamas. Worst still, he actually refers to them as "baby mamas."

During my lunch break I text James back.

March 7 at 12:03 p.m.

ALISON: GOOD. COLD. JEALOUS? YOU'VE CALLED ME BEFORE, SO ALTHOUGH I HAPPEN TO BE A VERY GOOD DETECTIVE, IT WOULDN'T HAVE TAKEN MUCH TO FIGURE OUT WHO THAT TEXT WAS FROM. . . . ALISON

JAMES: YOU'RE MEAN. BUT I FORGIVE YOU. WANT TO GET TOGETHER NEXT TUESDAY WHEN I'M BACK IN TOWN?

March 13 at 9:08 a.m.

Hey,

Look what I found in my coat pocket this morning! I thought I should give this whole "email" thing a try and see what it's all about.

Hope you had a quick flight home and that you're rocking a pretty sweet golfers' tan this morning.

Cheers,
Alison

March 13 at 9:31 a.m.

Wow - a communication breakthrough!!

Sadly, I am pretty much the same color as I applied a lot of SPF 30.

Do you have any movie requests for tomorrow or would you like to go out somewhere?

James

> March 13 at 12:50 p.m.

A couple things:

1. *I'm sick. I feel it is only fair that I warn you in the event that you prefer to be healthy for your weekly Florida trip rather than let me infect you with my germs. . . . I'll try not to be offended if you choose your health over the opportunity to see me. ;)*
2. *Should you decide to tempt a sickness-riddled fate, I'm happy to do any of the following: go to your place and watch you play guitar (hint, hint); go to your place and watch a movie; go to my place and watch a movie. I brainstormed the options, you pick.*

Cheers,
Alison

> March 13 at 1:29 p.m.

Thank you for the enticing list of activities. I will let you know what I decide on! A movie at your place might be a nice change of pace. I don't want to intrude on your roommates though . . . or show too much public affection. . . .

I'm sorry you are sick. I am definitely looking forward to seeing you, and I am not concerned about getting sick.

I began my morning workout regimen today and am going to try to follow up with it tomorrow at the gym . . . the goal is for a 6:00 a.m. wake up and 6:10 a.m. gym arrival!

Jim

* * *

"Ha! *This* is your 'not super-fancy studio'? This is, like, twice the size of my *three* bedroom apartment I share with Nicole and Cassie. And!" I gasp, "Those *windows*!" I rush toward the nineteenth-century casement windows. "These are *amazing*. They have to be original!"

James shrugs. "Well, I'm glad you like the place."

"Like? I *love*. Your apartment is gorgeous. You *totally* undersold it."

"Thanks. You wanna order dinner now? It will probably take a while to get here."

"And someone has to be up at 6:00 a.m. tomorrow, I must remind you." I smile.

He reaches over and pinches my side playfully. "I'm glad *someone's* on top of my workout regimen. Don't want me to lose all this muscle tone, huh?" I never really sized him up before, so I take this opportunity to, narrowing my eyes as I blatantly let them travel up and down his torso and then his legs. Nice. Lean.

We turn on *The Verdict* and sit on his couch watching while we wait for the delivery to arrive. Once it does, it is *the best* Italian food I've had in New York. The buffalo mozzarella is like a little pillow of perfection, the lemon-cream sauce on the shrimp and gnocchi is heavenly. I say as much.

"Yeah." James shrugs. "I order from here three or four nights a week. Or, rather, most nights when I stay in the city."

"*That* must be nice."

"It is."

"So you don't cook? Ever?"

"Have you seen my kitchen?" He points his fork at his minibar refrigerator. "Besides, I don't really know how to cook."

"Oh, following recipes is easy. It just takes practice."

"Well, you'll have to teach me one day. Or cook for me one day. Or both. You *know*, my birthday's coming up?"

"You want me to cook for you as a birthday present?" I ask, as I fork a gnocchi into my mouth.

"You don't have to. We can go out, or something. But if you *wanted* to, that would be nice."

"Sure!" I nod. "Of course I'll cook for your birthday. I just can't promise it will be *good* when I'm confined to your single-burner stove. So go light on the judging marks."

"Awww, you're just a regular Martha Stewart. I'm lucky," he says and leans in to kiss me. Except he misses and somehow ends up kind of kissing my eye.

"Bleh!" I flinch, laughing, though a little grossed out, too. "Slobbery eye . . . kiss-thing." I wipe at my eye with the back of my hand. "You're so weird!" I blurt out, not meaning to. But once it's out there, it seems easier to play it off as teasing, rather than to apologize.

He pulls his face back and searches my eyes while smiling. "Do you think I'm weird? I told my buddy Ross after our first date that I thought you found me weird." He says it half in jest, half-seriously, so I can't decide if he's being facetious or actually expects an answer.

I wobble my head from side to side as if debating. "I don't know. . . . Yeah, maybe a little weird." I wrinkle my nose and nod, smiling.

"I totally weirded you out with that whole stair thing, huh? It was really funny to me at the time. Actually, it's still funny to me now. Those weird," he shakes his head, "lacquered stairs to nowhere. . . ." Then he perks up. "But I *totally* weirded you out when I pretended to walk up them, right? I could tell. You looked kind of panic-stricken."

"I did want to pull my turtleneck up over my face and pretend I didn't know you, but . . ."

"But? . . ."

"But," I sigh, then pep up with a smile, "I'm here now, aren't I?"

	March 23 at 6:58 a.m.
ALISON:	HAPPY BIRTHDAY! HOPE IT'S A GREAT DAY AND THE START TO AN EVEN BETTER YEAR.
JAMES:	I CAN SAY WITH SOME SURETY THAT THIS WILL BE THE BEST BIRTHDAY YET. I'M REALLY LOOKING FORWARD TO SPENDING IT WITH YOU TONIGHT, AND I REALLY APPRECIATE THE FANCY MENU YOU'RE CONCOCTING.
	March 23 at 9:02 a.m.
ALISON:	AWW, SO NICE YOU ARE! LIKEWISE! . . . JUST DON'T DEVELOP LOFTY CULINARY EXPECTATIONS. THIS FORAY INTO COOKING IN A BACHELOR KITCHEN MAY NOT GO AS PLANNED.

After we finish the raspberry pavlova, I get up to clear the dishes. As I'm scrubbing the pan from the lamb chops, he asks, "What can I do to help?"

"Nothing," I say from the sink. "Or, maybe . . . how would you feel about providing background music?"

"Sure, let me set up my speakers."

"No." I look over at him while I continue scrubbing. "*You* be the background music. You still haven't played guitar for me. And you make it sound like you practice a lot."

"Sure." He retrieves his guitar from its case against the wall, tunes it, and starts strumming. It's a song I've never heard before, and I don't recognize the lyrics, but he's *good*. His voice is smooth and melodic, the song has a nice hook, and as I'm rinsing the plates, I feel a strange sensation, like a fist welling up inside my chest. I've never understood when girls swoon over musicians purely because they're musicians, but with this song, with James singing and playing this song, I think I get it.

I'm drying the dishes as he finishes the song and lowers his guitar. I applaud softly. "Wow. You are . . . *really* good. And that was really good. Encore?"

Without a word, he starts in on another song I don't recognize. I put away the dishes and sit on his floor cross-legged, my back leaning against his bed frame, and I watch him strum on his chair across the room. He goes through two or three more songs and my mind wanders, but I feel intensely calm, and sated, at the same time.

He claps his guitar strings with one hand. "Okay, okay. I've spoiled you enough tonight. And besides, I'd rather be spending time with you than practicing my guitar."

"That was amazing. I mean it. I'm not just saying that because I have to."

He puts his guitar down, walks across the room, bends down and lifts me from under my arms to a standing position, and he kisses me.

"Thanks for indulging me. I couldn't have asked for a better birthday." I nod. "Do you want to stay over tonight?"

"I . . ." I dread this conversation. "I do and I don't," I say slowly.

"Ohk*aaaay*."

I search for the right wording. "I *do* want to keep spending time with you . . . but I *don't* intend to let you get in my pants tonight. So if that's what you . . . anticipated when you said 'stay over,' then I . . . should probably go home." I quickly add, "Which is fine. Sorry, I know it's your birthday and all . . . I don't want to have any 'talks' or bring up any serious junk tonight."

His hands are still on my shoulders, and he grips them while staring into my eyes with a directness that makes me slightly uncomfortable. "I *do not* care. I asked you to stay over, not to do anything that would ever make you uncomfortable. You can be the pace leader."

I nod a couple times, smile bashfully, and mumble, "Cool, thanks."

March 24 at 10:17 a.m.

JAMES: THANKS AGAIN FOR A WONDERFUL BIRTHDAY. THAT'LL BE HARD TO TOP. I FORGET WHICH DAY YOU LEAVE FOR DISNEY WITH YOUR COLLEGE FRIENDS. . . . DO YOU HAVE TIME TO HANG OUT BEFORE YOU GO?

March 24 at 12:03 p.m.

ALISON: IT WAS MY PLEASURE! WEDNESDAY NIGHT, SO NOT MUCH TIME BETWEEN NOW AND THEN. WEEK AFTER?

March 30 at 9:52 p.m.

Dear Alison,

You always tease me about my "weekly trips to Florida," but look who's the big traveler now!

Are you getting to fish? (I think you said you and your friends might go fishing. . . .) Binge on turkey legs and then ride Space Mountain until your stomach aches?

Desperate to hear all about it,

Jimmy

March 31 at 9:40 a.m.

Hey there,

Yes, I am a very big traveler indeed. It's tour-as-many-countries-of-the-Epcot-arena-as-possible-in-6-hours or bust. With Mickey ears. That's always been my motto at least. . . .

Goin' fishin' tomorrow.

How are things up North? Or, I forget, you're probably in Florida this weekend too, as usual. Yes? ;)

Alison

"*Someone's* nice and tan!" he exclaims when I turn the knob and step into his apartment.

"Yeah, I didn't do too badly this time. This might be the tannest I've ever been. Which, I guess, is really sad. But . . ."

"No, you look great. Shimmery with your tan skin in your white sweater . . ." He hurries toward me from across the room, practically skipping, and envelops me in a bear hug. "I missed you," he practically yells in my ear before pecking my lips. "Did you miss me?" he begs.

I laugh. "Inside voices," I chide pedantically.

"Huh?"

"You're *yelling* in my ear." I playfully bat his face away and guard my right ear with my palm. "So how were things here?"

"Good."

I settle into the couch while he moves about unpacking his brief-case, plugging in his cell phone, folding clothing.

"I went home to spend some time with my brother." He folds a shirt and pauses, looking up. "Have I told you about my brother?"

I shake my head. "Not beyond the fact that you *have* a brother. Two," I correct myself.

"Yeah. So. It's kind of a long story, but my brother's got some prob-lems. . . ."

I nod, not sure if it's appropriate for me to ask the logical follow-up *what kind of problems?*, so I keep silent.

He nods to himself. "He's . . . well, it's not a big deal. But he's thirty and he still lives at *home*, and he's had a lot of drug problems, been in and out of rehab . . ."

"Oh," I say softly, nodding.

"Yeah, so . . . I think it kind of sucks for him. Being cooped up with my parents all the time. I mean, my parents are great and all. My dad is basically my best friend, he's so wonderful. But, my brother's single, and he can't drink because of his rehab program, so I think he probably gets a little stir-crazy living in his parents' basement in suburbia."

"Yeah, that would be . . . tough, I imagine."

He nods. "So, anyway, since he's been home the last year, I try to go home once in a while just to hang out with him."

"So what'd you guys do this weekend?" I ask, upbeat, hoping my upbeatness conveys that I'm not judging and agree with him that it's not a huge deal.

"We golfed."

"Oh? It runs in the family?"

"Yeah. Well, he and my dad golf. Not my mom and my other brother." He picks up a picture frame and hands it to me. "This is me golfing with them last summer."

I study the photo. "Wow. You look *nothing* like them. You're like me and my siblings and mom. My dad and I look pretty Nordic, but everybody else looks Mediterranean. Same goes for you . . . except more so."

"Well, that makes sense. I'm adopted, you know."

I turn to him. "Wait. Really? No, I didn't know."

"Yeah, I guess it's not something I really talk about. But. I'm *adopted*."

"Oh. Cool. What did . . . uhhh . . . how did . . ." I shake my head back and forth, hoping he'll proffer an explanation of the parts he's comfortable sharing, since I clearly don't know which questions are off-limits or on.

"Yeah," he jumps in, saving me and the conversation. "So my parents tried to have kids for a really long time. Like, years. And finally doctors gave up and told my mom that she couldn't get pregnant. So she and my dad adopted me."

"Do you know . . . anything about your . . . biological parents?"

"Kind of. Not really. My birth mother was a graduate student in New Mexico. She got pregnant, wasn't married, and didn't feel . . . equipped to raise me, I guess? So my parents found her through an agency."

"Were you really young then, when you were adopted?"

"Yeah, I was less than a week old."

"Have you ever . . ." I pause, debating whether to proceed. But he brought it up, right? ". . . talked to or had contact with your biological mother since?"

He shakes his head. "No."

"Are you curious about her?"

He shakes his head again. "She knows my parents' names and knows they live in Connecticut. She could try to find me if she wanted to. But since she hasn't . . . I guess I don't feel a great need to find *her*. Besides," he adds, "my mom and dad are the best. I totally lucked out, and they've been my family for as long as I can remember. Obviously."

"That's nice," I say. I turn my eyes back to the framed photograph. "But it's funny, your brother here actually *looks* like your dad. Is it like that thing where they say couples grow to look like each other, or dogs and their owners start to resemble one another?"

He chuckles. "No, but that'd be really uncanny, right? Since they *basically* look like twins. After I was adopted, my mom actually got pregnant. Twice."

"Awww, that's like a medical miracle!"

"Yeah. It was kind of a big surprise. A *big* surprise." He laughs. "But . . . I got brothers out of it. So that was cool."

I nod encouragingly, smiling.

"So. You want to go *out* tonight instead of order in?"

"Sure."

"Mexican?"

* * *

I'm panting on the treadmill beside Cassie again the next morning. "But, when we saw Evan and Hannah on the way to dinner last night, I just felt . . . I don't know how to explain it. Like, kind of . . . *embarrassed* by him?"

"How so?"

"I don't know. It's like, he was . . . too *peppy*. He's *always* too peppy. And loud, like he can't modulate his own voice. So . . . when we first bumped into them, I was internally panicking, hoping he wouldn't embarrass me in front of them. And they're my *friends*! . . . I don't want to be embarrassed to bring someone I'm dating around my friends."

"Are you just being ridiculous though? What's so embarrassing about him?"

"I . . . I have no idea. I'm being such a bitch," I sulk. "I know I am. I'm sorry."

"Al, you can *feel* however you *feel*, you don't need to apologize for that. Certainly not to me."

"Yeah, but I'm being ridiculous and unfair. And I know that if you were telling me this very same story, I'd say, 'Well that's a no-brainer. If you're *embarrassed* by him, stop seeing him.'"

"So why don't you stop seeing him?"

I up my speed arrow and meditate on this for a second. "I don't know? I guess because he's handsome. And smart. And he's a really good conversationalist, so our dinners are interesting. And he likes food almost as much as I do, so we get to eat really well?"

"Don't forget the guitar thing," she adds.

"Well, *obviously* the guitar thing."

"You want me to be a test pilot?"

"I was thinking about it . . ."

"Invite him to Ashley's 'summer-come-early' soirée next weekend. It'll be a lot of people, but they're either going to be your *really* good friends, who you know won't judge you for bringing him but will also be honest with feedback; or strangers, who you don't care about anyway."

"Yeah, I'd been toying with that idea as well. I guess I'll ask. I'll tell him to bring friends. Never know, maybe he has cute single friends?"

"Uhh, you were right about him having cute single friends," Cassie says as she hands me a plate that Saturday night.

"You brought me spare ribs? And a cupcake! I should date *you*."

"That bad, eh?"

"No, I was just kidding. I mean, at least, *I* don't think it's going badly. . . . Do you?"

"No. The opposite. Hang on. Nicole!" she calls to Nicole across the roof-deck. "Can you come here for a second?"

Nicole joins us. "What's up?"

"Okay, time to dish," Cassie says in a near-whisper. "I thought we should tell her what we were saying about James." I instinctively glance over at him. He's standing in a small circle with Ashley, Blaire, and

Ross, the friend that he brought. One of them is mid-story, and James is smiling, nodding.

"Yeah! Totally!" Nicole exclaims. "You ready?" she asks, as if she's bracing me for a letdown.

"Yes. Please, tell me."

"We think you're crazy," Nicole says.

Cassie nods vigorously. "Yeah, really crazy."

"Me? Wait, why?" I smile, anticipating their praise of him, secretly looking forward to this kind of affirmation, some kind of affirmation, which I'd been craving the past two months.

"He's *wonderful*," Nicole says matter-of-factly. "He's really attractive, and he's really gracious and polite, he has *nice* friends—"

"And he's really smart, *and* he's clearly very into you," Cassie adds. I can't help but smile.

"So we don't get why you're so . . . *paranoid* about him."

"It's not that I'm *paranoid*," I counter, "it's just that . . . well, he's not . . . quite as . . . calm? . . . as the people I'm usually interested in. Or used to dating."

"Yeah, and look how well *those* relationships worked out," Nicole says.

"I know, but . . . he's just not always normal. You know, he like, yells in my *ear* and kisses my *eye* . . . and the other night when we were out at Middle Branch," I confide sotto voce, "he took the olive from his martini and stuck it over his tooth so it would look like he has a black tooth!" I grimace. "It's . . . like . . . *weird*."

Cassie laughs, "Noooo, he's being *funny*. He's trying to make you laugh. And you *love* it when guys make you laugh. You always say they have to be funny."

"Yeah, but there's, like, smart-witty funny, and then there's I'm-making-you-laugh-because-you-don't-know-how-else-to-mask-your-discomfort funny."

"You are being *so* hard on him," Nicole castigates. "*Look* at him." She gestures her arm across the deck. Horrified, I lunge at her arm and push it down to her side.

"Don't let him know we're talking about him!"

"Fine. But look at him! He's, like, the stud of the party! Every friend you have here is charmed by him." I glance over and see him gesturing, if a tad wildly, while explaining something to Ashley and Blaire, who actually appear captivated.

"I think what Nicole's trying to say is go easy on him," Cassie says. "He was helping Ashley ferry trays up and down the stairs. I went down to get more rum and he was in the kitchen alone, loading her dishwasher."

Two days later we're having dinner in his apartment (that dreamy Italian takeout again), when he asks, "So what'd you do last night?"

"Huh?"

"Well, I saw you on Saturday, and now it's Monday, what'd you do yesterday?"

"Uhh . . . a couple things?"

"Like . . . ?"

I lick my lips and stutter, "I, uh . . . I—"

"—*I* got out of work, went to the gym, played guitar, and went to sleep. In Connecticut. Your turn. Come on, this is an easy one," he says in an educator's tone.

"Yeah, okay. So . . . I got out of work, I tutored, and," I hold my breath, "I went on a date?"

"Whoa," he says quietly to himself. "I wasn't expecting that answer."

"Sorry? I don't really know if we're supposed to talk . . . about these things? I don't know where we stand, so I figured I should still . . . keep options open? But when you asked me just now, I didn't feel like I should lie?"

"No. No, that's okay," he says, nodding to himself. "You're right, we never talked about it." He reaches over and puts his hand on top of my left hand, which rests on the table. "Do you . . . prefer to—ah, you're making me self-conscious. Let's drop it."

He clenches his jaw and loosens it, clenches it and loosens it.

"Don't be self-conscious on *my* account," I say softly. "You want to finish your sentence?"

"Nope. I take it back."

"Okay," I shrug.

"Except . . . I also think we should talk about this." He nods slowly, as if to himself. "Do you *prefer* to keep things open?" I wince, not sure what to say. "Let me clarify. *I'm* not seeing anyone else. I would *like* it if you didn't see anyone else either. But I obviously can't force you," he adds quickly.

"Okay," I say, nodding slowly, trying to process this.

"Ohkaaay let's leave things as they are? Or okay you won't see other people anymore?"

I keep nodding, chewing this over. "Ohkaaay the latter?"

James invited me up to his house in Connecticut for part of the weekend, and after riding the train together from Grand Central early Friday evening, we're sitting at a beachfront restaurant, enjoying the tides rushing in beyond the window and picking at a platter of oysters.

"So, my parents . . . nah, forget it."

"What?"

"No, nothing."

"Come on."

"No, I was going to . . . now I'm feeling self-conscious."

I roll my eyes. "Come on, what is it?"

"My parents live just five minutes from me . . . and I was wondering if you wanted to meet them for drinks tomorrow night?"

"Oh." I pause, surprised and flattered by his invitation. "Actually . . . I can't stay *too* too long tomorrow. Like, until lunch maybe?" I hesitate. "I've got some college friends coming into town tomorrow night, and since you mentioned you had a thing anyway, I told them I'd be back and ready to meet up early evening." I've never had someone arrange a meet-the-parents so soon. It's touching, and maybe a little strange? But I'm not going to be "that girl" who breaks plans for a guy.

"Do you . . . want to meet my parents another time?"

"I . . . guess if you *want* me to?"

"Would I be asking otherwise?"

I smile and reach for a wedge of lemon, not sure that this merits a response. "So. What'd you do the last couple of days?"

"I played half a round of golf after work Wednesday, met up with some friends for drinks yesterday. Work was boring . . . you?"

"Work-wise, same old same old. I've been at the Armory every day this week, trying to avoid the office, which is crushing my soul. Otherwise? I tutored, had drinks with Dave, I dunno." I shrug.

"Dave, as in, your ex?"

"Yeah, but, I think I've said this before, we are 100 percent utterly and truly platonic. He's a friend. I've known him forever, and I promise you it's not . . . untoward or anything. I remember our conversation from Monday night." I nod encouragingly. While I haven't closed down my Match account, my inbox is starting to fill up with unopened messages and winks. To say that I'm in a *serious* relationship with James would be an overstatement, but it at least feels like the start of a committed one.

"Does he know about me?"

"Yeah. I actually told him about you last night. So, *now* he knows."

"Wait. So, *my* parents know all about you. They've known about you for weeks. Maybe months. They're ready to *meet* you. And you just told your ex now?"

"Look. I don't think of him as an ex-boyfriend, so I don't . . . divulge information on a faster or slower timeline than I do with regular friends."

"But you had your other friends meet me at Ashley's, so they obviously know about me."

"Yeah, but if you remember, I didn't think of us as exclusively dating until Monday. I obviously liked you, or I wouldn't have kept seeing you, wouldn't have introduced you to friends . . . but I wasn't going to go around talking about you as 'my *boy*friend' when . . . I mean, you know, I thought we were still seeing other people." I pause. "But I don't tell Dave, or anyone for that matter, about every single date I go on."

"Uh-huh."

"Besides, I *did* tell Dave. Wasn't that the whole point of this? So, there's really nothing to be upset about." We look at each other, and he looks like he's mulling this over. "I'm sorry. I am. I'm sorry if you're upset. But I wasn't trying to be inconsiderate, or to pretend you don't exist. Dave *knows*. Right?"

Almost instantaneously, as if a light bulb went on in his head, he brightens. "Was that our first fight? Uh-oh, first fight? Maybe? I think that was our first fight."

"How was that a fight?" I can't tell if he's joking or not.

"Well, *I* have been placing more importance on this relationship than *you*, and *my* feelings were hurt, and *you* disagreed with me and—"

"That wasn't a fight. That's a differing of opinions."

"You can call it whatever you want, but you're *disappointed* in my reaction."

"I'm not disappointed. It's sweet. I was just trying to explain why I hadn't told Dave sooner."

"It's *fine*," he says, as if he's soothing me. He reaches across the table, pulls my head in, and kisses me on the forehead. "First fight," he whispers to himself.

Later that same evening, we sip nightcaps of bourbon from crystal-cut glasses before the crackling fireplace in his living room, which feels straight out of a Ralph Lauren catalog: brass-tacked leather armchairs, red-checked flannel throw pillows everywhere, overlapping animal skin rugs, an iconic Louis Vuitton trunk serving as the coffee table. When he opens a guitar case in the corner and crosses the room toward me, strumming as he sits, I know I'm toast. The cozy-classy lodge ambience permeated with the wintry scent of burning embers, his faint music drawing me to him like the Pied Piper—I'll be eschewing the Pants Speech tonight.

> *April 24 at 12:31 p.m.*
>
> *Subject: FW: James Hathaway added you as a friend on Facebook*
>
> *So I see you're hard at work today, too? ;)*
>
> *I actually just polished off a lengthy Word document chock-full of Florence recs, but now I'm pulling a you (Kidding. Kind of) and getting all self-conscious about sending it, in my case because it is ridiculously detailed and I think you might have just been being polite when you said, "Yes, Alison, I'd love to hear your advice on what to see & do when in Italy next month . . ."*
>
> *Cheers,*
> *Alison*

April 24 at 1:08 p.m.

Good afternoon!

Thank you for confirming me as your Facebook friend. Just so you know, I was not being polite when I said I wanted your list of Florence-related recs. I feel like you're an expert traveler, plus, you lived there! Please send me the email!

So, I hit a major wall 20 minutes ago but was able to drive through it with a 3rd cup of coffee. You wore me out this weekend. 8:45 will be my bedtime tonight as long as it isn't too light outside!!

The last 45 minutes of sleep we were able to get Saturday a.m. was one of the top 5 moments of the weekend. . . . That's a compliment, BTW.

JRH

April 24 at 4:55 p.m.

Funny - I'm having trouble comprehending how "I most enjoy spending time with you when you are passed out" is a compliment. . . . What were the other 4 highlights of the weekend?

Also, my Word document o' travel advice is attached. I lifted a few sections from a similar document I created for friends honeymooning across Italy last summer. I opted not to delete the sappy romantic suggestions, because I figured you can enjoy them by yourself, snap some photos, and Photoshop me in. Nothing spells romance like a good Photoshopped JPEG.

April 24 at 5:56 p.m.

1. *Intimate activities with you by the fire Friday evening*
2. *Waking up next to you*
3. *Dinner (everything except our first fight) and ice cream Friday evening*
4. *The anticipation of seeing you again after you left*
5. *Run/shower/breakfast Saturday*

The last 45 minutes of sleep yesterday a.m. was wonderful but was technically not part of the weekend. I liked it because it was so unplanned and totally mellow, comfortable, etc.

Yours,
Jamie

April 26 at 8:45 a.m.

Good morning!

Thanks again for accompanying me to the office party last night. I can't imagine that was any fun for you, but you were a very good sport. Plus, today at work everyone keeps telling me how I'm dating up.

I hope you're hanging in there. I know I slept like a rock when we got home last night, but I vaguely recall waking up to you reading by the lamp more than once in the middle of the night. How many hours do you think you slept?

Jimmy

April 26 at 12:02 p.m.

Hmm. I'd venture to say 6 hours? I think that's a PR for me in terms of our sleepovers, though. Mental high five! I'm proud.

Ooh! Did I tell you (I think I did) that my firm got an increased allowance to let me move forward with finishes analysis (i.e., paint, varnish, shellac, etc.) in unexamined spaces in the Armory? A very welcome respite from the dreariness/oppressiveness of the office! Happy day.

I have to swing by there at some point today or tomorrow. If you weren't kidding about wanting a personal tour on Saturday, I can try to arrange clearance for us with the security guards?

Cheers,
Alison

* * *

"Sooo, don't get all . . . freaky or whatever," James says, lifting his martini. "Oh, cheers, by the way." We clink glasses. "But . . . I was staying in Connecticut last night and my dad had to work late, so I had dinner with my mom. Somewhere near the dregs of the second bottle of wine—"

"Ooh, I'm impressed, maybe secretly *jealous*, that you and your mom can polish off two bottles between you! That's all fine and well for me and my BYOB-ing gal pals, you know, but my mom has the tolerance of a flea."

"No, my mom can kick it back like the best of them. See? I told you she's cool. Anyway—"

"Anytime *we* try to wine and dine my mom, we wind up calling it an early night before she makes it through glass two. Actually, it's kind of cute; she always tries to deny her lightweightedness, but then always winds up whispering to the hostess on the way out that her children got her drunk."

"That's cute. Are you going to let me finish my story?"

"Nope," I say smiling defiantly. ". . . Okay, fine. Go on."

"Anyway, somewhere near the dregs of the second bottle, I told her that I thought you might be The One."

I blink.

"And . . ." he leads.

I blink again and faintly smile.

"And this is the part where *you* say, 'Really, James? That sounds so nice. That makes me *happpppy*.'"

"Really, James? That sounds so nice. That makes me *happpppy*," I imitate.

"Come here, you." And he kisses me somewhere between my cheek and forehead, dangerously close to my eye once again.

Over brunch at Cowgirl in the West Village on Saturday of that same week, he reprises the subject. "So, when I brought up my conversation with my mom on Thursday, you . . . didn't say anything."

"Oh?" I dip a forkful of eggs into my ketchup.

"Way to be coy again," he says.

"I'm not trying to be coy. I'm sorry. I just don't know what to say to that? It was really sweet."

"Well, why don't you reciprocate the sentiment?"

I understand and nod okay.

"Are there things you want to change?" he queries.

"Want to change?" I echo. "Well. Now that you mention it . . ."

"Uh-oh. What do you want to change about me *this* time." He rolls his eyes, pretending this is a constant cycle.

"No. Nothing. But . . . I just want you to be . . . more considerate. Like, a little." I quickly add, "Not a lot. And no, I'm not angry."

"Considerate how?"

"Well . . . a few times recently you've broken plans. Or pushed them back to really late. I *know*," I look him in the eye, "that it comes from a good place. And I *know* that you have to get work done *and* that you want to see me. I just wish . . ." I sound it out slowly, trying not to frighten him or elicit his "this is a fight" routine, ". . . that you could *plan* a little better. Like if you know you're going to have tons of work one night, just say so. And we can meet up late-night, or just not see each other that night."

"*Really?*" he says sarcastically. "Like you wouldn't be annoyed if I called you at 11:00 p.m. Like you wouldn't treat it as a 'booty call.'"

"I kind of," I wrinkle my brow, "think we're past that at this point, no?" My mind flickers back to our sexual escapades—on the rug before his fireplace last weekend, tangled up in his bed sheets throughout this week. I blush. "And besides, if I'm telling you now it's okay, then it's okay." I read his eyes, he nods. "The problem is that *even* though I know it comes from a good place, when you cancel on me last minute, it means I'm out the time when I *could* be seeing friends, or staying late at the office, or tutoring."

"Is this our *second* fight?" he asks, eyes wide, faux-disbelieving.

I force a half smile. "No." I sigh. "It's not a fight. I'm not trying to fight. You are a very good guy. Man. And I know that you try very hard to make me happy. So I'm just telling you this . . . one . . . *little* thing that would make me happy if you tried to work on it a teeny tiny bit."

"And that is?" he asks.

Gah! Is he not listening to me? "Trying to plan your time out a little better. Even if that means not making plans with me, if you think there's a chance you'll get stuck working late, or not wanting to come into the city."

"Okay. I can do that."

"See? That wasn't so hard!"

"For *you*," he says. "Second fight. You won again."

	April 29 at 10:51 p.m.
JAMES:	HEY! WEDDING'S OVER. YOU STILL OUT WITH BEN? WANT TO MEET UP?
ALISON:	OOH. CAN'T WAIT TO HEAR ABOUT THE INDIAN CEREMONY. WE'RE AT MCSORLEY'S. YOU CAN MEET BEN!
JAMES:	ON MY WAY. PROMISE NOT TO BE LATE THIS TIME!

"I think your brother and I could be good friends," James tells me as we kick off our shoes in his apartment later that night.

"Oh yeah? He's pretty great."

"Does he golf?"

"I can't tell if you're asking as a joke? Like a blue-blood bro code? But yes."

"Does he—"

"No, he doesn't play squash, and he's never rowed a day in his life."

"We're feisty tonight."

"No, just playing. Sorry." I bite my lip. I start peeling off my tights. "What time is it?"

He checks his watch. "Yikes, close to three."

"Okay. I'm gonna go brush my teeth and wash up. Do you want first bathroom?"

"No, it's okay. You go. I'm kind of amped up from all the liquor. Do you mind if I play guitar?"

"Of course not! Serenade away!" I call from the bathroom.

I reenter the room and climb onto the bed, then wrap his comforter around me. He's playing and singing, and again, his music is oddly moving.

Suddenly, mid-song, he claps his hand over the strings and says, without looking up, "We have to talk."

A knot plunges to the pit of my stomach. "Oh?"

He stands up, drops his guitar to the ground, where it clangs discordantly, and starts pacing back and forth. "Yeah. I'm just . . . I'm just . . . the wheels have been spinning up there all day." He gestures a crank next to his temple. The same gesture we used as kids to say, "*Looney Tunes!*"

I nod.

He raises both hands to his forehead and presses his palms against his temples. "And . . . I'm just . . . I'm just really . . . *tweaking out* over here." He lowers his hands into fists and clenches them with each word "tweaking," "out," "here." His voice amplifies. "I've just. I've just got . . . so . . . much . . . PRESSURE . . . on me from all sides right now. And . . . it's feeling really *freaky*." He growls the word "freaky" through gritted teeth, instantly conjuring an image of Heath Ledger's rabid Joker intoning it the same way. "I've got *pressure* to do well at work! My boss keeps putting *pressure* on me to bring in new clients! I've got *pressure* to take care of my younger brother!" He stops pacing and kicks his guitar, which skips across the carpet. His voice rises to a fever pitch and he punctuates each phrase by hitting his right hand into his left palm. "Who's a fucking MESS. . . ." he barks. "There's really nothing I can do to help him, since he can't help himself." He resumes pacing, his chest puffed up and fists above his elbows. "He's a *drug addict* for crying out loud! What am *I* supposed to do to help him? And I've got PRESSURE to pay for the renovations on my house! And PRESSURE from my parents to settle down . . . and now there's PRESSURE from you!" On the word "you," he points at me accusatorially, his eyes maniacal. "And—"

I sit up straight on the bed and choke out, gently, hesitantly, "I'm . . . sorry? I don't *want* to get in the way of you and your—"

"NO! But you're *always* trying to change me! Trying to make me . . . *be* more attentive, and *do* . . . *more* of this, and *less* of that." He smacks the back of his right hand into his left palm with each emphatic phrase. I glance around the room, keeping track of where the knives and dangerous objects are. "And I'm *not* getting any younger," he howls, "and my *hair* is starting to fall out and—" he goes on. Yelling. But he lost me in this kitchen sink of a meltdown when he started talking about losing his hair.

I slowly, subtly, start gathering my clothing from the chair, keeping my eyes fixed on him as I start to pull my tights on, then my boots.

"—It's like everybody *wants* something from me! And does anyone ever ask what *I* want?" I'm guessing the answer is no. "I NEVER get time to think about what *I* want! Nobody ever asks ME what *I* want!" he clamors.

"Okay," I say softly, abruptly. "I'm going to go." My coat is on, my purse in hand, and I inch slowly, backward, to the door.

He clenches his jaw then relaxes it. Then clenches it again. His face is beet red. And terrifying.

"Bye." I exit through the door, close it behind me, and call the elevator. I'm practically hopping from one foot to the other as I wait for the elevator to ding and its doors to open. But he comes out first.

"Hey. Can you come back in here and talk?"

"No," I say, as calmly and gently as possible. "I don't think now seems like a good time to talk. I mean, for you."

"Can I at least walk you downstairs?"

If I say no, he's going to get incensed. And there's nobody here since it's the break of dawn, so I'm not protecting myself by verbally rebuffing him. He can and will follow me if he wants to.

"Ummm. If you like?" We ride the elevator down in silence, while I scan the ceiling for a security camera. His face is still red, he's still clenching and unclenching his jaw, and he keeps raising his eyes to the ceiling, too.

My eyes are watery and I feel a wave of relief wash over me as we step out onto the sidewalk. Doormen! Never have I been so happy to see other people's doormen! I can feel my body trembling. Traffic on his street is heavy, so nearly as soon as I've stepped off the curb and extended my arm, a cab pulls over.

"Do you . . . want cash?" he asks.

"Uhh . . . yeah, I guess? I don't think I have any on me. . . . Thanks." He pulls out a twenty and slips it into my hand. Once safely inside, I shut the car door behind me without saying another word.

My pulse races uncontrollably throughout the ride home. Before I know it, we're stopped in front of my building. It's only when I pull out my wallet to pay the cab driver that I realize I didn't need cash from him. All cabs take credit cards. I don't know what I was thinking. Or what he was thinking.

I rush into my building, fly up the stairs and into the apartment, lock the door behind me, and then flip the dead bolt. I lean against it and wait for my pulse to stop racing. But it doesn't. I close my eyes and take three deep breaths.

I change into pajamas, tiptoe down the corridor, and knock on Cassie's door softly. I open it a crack. She's sleeping. I tiptoe over and climb into the empty side of the bed.

"Are you okay?" she mumbles, half asleep.

"I think so," I say.

"Where's James?" she mumbles again.

"At his place. Having a navel-gazing nervous breakdown straight out of *Brief Interviews with Hideous Men.*"

"Oh no. Do you want to talk?" She starts to rouse.

"No, no, go back to sleep," I whisper.

"Are you okay?" she mumbles again.

I think. "I am now," I whisper. Then I pull the blanket over me, roll over toward the window, stare at the glass, and try to calm myself by focusing on my breathing.

May 1 at 12:27 p.m.

Are you OK??? Would you like me to make a voodoo doll named James? I would put a Viking-sized ax right between his legs.

I'm afraid my week is swamped, but are you free late-night this week? You know I will sacrifice my sleep if you need a tequila shot buddy.

Xoxox
Nicole

May 1 at 12:59 p.m.

Hi hi,

You are super sweet. Thanks! No need to sacrifice your sleep, but I appreciate the offer. ;) It's a very long story that we don't have to talk about if you don't have time, but in brief,

I'm somewhat disappointed in humanity. And I'm freaked out that my judgment failed me.

With this whole "dating strangers" thing, I proceeded super cautiously on all fronts. Or tried to. I didn't kiss until fairly late in the dating sequence, I didn't fall hard, didn't push it forward, continued to play the field for the first two months of daTing him (capital T as in "going on dates," not to be confused with dating, as in "you are my boyfriend"), etc.

Before committing to him in any way, I made sure he had some degree of accountability (met friends, received multiple emails from his work account, thereby proving he had a real job at a real place, saw his house, saw his dad's office, knew his family history, asked about his prior multi-year relationships and subsequent breakups, asked about future goals, etc.). And then, just as I started to get comfortable, tell friends that he existed, told DAVE because I was trying to do the right thing, he did a complete 180 on Saturday night.

Again, longer story for in person, but he met up with me and Ben. Was his usual spazzy but super-affectionate self. Told me he thought he and Ben could really be friends, etc., etc. Then we're at his place, he's playing guitar, he puts it down and basically launches into a nervous breakdown without me saying a word. It was scary, and my pulse didn't stop racing until Monday morning.

My mom asked me if I was most disappointed in:

a. my judgment

b. losing him, just as I'd started to care

c. the world

The answer is definitely NOT (b). Whether this episode occurred two weeks ago, in three more months, or in three years, I don't see how I could ever get back to a point where I could care much about him.

As for (a), perhaps I should have seen the fact that he dumped his girlfriend three days after she moved in as a red flag? But I took what he said at face value and accepted that she was intense and overly self-centered. I feel like I spend 95% of my life trying to be in control; I guess I'm just ashamed that I got this all so wrong. There have to have been other red flags; how did I miss them all?

I keep replaying all the sweet things he did and said (he told me on Thursday - two days before this - that he told his parents I was "the greatest person he'd ever dated," and that he thought I might be "The One"), and I fear that even knowing what I know now, I can't pick out a turning point where I should have seen the signs or done things differently. Nevertheless, I rue the timing of it all. Why, oh why, did I decide this was a relationship - a relationship with promise - SEVEN DAYS before this meltdown? If I could go back and do it again, clearly I'd omit this week's whole jumping-in-the-sack part. Welp, another notch on the bedpost for me. Ugh, I hate you, timing!

Although (c) is really a crappy way to feel, it's the right answer to my mom's question. . . .

WOW, was that a vent. Sorry! I've had issues talking about it, and word vomiting via email to you just made that all so easy!

If you need to find me, I intend to spend the rest of the week self-censuring in the fetal position under my desk. With a flask of bourbon.

Love,
Alison

May 1 at 3:11 p.m.

1. You said "sorry" two-too-many times in the last sentence! Don't ever be sorry for venting or email-word-vomiting!! 99% of the time I prefer to email-vent than chitchat-vent, because my chitchat-venting is so mucky and email-venting is so therapeutic.

2. I like "daTing." I've never seen that before. But why is it the "T" that's capitalized? This topic so-shouldn't be #2, it's not important. I'm demoting it to #37 in this list.

3. *I'm so sorry, that's really shitty. Especially because you did everything right, to a T (ha! Get it? Like daTing). There's no way that the answer to your mom's question should be (a) - and I hope there's not even an inkling of self-blame. Maybe his spazzy exterior also translates into a spazzy/schizophrenic interior?*

4. *I liked him too, remember? I was probably a bigger fan of his than you were! And as we puzzle through how to eschew situations like this down the line, maybe we chalk this experience up to a not-so-fun reminder that we never really know 100% what's going on in someone else's head. Sorry to wax all philosophical on you . . . but it's weird, right? Someone you know very well might totally surprise you by freaking out, or by proposing to someone else, or by buying you a wedding dress. These things have now officially all happened to VERY good friends of ours! There wasn't any real advice to this comment, but I think acknowledging the impossibility of knowing for certain what the other is thinking makes these shockers a wee bit less shocking.*

5. *Did you realize you wrote your whole email without saying his name? You go, girl! Let's erase him from your life!!*
   ;-)
Xoxoxox
Nicole

Three weeks have gone by since I last saw James. This morning I found this note in my inbox.

May 22 at 7:33 a.m.
I know we're not supposed to be friends, so I don't really expect to get a response, but I just wanted to say hello and see how you were doing. I'm off to London tomorrow and plan to use your great travel itinerary when I get to Florence! I'm sorry for how things ended up between us.

James

May 22 at 9:08 a.m.

Um, WOW! I cannot believe he wrote an email to you. Part of me is glad that he did because it shows some humanity from him. The other part of me is not glad because I want him as far away from you as possible.

What are your mom's theories on why he wrote? Wow! Wow! Wow!

~Cassie

May 23 at 12:49 p.m.

Update: since receiving and forwarding that email yesterday, I also received a missed call from him (he rang the moment I walked in the door from tutoring, and I ran to your window to scope the street, on the brink of a heart attack thinking he might have followed me home). I went ahead and blocked his number so they always go straight to voice mail from now on. Anyway, back to fun stuff like hypothesizing!

My mom thinks it's EITHER:

a. *He feels remorse. As he's going through his travel shit and found this really funny, long Florence recommendations email I tailored to his interests, he realizes his about-face was unnecessary, and he's embarrassed.*

b. *She's not entirely sure she believes (a) since he said he'd never been friends with an ex. So why bother reaching out to me? Therefore, she thinks he let the dust settle, pondered his loss, is gearing up for this trip to Europe solo, and wants to have something to look forward to coming back to (i.e., me).*

I think his internal monologues defy better logic, so I don't think psychoanalyzing his motives is especially productive; because with him, we can't REALLY ever know what he's thinking and why.

As a psychology major, what's your best guess?

Love!
Alison

May 23 at 12:50 p.m.
It's been nearly a month — does he realize that? I think he felt really badly immediately after the incident, but he was too embarrassed to do anything about it. I don't think there was anything he could have done that Saturday to win you back, but he could have saved himself some dignity had he at least apologized.

I think he thinks enough time has passed that he can address you again without feeling utterly foolish. I agree that he may be trying to win you back (one very small step at a time). Do you have any desire to try to work on things with him?

~Cassie

May 23 at 1:06 p.m.
EWWWWW!
NOOOOO!
Wait . . . seriously?

EWWWWW!
NOOOOO!

If I'd said yes, I hope you would leave your office, come down to mine, duct tape me to my chair, and beat some sense into me. Immediately.

There are a couple really positive things I know I will miss in future relationships now that I've experienced them - namely, having my ego stroked constantly with praises and compliments was nice (until I realized the person they were coming from was insane, which negated all of them), and also feeling like someone is totally physically attracted to you like a magnet and always wants to touch your hair is kinda nice, too. Sometimes. Not when they overdo it in public though. Gross.

I know it's easy to say "other people can do this, too!" but the reality is I don't really like people who are like that. I

shy away from romantic types, and, let's be honest, roman-
tic gestures make me do the awkward dance. My conclu-
sion is that James's delivery was so outlandish and funny
that it stripped away the awkwardness - but that's really only
because I grew used to always feeling puzzled by his ges-
tures (like kissing my eye and yelling in my ear) and learned
to appreciate the humor in the situation. So I doubt the per-
son I end up with will be as overtly affectionate and enam-
ored. Sigh.

On the bright side, I look forward to meeting some man,
someday, who doesn't make me embarrassed at all.

Oy.

Alison

* * *

A month after that email to Cassie (nearly two months post-James'
meltdown), I receive the following voice mail:

"Hey. It's James. I'm back from London and Italy, and I wanted to tell
you that your itinerary was amazing. I did almost all of it, including the
run along the Arno up to San Miniato al Monte. Anyway, thanks for
that. And if you ever want to talk, please know that I'm sorry and that
I'd like to make it up to you."

I play it once and hit DELETE.

myownmaster05: Brooks, the Epistoler

Sometime while I was dating James, but before we stopped seeing other people, I had a lengthy email exchange with Brooks.

April 3 at 5:31 p.m.

Dear Alison,

I'm so sorry - more for my sake than for yours, but also for yours - but I have to cancel our date for Wednesday. I had my wisdom teeth out before the weekend, and though the dentist said swelling goes down quickly, mine hasn't. So I was already planning on meeting you looking like a chipmunk and hoping that you might, by some stretch of the imagination, be able to overlook my bloated appearance. But then, to reduce swelling, they put me on a prescription that has wreaked all kinds of havoc on my system. Also, I still can't chew, so our dinner date would have been problematic. Or a flash-forward to life together when we're old and gray and you have to spoon-feed me everything. . . .

I'm taking off to visit my dad in Arizona on Thursday, so although I feel terrible punting our date off, on the bright side, when you see me, I will have a sexy refined jawline and be nicely tanned. Silver lining for both of us?

Anyway, promise you won't fall in love while I'm gone. And to make it up to you, I'll upgrade our date from Chipotle to a cloth-napkin venue.

Best,
Brooks

April 4 at 10:58 p.m.

Bummer! But no worries, I completely understand. Besides, this soon-to-be-new-and-improved version of you sounds way better, so I shouldn't complain.

I'll try my hardest not to fall in love between now and then, but no promises. How about this: even if I do, I'll at least give the post-Arizona version of you a chance to be my friend? ;)

Cheers,
Alison

When Brooks returned two weeks later, I received the following email:

April 19 at 2:14 p.m.

Hey Alison,

I am still sitting on the tarmac, waiting to deplane. Didn't want to waste a minute here: How about Tuesday night. Candle Cafe?

Fondly,
A tanner, less swollen Brooks

I wrote back:

April 19 at 10:16 p.m.

Subject: Well, they say that timing is everything . . .
Hey,

Welcome back! Glad you're feeling better.

Perhaps you jinxed it by making me promise not to fall in love, but while you were away, things became a bit more serious with a guy I'd seen a few times before you left. You sound terrific. But unfortunately, I'm off the dating market, for now at least.

Sorry!
Alison

To which he responded, in 24-point Olde English calligraphy:

April 20 at 7:57 a.m.

Dearest Alison,
Indeed 'tis true that timing is everything, and I am kicking myself for letting it obstruct our blossoming romance. Yet they say that the strongest tales of passion and love are those that were begat through epistolary correspondence, so perhaps our story doth not end here. . . .

Yours truly,
Brooks

P.S. Call me if he snores.

I'm walking home from tutoring in the dark, cool night. Now that my heart rate has resumed a seminormal level thanks to two days' distance from James, I loosen my grip on my cell phone and breathe. Then dial.

"Hello?"

"Brooks?"

"*Yeeeessss?*"

"Hey! It's Alison. From *Match.com.*"

"Uhh. Hi! How're you doing?" His voice is pleasantly deep and masculine, attractive-sounding.

"Uhhh." I laugh nervously. "Good?" I breathe in. "*Soooo.* This is a little strange, and I know that that lasted a hot second, but, I'm single again? So, I thought I'd take you up on the postscript from your epic epistolary correspondence . . ." I laugh, and he, thankfully, joins me in laughter, "and call to see if *you're* still single and maybe want to meet up? Sorry, this is incredibly odd. And somewhat embarrassing."

He laughs. "Oh! No! That would be awesome. I'd love to meet up!" He pauses. "Also, I'm sorry to hear that," he says. And he sounds genuine. "But I'm happy for me. . . . Yeah, that was clever, right? I felt like when I discovered you could change the font on Match mail, I knew that email was going to be epic."

"I *was* kind of tempted to print it out and hold onto it for posterity," I agree.

"So. I don't want to rush you. Do you think you'd be ready to meet up later this week? Like, Thursday?"

"Yeah. I could do Thursday."

"Excellent. But, you actually caught me at a weird time. I'm in the gym, and now I should probably go so I'm not that douche at the gym who's yammering on his cell phone while lifting weights."

"Oh, yes. Go. Sorry!"

"No, I'm really glad you called. I'll shoot you an email with a time when I get home."

"Okay, bye!"

"Bye."

I hang up and walk down the street. Thank *goodness* he didn't ask me what happened. How would I have responded?

Later that night, I receive a blank email with no subject line from Brooks. I write back:

> *May 2 at 9:50 p.m.*
>
> *Re:*
>
>   *I have to say, I think your last email was better. . . .*
>   *Good talking to you, though. Glad we can finally meet face-to-face!*
>
> *Cheers,*
> *Alison*

> *May 2 at 10:22 p.m.*
>
> *Hi Alison,*
>
>   *Ha! Sorry about that ghost email. I got a little overeager and hit send before writing anything. Don't read too much into that. . . .*
>   *Because I feel like we have made some kind of cyber–cell phone connection, it's important to me to be honest*

before we flesh-and-blood meet. So here goes: I'm 45 not 35. I totally understand if you don't want to go to dinner with me now. But I really hope you don't change your mind. My photos are recent. And if you are still willing to meet, I won't lie to you about too much other stuff.

Idiotically,
Brooks

May 3 at 6:43 a.m.

That's so funny! Because I'm actually 17, not 27.

OK, just kidding.

This is a big bummer. The reality is that your emails have ranked among the top emails I've ever received. And you seem really smart/nice/charming. But I recently corresponded with a 37-year-old on Match and felt weird about that, so I think that I'm probably not in the right mind-set at this moment to be worth you wasting time on.

Thanks for being honest. Even though this is a sucky response, I do appreciate it.

Cheers,
Alison

poplockandroll03: Doppelgänger Greg, Continued

April 16 at 12:43 a.m.

GREG: RANDOM BUT I THINK I SEE YOU OR YOUR DOPPELGÄNGER. ARE YOU AT GRAY'S PAPAYA ON WEST 4TH?

GREG: DID YOU JUST WIN THE HOT-DOG-EATING CONTEST???

ALISON: AS A MATTER OF FACT, YES! I WAS INSPIRED AFTER TRYING THEIR RECESSION SPECIAL, AND MY FRIENDS ROPED ME INTO IT.... ARE YOU STILL HERE?

As he is wont to do, Greg doesn't respond. But a month later, I'm at a Rosanne Cash concert. She has these Teutonic-looking twin-hipster guitar players, which for some reason I find very amusing. Which for some reason, makes me think of Greg.

May 13 at 9:16 p.m.

ALISON: WHOA. WAY TO ROCK OUT ON THAT GUITAR SOLO! ROSANNE CASH IS GREAT & ALL, BUT I CAN'T STOP ADMIRING YOUR NEW COIF & PLATINUM HIGHLIGHTS.

Naturally, because it's Greg, I don't hear back until Tuesday morning.

May 16 at 8:50 a.m.

GREG: IF YOU THOUGHT I LOOKED GOOD SATURDAY, HERE I AM WITH RC OUTSIDE THE OLIVE GARDEN TIMES SQUARE LAST NIGHT. I ATE 32 BREADSTICKS AND GOT MINESTRONE IN MY FU MANCHU.

He's attached a photo showing Rosanne Cash in Times Square along-side a ZZ Top look-alike with a multi-foot-long beard.

May 16 at 5:47 p.m.

ALISON: I KNEW IT WAS YOU AND NOT YOUR DOPPELGÄNGER THIS TIME! BUT WHAT OF THE BLEACHED HIGHLIGHTS? THEY WERE *NEARLY* AS SEXY AS THE FU MANCHU. . . .

ga2nyluke: Older Luke

"Uhhh. Uh-oh."

"What?" Nicole asks.

"Eesh." I frown at my computer screen. "Okay. So, I've been corresponding with this guy, Luke, and we just set a date for Sunday. . . . But now I'm looking back at his profile, and I just realized he's *divorced*." More to myself than to her, I wonder, "How did I miss that?" I continue scanning his profile. "I mean, I already knew that he's . . . kind of old? Thirty-seven. I guess I was so focused on his age when I checked his profile after he emailed me, I totally missed the 'relationship status' section. Crap."

"Is that a deal breaker?"

"I don't know. I've never dated anyone who's been *married* before. I can't decide if that means I should just flake out and cancel?"

"Does he have kids?"

"Gosh, I hope not. I doubt I'm ready for *that* quite yet. Let me check." I scroll through his profile quickly. "Nope, no kids. Phew." Nicole leans over my shoulder to check out his profile page.

"He's *hot*!"

"Yeah, and a doctor. But he's old. And apparently divorced?"

"So, *is* that such a big deal? The divorced part?"

"I don't know. Kind of. I guess I sort of assumed that whoever I wound up with, I'd be their first . . . you know, *great* love. . . . But he's had that before."

"Yeah, I guess I would want that, too. But we can't always control people's pasts . . . including our own." She smirks. "You've already got the date set up. *I* think he's too hot to ignore."

I glance around Trinity Pub and spot him at a low table in the back of the room.

"Luke?"

"Hey, Alison." He gets up from his chair and gives me a hug with a hard pat on the back—the kind you give a teammate after a soccer game. "It's nice to meet you."

"You, too!" The combination of his buzz-cut brown hair, his rippled biceps peeking through his NAVY T-shirt, and his Southern twang remind me of quintessential military men, like Channing Tatum in *Stop-Loss,* or Channing Tatum in *Dear John.* We order pints and make small talk. He's an only child, a former ROTC, a psychiatry resident hailing from Georgia.

"I know this sounds weird," I say, "and I'm not trying to flatter you, but I have a disproportionate number of friends from Georgia. It's like everyone I've ever met from that state is super polite, super warm, and super genuine. . . . No pressure to reciprocate the compliment," I add quickly, ". . . or to embody it. . . . I'm pretty sure the same can't be said of New Yorkers. Or suburban New Yorkers."

"Yeah, New Yorkers are tough nuts to crack," he says. "I've been here for three years and have found it really hard to make friends outside my program. And, as you probably could guess, I'm kind of in a different age bracket than most of the other residents."

I nod slowly and take this to mean it's alright to ask, "Yeah. So, that *is* kind of late to be in residency. Quarter-life crisis?"

"Sort of. My life changed a lot eight years ago, and I was really craving a fresh start. I already had a master's in chemistry, but the work I was doing for a petroleum company wasn't fulfilling and didn't have a lot of growth potential. So I decided to apply to med school, if a bit late, and try to become a doctor."

"Do you mind if I ask what triggered the 'fresh start' craving?"

"Yeah, I wouldn't have said it if I wasn't comfortable talking about it." He shakes his head for emphasis. "My ex-wife and I decided to get divorced at that time. So much of my life was anchored in our small town, I felt like I needed to . . . cut the cord geographically, professionally . . . emotionally."

I nod. "How long were you married for?"

"We started dating in college. And we were married for seven years."

"You didn't have kids?"

"No. I think we both knew the marriage wasn't perfect. Or, rather, was *im*perfect. So we never tried for kids. If I'd analyzed it more closely at the time, I might have seen that decision as symbolic of the larger problem that we should have addressed earlier. Rather than stay in a tumultuous marriage for all those years."

"And *was* it tumultuous? Is that why you got divorced? . . . Sorry, I don't mean to pry—"

"No. Please, ask as many questions as you like. We were young and hotheaded. We fought constantly. It wasn't a good relationship. She was really good at getting under my skin . . . and I did the same to her."

"Did you guys . . . ever seek help? Like a counselor or psychologist?"

"No. We were young and . . . it was kinda like puppy love. If I were going through it again now, I definitely would. But, on the other hand, I'm glad I'm older. And not in that relationship anymore."

I nod.

"What about you?"

"Me?" I point to myself.

"Yeah. Have you had any long-term or serious relationships?"

"A few. Importance-wise they all pale in comparison to a *marriage* though."

"No, that's not necessarily true. Have you had . . . one? Or many?"

"Only two significant ones. And one was in college, so I don't feel like that counts anymore."

"That counts." He nods encouragingly. "What was your post-college one?"

"A three-plus-year thing. It ended in January."

"Do you feel like you're over it?"

"God, I *hope* so. It's been nearly five months."

"Yeah, but relationships can have profound or far-reaching effects on us."

"Spoken like a true psychiatrist." I raise an eyebrow and take a sip of my cider.

"Are you skirting the question?" he asks, winking.

"You're making me feel like I'm on the couch." I half smile. "And no. I'm fine. I'm not sure there's a whole lot to say."

"*That's* not true," he brushes this off. "What was he like?"

"I don't know . . ." I wait to see if we can drop the subject, but since he doesn't say anything, I take it as a cue to continue, if begrudgingly. "Smart. Adventurous. Generous. We *really* don't have to talk about this. . . . Tell me more about your life in New York so far."

"Well, I live down by the hospital in resident housing. I've been in the same place for three years. I've got a rescue dog; his name's Boomer. . . . My ex-wife and I shared custody of our dog, back when I did med school in Georgia. I'd get the dog every other month. Then when I moved to New York, the worst part was that the distance precluded that. So I got Boomer." He adds, "But I really miss my other dog."

"Have you seen him since you moved?"

"Nah. That would entail seeing my ex-wife, and it doesn't really seem worth it, since she doesn't live near my parents or other people I try to see when I go home. What about you? Do you get to go home a lot?"

"My parents live two blocks away, so yes. It's not the home I grew up in—that was sold a few years ago—but their place feels like home now." He asks about where I grew up. I talk about their reverse migration again, and it sort of rolls off my tongue like a script.

"Do you have any big vacation plans or summer travel coming up?" he asks.

"My big one is a trip to Turkey later this month with my parents. And then in July I'm flying to Napa to be maid of honor in a friend's wedding." He asks me how I know the bride- and groom-to-be.

"The bride, Catherine, was a roommate of mine in college; Andrew, her fiancé, she met out in California."

"What's their relationship like?"

"Interesting question. . . . I'm not sure I ever thought about it before." I describe the bride, and her lovable idiosyncrasies and her strengths, also her needs and insecurities, "Which I think are just . . . complemented, or fulfilled, by him in the best of possible ways."

"How so?"

I explain her messy family background, contrasted with the stable, all-American, close-knit family the groom hails from. I describe her creative, sometimes frenetic, energy, which seems to be endlessly inspiring and intriguing to her groom. "I think it's actually a pretty ideal situation. She needs someone who is, at the end of the day, loving, forgiving, and stable. And he . . . he just feels like he hit jackpot with this beautiful, ethereal, intellectual woman, and you can tell that nothing will ever change that feeling."

He stares at me. I blush. "Sorry! I can't believe I just droned on and on about that. Next time, will you cut me off, please?"

"No." He nods. "I was just thinking. Well, I was listening, but I was also thinking: You're kind of an old soul, huh?"

I blush deeper. "Yeah, I get that sometimes. Sorry, didn't mean to be so deep or serious."

"No, not at all. I'm impressed. You could be a psychiatrist."

"I think one's enough for this table."

"Have you always been an old soul?"

"I don't know. Kind of?" I pause to think this over. "Ever since I was in high school, I've kind of always felt . . . old. Like, I *loved* my friends! And I *loved* playing bonding games at volleyball retreats, and going to field parties in the woods. But, I also kind of felt like, 'Gosh, so much of what we're talking about is so inane and . . . senseless?' Like, maybe I was a thirty-year-old stuck in a sixteen-year-old's body? I never *cared* about who got drunk or who hooked up with who. Whom. . . . But my friends did. And that sentiment reared its head again regarding sorority politics in college and . . . ugh. Why am I telling you all this? I sound like the most boring, *negative*, plaintive person you've ever met!" Seriously. *Shut up, Alison.*

He laughs. "Hardly. In analyst-speak, we talk about the contrasts between someone's mental age and their physical age. It's a common basis for assessment, especially in terms of child and teen development."

"Yeah, but I think . . . hope? . . . I'm a fully formed human by now, and I *know* I sound like a Negative Nancy." I look down at my lap, ashamed. "Can we talk about something else? Like . . . what mental age do you think *you* are?"

"I'm thirty-seven years old, and I kind of feel thirty-seven mentally, too. But . . . maybe not? Given my life stage, I'm probably closer to early thirties."

I nod repeatedly, still chewing over my horrendous monologue from a minute ago.

"That was a joke." He smiles. "To justify why it's okay for you to date me."

"Oh. Oh! Gosh, sorry! I just keep trying to devise ways to extract my foot from my mouth."

He laughs. "I actually think, or at least hope, I'm a bit ahead of the thirty-year-olds. I'm hoping it's not too much longer before I can settle down again. This time for keeps. And maybe have kids. . . ." he trails off. "What about you?"

"Hmm?"

"Do you want to settle down? What were you looking for when you signed up for Match?"

Without giving it much thought, I rattle off my now-near-rote explanation of wanting to "branch out beyond the alumni population of my college"; I mention my theory about timing, and "porch swing candidates." It's really starting to feel like I'm dating myself.

May 7 at 8:30 p.m.

Hey Alison,

I really enjoyed having drinks with you this afternoon, so much so that I came home and told Boomer all about you. Boomer asked me if I was uncomfortable about our age difference. I told him I wasn't, primarily because you seem wise beyond your years. In fact, I think you're possibly wiser and more mature than I am.

Boomer then asked if you were uncomfortable about our age difference, and I said I thought you might be, but that you're a good actress. Boomer wanted me to tell you that I still run around and tumble with him in the park most days, and that I have really good genes. My dad hasn't gone gray yet, so hopefully I've got a few good decades in me still.

On a more serious note, I think you seem really interesting, really thoughtful, and kind. So if you want to talk the age thing through on a more serious level, or ask any more questions about my divorce, I'm always happy to discuss.

Finally, Boomer asked if he could meet you. I'm on call Tuesday, but the second half of the week is free. Let me know if and when you're free, and I'll tell Boomer so he can start getting excited.

Best,
Luke

May 9 at 10:21 p.m.

Hi Luke!

Apologies for my tardy reply – please don't think I didn't appreciate your email. Unlike for normal people, summer for me means significantly longer hours, since that's when all the scaffolds are up and the chemicals flying. So right now we just kicked off my most exciting/happy time of year (I'm no longer confined to the office) but it's also the most sleepless time of year, which is a bummer since I'm really good at sleeping.

But! We certainly don't want to keep Boomer wagging his tail for weeks on end, overly eager to meet me (sidenote: Eek! Pressure!). Is 9:00 p.m. on Wednesday past Boomer's bedtime, or would that be OK?

Cheers,
Alison

May 11 at 7:14 a.m.

Subject: Positive Feedback
Alison,

I thought about what you said last night about keeping a conversation flowing. That's an insightful comment. Without good conversation things will be limited. What I'm trying to say is that I'm impressed by your observation. Also, I think that so far we have had nice, interesting conversations. I like that you make an attempt to keep the conversation equal and make sure we talk about you and me. Thanks.

As far as Sunday is concerned, can we do 5:45 at the entrance to the Reservoir? Let me know if that works.

-Luke

May 12 at 10:01 p.m.

Aww, sweet and thoughtful email. Thanks!

As for me making an effort to talk about you, it's not something that deserves a "thanks," because really it's just selfish on my part - I have no interest in dating myself. . . . The only problem is that you have this tremendous ability to elicit lengthy anecdotes, descriptions, and opinions from me, despite the fact that the last two times we hung out I secretly vowed to give you the silent treatment in order to force you to take the conversational reins. It's like that magicians' trick, where they pull multicolored paper out of their mouths in a long string. I close my mouth, mime not talking, but then you pull the words out of me and they don't stop. It's magic!

5:45 is totally fine. I'll look for you and Boomer in that vicinity. ;)

Hope you're having a good day!

Cheers,
Alison

"Hi, Boomer! How are you?" I bend over and scratch him, tentatively, behind his ears. Boomer is a terrifying beast of a pit bull who attacks everything in sight and is bigger than I am in every which way. But I pretend to like him a whole lot. "You look pretty energized today!" I squeal, as if coaxing an infant. "Did you maul any puppies on the dog run this weekend like you did Wednesday? Bad doggie."

"*Annnnd* hi, Luke!" I straighten and give him a hug. He pats my back again, like a teammate coming off the field.

"How was your weekend?" he asks.

"Good! Busy. Happy it's not over *quite* yet. You?"

"Low-key. Boomer and I explored Bear Mountain State Park with some of my colleagues. Have you been there? I feel like you'd really enjoy it."

"I *have* been there. Yeah, it's crazy how close we are to . . . *real* wilderness, just a short ride from this . . . manufactured kind." I gesture to the Reservoir path we're circling. We swap tales from hiking trips gone by, he talks about his rock climbing and cycling, and we make our way out of the park and toward the nearest Starbucks.

"Okay, wait here. I'll go in and buy our coffees. You hold Boomer."

I hesitate. "What if we swapped tasks?"

"Nah, I want to pay. And besides, I could use the bathroom, too."

"Umm."

"Do you not want to watch Boomer?" he asks, lowering his face to read my expression.

"No, uhh . . ." I scratch at my neck, "it's not that. It's just. Boomer weighs a lot . . . and is exceptionally strong. . . . How am I going to restrain him? I'm, like, a weakling compared to you."

He laughs. "Hold his leash like this." He loops the leash handle around his wrist twice. "Then give it an upward tug if he misbehaves. It's got these spike-like things that dig into his neck. It doesn't hurt him, but it makes him behave."

I contort the left side of my mouth into an unconvinced frown.

"You'll be *fine*!" He laughs. "I promise."

In the time it takes Luke to get through the bathroom line and the coffee line, Boomer lunges and barks maniacally at no less than three dogs and two pedestrians who pass by. I scold through my teeth, I try that upward jerk of the leash, I loop the leash handle around my wrist three extra times for good measure. And I feel so nervous I could cry.

Luke comes out with coffees in hand. He's laughing. At me, I think?

"Here, you deserve a reward." He extends a large iced coffee. "I'll trade you, the leash for the cup?"

Relieved, I relax my shoulders and try to smile, feigning an easygoing calm. "Do you have the leash?"

"Yeah, I've got it."

"Are you sure?"

"Yes, I'm sure."

"Are you sure sure? Like, positive?"

"You're *funny*. Yes, I'm sure. Do you know I watched you through the window while I was in line? You looked like you were trying to herd a grizzly bear."

I blush. "No. I wasn't *that* bad."

He nods. "You were. Every time he turned his head, you looked like you were going to have a panic attack. When he barked, I worried you might take off running in the opposite direction. It was really cute." He laughs.

"Well, laugh it up. I wasn't trying to be cute. During those two-point-five minutes, I summoned more courage than I have in my lifetime."

"Just standing still?"

"Just. Standing. Still. . . . Hey, that was hard work! Perfecting my defensive stance, feet firmly planted . . ."

"Okay. I promise not to make you do that again. But hey, Boomer loves you!"

"*I* . . . am not sure that's totally true."

"No, it is. Look at your pants."

I glance down. "Ew! How did that *happen*?" My black pants are streaked with huge white swaths of slobber. It looks like they've been tie-dyed.

"Alison, don't let Boomer hear you say that!" Luke says, bending down and pretending to cover his dog's ears. "It means he *likes* you. He's nuzzling your legs every chance he gets."

"Mmmhmm."

"Well, I needed you to pass the Boomer test, and I'd say your pants are telling me you did."

groovymonday80: Younger Luke

May 10 at 9:49 p.m.

Hey there,

I'm sure you get a lot of messages on this site, and I'm sure a lot of them ask you all about your pet hermit crab, Poseidon (that's the lie, right? Back me up here). Rather than make you talk about the same stuff as every other guy, I'll cut to something more fun: it's about to be summer soon. Are you doing anything exciting this summer?

Stick to the true stuff, though, no more lies. Let's get off on the right foot here.

-luke

May 11 at 10:31 p.m.

Hey Luke,

Yes! You are actually the first person to get that right. I used to have a pet hermit crab. I bought him at Myrtle Beach. His name was Romeo (RIP).

To answer your other question, I am very, very much looking forward to summer. It's good for me job-wise (it's our busy season in the construction-conservation industry, so I get to be out of doors all day and climbing around on the outside of buildings, rather than chained to my desk), and also I've got some fun travel plans. Mostly to destination weddings (Napa; an island off the coast of Maine; Newport, R.I.) but also a trip to Europe in a few weeks.

How about yourself? Same rules apply: true stuff only. ;)

Cheers,
Alison

May 13 at 12:33 p.m.

Hey Alison,

You're not a very good liar. That means your list was really 2.75 truths, and only 0.25 lies.

As for me and my summer, I'm spending the next month and change studying for a financial exam. It's pretty depressing stuff, having to spend all of my free time cramming. My brain hurts enough from work as it is. But I'm trying to be a light at the end of the tunnel kinda guy. The end of the tunnel is a killer trip to Vegas with my high school buddy after the exam. We're going to cycle through the desert, try our hands at blackjack, chill by the pool . . . cannot wait.

How many times are you going to get married this summer? I could really use a blender. Not the crappy kind, but a really nice one.

Sorry to hear you're busy right now. Also, based on your photos, wondering how you manage not to get burned to a crisp every day if you're working outside. Anyway, I went to the Turkish baths (Russian? I forget) this morning and am spending the rest of the day with my financial textbooks. Until you free up, I'll just be here, studying, waiting for my blender.

May 13 at 3:46 p.m.

Hey Luke,

Such a happy coincidence in that email - the Turkish (Russian?) baths reference - because . . . (drum roll) . . . I actually just finalized my flight to Turkey this morning! In two weeks I'm journeying through Istanbul, Cappadocia, and Ephesus. . . . I'm excited about the architectural, culinary, and climatic aspects, but also, just think: such fabulous

opportunities to furnish my bedroom! (Kidding. Kind of.
Though, I might actually need to carry on an empty suitcase
on the way over.)

So! Back to your bathing experience. I've never been
to the baths of NYC, but have long yearned to experience
them. However, a dude friend recently went to the one way
downtown and said it was just like a scene out of Eastern
Promises (i.e. overrun with foreign mobsters), plus he got
flogged so hard with twig branches that his skin was purple
for weeks. Can you confirm or negate this?

Not related at all to bathhouses are the following ques-
tions/observations:

1. *I'm sorry to hear you're suffering through the prep work*
   for a tedious exam. Am I to assume it's the CFA? Also,
   remind me exactly what you do job-wise?

2. *Your Vegas adventure-to-be sounds fantastic. . . . Last*
   time I was in Vegas I was ten, so suffice it to say you're
   going to see a different side of the city than the one I'm
   familiar with. You will have to take many photos of your
   desert adventures, and I shall have to live vicariously.

I think I'm forgetting to respond to a whole bunch of things.
Oh, I know I am. Your blender request, my once-in-a-life-
time tan, etc. But this is turning into the longest Match mes-
sage I've ever written, so I'll hold back until you reply.

Cheers,
Alison

May 13 at 7:57 p.m.

Hey Alison,

I love your long message. You're like the pen pal I never
had. Also reading your stories means I get to ignore my
studying for a little while.

That is hilarious, btw. The baths are great, but definately
reminiscent of Eastern Promises. There are two that I know
of in the city. I think you'd definately like the one in downtown

more than the one in the E. Village. Its much bigger and there are lounging areas.

As for amazing furniture, I sometimes procrastinate by searching online for interesting furnishings I could never afford. Check out http://berbereimports.com -- they import mostly from the middle east, africa, and india. Pretty incredible stuff. Someday I plan on buying out half their showroom.

Work-wise, what I basically do is follow the aviation sector and invest in related companies. Boeing aircrafts and aircraft carriers, stuff like that. It's kinda boring, but if you don't mind being bored, we can chat more about it when we meet up.

Speaking of which, I'm going to quiz night with my office tomorrow night and then have test prep Monday (yes, CFA. How did you know that?). Any chance you're free Tuesday? Let me know. OK, this is without a doubt the longest match message I've ever sent. Looking forward to hearing from you soon. My cell number is below.

-luke

May 14 at 10:45 p.m.

Hey Luke,

I surfed your favorite site and have decided that when I next win the Mega Millions, I am springing for the Opium Bed. What are you adding to your registry from the shop? Right now, I think you've just got one measly blender on there.

How was quiz night? Did you manage to stun your team with a vast knowledge of obscure musical groups and irrelevant historical events? (My claim to fame the one time I played was knowing the plot of It's a Mad, Mad, Mad, Mad World . . . until I failed to contribute anything of value for the rest of the night. Oops.)

OK. I'm cutting myself off and ending here. After all, I need to save something to tell you about on Tuesday, because, you know, our Match messages are so short as it is, what if we run out of things to talk about? My cell number is below, too.

Cheers,
Alison

P.S. That was my way of saying "Yes, Tuesday works." Where and when?

	May 15 at 6:08 p.m.
LUKE 2:	ARE WE STILL ON FOR TOMORROW? HOW DO YOU FEEL ABOUT WHITMAN & BLOOM ON THIRD AVE? 7 P.M.?

	May 15 at 7:33 p.m.
ALISON:	ANYTHING I SHOULD KNOW? LIKE WHERE TO FIND YOU ONCE I'M THERE?

LUKE 2:	IT'S CASUAL. SO NO NEED TO WEAR A PROM DRESS OR ANYTHING. I'LL BE AT THE BAR.

I walk in and scan the occupied bar stools. I see someone give a short wave, "howdy" style, and I walk toward Luke #2.

"Hey, I saved you a seat." He nods his head at the empty stool next to him.

"Perfect." I add, "Such a gentleman."

"Yeah, I try." He shrugs. What is it about Henley shirts on men that gets me every time? Such a cute look. The fit of the shirt enhances his lean, muscular shoulders, and the worn-out gray matches his eyes, which are offset by these extra-long, extra-dark lashes.

I pull off my jacket, hang it on the hook beneath the bar, and sit beside him.

"So how'd you know I was taking the CFA?"

"Oh." I shrug. "You're not the only banker in New York, you know."

"But it's funny that you'd know that. *I* don't know a ton of people who have taken the exam."

"Huh. I don't know. I have a ton of college friends who work in finance, and a few of them griped about it last year or the year before."

"That's odd. I don't think I have *any* friends from college who went into banking. Where'd you go to college?"

"Uhh, Yale? It's in Connecticut."

"That's cute. Do you always say that? As if people might not have heard of it?"

I blush and bite my lip. "I *do* actually always say it that way. I feel like it's so cocky if you just say, 'Yale,'" I say flatly. "Period. Like, 'I know you've heard of it because it's so great and all. . . .'" I roll my eyes. "I feel like most of my friends say it that way: followed by a question mark, and with geographical positioning."

"Why did I think you went to Columbia?"

"Uhhh. I guess because I went to grad school there? Maybe I said that in my profile?"

"Wow. So you seem like you need a little ambition or something. Like you could, you know, *try* a little harder?"

I blush further. "There aren't that many people vying for the architectural conservator slots. I feel like everyone who applied my year got in."

"I got in," he says, matter-of-factly.

"To the Historic Preservation program?" I ask, bewildered. "*Really?*"

"No, to the School of Journalism."

"Oh . . . wait. *Really*? But that's, like, the best program in the country. Or so I've heard. . . . Did you go?"

"No. I wound up going to business school instead. But I got in, and that's probably my single greatest achievement to date. You've got your Columbia diploma, I've got my Columbia acceptance letter . . ."

"Potato, potahto," I say and he laughs. "So where'd you go to business school?"

"Actually just up in the Bronx at the Gabelli School of Business. It's part of Fordham University."

"I know it." I nod. "But see, *you* gave geographical description, too."

"That's because I thought you likely *hadn't* heard of it," he chuckles. "You did it backward."

"Hmm." I pick up the menu and scan the drink list. "So what's good here?"

"I got a beer, but you should get a cocktail. Or two."

"Thanks, I think one's good for now." I smile and try to get the bartender's attention.

"So you probably get this question all the time, but how'd you choose your screenname on Match? Sorry," he adds quickly, "I don't want to talk about *Match.com* all night, but it's an unusual name, so I thought there might be a story behind it. You know, better than the story behind GroovyMonday80."

"Play on The Smithereens?" I ask as the bartender approaches. I place my order and turn back to Luke #2.

"Yeah, how'd you know?"

"Lucky guess." I shrug. "I was going to Google it to see if it meant something else, but I never got around to it."

"So what was yours all about?"

"Oh, it's kind of a long, weird story." I swivel my stool to face him.

"Aren't all your stories long, weird stories?"

"Hey! That's not very nice, you don't even *know* me!" I pretend to be offended, which I kind of am.

"I'm kidding. Ki-dding," he sounds out the word. "You write very good emails," he says in an overly serious, professorial tone.

"*Anyway* . . . Okay, now I can't tell you. It's a long story, and I'm embarrassed."

"Oh, come on."

"Nope! Stage fright." I avert my eyes from his.

"Come *on*. How about I'll tell you an embarrassing story about myself next."

I look up brightly. "You promise?"

"Promise."

"Okay, so. A really long time ago I was out on a double date with my then-boyfriend and his coworker, plus his coworker's girl-friend." Luke #2 nods. "I can't remember how it came up, but we started talking about mail-order brides and couples who meet in chat rooms, and . . . that kind of stuff. The men started talking about this site. I forget what it's called. True Life? Second Life, something like that—"

"—Second Life." He nods.

"Yeah, Second Life . . . you know it?" He nods again. "Well, anyway, the site sounds . . . nuts. Fascinating, and nuts. But they were talking about some article they both read about the site, and the coworker said that he's on it. It was kind of funny, you could see the look of surprise, or, horror and surprise, cross his girlfriend's face. Evidently, this was the first she'd heard of him spending his time on Second Life, and they *live* together. You could tell they were definitely going to have a fight about it later. . . . But anyway, we asked him what he did on there, and he said he set up a soda shoppe, like an old-fashioned soda-jerk kind? I don't know how these things work, but you can, I guess, buy fake money with your real money and become an entrepreneur. In Second Life?" I wave my hand in the air to indicate that all these details are fuzzy to me. "So we asked him what his avatar looked like, and he said it looked like him, only miniature. And we asked him what his name was, and he said 'Erstwhile,' which at the time, I just thought was a really funny choice for some reason."

"So that's why you chose it?"

"Well, kind of. . . . Not really. So a few months later, my brother signed up for Match and because I'm, you know, a really *good*, caring, and concerned sister . . . I insisted on helping him with his profile. But in order to view *anyone*'s profile, you have to set up your own Match account. It's free if you're not winking or messaging anyone, but you still need a username. I was still with my boyfriend, so this was purely for sisterly help, but I created a Match account under Erstwhile701. My birthday, seven-twenty-nine, was taken."

"So there's an Erstwhile729 on Match, too?"

"Apparently? I know, I found that really weird, too." I laugh. "Anyway, when I went back to sign up . . . you know, 'for reals,'" I hold up finger quotes around this phrase, "my browser couldn't log me out and create a new account. It was dead set on me keeping this really dumb moniker. . . . So . . . that's me!" I feign excitement, then bite my lip in embarrassment.

He chuckles audibly. "Good story. I bet there are a lot of people who don't even know what that word means."

"Oh, for sure. You wouldn't believe the number of emails I get that begin, 'Dear Erst.'" I crack up laughing, and Luke #2 does, too. "Okay, your turn! Embarrassing story. Go!"

"Well if you want it to be about Second Life . . ."

"No! Get out." I slap him on the shoulder without thinking, then realize what I have done. "Sorry! Got excited . . . *You* use Second Life?"

He laughs. "Would that be so bad?" I narrow my eyes, then nod vigorously. *Yes, yes it would be.*

"Well, if it makes you *feel* better," he says slowly, "I'm not on it anymore. Or, at least, I don't think I am. . . . I read about it, too, and I just, you know, wanted to see what the kids are up to these days."

"So what's *your* avatar's name?"

"I don't even remember," he says.

"What does he look like?"

"Kind of like me. But I didn't spend too much time on that part. I just wanted to take a stroll through Second Life town, see how it worked."

"What'd you do there?"

"I met some people."

"Anyone interesting or cool?"

"A large Nigerian prostitute, a—"

"—Should you be telling me this on our first date?" I ask inquisitively.

"I didn't *do* anything with the prostitute."

"Then how did you know she was a prostitute?"

"Well, she was dressed in a stripper outfit, and they have these little speech bubbles, and when I wandered over to her, she offered me sex for money."

"Well, I guess that would be *one* way to know." I laugh.

"Yeah. I met a few shop owners. They give you some currency when you sign up. Or at least they did when I signed up."

"Ooh, what'd you *buy*?"

"Glow sticks," he shrugs.

"*Glow* sticks?" I echo.

"Yeah. I wanted to see if my avatar could twirl them or, you know, do a mean glow-stick routine at a Second Life rave."

"And?"

"Yeah, he could. I could."

"So when was the last time you went on?"

"Gosh." He strokes his chin, trying to calculate. "At least three years ago. I don't even know if I ever closed my account. I'm probably still there, walking down Second Life Street, twirling my glow sticks."

I laugh. "So are you, like, the raving, glow-stick-slinging, tattooed type in *real* life, too?"

"Yeah, that's me in a nutshell." He smiles and flicks at his straw. "Oh, except I do have a tattoo. In real life."

"As opposed to in Second Life?" I smile, he laughs. "Where is it? Tramp stamp? You *totally* have a tramp stamp." I nod vehemently. "Am I right?"

"No, I've been dreaming of getting a tramp stamp, but for now just the . . . the other one."

"Ooh. What's the *other* one? Where is it?"

He shakes his head no.

"No, you won't tell me?"

"You'll have to find it for yourself one day if you're so curious." He raises an eyebrow. I blush and look away.

"Uhhh, what's it of?"

"It's . . . a design. I designed it myself."

"What of?"

"Just black lines that make a shape I liked."

"Huh."

"So what about you? What's your tramp stamp of?"

"Wouldn't *you* like to know."

"Wait—you actually have one?" He looks at me askance.

I shake my head no and smile. "I mean, I guess I could say, 'You'll have to find it for yourself one day if you're so curious,'" I say in a dumb-jock-sounding deep voice, "but . . . I don't actually have one."

After two more rounds of cocktails, Luke asks if I want another.

"Three's enough for me in one night, I think. But thanks! I should probably get going soon-ish anyway."

He gets up to go to the bathroom.

When he returns, he heads straight to the cash register to settle the tab. While he's waiting for the bartender to ring up his credit card, he bops, ever so faintly, in time to the music, his head and knees moving in time with the song. The bar is much darker now, and when he walks back over, he shakes his head slightly as his eyes readjust to the light where we're sitting. "Oh!" he exclaims pleasantly. "You're still here."

I smile. "Was I . . . not supposed to be?"

"No, I just wondered what you were thinking of the date. You know, if you were going to bolt while I was in the bathroom."

"Yeah." I raise my eyebrows and tilt my head as if weighing this option. "I thought about it, but . . . you seemed too nice to do that to, so I thought I could at least walk out with you. Civilly, cordially, you know."

He smiles.

"But I caught you dancing in front of the cash register, by the way. Don't think I didn't see that."

"Oh, you did." For once I'm not the one blushing. "I'm . . . kind of not a dancer. Well, I dance, but I'm, like, a closet dancer. You will *not* get to see that repeated in public," he assures me.

"So you *don't* want to go to the Joshua Tree? It's so close *by* though. So tempting!"

"What's the *Joshua* Tree?"

I clap my hand over my mouth in astonishment. "*You*'ve never been to the *Joshua Tree?*" I sound out slowly. "Oh, I used to go there every weekend when I still pretended I was in college. It's all eighties songs, usually paired with the music videos projected on the walls. And you just . . . dance stupidly all night until they kick you out at 4:00 a.m."

"Yeah, right. See you there sometime," he rolls his eyes.

We're walking to the subway and I'm midsentence when he steps in front of me, turns to face me, and kisses me. I'm so startled, when he pulls away, I can't even remember if I kissed him back or not. I don't know what to say, so I don't say anything. He straightens up, towering above me but looking in my eyes skeptically. "Too forward?" he asks.

"Uhhh . . ." I shake my head in confusion. ". . . Yes? I guess? I don't know. Not bad, just . . . surprising. Sorry."

He laughs. "Note to self: Don't do *that* again."

"No." I laugh, glad he took the edge off the moment. "It's not that. I'm just . . . not the kiss-on-the-first-date type. But it's fine."

"Well, if it makes you feel better," he volunteers, "I'm not that type either. I don't know what came over me. It just felt right, I guess," then he adds quickly, "for one of us."

I smile.

"So, I know you've got a busy social calendar and all. When do you leave for Turkey?"

"Next Thursday."

"And, I can't remember—are you here this weekend?"

"No, I've got a friend's wedding in Newport."

"Do you want to do something one night next week before you leave then?"

"Sure."

"Okay, I'll be in touch. . . . Bye." He leans in and gives me a hug. A really nice, enveloping tight squeeze. When we separate, I wave like Paul Pfeiffer and descend into my subway station.

"So how are you going to keep them straight?" Cassie asks when I return home from my date with Luke #2.

"They're not really very similar, other than in namesake."

"But, like, even in your phone? Do you know their last names yet?"

"Older Luke is Luke Edmonds. I don't know Younger Luke's last name. I'll just call him Younger Luke."

"Oh. I don't think I realized that he's younger—"

"—No, he's old. He's just *younger* than Older Luke."

"How old?"

"Thirty-three? Thirty-four? One of the two. . . . Older Luke is thirty-seven."

"Just be careful not to slip up. That'd be bad."

"What, slip up and accidentally call Older Luke 'Younger Luke' to his face? I don't think we're in grave danger of that here. . . ."

"You know what I mean," Cassie says.

May 19 at 5:41 p.m.

YOUNGER LUKE: HEY THERE, ANOTHER WEEK DOWN, ID HAVE TO SAY TUESDAY WAS THE HIGHLIGHT. HAVE A GOOD WEEKEND.

ALISON: HA, I'LL BET YOU SAY THAT TO ALL THE GIRLS. HEADED TO NEWPORT FOR THAT WEDDING-YOU STILL UP FOR SOME PRE-TURKEY HANGOUT TIME WHEN I'M BACK?

YOUNGER LUKE: ONLYTOBLONDARCHITECTURALCONSERVATIONISTS.IAMIFYOUARE.

"Sorry, you beat me to our date *again*," I apologize as I pull out the chair across from Younger Luke at Toloache. "And this time you had a lot farther to travel!"

He holds up his glass. "I just wanted to get a head start on the drinking without you."

"Oh, is that so?" I say, attempting to sass him. "Wait, what are you drinking?"

"A coconut margarita."

"Isn't that . . . a little girlie?"

"Yeah, I think that's why they served it to me with this little umbrella, but, oh well. They're surprisingly delicious," he says persuasively. "If this is what girls get to drink all day, I've really been missing out. . . ."

My cucumber-jalapeño margarita arrives shortly. "Hey, look!" I point out, "no umbrella!"

"They probably got our drinks confused. I'm sure your spicy drink was supposed to get the umbrella. Here, let me trade it for the chili pepper on the edge of yours." He reaches across the table and swaps our garnishes. "There, much better. The way God intended."

I laugh.

The waiter returns, and we order our dinners.

"Fish tacos, huh?" he asks.

"Oh, I *love* fish tacos. And they're really good here."

He looks at me suspiciously, then looks down to my chest, then up at my eyes again.

"What?" I instinctively cross my arms over my chest, resting my hands on opposite shoulders. "What?"

He nods, slyly. "No. I just . . . I like your *style*," he says.

"Huh?"

"Ordering fish tacos with a . . . what do you call that . . . cowl-neck top? Cut straight to the messiest entrée you can find . . . wear a shirt that very likely will wind up filled with mahi mahi and guacamole. . . . I *like* your *style*," he says nodding.

My discomfort evaporates. "I don't know, I . . . might get hungry later?" I gesture to the swooping bowl of my cowl-neck. He laughs out loud at this. "But, my God you were so *creepy* staring at my chest like that. Ehhh! Also, how do you know the word 'cowl-neck?' Most men don't even know the difference between a skirt and a dress."

"I've got a sister. And a niece. And a mom." He shrugs, still smiling as he rests his chin on both his hands and leans into the table.

"Well," I start defensively, "if you get to critique my order—"

"It's not a critique. I'm actually really impressed. You're not like most girls." *Hmm, I've been getting this a lot lately, and so far, it hasn't ended well.*

"If you're trying to say I eat like a man, well, unfortunately, yes, that's true." Younger Luke smiles and nods at this. "But you might as well find out now rather than be surprised later. *Anyway*, if you get to critique my order, should we return to the subject of *your* drinks, adorned with pink umbrellas, Mr. Macho?"

"I told you: They're delicious. No regrets. In fact, I'm going to order a second one just because you said that."

Six tacos later, and the conversation's still going strong.

"So you have a big vacation coming up, right?"

I nod enthusiastically.

"Tell me about it. Who are you going with?"

"It's . . . it's a long story, but I'm going on vacation with my parents. I haven't traveled with them in ages, except for family holidays, and I know you're kind of not supposed to do that when you're twenty-seven, but secretly," I lean in, as if confiding, "I'm *really* excited about it."

"And you're going to . . . Turkey?"

I nod again.

"Turkey the country?"

"Everyone's been asking me that lately. I keep wanting to say, 'No, the sandwich meat.'"

"Good point. I wonder why I asked that?"

"At least you're not alone."

"So why is it a long story that you're traveling with your parents? And, for the record, I think it's cool that you are. Are your siblings going, too?"

"No, my siblings aren't going. And, basically, my work instituted this draconian policy where you have to block off your vacation for each year the year *prior*. Which is, like, totally ridiculous if you think about it. Who knows where they want to go—or have to go—for holidays, weddings, et cetera twelve months in advance?"

"Yeah, that's ridiculous."

"Right? So anyway, in December, I was still with my ex-boyfriend of a while, and we calendared these eight days in May. . . . *But* then we broke up, and now I'm stuck with these vacation days that are set in stone, and it was a use-'em-or-lose-'em kind of thing and . . . yeah. So I'm using them."

"With your parents? Not your ex-boyfriend."

"Oh, gosh no. Not with my ex-boyfriend. With my parents. I think they felt bad for me given the whole work situation and breakup, my mom acted like, 'Ooh. This is a *wonderful* confluence of events. Wouldn't it be such fun to travel together again like we used to?' They're really nice."

"Have you been to that part of the world before?" Younger Luke asks.

"Kind of? Greece is probably the closest? And I've been to Morocco. I know they're not even that close by, but in my head . . . the markets, spices, carpets . . . I kind of feel like they're similar. Have you been?"

"No, but I've been to Morocco, too. I loved it there. Did you?"

"Oh, yes. I thought it was *incredible*. The colors, the sounds, the architecture . . . one of those places that made my heart swell with excitement just walking down the street."

He nods. "Yeah, it's a fascinating place, but we had some really odd experiences there."

"Odd how?"

"I was with my brother, and we got pulled over on the highway—"

"—We got pulled over, too! ALL the time!"

"Did you get pulled over and held at gunpoint and forced to buy hashish?" Younger Luke asks.

I look at him blankly. "What?"

"We got pulled over and held at gunpoint. We couldn't figure out what was going on, but they demanded our money. So we gave them some of it, and then they handed us a bag of hashish and sped off."

"Wait. *Really?*" I cock my head, and he nods in response. I ask again, "Like, *really* really?"

"Really really," he says matter-of-factly.

"Oh. No." I sit back. "That's nothing like what happened to me. . . . *Why* did they force you to buy drugs at gunpoint?"

"No idea. Afterward we wondered if maybe they thought we were someone else."

"And the reason they'd be pulling over someone *else* and forcing *them* to buy drugs at gunpoint is . . ."

"Dunno. The world's a crazy place, you know. You'd better be careful out there." He dunks a tortilla chip in the guacamole and pops it in his mouth. "So what happened to *you* in Morocco?"

"Oh, many things. Not nearly as good as your story. . . ."

"I'm listening."

"No, we just . . . well, my ex-boyfriend has coloring like mine, so we . . . kind of stand out in Africa, you know? So we drove in a big loop, from Casablanca to Essaouira . . . to Marrakech to Fes and back. We were only there for maybe . . . nine days? Only driving for, like, four of those days. But we got pulled over and ticketed eight times. Eight! I think they just knew they could take advantage because . . . what are you supposed to do when alone in the desert with a police officer who demands to be paid on the spot for a ticket? We stopped carrying cash at one point for this reason, but then the next officer took credit cards. It was crazy."

"Is your ex-boyfriend a NASCAR driver?" He smiles as he picks up another tortilla chip.

"That's the crazy part: one time, we got ticketed for going two kilometers over the speed limit. That's, like, one mile!"

"That's whack."

"I know." I nod repeatedly. "I think we paid more in speeding tickets than we did for the rental car. Or maybe even for our flights."

"There were a lot of things I found quirky and lovable in Morocco," he muses, crunching on another guacamole-piled chip.

"Ooh. Fun game. Like what?" I grab a chip from the basket.

"Well, like, for starters, everywhere we stayed, I kept seeing those vibrating workout machines. You know? The ones from the fifties with the belt you wear that . . . shakes off the fat?"

I laugh. "They have it in the Carousel of Progress at Disney World, so yes, I know what you're talking about."

"When was the last time you were in Disney World?"

"A month or two ago." I add quickly, "Don't judge me."

"Judging. But fine. With, like, a boyfriend? A boyfriend and your kids?"

"*No*, with my college friends. . . . Remember," I point my tortilla chip at him, "no judging."

"Right. Anyway, so that's what I remember from Morocco. That, and hammams. . . . Have you ever been to a hammam?"

I nod. "In Marrakech."

"So mine was . . . unique," Younger Luke says thoughtfully.

"Unique how?"

"Well, instead of it being in a private room, while lying down on a table or chair, you got scrubbed down on this platform in a room full of naked people."

"Was it coed? That sounds so . . . un-Moroccan."

"No, but still, it's kind of . . . incredibly unsexy to get scrubbed down in your birthday suit in front of a dozen other dudes who are watching."

"I've never been to one like that but . . . agreed. It sounds pretty unsexy. Oh! Except, I actually saw a mooooovi—" I cut myself off. "Nothing."

He chokes on his sip of coconut margarita as he laughs. "What was that?"

"Nothing," I say quickly, blushing.

"You saw it in a *mooovie*?" he sounds out slowly.

"Ugh! I do *not* want to be telling you this story."

"Come on."

I shake my head back and forth.

"Come on. You're making it *more* awkward by not saying it. Now my imagination is going to . . . run wild. Get the better of me."

I groan. "Okay, fine." I breathe in. "This, too, is a long story. But last year my brother was trying to come up with a venue for his birthday party. I'd just gone to a party on the Lower East Side at a place that I thought was pretty neat. . . . It's just a bar, but they had good cheap drinks, nice lighting, you know. Important party stuff."

He nods.

"Anyway, I told Ben the name of the bar and he was like, 'Don't they screen porn there?' and I was like, 'What are you *talking* about?

Of course they don't screen *porn* there.' And he was like, 'I've been there once. I'm pretty sure they do.' And I told him he was nuts, and I had just been there, and it was delightful."

"Sooooo . . .?"

"So we get there for his party, and there's totally porn screening on the televisions. Porn on three of them, *West Side Story* on the fourth. It was so weird!"

"So had they *not* been showing it when you were there before?"

"No. I asked friends who were there with me, after the fact. Apparently they showed porn that night, too! I was just so excited to be reunited with some old friendly faces, I totally didn't pay attention to what was flashing on the monitors."

"That's really funny."

"Yeah, and my brother's friend blogs for *The Daily Beast* or *Buzz-Feed* or one of those sites, and he wrote a post about it the next day. Like 'last night I went to a really weird birthday party on the Lower East Side where they showed porn and *West Side Story*.' So, you know, the party's now kinda famous, I guess."

Luke laughs, and it's not just a polite laugh, it's genuine.

"So anyway, getting back to the *original* point of my story, one of the porn flicks showed woman-on-woman action inside a bathhouse. Which was maybe like the ambience you experienced at the hammam in Morocco?"

"No, no," he says quickly, "nothing like that."

"I didn't mean for you, *personally*."

He relaxes. "Ahh. Right. Right. Then, uhh, yeah. Maybe?"

"So what else did you notice that was . . . quirky or different in Morocco?"

"Their Doritos are pointy."

"Aren't *all* Doritos pointy?"

"When was the last time you opened a bag of Doritos?" He looks at me quizzically.

"Is this . . . a trick question? Because I have no idea where you're going with this. . . ."

"No, it's just they started making Doritos with rounded edges years ago. It was, like, a choking hazard or lawsuit issue or something."

"What?"

"No, it's true. Anyway, I miss those pointy Doritos," he says long-ingly. "And I was surprised that Morocco can get their own special batch of pointy ones. They probably make them for other places, too. Like Turkey."

"Okay." But he doesn't say anything. "*And*?"

"And, what I'm trying to say is: I want to pay for dinner tonight. But in exchange, if you can find the pointy-edged Doritos, bring me back a bag. I'll reimburse you, of course."

"Noooo, that's okay. I think I can afford *one* bag of Doritos. . . . And thanks for dinner?"

He walks me home, and I thank him again for dinner and for trekking to the Upper East Side midweek.

"It seems only fair. You've got a busy week and packing to do. Besides, it was worth it." And this time, when he kisses me, it *doesn't* surprise me or make me nervous. He places his hands on my waist, and I wonder to myself, *should I touch his face? Don't touch his face? Touch his face?* I reach my hands up and place them lightly on either side of his face and we stand there on my doorstep, lips locked, still as statues.

Greetings from North America: Older Luke

Subject: Hello, it's Luke, Greetings from North America

Alison,

I'm really sorry we missed each other's calls yesterday and today. I hope you had a safe flight.

How many days are you staying in each place? What's the area you're in like? What types of buildings are you staying in?

By the way, you should tell your friend Jason that he's on to something with his idea about a male-centric *Sex and the City*. I think the act of trying to analyze single male behavior is interesting and might get traction. He could have been a psychiatrist! I hope you'll introduce us when you're back.

Speaking of psychiatry, I read this interesting article in *The Atlantic* about a psychiatrist who followed some now-septuagenarian men, starting at Harvard undergrad and into old age. The premise was to find the secret of happiness. He noted that men who possessed at least five of the following characteristics were happiest: low weight, some exercise, education, stable marriage, nonsmoker, and no problems with alcohol. Ironically, the psychiatrist himself seemed to be plagued with unhappiness and was divorced three times.

Boomer went to the dog park for visit #3 yesterday. He did pretty well until he and a Rottweiler got into a metaphorical pissing contest and both turned violent. Baby steps . . .

I look forward to hearing back from you. I have to tell you I've been really impressed with the maturity and intelligence

you've shown in our conversations. For me, that stuff goes a
long way and I hope to continue such conversations.

Hope you are having a great time,
Luke

My brother warned me that whenever his dating prospects go on vacation, they somehow manage to disappear, never to be heard from again. After borrowing my dad's iPad and finding Older Luke's thoughtful note in my inbox, I make a point of setting aside time the next day to get to the hotel business center and type out a semiworthy reply. I'd like to keep this (potential) relationship going, vacation be damned.

May 26 at 10:59 p.m.

Hi Luke!

Apologies in advance for the many typo☒ certain to sprinkle this email, a☒ I'm writin☒ fröm a funky keyböard and my time at the kiösk i☒ about to expire.

Much to see/do/soak up in Istanbul, so we've been moving at an uncharacteristically speedy pace (not bad though, oddly invi☒oratin☒). Things should calm down tomorrow when we leave the bi☒ city and head into the smaller coastal towns and ancient ruin sites. . . . In brief, the weather's been much cooler than predicted (low 60s) which means I pretty much packed entirely incorrectly and am shivering in all the photographs. But! ☒ have made several wonderful di☒coveries about Türkish history and\or culturë| (hmm, can't find the colon symbol)

1. *A 52-karat diamond really just looks like a Ring Pop, only clear. An 86-karat diamond really just looks like three Rin☒ Pöps lined up ☒ide by ☒ide.*
2. *Being the imam in the Topkapı Palace who reads the Qur'an aloud ceaselessly before tourists for 500 years would be a pretty undesirable job. Not as unde☒irable, höwever, as being part of a dying sultan's harem, since you know your fun will end when you'll be drowned the day after he kicks the bucket. Also, the*

sultan had a 4-ft. circumference, if his robes on display are any indication . . . so that's another drawback of the whole harem-job thing, too.

3. *Beautiful tiling, architectural detail, plasterwork, and mosaics abound at every corner, and I'd forgotten how addictive Türkish cöffee is.*

Off to Cappadocia tomorrow, more to follow if/when I have email access again. Happy to hear that Boomer's continuing to make social progress. Hope all is well on your end!

Cheers,
Alison

P.S. Do you think you possess five of the six secrets to happiness? Just curioüs ;)

May 29 at 6:43 a.m.

Hey Alison,

Great to hear back from you! I hope you're still having a nice time. In answer to your question, yes, I have five of the six qualities: low weight, exercise, education, nonsmoker, and no problems with alcohol. I'm missing the marriage piece.

Where have you visited since you last wrote? What's been your favorite, or favorites?

When you get back, I'd like to go with you to the Jasper Johns exhibit at MoMA. It includes photographs and works by Francis Bacon. I imagine you've studied Bacon in your art history classes; I always found his works to be grotesque yet compelling. I'm curious to see what kind of dialogue he and his works created with another painter. Just in case you're unfamiliar with this work, here's an example: *http://www. artknowledgenews.com/files2009a/Bacon_Pope_Inno- cent_X.jpg*

Bacon's style never changed over the course of his career. I always find that interesting and somewhat depressing, when a talented artist fails to evolve.

Ring Pop: I had to Google it. You're talking about a ring lollipop, right?

Harems . . . many thoughts. One, do you think the women are depressed or anxious? How are their attitudes related to their inherent dispositions?

Are you taking pictures of all the various architecture? What's been your favorite so far?

So, I know you can't answer all these questions with your limited Internet access. I would like it if you give this one a try, though: If you had to say what the six keys to happiness are for women, what would they be?

Take lots of photos, I'd like to see them when you're back. You return Sunday? Glad you're having a good time, may it continue.

-Luke

May 31 at 11:07 p.m.

Hi Luke!

So much good stuff to respond to, I'm not sure where to begin (though my time's once again limited, it should be somewhat smoother--if less amusing for you--since this keyboard is Americanized). . . . In order of your inquiries/thoughts:

Yes to Francis Bacon (and Jasper Johns)! I actually made a mental note several months ago to see that exhibition when it opened at MoMA. I'm not sure whether or not I consider myself a Bacon "fan," but suffice it to say I find his work interesting. I always kind of thought of him as the modern-day version of Hieronymus Bosch. And he's oddly referenced a fair bit in neorealist Italian cinema critique from the 1960s/70s, hence my piqued interest. Good suggestion!

You had to Google Ring Pop (yes, lollipop)? Don't you remember the annoying commercial jingles at the very least? C'mon, I'm not THAT young.

OK, so this is a major cop out, but I've been giving a surprising amount of thought to the psychology behind job happiness (based largely on my learning about imams, harems, and whirling dervishes this week) and then relationship happiness, and ultimately life happiness, and I'm saving all my answers for the harem question for a longer conversation to be had in person. Although not in The Atlantic, I literally just read all about the Harvard study of the 268 men last week in an in-flight magazine.

So, I haven't read the scholarly version *yet*, but based on the more mainstream rendition I saw . . . I think the conclusions are kind of, well, cheap? Marital stability can't be one of six factors of happiness, on equal footing with weight. Having a stable relationship is going to make you happier. It's pretty much the predominant factor, or maybe second if you're of the camp where professional happiness is paramount. . . . So while I thought the article was a worthy - if depressing - read, and I was interested in the idea of a 60+ year longitudinal study (and the evolution/growth/decay of the study itself), that concept of the six factors should be reworked, in my extremely amateur opinion. . . . What was your take?

Yes, way too many pictures of buildings and not nearly enough of people (as is always the case when I travel) but I'll gladly give you a slideshow when I'm stateside again. We just left Cappadocia, which is famed for its unique geological formations (long explanation that requires me to draw on a napkin. I'll save that, too). We actually stayed in a converted cave hotel -- my favorite example thus far of adaptive reuse. We got to do some quality rock climbing outside and inside the caves, and enjoyed some really wonderful hikes through the valleys of these structures/formations (one was alone with my dad for several hours. You'd be proud of me! All trip I've been working on that four-minute probing-conversational approach you recommended; really got in some good ones with him during the multihour hike). Also hot air ballooned through the valley, which was quite different perspectively (is that a word? It's not. Oh well, I shall employ it thus).

Okay, so the man waiting for the kiosk is glaring at me, and this has officially become the world's longest email, so I should go. But before I do, how are YOU? Any big stayca-tion-y activities over the three-day weekend? Quality time with Boomer? I assume you were off from work for some - if not all - of that time?

Hope all's well with you! Yes, back on Sunday afternoon.

Cheers,
Alison

In a bookstore in the Ataturk Airport in Istanbul, I purchase a copy of *When Nietzsche Wept*, a historical fiction novel that melds philosophy and psychotherapy. In fairness, I had already exhausted all the reading materials I packed for this vacation, so I needed *something* to occupy me on the eleven-hour flight home. But I'd be lying if I said this pur-chase wasn't at least partially motivated by eagerness to have a new talking point with Older Luke.

While admittedly it's far better to buy a book than a new wardrobe addition to impress a man, I can't recall the last time I purchased any-thing with the intention of impressing anyone. But I also can't recall the last guy who really got my intellectual juices flowing. I feel a bit out of my cognitive league with Older Luke. And I like it.

Hey, Did You Find My Doritos Yet?: Younger Luke

May 24 at 12:38 p.m.

Hey Luke,

I bumped into my dad at the gym this morning (running into family members at various Upper East Side locales happens more often than you'd think when you live within a three-block radius) and he shared two good pieces of news with me:

1. He somehow convinced his doctor to prescribe him high-dose Ambien last week, which (per your recommendation) means . . . happy flying for me!

2. I relayed your request, and he and my mom are totally stoked for you to join us. Their only request is that you play negotiator should we get pulled over, held at gunpoint, and forced to buy pot. They're really not so good at handling stressful situations like that. And if my eight Moroccan speeding tickets are any indication, I'm pretty chicken myself.

So. See you at the Delta check-in circa 4:30 tomorrow?
Great. Looking forward to it. ;)

Cheers,
Alison

P.S. In seriousness, good luck with the CFA studying and with pulling off your surprise visit to Tacoma. Much to catch up on upon my return.

P.P.S. Thanks again for dinner & for trekking to the Upper East Side!

May 24 at 5:40 p.m.
Perfect, see you in the security line. So, should I bring my swimsuit for the beaches or is euro style cool with the folks?

Well, all I can say of your taking ambien is make sure someone locks you into your seat, and that your not near the emergency exit.

Anyway, yes last night was fun - enjoyed too much coconut margarita thoroughly (just had the urge for fruity drinks, still can't explain). Hope you enjoy your trip and I look forward to hearing about it. (Emailing from my phone, hence the brevity.)

Talk soon,
Luke

May 26 at 11:21 p.m.
Apolo⊠ies in advance for the many typo⊠ certain to riddle this email, a⊠ this keyböard's somewhat funky, and my time at it i⊠ about to expire. . . . But! ⊠ couldn't resist relatin⊠ the following di⊠covery| (hmm, can't ever seem to find the colon symbol)

The Sültan's winter cöttage at the Topkapı Palaçe contained four rooms (the entire palaçe had 100+): a library, a throne room, a harem room, and -- drum roll -- the Room for Sweet Fruit Beverages. Based on your proclivity for coconut margaritas, I'm thinkin⊠ you take a page from the Sultan's book and design a "Room for Sweet Fruit Beverages" in your apartment? I took pictures if you need desi⊠n in⊠piration.

Yep, that was my ⊠roündbreakin⊠ cultüral öbservatiön. Oh. Al⊠o, Turkish hammam experience was markedly different from Moroccan one. Way more like a scene they'd screen at the bar I forçed my bröther to have his party at. I'll save the details for another day.

Hope all's well on the home frönt. Any good ⬚tories?

Cheers,
Alison

May 28 at 6:10 p.m.

What you can't use a Turkish keyboard? And you call your-self an American?

I actually don't think the sweet beverage room would be too difficult - I mean I've already got the harem, so I'm half way there. But I would definately linoleum that floor - you know, jazz it up a bit more. . . . Anyway you know what they say about great minds . . . I could get use to being called "Sultan."

Per our conversation last week, I just googled the Room for Sweet Fruit Beverages in the Topkapi Palace. Sorry, had to do it, just cause I was curious if my theory holds. OK, so be honest. Whose photo is better, mine or yours? Maybe I could crop myself into it holding a pina colada.

I get the feeling that place is overwhelming your archi-tectural senses, so I hope you're not driving. You need to pace yourself.

Wish I had some exciting stories to share, but I've basi-cally been doing the mental preparationing 24/7 and need to enter a long weekend of attempting to be disciplined and study (while catching the playoff games which require me to attend bars because I don't have cable).

I did pay a visit to the old iTunes and buy a Bloc Party album - pretty good stuff - the highlight of my week. Hardly compares to yours I'm sure.

Safe travels. Hey, did you find my doritos yet?

luke

May 31 at 10:46 p.m.

I mean, I see your point - why travel halfway across the world to soak up culture/art/life when you can do it from your office desk, so long as you type in the right keywords? But the compositional framing of my photo is so much better! And the shadow effects coming in from the window? No light blotch things marring the lower right corner of mine . . . not to brag or anything.

That being said, you inspired me to do some online photo hunting of my own (did you know you're in the Google Images database?). Please see attached. I'm pretty sure this is an attainable aesthetic. From an architectural perspective, I think the gilded plasterwork and decoratively painted floral/ fruity motifs would nicely complement your checkered lino- leum flooring. Think your landlord would dig it?

I figured with all the chaos & Excel sheets that must be flying across your desk, a moment of Zenlike daydreaming of coconut margaritas served in a harem straight out of your apartment might appeal to you.

Ah well, another productive morning catching up on work emails for me. Good luck plowing through the earnings.

Cheers,
Alison

P.S. I went to the hotel gym this morning and you will NEVER guess what I spied. OK, maybe you will. But I'll give you a hint: it's prominently featured on the Carousel of Progress. I plan to track one down on eBay when I get back and have it shipped to my apartment. Think of the money I could save if I relinquished my monthly gym membership!

June 2 at 7:31 p.m.

Thanks for the moment of zen. I might make that my desk- top background. I like how you photoshopped my face onto some other dude's body. It actually took me a moment to realize that wasn't my shirt. I take it google failed to deliver a photo of me clutching a now much-needed pina colada? That coconut filled harem sounds pretty nice right now. But I try not to think about such things when I'm waste deep

in spreadsheets. Though the doodles I create during con-
ference calls somewhat resemble the designs in this room
here.

Didn't I tell you I already own the fat-jiggling machine?
You might want one of your own, but your welcome to come
borrow mine any time.

When do you get back here anyways?

luke

The Verrrry Slooooow Dater: Older Luke

After I unpack and put up my laundry, I make plans to meet up with Older Luke the next night.

"Well it sounds like you had a wonderful trip. Don't forget, I want to see photos."

I nod.

"So when does the bride arrive, and when do the festivities start?" Older Luke asks.

"Catherine gets in Thursday night, and we've got some quality time just the two of us. Maybe with Cassie, too." I reach for my water glass. "The other girls get in on Friday after work."

"What do you have planned for the bachelorette party?" he asks. I rattle off details about Southern barbecue dinners, the Russian bathhouse down on Wall Street, a burlesque show, and a lingerie bridal shower.

"That's pretty comprehensive. Whatever happened to the singular night of dinner and drinking on the town?"

I shrug.

"Well, it sounds like you've planned quite the weekend. Is this the first bachelorette party you've hosted?"

"No, I cohosted my sister's. And I've been to a handful of others. But this is the first time I'm doing all the planning solo."

He nods. "It's weird when the wedding circuit begins. I still remember the year I went from having, like, zero weddings to being in and attending what felt like dozens all at once."

"Yeah." I sigh. "The save-the-dates and invitations slowly started trickling in recently. . . . It makes me feel *old*. Like I blinked—" I blink hard then shake my head, miming discombobulation, "—and, all of a sudden, my friends were all grown up."

Older Luke agrees.

"Life moves *fast*! . . . And then, sometimes I think it moves slowly. . . . Somehow both seem true?" I laugh at my own convoluted assertion.

He smiles pleasantly and again agrees.

As the server's placing our dinners before us, my cell phone rings. The screen flashes JASON. "Oh, it's Jason. . . . Do you mind if I pick up for a second?"

"No, go ahead," Older Luke encourages in his harmonious twang.

"Jason! Hey. What's up?" I watch Older Luke, who watches the pedestrians go by. "No, I'm just having dinner with . . . Luke. . . . Yeah, I don't think you've met him before. You guys would get along well, though! He's all science-y, too, *and* trained as a marine." I cover the mouthpiece of the phone and whisper, "Jason wants to know if we want to meet up for drinks later. . . . Do you want to? If not, I can easily say no." I shake my head for emphasis. "So. No pressure."

"No, I told you I wanted to meet Jason. Pick a place near here where we can find him after dinner."

"Hey, Jason? We just ordered dinner, so we need an hour or so. Do you mind trudging to the Upper East Side?" I wait for his reply. "Okay. Auction House? Have you been there?" I cover the mouthpiece again and whisper, "Is Auction House okay?"

Older Luke nods.

"Cool. Yes, we will see you there. . . . Nine. . . . Okay. Bye!"

"That's great." Older Luke smiles, seeming genuinely enthused by this idea. "When you said I trained as a marine, did Jason do that, too?"

"No, but he spent summers at Officer Candidate School, so you guys have all that bootcamp experience in common. And probably make equally perfect hospital corners on your beds."

"He's a college friend?"

"Yep. And a biomedical engineer, so you two have that shared zeal for pharma-medical stuff, too."

"Well, as we discussed, I could use male friends. Is Jason single?"

"Are you looking for a wingman?" I ask, half-teasing, half-serious, because I actually *do* think Older Luke and Jason would get along. And be a dynamic duo out on the town.

"Not right now," he says. "But maybe some unmarried guy friends who like . . . throwing around a baseball or cycling, whatever."

"Maybe. You'll have to ask him yourself."

I see empty glasses before Jason and Older Luke, so I offer to go get the next round. I come back, awkwardly clutching three glasses in hand, and I start to distribute them to the men, who seem engaged in rapt conversation, but lighthearted, smile-filled rapt conversation.

"Hey, we were just talking about you, friend," Jason says.

"Oh? I can . . ." I gesture to the bar, "go get napkins or . . . hit the bathroom, if you want to continue talking about me? . . ." I smile.

Jason laughs. "No, I was just saying how . . . *amusing* it's been to watch you ease back into the dating pool."

My eyes widen, and my heart quickens. "Uhhh," I stammer. "Oh?" *Shut up, Jason!*

Jason and I have long acted as sounding boards for each other. He's keenly analytical and approaches problems like a management consultant, asking targeted questions and offering pointed, novel suggestions or advice—often served up with a healthy dose of optimism or cheer. I confided in him about the craziness that was James, but between wedding travels and Turkey and the Lukes, life's been so hectic lately, I haven't had the chance to bring him up to speed on who Older Luke is, or that I've been going on dates with him. I now regret not having filled him in.

"Yeah. Well, you know." Jason shrugs. "I met you when you were in a serious relationship freshman year. And for the years I've known you since, you were always still 'taken.' So I feel like this social blossoming . . . newly high jinksed life of yours is a whole new side of you."

I stare at him, my heart pounding in my chest. My widened eyes pleading, *Yes, I know I didn't tell you that I was on a "date" with Older Luke, but just please, PLEASE stop talking.*

"Oh, come on, Alison. I mean it in a *good* way. Your life is way funnier now."

"Ha? Ha, ha," I force out mechanically, through a frozen smile. "I'm glad you find it funny." Older Luke looks at me, and I look nervously back and forth between him and Jason and him again. He raises his eyebrows playfully, as if saying, "No big deal. This Jason character is hilarious!"

"So anyway, as I was saying." Jason turns to me and says, "You don't mind, right? You always make fun of yourself anyway—" I wince, open my mouth, but am too paralyzed to speak. "—Alison is a verrrrry slooooooow dater. She amasses all these guy friends left and right, then strings them along for*ever*, then gives them the Pants Speech, and it's like an endless, Sisyphean task for all those dudes who try to date her."

I instantly palm my forehead, then realize they're watching me, and slide it down my face, trying to play it off as rubbing fatigue from my left eye.

"So, how do you guys know each other anyway?" Jason asks.

Chasing the Free Case of Beer: Younger Luke

While I was in Turkey, it felt like Younger Luke was everywhere. I found myself constantly searching gas stations for Doritos, ever aware of the belted vibrating workout machines, and actually thankful that my mom and I had such an awkward hammam experience because it would give me another funny story to regale him with after the fact. So once I returned to my apartment, I didn't last minutes before I picked up my phone to call him.

"Hey Luke, it's Alison. Just got back from Turkey and have many a good story for you. Like . . . did you know that Doritos aren't the only differently shaped snack food overseas? Yeah. So, clearly, much to discuss when you're back. . . . I'm digressing, though—the point of this message was to say: I hope your surprise visit went off without a hitch and that you're having fun in Tacoma with your family."

He calls back shortly, and we talk for half an hour. It's all giggles and story one-upmanship.

"And? The surprise? How'd it go?"

"Yeah." He laughs. "They were pretty surprised. It didn't have quite the impact I expected because my mom was outside gardening when I arrived, so she saw me coming up the driveway. I was kind of hoping to surprise her and my dad together, in the middle of their party. But I got there a bit early."

"Gosh, I can't think of the last time I was on a flight that landed *early*. What are the chances?"

"I know. But, they seem pretty stoked I'm here."

"Should I let you get back to them? You must have a red-eye to catch soon."

"Yeah. I should probably go. I've been studying all afternoon, so I want to get in some quality son time before I head to the airport. . . . But thanks for calling. I was wondering how you were finding things in Constantinople. Wanted to make sure you didn't, you know, explode from sensory overload."

"Close. Not quite, but close. . . . Oh, also good *luck* with your studying. When will this whole CFA thing be over with anyway?"

"That was a joke, by the way. You know it's not called 'Constantinople' any more. And uhh, next Saturday and Sunday."

"I just came from there, remember? So, yeah. I know. Also, there's a famous They Might Be Giants song about it. . . . But, that's soon!"

"Look at you and your knowledge of passé music. Not bad. . . . But yeah, it's soon. I'm starting to get nervous."

"Well, at the very least, it'll be over, right? Pass or fail, over?"

"Yeah, I guess."

"Now *I* was kidding. You'll pass. . . . Come on, of *course* you're going to pass. But also, it will be *done*. No more studying, no more nerves after Sunday, so *that'll* be nice."

"Such an optimist. Okay, now I really gotta go. Have a good *niiight*," he says in a singsong.

"You too. Safe travels."

June 11 at 7:43 p.m.

YOUNGER LUKE: FYI - THIS PLACE IS KIND OF FANCY. THERE'S A BOUNCER.

ALISON: SO YOU'RE SAYING I SHOULD WEAR MY PROM DRESS?

YOUNGER LUKE: GOD YOU'RE ALWAYS SO EAGER TO GET EXTRA MILEAGE OUT OF THAT THING.

I see Younger Luke sitting in the cobblestone courtyard reading his phone. He looks up and sees me, too, as I walk in.

"How did it go???" I exclaim, running over to give him a hug.

He wraps his arms around me, lifts me off the ground, and kisses me hello, surprising me with this easy affection.

"It was good. It's over." He shrugs.

"Do you think you did alright?"

"Yeah, I think I did okay. . . ." He nods. "I guess I did. I hope I did?"

"Yaaay!" I instinctively pump a fist in the air. "I'm so happy to hear that. I'm so *glad* for you that it's over."

"Thanks again for your good luck call Friday night. That was really sweet."

"Oh, don't be silly. . . . So, what do you do with your results? Like . . . once you become a CFA, does anything change at work?"

"No, but it gives me greater potential for upward mobility . . . one day. . . . Sorry, do you want to go up to the bar now?"

"Um, of *course*!"

He places his hand on my lower back and guides me in the right direction. A happy tingle runs up my spine.

"Sooo, did you learn anything . . . interesting? . . . from your exam prep? Stuff you can apply to work?"

"Some stuff, maybe. Not really though." He opens the door for me.

"Thanks. That's . . . disappointing, I guess. To put all that time into something for a credential. . . . Though," I muse aloud, "I guess that's what grad school was for me. A credential. Dunno." I shrug. "Deep thoughts. . . . Anyway! Do you think you'll work in finance forever?"

"I don't know what else I'd do," he breathes out, slightly winded from the multifloor climb to the rooftop. "You probably gleaned some of this from my profile, but I always thought I'd be a musician."

"Right . . ." I say thoughtfully. "I *kind* of remember something about that." He shoots me a glare and an eye roll.

"What?" I ask defensively. "I haven't looked at your profile in . . . a really long time. At least a month!" The waiter escorts us to a banquette overlooking the Hudson River, and we sit down. "If you don't believe me . . . you can check. You know they let you see a list of, like, the hundred most recent people who have viewed you."

"A-ny-way," he spaces out the word, feigning aggravation, "I moved to New York to pursue . . . 'my dreams,'" he says in a falsetto, clutching his hands over his heart, "and I got quickly sucked into the music scene. I had a stage name, and a tiny backup band and—"

"Ooh!" I perk up. "What was your stage name? Should I guess?"

"Nah, you'll never guess. It was Nat Rivers. Nathaniel's my middle name, Rivers is my mom's maiden name." He picks up a menu and hands me one.

"Why did you want a stage name? Why not just be Luke Watts?"

He pauses in thought, then shakes his head. "I don't know. I never really thought about it. It just seemed like," he pauses again, "a cool thing to do," and shrugs.

"So you were a starving-artist folk singer type? Or a bad-boy rocker type? Or . . ."

"The former. A sexy starving-artist folk singer."

"I didn't say sexy." I shake my head. He elbows me in the rib. "Ow!"

"Yeah, I played at The Bitter End and some other cool places you've probably heard of or been to. I played a lot of Dylan covers . . . but also wrote a bunch of my own songs."

"Cool."

"Yeah, it was cool. For a while . . . but you can't make money, so I had to also work as a bike messenger, and after a few years, I was tired of . . . well, starving. So I applied to business school, went—"

"—business school *and* journalism school."

"—Right. Went straight into finance, and that's . . . what I've been doing ever since."

"That was how long ago?"

"Seven or eight years."

"And you've been at Bank of Tokyo ever since you graduated?"

"Yeah."

"Do you like it?"

"It's fine. I mean, I don't like it the way *you* seem to like *your* job, but it's steady and it pays. . . . I don't see why I'd leave it. Unless they fired me."

"How did we get on this?" I squint, trying to remember. "Oh right! Did you always want to work in finance? . . . So I guess the answer's n—"

"No," he says. I nod quickly. He smiles. "When I was little, I wanted to be a spy. For as long as I can remember, I wanted to be a spy. Every year for Halloween, I insisted on having the same costume."

"Saves time and money for your parents." I nod, sipping my ginger mojito. "How'd you dress up?"

"I wore big dark sunglasses and my dad's trench coat. And I carried a plastic gun, maybe a water gun?"

"*You'd* get kicked out of school for carrying such an accessory these days. . . ."

"I know, right. But what about you?"

"What was I for Halloween? Oh, all kinds of things: a *Viking*, Harpo Marx . . ." I smile.

"No, did you always want to work in conservation?"

I have to pause to reflect on this before speaking. "As a kid, I wanted to be a glassblower. *Really* badly. I went to Venice with my family when I was maybe ten or eleven, and this glassblower at a factory in Murano brought me a small deer. I'm sure it was imperfect or flawed and they were gonna trash it anyway, but it was this . . . *amazing* gesture to a ten-year-old. My family didn't speak Italian, so he tried to communicate by putting his hands up," I mime being a deer, "and saying 'Bambi! Bambi!'"

"—Wait, that was really adorable. Do it again," Luke interrupts.

"Do what again? My impression of a glassblower's impression of a deer?"

"Yeah," he nods vigorously, "do it again. It was really cute."

I shrug and do it again. "A-ny-way," I continue, mimicking his aggravated tone from earlier, "I was hooked. I spent some summers glassblowing, and there was a point in time when I really thought I might up and move to Venice to apprentice there after college."

"So what happened? Why didn't you go?"

I shrug. "Life gets in the way, I guess. . . . I don't have a good answer for that. I guess I'm not as brave as you, striking out on my own without an income to pursue my craft, or passion. . . . I *do* love what I do now. But I'm never going to meet a glassblower and not have pangs of envy."

"You could change it up, be a glassblower now?" he suggests.

"I know. I still rent studio time every now and then, but . . . I guess I don't have any regrets about it? I think there are myriad paths that can make you happy, it all just revolves around where you are when." I pause, then add, "It's like my Pachinko theory."

"Your what?"

"Pachinko, those Japanese pinball games?" He shakes his head, indicating he has no idea what I am talking about. "Okay." I hold my left hand up, spread my fingers out, and explain, "With American pin-ball machines, there's a goal, right?"

He nods.

"You're trying to get the ball to certain places for bonus points and away from others for penalties, but you always wind up at the same final destination, the bottom pocket of the machine."

"Okay."

"But with *Pachinko*, you have all these tiny pins, and the same sized ball will bounce around them," I jump my right index finger between the open slots in my left hand, "and almost never take the same trajec-tory twice, *and* it can end up in a variety of different slots at the bottom. Like, ten, or twenty." *Though I could be making that up. I haven't seen a Pachinko machine since high school in my friend's basement.* "And, I think life is like a Pachinko machine." I shrug, dropping my hands.

"Ahh, Forrest Gump." He nods, teasingly.

"No! But, one day, you could bounce off a pin to the right, the next day to the left, and it will affect where you land. But no matter where you land, you're always on the same level as all the other pinballs, just . . . in a different slot. So . . . it's like you can be happy—i.e., at the same *level*—with a plethora of outcomes. It's not predetermined, you just need to make the most of whatever trajectory you take, so that it's a good ride."

"Huh. I've never heard that."

"That's because I made it up." I smile proudly. "It's not like it's an official theorem or philosophy."

"Cult of Alison."

"Eek, I hope not."

"So do you think dating or love is that way, too? That there are dozens of different outcomes that can make us happy?"

"Oh, *absolutely*."

"I like that." He nods. "I might steal that theory and pretend it's mine."

One round of ginger mojitos and two rounds of jalapeño margaritas later, the sun has set, leaving us with a twinkling view of the New Jersey waterfront.

"God, I love this view," Luke says as he pushes back my hair and kisses my neck.

"Yeah, not too shabby."

"Not that view, this one." He kisses my neck again.

"What a *line*," I mock, and he raises his eyes to meet mine, then kisses me deeply on the lips. We embrace for a while, for long enough that we've probably grossed out the poor waitstaff. His hand wanders up my legging-covered thigh and his fingers toy with the elastic waistband under my shirtdress. He slides his hand under the waistband and down my lower back. Wordlessly, I shift my weight off of my left arm and flick at his hand. Twice.

He smiles through his kiss and moves his hand back to my—covered—thigh.

"Do you want to run away to Vegas and elope? C'mon, let's make it a forever," he whispers into my ear.

Yes, please!! But maybe once I've gotten to know you a tiny bit better? Can we sit down and talk about your values first, please? I turn, look into his eyes, and say, "I mean, I don't know if you learned anything from *The Hangover* movies . . ."

"Well, I was hoping you didn't need so much convincing, but I hear they give you a free case of beer when you get married at one of those Elvis-y wedding chapels." He half-sings the word "chapels" as if dangling a carrot or temptation before me.

"Why didn't you lead off with that information? In that case, heck *yeah,* let's hop on the next flight!"

As we walk to the subway, in a slightly bizarre effort at small talk, Younger Luke asks what I'm doing for the rest of the night. I glance at my watch.

"Crud! It's after midnight! Well, I gotta get to my next date. Sorry! But . . . thanks for everything. Hope you have a good week!"

"Okay, *fine*." He pokes my clavicle teasingly. "Dumb question. A-ny-way, I had fun. And I needed that after two days crammed behind a tiny desk inside the Javits Center. So, thanks."

June 12 at 12:32 a.m.

ALISON: THANKS FOR THE DRINKS & THE ROOFTOP ROMANCE. A GOOD CHOICE.
I'M ON TO DATE #2 FOR THE EVENING, BUT WE'LL BE IN TOUCH SOON.

YOUNGER LUKE: I HEARD HE'S KIND OF A DOUCHE, BUT HAVE FUN. COULD HAVE STAYED ON THAT ROOFTOP ALL NIGHT

After brushing my teeth and changing, I climb into bed and see my cell phone light up and vibrate on the windowsill. YOUNGER LUKE flashes on the screen. I swipe at the screen.

YOUNGER LUKE: SO I'M THINKIN' OF CATCHIN' THE NEXT FLIGHT TO VEGAS. YOU WANNA COME WITH?

YOUNGER LUKE: OR ARE YOU GOING TO LET THE WEREWOLVES GET THE BEST OF YOU?

What on earth is he talking about? Was there a full moon tonight? Did we even talk about this? I ignore the second text and respond to the first:

ALISON: A FRIEND ONCE TOLD ME THEY GIVE YOU A FREE CASE OF BEER IF YOU TIE THE KNOT IN VEGAS. . . . ER, OR AM I GETTING TOO FAR AHEAD OF MYSELF?

Except, four (strong) cocktails and no dinner have gotten the best of me, and when I hit SEND and return my cell phone to the windowsill, I knock it *off* the sill and behind my bed. "Crud!" I exclaim aloud. I hop out of bed and try to push my bed frame away from the wall. It moves about an inch and gets snagged on the carpet, and I decide I'm not in great shape to do this right now. So I climb back in bed and go to sleep, hearing my phone vibrating somewhere beneath me.

The next morning I recover my phone.

June 12 at 1:06 a.m.
YOUNGER LUKE: YOU JUST CAN'T PASS UP THAT FREE CASE OF BEER - I LIKE YOUR STYLE. BREAK A LEG TONIGHT, DON'T FORGET THE BANANAS.

What *happened* to me last night? Bananas? Werewolves? So although I don't remember these conversations at all, apparently I informed

Younger Luke that I am giving a talk at the Armory tonight . . . but what bananas?

* * *

The following week, I am sitting by the microscope at work when I receive the following text:

June 20 at 2:43 p.m.

YOUNGER LUKE: MEET ME BY THE TWO TAILED ELEPHANT WHEN THE RED CROW SINGS IN THE RAIN

ALISON: AWW NUTS-YOU'RE JUST AS CRYPTIC AS YOUR HALLOWEEN COSTUME WOULD LEAD ONE TO BELIEVE. BUT I THINK I CRACKED YOUR CODE, SO, COOL, I'LL SEE YOU THEN.

YOUNGER LUKE: JUST TO BE CLEAR, WERE YOU HEADED TO THE ANGELIKA ON HOUSTON FOR THE 8 PM SCREENING? CAUSE THAT'S WHERE ILL BE.

ALISON: OH. WELL, THE MYSTERIOUS LINGO HAD ME HEADED FOR A MIDNIGHT SCREENING OUT IN QUEENS. GOOD THING YOU CLARIFIED. NOTE TO SELF: HONE SLEUTHING SKILLS.

YOUNGER LUKE: YEAH, I MEAN, THAT WAS PRETTY FAR OFF. WHOA - WAY OFF. AND THAT WAS AN EASY ONE. . . ITS OK, YOU'VE HAD A ROUGH WEEK.

Work *was* rough this week, and I told him so—albeit in an abridged, far sunnier edition of what actually transpired: in advance of my annual review meeting, I received a written performance evaluation, authored of course by Joanne, which was both inaccurate and scathing. Thankfully, the meeting itself isn't scheduled for another eight weeks, leaving me fifty-six days to mentally prepare. Read: panic.

After irrationally crying first to my mom, then to Nicole, I tried to broach it with Younger Luke over the phone in what Nicole and I now refer to as "our first feelings talk"—or, rather, *my* first feelings talk, since Younger Luke seemed pretty nonplussed by the whole thing. Although I omitted the most depressing and pathetic details, I wanted to see how he'd handle a display of any emotion other than sarcasm, passion, or bliss. It wasn't the heart-to-heart Nicole and I had hoped for, but there *was* a lot of laughter, which was a positive by-product.

Happily, the prospect of an easy-breezy movie date makes the work headaches slightly easier to endure.

A Saturday night out in his neighborhood, Williamsburg, has begun to resemble a veritable pub crawl. An evening that started off classy with oysters and champagne gave way to two rounds of cocktails at a speakeasy-style bar, which devolved into multiple rounds of drinks and Skee-Ball at Barcade, and now we're walking home in the rain after the last bar closed at 4:00 a.m.

"Luke!" I scold, pointing at him. "We've been drinking for eight and a half *hours*. Why do our dates always end in your administering me . . . a giant dose of mind-erasers??"

"What?" He laughs.

"Sooooo. Remember your texts from last week? Or the week before?" We finally reach his front door, he turns the key, and we escape the rain, drenched though we may be.

"Yeah?" He starts climbing the stairs to his apartment.

"Werewolves? Bananas? . . . I don't remember *any* of these things. None."

"So you're *saying* that you don't listen to a word I say," he teases as we reach his apartment door.

"No, what I'm *saying* is that you are using Jedi mind-erasing tricks on me!" I add quietly, "And, I'd like you to stop."

"Awww," he says sympathetically, and he turns and wipes the rain off my forehead with his fingertips. "Someone can't hold their liquor."

"*Someone* needs to . . ." I search for my words, "stop making me drink so much."

He laughs. "It's a free country, you know. You don't have to try and keep up with me. You are, you know, a wee bit littler than me." He turns the key in his door, and we walk into his apartment.

"Oh my God!" I exclaim. "You actually *do* have checkered linoleum flooring!"

"Yeah, you put it in my Room for Sweet Fruit Beverages. Or did you forget that, too?"

"Yeah, but . . . but I thought you were kidding, and I was just making a joke about it."

"Nope. It's all here. Complete with the nineteen-sixties red kitchen cabinets."

"Your apartment is . . . so *strange*," I say, not meaning to offend, but not sure how else to complete that sentence.

"Thanks. I kinda like it. I think of it as a nice outdated man cave. Lacks any element of the female touch."

"Yes I *see* that," I say, noting his music posters and the strange mismatched furnishings and décor.

"Where can I hang this?" I hold out my coat, and he takes it to the closet by the door. I kick off my shoes, and Luke has me up over his shoulder—my torso upside-down against his back, my legs dangling close to his face.

"Where are you taking me?" I ask. He carries me across the threshold of the apartment, through the living room, and into his bedroom.

"Aww, look at you, my knight in shining armor," I say, the blood rushing to my head.

"Yeppppp. Yep yep yep yep yep yep yep," he replies in a quick monotone.

"Drunk speak?" I ask. "So who can't hold *their* liquor now?"

"No! I'm the Martian from *Sesame Street*."

"Soooo, yes, drunk speak."

He shakes his head from side to side, still carrying me.

"Is this the only way you're going to talk to me?"

"Yepppp. Yep yep yep yep yep yep yep yep."

"Cool. Okay. So from this point forward, I would like you to only communicate via binary speak. Don't worry! It will *never* get old."

"Yeeeeeppp. Yep yep yep yep yep yep yep yep."

"Okay, but Luke?" I struggle to push myself up off his back so I am oriented at least semivertically.

"Yeppp? Yep yep yep?"

"I forgot to tell you that you're not getting in my pants tonight." We've reached the bed, and with this, he maneuvers me off his shoulder and into a sitting position on the bed. He stands facing me and cocks his head sideways.

"Nope nope?"

I smile. "Nope nope. I hope that's okay. I probably should have told you sooner, like *before* I'm sitting on your bed at 4:30 a.m. . . . but I just got, I don't know, carried away by the fun of the night. . . . Ha ha, get it?" I say, reaching out and poking his stomach with my finger.

He nods twice.

"So. Is that okay? Do you want me to . . . leave?"

He shakes his head from side to side.

"So. We're good," I say, looking at him askance.

"Yeeppp. Yep yep yep yep yep." He goes into his closet and takes off his shoes.

June 25 at 12:16 p.m.

YOUNGER LUKE: JUST TOOK MY SECOND COLD SHOWER SINCE YOU LEFT. HOPE YOU EVADED THE MARSUPIALS ON THE SUBWAY THIS MORNING.

ALISON: HMMM. JEDI MIND-ERASING TRICKS AGAIN! . . . OR ARE YOU MAKING FUN OF ME?

YOUNGER LUKE: NOOOOOPE. NOPE NOPE NOPE NOPE NOPE NOPE NOPE NOPE NOPE.

* * *

In stark contrast with Older Luke, all Younger Luke and I can seem to do is drink, laugh, drink, laugh some more, and make out. I have probably consumed more alcohol with Younger Luke in the past two months than in the prior two years. My poor liver. So when we're playing Trivial Pursuit on the floor of his living room the following Friday night, a bottle of red wine in front of us and takeout Thai on the table, I sip from my wineglass and ask, as casually as possible, "How was your day?"

"Fine."

"Do you want to talk about your day?"

"Nope." He shakes the die in his hand.

I nod slowly then begin. "Sometimes," I use my most instructive, pedantic voice, "*sharing* can help us feel even more excited about *good* things that happen, and *better* about *bad* things that happen."

"Old man's turn to roll the dice."

"Oh? You think you're an old man, too?" I smile and nod. "I was just about to say that . . . but, now you go first: Why do *you* think you're an old man?"

"In comparison to you I am." He shrugs and rolls the dice.

"Hmm." I swirl the wine in my glass and look at it, trying to figure out how to proceed. "So *I* think you're like an old man because you are very set in your ways."

"Oh yeah? How."

"Well, you seem to have us on a more or less strict dating regimen, wherein we only see each other once a week, usually on weekends."

"Yeah, but that's because I have to get up so early for work."

"I know. But that's not . . . typical? Like, *sometimes* if you like spending time with someone, you might . . . I don't know . . . see them *twice* a week?"

He watches me and smiles.

"*What?*" I moan.

"Nothing. Keep talking." He sips his wine and swishes it through his teeth before swallowing.

"Also because you don't seem to need . . . I don't know . . . people? Like you've created your own little compact life here, in your self-proclaimed man cave," I gesture to the room around me, "and you don't want to . . . I don't know, talk about real things? Like day-to-day stuff. . . . It just kinda seems like . . . you've got yourself, and that's all you need."

He watches me and nods, then turns his attention to his plate and goes back to eating. "I think it's your turn to read me a card."

I roll my eyes in mock—grounded in actual—frustration, and read from the deck.

"So *our* Trivial Pursuit up in the Catskills house is . . . maybe, thirty years outdated? Thirty-five? Anyway, it's impossible to play with anybody except my parents. The questions are all about, like, the 1976 Olympics in Innsbruck. Or the USSR."

"That sounds terrible," Luke says.

"It is. But it's also kind of fabulous getting to watch my parents play together. You'll read a card, and the rest of us will all look around at one another scratching our heads, and my mom and dad will jump in with the right answers like it's the lightning round. They get so excited they're finally beating their kids at a board game. . . ."

"That's cute."

"This one time—my *favorite* time—there was a clue about some Swedish porn film, and my mom literally jumped out of her seat at the question and was like 'Yellow!' My brother studied the card, and my mom was like, 'I am Curious. Also called "Yellow"!' She was so proud of herself for getting it right, meanwhile we were all like, why does Mom know both the main and alternate titles of a Swedish *porn*?"

"That's really funny," Luke says, rolling the dice. "I'm going to call *you* 'Yellow.'"

"Because I look Swedish? Or like a porn star?"

"Because your hair is yellow."

"That's funny, if you try to get my three-year-old niece to say her colors—'What color is the sky? Blue,' 'What color is the grass? Green,' 'What color is Aunty Ali's hair?' she always says, 'White.'"

"Nope, you'll always be 'Yellow' to me."

"I feel like you're trying to be romantic," I pause for effect, "but it just sounds racist . . . or dirty . . . or both?"

"*No.*" He shakes his head. "That's romance, Yellow." He lunges over and tackles me backward to the floor, pinning my arms and reading my eyes before he kisses me.

* * *

July 1 at 5:50 p.m.

YOUNGER LUKE: YELLO

ALISON: YELLOASIN"HELLO"ORASINMYMOM'SFAVORITESWEDISHPORN?...
OR ARE YOU TRYING TO ROMANCE ME AGAIN WITH PET NAMES?

YOUNGER LUKE: ALL THREE. LET'S SAY WE GET TOGETHER BEFORE YOU SKIP TOWN.
WEDNESDAY?

This coming weekend I'm flying to Napa for Catherine's wedding, where, I was informed two days ago, the best man and I will be the only people toasting the couple. As someone with a morbid fear of public speaking, I have spent every moment since obsessing over my maid-of-honor toast. In a frenzied panic, egged on by Blaire and Ashley at a BYOB dinner on Saturday night, I decided I would deliver my toast via a puppet show. Our giddy high based on the brilliance of this idea continued into the subsequent morning, when we met up at Michael's arts-and-crafts store to stock up on pipe cleaners, fabric, and glue.

It was only on the subway ride to work this morning that the high started to wear off, and I started to worry that this is the worst idea ever. I'm still going to make the puppets tonight, knowing full well that I may jettison them in favor of a more traditional speech by tomorrow morning. But I desperately need a second opinion on my speech.

Meanwhile, Nicole's advice is ringing in my ears: *Find a way to engage Younger Luke in your real life. Push him to give advice, show thought. He may be incapable of moving this forward on his own, so push him to emote, or to at least be supportive.*

July 3 at 12:31 p.m.

Hey Luke,

    Saturday after I left your place, this week's bride-to-be left me a voice mail asking if I could toast her at the wedding. More specifically, if I could "you know, do something different or creative, like rhyme."

    Naturally, I wrote a puppet show.

    Given that the only person who worked on this thing is me, I could really use a second pair of eyes. And since yours don't know the bride & groom, or the audience, I thought maybe you could provide some feedback/constructive criticism. Anyway, drop a line if you wouldn't mind giving the script a quick read.

    I may literally die of stage fright on Saturday. In which case, it was nice knowing you. . . .

Cheers,
Alison

July 3 at 12:57 p.m.

YOUNGER LUKE: GOT YOUR EMAIL. LOVE THE PUPPET IDEA... LOVE IT. BUT YES IT COULD
BOMB TREMENDOUSLY. SEND IT MY WAY. I'LL DUST OFF MY RED PENS
FROM MY DAYS ON THE UDUB NEWSPAPER.

July 3 at 7:12 p.m.

Hey Alison,

Well, it's certainly going to be memorable. I spent my lunch break going over it, my edits are attached.

Lot of pressure though, you sure you're up for it?

L

July 3 at 11:10 p.m.

Stop it! You are stressing me out MORE! Shouldn't you be saying, "Well, Alison, you are so massively talented and funny that if anyone could pull this off, it would be you . . ."? Shame on you for contributing to my impending sense of doom!

But thank you for the edits.

Cheers,
Alison

P.S. My, my, someone's a stickler.

With the Googly Eyes: Older Luke

Wednesday morning in the Armory Drill Hall, I hop off the boom lift and shed my harness for a coffee break. I pull out my phone to find a text from Older Luke.

July 5 at 9:16 a.m.

OLDER LUKE: GOOD MORNING. KEEP YOUR EYES PEELED, I PLAN TO SEND YOU A SELF-DEPRECATING EMAIL SOMETIME THIS MORNING.

July 5 at 11:37 a.m.

Hey Alison,

I'm not on call until Friday. Are you free tomorrow night?

I've been thinking a lot about your work situation. I appreciate how open and candid you've been with me, and I hope I helped you talk through some of the difficult issues you're facing. That said, I think I've come up with a couple additional points you should make to Joanne, either before your annual review or during it. Rather than write them all out, maybe we can discuss them when we next get together. Also, I'm confident this is just a temporary stumbling block. You are immensely bright and talented; anyone can see that. Joanne will too, someday.

Now for the awkward part, I'm pretty sure in your 27 years of living you've never heard something this goofy. There is always a first, though. Here it is: I have a problem with initiating hand-holding/kissing. But, only with you. I know, how weird. Let me explain. It's because I think I could really like you. Whenever I feel that way about someone, this happens. Meaning that it seems like I know that I'm going to enjoy anything physical with you, so I want to make sure the other stuff is there first. Almost like, since I do like you, I have too much respect for you and this happens. Who goes on nine dates (I think that's the number) and doesn't even initiate hand-holding? What a schmuck!

I definitely don't feel the need to talk about this with you, I just wanted to put it out there so you don't think I'm not a physical person or that I don't enjoy showing affection. I actually do, a great deal. Verbalizing this helps me see how silly this is and will help me overcome it. At any rate, it would be nice to be more affectionate with you someday and who knows, maybe I'll even try!

I have to say that I find your company to be exciting and soothing at the same time. Maybe I can bring this paragraph around with a good ending: Alison, you should know that you have really beautiful bright blue eyes, so it's a little hard not to get mesmerized at times and lose track of what we're talking about. ;-)

Let me know if Wednesday works, as always I'll look forward to seeing you. The Brooklyn Bridge was nice, thanks for walking along it with me last night.

-Luke

July 5 at 5:36 p.m.

Rushing off to tutoring right now, but didn't want to let your email go unresponded to:

<<What a schmuck!>>

Ha. That's what I was thinking!

Just kidding. . . . Actually, I was holding Jason responsible -- I thought it was his whole "Alison is a VEEEERRR-RYYY slooooow dater" comment that scared you off. Interesting to learn that it was just me scaring you off.

At any rate, thanks for sharing. In a humorous fashion. This was a good read and I shall cherish it forever in my "keeper emails" folder. ;)

Look forward to seeing you tomorrow.

Cheers,
Alison

	July 6 at 8:11 a.m.
OLDER LUKE:	HEY, IT'S THE SCHMUCK. JUST WANTED TO GIVE YOU A NERDY HELLO. HOW GOES THE WORK, AND DO YOU STILL WANT TO GET TOGETHER TONIGHT?
ALISON:	I'M SWAMPED WITH ARTS & CRAFTS. IN LIEU OF ACTUALLY DOING SOMETHING SOCIAL, THOUGH, WE COULD WATCH A MOVIE OR TV WHILE I SIT ON THE FLOOR AND GLUE CLOTHING ON MY BRIDE AND GROOM PUPPETS?
ALISON:	P.S. IF EVER THERE WERE A TIME THAT I MADE OUR AGE DIFFERENCE FEEL VAST, I'M THINKING TONIGHT'S THAT TIME. . . .

I'm sitting on the floor of Older Luke's apartment, gluing googly eyes down on my paper bag puppets next to Boomer, who keeps trying to eat their yarn hair. Luke is sitting on the couch behind me, occasionally kneading my shoulders or upper back with his fists as we watch *Doctor Zhivago*.

"Do you think I need to cut out an additional costume change? For the final scene, when they have puppet babies?"

"I think that would be cute, but not necessary."

"Well, my hand hurts from all the cutting, so I think they're just going to have to birth their puppet babies in their wedding attire."

"How many costumes did you already make?"

"They each have three, not including the original ones, which are glued down."

"I'd say that's plenty. Are you sure you don't want me to help?"

"No, I'm good." I pause and look up from my gluing. "But you did a really good job coloring in puppet Andrew's Speedo!" I encourage.

"Thanks, I guess I'm just a natural." He smiles. Our eyes lock, and now would be a good time for him to lean in and act on his last email. But . . . nothing.

"Well, it's after midnight." I start brushing my supplies off his coffee table and into my canvas tote bag. "I should probably go. How much time is left in the movie?"

He pauses it to check. "Less than five minutes, actually."

"Okay. I think I can wait *that* long." I stand up and stretch my legs and back. Boomer has again drooled all over my pants, and though this is mildly revolting, I am trying to learn to embrace it. And to do laundry more frequently. I clamber onto the couch cushion next to Older Luke. Still . . . nothing.

The credits start rolling. "Okay. Now it's *really* time for me to get going." I stand up. "I'll . . . see you sometime after the weekend?"

"Do you want me to walk you home?"

"You don't have to." I shrug.

"It's really late. Come on, I'll walk you home." We grab our coats and head off into the night. We've walked all eight blocks to my apartment and still . . . nothing. No hand-holding. No arm-grazing. And yet I'm too nervous myself to take any initiative. Also, I feel like based on his email, he wants that initiative to come from him anyway.

We stand on my front stoop. I lean in to give him a hug. "Okay, well . . . it was good to see you again! Thanks for helping with my crafting. . . . Sorry if that was kind of boring for you. And juvenile. I just needed to get it done befo—"

"—Sorry, I just have to do this." And finally, after ten dates, Older Luke kisses me.

My stomach flips, but I think only because this moment has been so oddly built up, I'm anxious to finally get it over with. The kiss is gentle, and sweet. It's not bad, but it's not filled with fireworks either.

"Gosh I've been wanting to do that for so long," he says quietly.

I nod and smile. "Yeah, you mentioned that."

He kisses me again, hands me my bag of puppets and gives my hand a squeeze, and watches me step inside.

And He Can't Even Spell: Younger Luke

July 7 at 2:17 p.m.

YOUNGER LUKE: HOPE YOU FIND SOME TIME TO GET SIDEWAYS OUT THERE. YOU GOT
TOMORROW IN THE BAG (PUN INTENDED).

It's Friday, and after a long flight and drive to the midday wedding rehearsal, we have the afternoon to ourselves. Cassie and I decide to bike and wine-taste our way through Napa. The sun is shining, there are beautiful vineyards all around us, and though we only have a few hours until the rehearsal dinner, it somehow feels like a true vacation.

"So, we don't have to talk about this now, but . . . how are you going to decide between the Lukes?" Cassie asks as we lounge on the grass by V. Sattui Winery.

"I have no idea."

"You want to make a mental pro and con list?"

"They're just too different. It's not apples to apples. As Ashley would say, it's 'apples to donkeys.'"

"They're not *that* different."

"They are, though!" I protest. "It's like, if I want someone who is supportive, and thoughtful, and *really* smart, and kind to my friends and the people around him . . . that's Older Luke."

"But Younger Luke's smart."

"Not really. Not in the same way. He has an undergrad degree in journalism and he can't even spell. And I don't think he likes his job, or finds it rewarding or challenging, and I don't think he'll ever feel compelled to change jobs." I sigh and concede, "He's sharp and witty, but he doesn't like to think about things deeply. Or at all. We make each other laugh and laugh and laugh, and we can talk for hours on the phone at night about *nothing*. And the chemistry is . . . more than palpable. It's . . . *electric*, and *exciting* . . . but also scary, because it's . . . eerily addictive. I've never had that before."

"Why scary?"

"I feel like—I feel like a *girl* . . . or a woman or a female or whatever, but you know, someone who has to *think* before she texts a guy back or says something that might be taken the wrong way. With Older Luke, and everyone else I've ever dated in my life, I don't *care* what they think of me. I mean, I care, but, I don't . . . worry? Or . . . strike that: I *don't* care. I don't worry about what happens if I . . . say one thing that rubs them the wrong way, or makes them freak out, or end it. I told him I honestly think I might get fired. I would *never* confide that in Younger Luke—what would he think of me? With Older Luke, I am who I am, and if he doesn't like it . . . '*tant pis*,' as the French say. With Younger Luke, I feel like I have to *try*. And it's *so exhausting*!" I quickly add, "And yes, I *am* aware I'm whining. Sorry." I pout.

"But that's what dating is *like*. Or what it's always been like for me. You always date friends, so you know you can be yourself right off the bat, and forever. This is . . . kind of how it is?"

"But it *wasn't* that way with James or Older Luke. Why is it that way with Younger Luke and only Younger Luke?"

"He's different." Cassie shrugs. "Everyone else you mentioned wants to be in a relationship. . . . Well, scratch that. Everyone else you mentioned *thinks* they want to be in a relationship, even if they don't know how to do that . . . or don't have fully formed amygdalas or hippocampuses. Younger Luke, on the other hand, can take it or leave it. So even if there's no one else in the picture, you seem to think he'd be just as happy being single as dating—be it you or anyone else."

"Yeah." I nod. "I mean, I *do* think that's true. Annnnd?"

"Well that's . . . different. You know I couldn't date someone like that. I'd run in and try to change him, and force him into a reliable, affectionate, steady boyfriend. We'd have had The Talk by now, and I would have made him meet all my friends, maybe even my parents."

I laugh out loud, impressed by how well Cassie knows herself. "You WOULD!" I agree teasingly. "I wish I could," I sigh, "but he's just different. Which also makes it hard to compare them. You know, Older Luke calls or texts *every* day. And if I'd let him, he'd probably try to *see* me every day, too. Younger Luke has me on this strict once—max twice—a week schedule . . . and it's *cool by him* if two or three days go by without communicating. . . ."

"But you and I are different. And if you don't need those things, then it *can* work. But it's going to be different from every other relationship you've had, because he may *never* want to see you on a weeknight. Even if you project forward two years and you're living together, or married, you might just be one of those couples who love each other but do most things independently."

I grunt.

"Would that work for you?"

"I don't think I know him well enough to write off the possibility that he could . . . or couldn't . . . give more if we date for longer . . . and I guess I just find him so funny, and so magnetic, that I probably can't bring myself to walk away until I know more."

"But would it work for you?"

"Probably not. . . . No," I admit.

"You should make a point of trying to tease out some of his issues then. Gently, if you don't think he can be probed, because you're making him sound like a minefield of red flags."

"He *is*."

"So then why would you *ever* choose him over Older Luke?"

I exhale deeply and say through gritted teeth, "Pheromones. *Stupid* pheromones." I close my eyes and shake my head, more to myself than to Cassie. "His are like . . . a highly addictive drug for me. It feels as if my brain is working overtime trying to convince my limbs to motivate and walk away, but then, every other fiber of my body wants to, I don't know, stick around? You know, because of his powerful pheromones and all." I roll my eyes. I can't even decide if this is just silly self-justification, or truth masquerading as silly self-justification.

I continue, "Remember when ABC restreamed Trista's season of *The Bachelorette* last spring, and we got really absorbed in the show, lamenting how life was *so* hard! 'Her head was with Charlie, but her heart was with *Ryan*!' I feel like—"

"Older Luke is Charlie."

"Yep."

"And Younger Luke is Ryan."

"Yep."

"Well, then I think you have your answer."

* * *

July 8 at 8:36 p.m.

YOUNGER LUKE: YOU'RE EITHER . . . DITCHING THE WEDDING TO TIE THE KNOT IN VEGAS RIGHT NOW . . . OR SPEAKING IN FRONT OF A LARGE GROUP OF PEOPLE WITH A PAPER BAG ON YOUR HAND.

July 9 at 1:05 a.m.

ALISON: IT WAS SUPPOSED TO BE A SURPRISE! I THOUGHT YOU'D BE FLATTERED THAT I THOUGHT OF YOU AND BROUGHT YOU BACK THE FREE CASE OF BEER AS A SOUVENIR.

July 9 at 9:27 a.m.

YOUNGER LUKE: YELLOW, I THOUGHT WE HATCHED THAT VEGAS PLAN TOGETHER . . . DID YOU KNOCK THEIR SOCKS OFF?

July 9 at 11:16 a.m.

ALISON: WHAT DO YOU THINK?

YOUNGER LUKE: DEFINATELY.

What Part of This Love Boat Are You On: Luke

As planned, when I exit my office, Luke is standing across the street waiting for me. He watches me as I cross West 24th Street and reaches for my hand as we walk the city blocks to the subway. *Be still, my heart.*

It feels like I'm struggling to catch my breath the entire subway ride as we head out to Williamsburg together. I fill him in on the puppet show and other highlights and comic errors of the past weekend, and through it, my heart races on. When I returned from California, he suggested he cook me dinner this week. I protested, saying that it was my turn to make up for his generosity in food and drinks over the last few months, but he insisted. And then he justified it as not wanting to be cooped up with roommates he didn't know.

When we get to his apartment, he has the meat marinating ("I got it ready before work this morning, aren't you proud of me for planning something in advance?"), and his fridge is far fuller than it's been before ("I hit up Trader Joe's. I know how you females love organic food"). He refuses to let me touch anything ("I wanted to cook for *you*, remember?"), so I sit on the couch with a glass full of wine in hand, ask him about his week, and tell him about mine.

Once the various pans are cooking on the stovetop, he suggests we turn on the TV and moves to join me on the couch.

"I'm going to lie down," he says. "You can join me, if you want."

"Umm." I look around for somewhere to put my glass down.

"Or you don't have to." He adjusts his position, extends on the couch, and rests his head on my stomach while I sit upright.

"Dude, your heart is *racing*," he says, and I am mortified. *He knows! He knows how nervous I am, how nervous he makes me!*

"No it's not. It's normal," I say defensively.

"Are you nervous?" he asks, looking up at me. Then smiling, teasing, he asks, "Do I make you *nervous?*"

"Shut up and watch TV," I say, feigning anger. *But he knows. I've shown my hand, and now he knows.*

I wash the dishes after dinner, and while he's helping me dry them, he suggests, "Hey, should we get some tunes going?" He goes into his room, and I can see him through the doorway plugging in his iPod, clicking his computer mouse. I recognize the first measures of Coldplay's "Yellow."

I can't help but smile. "Ha *ha*. Very funny. How long have you been planning *that* for?" I call out.

He comes back in wearing a blank expression on his face and playing dumb. "Huh?"

I shake my head and acknowledge, "That's funny, though."

"I just . . . like . . . Coldplay. I don't know what you're talking about." He comes up behind me, takes the sponge out of my hands, and puts it in the sink. I quickly dry my hands on my jeans. Standing behind me, he then lifts my hands from my sides, interlocks our fingers, and studies them for a moment. "Yeah, this song came on my iPod a few weeks ago, and it made me think of you, Yellow. It's kind of become my new jam, even though it's old. I thought you'd get a kick out of it." Then he turns me around, kisses me, picks me up, and carries me to the couch without breaking embrace, and I get lost in him for several songs.

"Do you want to . . . move to the other room?" He nods his head to the bedroom.

"Oh, *I* see how it is. Coldplay's your lead-up. Your . . . Barry White or Marvin Gaye or . . . Dave Matthews Band." I smile.

"Yeah, except . . ." He looks down, and then up at me again. "I don't think we should sleep together tonight."

"Wait—that's *my* line."

"Nope, I said it first. Now it's *my* line." With that, he stands up, leans over the couch, scoops me up, and moves to his bedroom, carrying me across the threshold newlywed-style.

As we lie entwined on his bed, his hands wander under the covers, like he wants to memorize entire areas of my skin. Random creases, like the insides of my elbows and the webbing between my fingers. He kisses my neck, kisses my ear, then groans.

"What?" I laugh lightly.

"No. I just . . . don't think we should sleep together tonight."

I prop myself up on my elbows. "Yes, you keep telling me that. But first of all, quit stealing my line. Second of all, you've said it three times now, and it's starting to feel offensive."

He climbs on top of me and meets my face with his. "It's a good thing. I promise." He kisses me again, and it's bliss.

***

July 17 at 12:18 p.m.

LUKE: WHATCHA MAKIN TONIGHT, YELLOW? AND CAN I BRING ANYTHING? WINE? MANWICHES?

ALISON: WHAT'S A MANWICH? THOUGH I'M PRETTY SURE THE ANSWER'S NO.

LUKE: YOU EAST COAST GALS MAY CALL THEM SLOPPY JOES.

ALISON: AH. OK, NO MANWICHES. BUT HOW KIND OF YOU TO OFFER! STRANGE REQUEST, BUT CAN YOU PICK UP MILK? I USED IT ALL AND WE MIGHT WANT SOME TO CUT DESSERT.

July 17 at 5:46 p.m.

LUKE: MY BAG IS FULL OF MILK AND I'M BRINGIN IT OVER - TOOK IT OUT OF THE CARTON TO MAKE IT EASIER TO CARRY, DON'T THINK ANYONE SAW.

July 18 at 1:02 p.m.

LUKE: THANKS FOR SOME SPECTACULAR EATS LAST NIGHT. STUFFED MYSELF WITH LEFTOVER MERINGUES FOR LUNCH THIS AFTERNOON. MY TURN NEXT.

ALISON: MY PLEASURE - ANYTIME. MAYBE YOU SHOULD TRY DUNKING THE MERINGUES IN MILK, YOU KNOW, SOP UP SOME OF THAT MESS IN YOUR BAG?

LUKE: NICE, BUT I ACTUALLY DUMPED A BOX OF YOUR CHEERIOS IN MY BAG ON THE WAY OUT THIS MORN FOR THE SUBWAY - GOT SOME FUNNY LOOKS THOUGH.

ALISON: HUH. WONDER WHY.

* * *

Luke is out in Las Vegas with a friend this weekend while I'm up in the Catskills with Ben and a group of our friends.

July 22 at 1:35 p.m.

LUKE: KNOW U HAVE A BUSY WEEKEND OF HOSTESSING, BUT JUST BIKED THRU THE JOSHUA TREE FOREST AND KNOW HOW U LOVE JOSHUA TREES. MADE ME THINK OF U

ALISON: AND HERE I WAS THINKING OF YOU. WE PLAYED TABOO, AND I GOT THE "SPY" CARD. I SAID, "IF YOU DRESSED UP AS ONE FOR HALLOWEEN, YOU'D DON A LONG TRENCH COAT AND CARRY A PLASTIC WEAPON."

ALISON: FIRST GUESS WAS "ASPIRING PEDOPHILE," THEN "EXHIBITIONIST." WHAT WAS YOUR MOM THINKING LETTING YOU WEAR THAT TO SCHOOL?

* * *

"But I don't *want* to invite him," I whine. "I know I'll just be nervous if he's around. And I've been so nervous all the time lately, I kind of just want to relax, and see all my friends, and not think about . . . *feelings*."

"But if you *don't* invite him, you're sending such a clear signal that you're not interested," Nicole argues.

"But he doesn't have to know!"

"Hi, Facebook! Or accidentally letting it slip out. Or me or Cassie accidentally letting it slip out!"

"Uggggh. Fine." I sigh. "But now I have to try to look cute. UGH!!" I tap my elbow twice, mimicking WWF wrestlers before they drop on their opponents with their elbows. Cassie and I invented this move in college, and it goes a surprisingly long way toward communicating aggravation or anger.

"*Hey*," I say.

"You calling to tell me how much you miss me?" Luke asks, and I can hear him moving to quiet his speakers in the background.

"No. Was that your way of trying to tell *me* that you miss *me*?"

"Maybe."

We make small talk about our respective weeks before I begin, "So, I just wanted to tell you something, but I don't want to put any pressure on you . . . or on it . . . or whatever." He's silent. "I'm having a birthday party this Saturday. I have one every year—"

"—A birthday? Get out! I have one every year, too."

"—and it's nothing extravagant, just a good excuse to get all my friends in one place, drinking, out of doors. Anyway, I know you and your old man ways don't like socializing, so if you have to be some-where else or . . . need to wash your hair . . . I totally get it and won't hold it against you. But I just didn't want you to *not* be invited. Soooo, no pressure. Okay?"

I can practically hear the crickets before he breaks the silence. "Can I bring a friend?"

"Umm, sure. Yeah. It's not, like, formal or anything—"

"So you *won't* be wearing your prom dress."

"I mean, I *might*. I haven't decided yet. But it's just at a bar on an old boat that docks near Chelsea Piers. I'll add your name to the e-blast. I just didn't want to add you without talking to you about it first, because I didn't want to . . ." I trail off.

"Pressure me. Yeah, you mentioned that. I'll be there. I don't know if my friend can even come or not, but I'll be there."

"Okay."

"Wash my hair?" He laughs to himself. "Do you really think I'd skip your birthday to wash my hair? Play guitar, maybe. . . ."

* * *

My birthday rolls around, and I receive the following text from Luke:

	July 29 at 3:17 p.m.
LUKE:	AWKWARD VOICE MAIL. DO NOT LISTEN.

Nervously, I punch in numbers to play the voice mail, my stomach jittery.

"Hey Alsy . . . Al . . . Yellow . . . You . . . So, uhhh, it's Luke. And I just wanted to say that I hope you have a really happy birthday. And I'm really looking forward to seeing you tonight. And to . . . socializing among your . . . friends. Or family. Or whoever's going to be there tonight. So . . . yeah. I'll see you later. Best wishes, Alsy. Oh yeah, this is Luke. Did I say that already?"

ALISON:	WITHTHATKINDOFLEAD-IN? AREYOUKIDDING? OFCOURSEILIS-TENED BEFORE TEXTING YOU BACK.

ALISON:	P.S. I SHALL CHERISH THAT VOICE MAIL FOREVER.

	July 29 at 9:22 p.m.
LUKE:	WHAT PART OF THIS LOVE BOAT ARE YOU ON?

I'm mid-conversation with some work friends when, out of the corner of my eye, I see him walk onto the boat. My stomach knots again, and I continue conversing with my colleagues. Before too long he makes his way over to our circle and kisses me hello, and introductions are made all around. I part from the group and gather Cassie, Nicole, and Ashley so they can finally meet him. While they talk, I gather Ben, my sister, and my brother-in-law so *they* can meet him, too. Not surprisingly, my sister, who shares my ability to talk to a doorknob, hits it off with Luke immediately and is trying lovably hard to make him feel at ease. "So, Ali said you're from Tacoma, yes? My husband lived in Tacoma for . . ." ". . . Did Ali say you have nieces and nephews, too? Where do they live? . . . Oh, what fun ages! My daughter is . . ."

The hours fly by as college friends, high school friends, and city friends come and go. I see Nicole waiting solitarily at the bar, and I make my way toward her.

"So how do you think it's going? You know, with *Luke*?" she asks.

"Dunno." I shrug. "I haven't seen him in a few hours."

"Oh, he's over there by the front of the boat." She gestures in that direction. "Who are those guys he's with?"

I scan the circle of men he's hanging out with. "That's funny. It's like all of my Match friends instinctively gravitated toward one another."

"Well, I guess they're kind of the odd men out, right? They're the only ones that don't fit into a group—college friends, grad school friends . . ."

"Yeah, but, they're all *single*. Shouldn't they be hitting on the single *girls* here? Instead of on each other?"

"So who are all of them? Now I can finally put faces to names!"

We turn to scope out the circle. "Okay. The dark-haired guy on the left is Justin, then Jake, Luke you know, then some guy I don't know. I thought Greg was coming, but . . . oh well."

"Who are Justin and Jake again?"

"Justin is the one who took me to the University Club and gave me a private architecture-themed tour. And, Jake . . . I don't really know how to describe him. He's an anesthesiologist? They're both really wonderful. Actually, you should meet them! Wanna meet them?"

"Yeah, let me just wait for my drink."

I nod.

"Well, at least if nothing comes out of *Match.com* romantically for you, you've collected enough friends to fill up a bar. Oh, by the way, all your college friends keep talking about how Luke looks like Armie Hammer."

"Ha! I wish. But, yeah . . . he's cute."

"I think he brought a birthday present for you."

"Huh?"

"He's been carrying around this big envelope all night. It's gotta be for you, or else why would he still be holding it?"

After midnight, thunder rumbles and the skies open up to a downpour. Guests start running for cover, but there's not much to be found on the boat.

Cassie sprints over to me through the rain. "Should we relocate to an after-party bar?"

"Sure, what's around here?"

"Nothing, we're on the West Side Highway. . . . But maybe if we make a run for it, we can get to The Half King?"

"Where is that?"

"Just a few blocks up 23rd Street."

I nod. We rally the partygoers that remain and make a collective group run for The Half King.

When we get into The Half King, I stand near the doorway with the other girls as we wring out our dresses and our hair, giddy and winded from having sprinted through the rain. Luke comes out of the bathroom, and when I stand up, the hem of my dress still in hand, our eyes lock. I smile and shrug, as if to say, "Kinda messy, but fun, right?" I walk toward him, and he wraps his arms around me, leaving his hands on my butt.

"Not *here*," I chastise. "Not in front of my brother and sister . . . and all my friends."

He kisses me. "Sorry, I couldn't help myself. I felt like I was watching you from across the bar . . . across the boat . . . all night. It was getting me . . . excited," he whispers in my ear. "So!" He straightens and releases me. "Can I buy you a tequila shot?"

"I'd rather not forget tonight." I smile.

"Come on. One tequila shot. Besides, I want to show you something."

"Okay."

We walk over to the bar and climb onto the stools. Luke orders two tequila shots. "Here, this is for you." He puts a large manila envelope on the bar. "Sorry it's kinda wet now. It's wrapped inside, so hopefully it's okay."

"You want me to open it . . . now?"

"Yeah."

"Okay." I slowly tear open the flap and slide out a rectangular gift-wrapped package and another envelope. "Which should I open first?"

"The package."

I nod, and my fingers fiddle with the tape and seams. "Oh. *Oh.* This is *so* cool!"

"Yeah, I've been reading about this guy, and I thought you might . . . find his stuff kinda cool." It's a coffee table art book on Banksy.

"Oh, *way* cool! I thought his . . . 'residency' or whatever in New York was amazing. And . . . did you see *Exit Through the Gift Shop*?" He shakes his head. "Anyway, it's a documentary about him. And other street graffiti artists. We should watch it sometime."

"Yeah, sure. . . . So I bought this because . . . well, I thought that you like art, and you *do* art for a living, but usually, higher-brow stuff. I thought this might appeal to your more . . . alternative or gritty side."

"No, yeah. It's *awesome*. *Thank you*. Really. *Thank you*."

"Nah, it's no big deal. But I was kinda excited to give it to you."

"Now should I open the card?" I ask brightly.

He nods. "But first, tequila shot!" He hands me one, and we clink glasses. "Happy birthday."

I smile and down the small glass.

When I open the card, decals and stickers tumble out onto my lap. "What is this?" I laugh. "Have you been scrapbooking?"

"Read the card."

I read the card slowly to myself, then close it and look up at him. "That was so thoughtful! You are so sweet!"

"Can we go through them now? . . . Here." He picks up an American flag decal. "See, so I figure you could put this one on your helmet, and—"

"—my *hard hat*?"

"—yeah, your helmet." He pauses and looks at me, smiles, and continues, "And this way, all the construction workers will see your flag and know you're a solid, God-fearing *Amurrican*. It's like an instant 'in.'. . ." He riffles through the pile spread out on the bar and on my lap. "Or they'll see . . . *this* one," he pulls out a cartoon sticker of the Beatles on the yellow submarine, "and join you in whistling rounds of 'Yellow Submarine' on the scaffold."

He walks me through explanations of the rest, but I kind of stop listening and just enjoy watching him so animated, so at ease, and also, at the root of it, so thoughtful.

* * *

The next morning, we're lying in bed, alternately joking, kissing, and trying to fall back asleep.

"So, let me get this straight: All those guys I was hanging out with last night—you met *all* of them on Match?"

"I mean, not all of the guys at the *party*. Just the ones you happened to be hanging out with."

"Why'd you stay friends with them, if it didn't work out romantically?"

"They're great. They're *really* great. Just . . . not great for *me* romantically. . . . I like to think of it as performing free screening tests for my single lady friends."

"How long did you date them for?"

"Just once. But, don't worry—I never kissed any of them, or even held hands. I just . . . I thought they were really interesting, really good people . . . so why not be friends?"

"Don't you think you have enough friends already? That boat was pret-ty crowded last night."

"We can't all be old man hermits like you. People who don't need people . . ." I sigh in mock reverie.

"Soooo. Are you still . . . *on* Match?"

I swallow nervously and nod once. "Kind of. Are you?"

"Well, look, I don't want to tell you what to do, but I took myself off Match shortly after I met you. But you should, you know, still use it for social networking purposes . . . or whatever."

"Social networking purposes?" I laugh out loud. "Like . . . finding potential clients. Or book clubs?"

"Yeah, or whatever."

Is he saying he wants to be exclusive? And what is it about him that stops me from asking this question out loud? Unfortunately if I ask that question, a question that might solve *everything* for me right now, he's going to run the other way. I know he will, what with his hermit-y "old man" tendencies and all. So I soften it:

"You've got these . . . old man ways. No socializing on school nights because it's early to bed, early to rise. . . ."

"You know, I always thought I took after Ben Franklin."

"Anyway, you and I call these your 'old man' ways." I nod and look to him for confirmation. He nods back. "So, I've gotten the sense that you never *want* to see me more than once a week. Sometimes twice, when I'm lucky." I poke his arm, trying to turn this into lighthearted ribbing. "But. I don't know what you're doing with the rest of your time . . . and you don't have to tell me . . . but now that you *are* telling me that you aren't advertising yourself to the ladies anymore . . . can I *see* you more than once a week?" I raise my eyebrows. He's silent. "Like . . . maybe twice?"

"I don't know. Maybe."

"So . . . you said you had a long-term girlfriend before. Did you ever see *her* more than once or twice a week?"

"That was a long time ago, and it was different."

"Different how?"

"She moved out from Tacoma with me. We packed my car and drove across the country together, we had no money, so we lived together. So . . . yeah, I saw her every day. But it wasn't a good relationship. And I don't want to repeat that."

"How long were you together?"

"Four years."

"And have you dated anyone since?"

"Yeah. I saw another girl maybe three years ago."

"For how long?"

"Five months, give or take."

"Why did you guys break up?"

"It was different than this." He points back and forth between us. "It was more of a . . . casual thing."

"But five months is a long time," I posit.

"Yeah. But, it didn't really require a conversation when it ended. It just ended."

"You gave her the fade-out after five months! Luke, that's . . . mean!"

He shrugs. "I don't think she was upset. It clearly wasn't going anywhere. And it's not like she called *me*."

My stomach's knotting itself again, and I try to steel myself as I ask, "So, then . . . how do I know *we* won't . . . just fade out?"

"I . . . can't answer that."

"Well. Why not?" I add softly, "It would probably help me if I understood a little better."

"I don't know. I'm not an astrologist."

My shoulders sink, and I feel my eyes start to water so I sniff quickly to clear them, disappointed in this answer, disappointed in him.

"Aww, Alsy." He lifts my chin with his hand and kisses me. "Don't worry, babe. We'll get there someday."

I blink, and he continues. "Look, I know this sounds weird, but if I didn't like you so much, I would have had sex with you by now."

I grimace. "Have you given the fade-out to other girls between the five-monther and me?"

"There hasn't *been* anyone between the five-monther and you."

I squint skeptically. "Really?" *Really? In three years?*

"No. Maybe a few random dates here and there, but I haven't gone on a second date since her . . . until I met you."

I continue to narrow my eyes suspiciously. "In three years?"

"This is the part where you say, 'Awwww, Luke. You're so romantic.'"

"Yeah, whatever." I roll my eyes. "So. Going back to your question . . . a large part of me is perfectly happy to close my Match account, if that's what you're asking. But a *larger* part of me doesn't want to be a super optimist who puts all her eggs in one basket . . . when that basket fades out on people."

He nods.

"Also, if I close my Match account *now*, then I don't get my free six months."

"I forgot you're a newbie at this."

"And a cheapskate, too."

"Ha."

"Sooo . . ."

"Look, like I said. Mine's down. Yours doesn't have to be. I can't tell you where we'll be in a few months. Or, where you'll be in a few months."

"Right, because you don't like astrology," I say quietly.

Over brunch later that morning he asks, "So, is there anyone else I should know about from your Match past? Anyone who was notice-ably absent last night . . . or is still present in your life?"

"Well, I have a couple of ex-boyfriends still present in my life, but I didn't meet any of them on Match."

"Mmmhmm." He nods.

"I still consider my college ex-boyfriend one of my best friends, though he doesn't live in New York. And my other ex-boyfriend,

Dave, who I think I mentioned before . . ." He nods. ". . . was there last night."

"Wait." He looks taken aback. "He was on the boat last night?"

"Yeah."

"Why didn't you tell me?"

This reaction surprises me. "I don't know," I stumble, "I . . . I didn't think it mattered. He's a friend, I wasn't going to introduce you two and say, 'Ex-boyfriend, meet current . . . man friend.' What would be the point?"

"Do you still see him?"

"Yeah." I nod.

"Are you sleeping with him?"

"Wait—are you *serious*?"

"I mean, if you're not . . . why be friends?"

I breathe in, trying to figure out how to explain this sufficiently. "I mean, we like, have dinner together. Or lunch. We share a lot of mutual friends. I love his *family*. I don't know. . . . I guess I never really understood how most people can just flip a switch that's like, 'Ehh. Done with you. No more.'" I mime clapping dust off my hands.

"But attraction is such a big part of things. You can't flip a switch on that."

"I don't know. With self-restraint you can, or I can. . . . I mean, I know everyone is different, and I can never presume to know what goes on in other peoples' relationships, but . . . if someone plays such a big role in your life for so long . . . they basically become your best friend by default, right?"

Luke tilts his head from side to side, weighing this.

"You go *through* stuff. You grow, and you change, and . . . in a large part . . . you do a lot of that growing *together*. And the same way that you amass friends from that stage of life, because you've grown up together, I . . . I don't know . . . I guess I see them as part of who I am."

Luke looks mystified, so I follow up, "I mean, I don't hang on to people I've just gone on a few dates with—"

"—Well, except the guys from last night."

"—Well, right, but that's not *dating*. That's more like . . . meeting someone once for coffee or a drink. But anyway, for the people who've been *really* intertwined in my life . . . they're great guys! I dated them for a reason. I love having them as friends . . . still." I pick up my mimosa.

"Yeah, but they're guys. The attraction can't die for them," he counters.

"I don't know, for me it *does* . . . though I guess I'm very black-or-white. And I suppose I don't know what they're thinking." I take a sip from my glass. "But if you set really firm boundaries from the start—well in *my* experience at least—you can transition the friendship into a normal one, talking about people you're interested in, doling out advice. . . . I think you can crop out the romantic stuff and treat it like any other friendship."

"But if the breakup is rocky—"

"No, of course. If things end *badly*, like with lying or infidelity . . . you'd have no reason to want to be friends. Obviously."

"And have your relationships really all ended well?"

"The important ones, yeah. I guess I've been lucky? . . . I don't know. The point *is*: I just think that if you love someone, or love*d* someone, that shouldn't just vanish," I gesture a "poof" with both hands, "in a day. You can still value everything about them that you originally liked, just minus the physical-sexual stuff."

"I don't know . . ."

"Could you imagine if we just . . . broke up with our best friends? Like, all of a sudden, one day, 'End of friendship. Terminated.'"

"I don't know. It still just makes me uncomfortable."

"That I'm still friends with Dave?"

"Well, yeah."

"But you trust me though, right?"

"Look, I have no claim to you. You're not my girlfriend." My heart sinks with these words. "So I can't tell you what to do, but yeah. It makes me uncomfortable."

Changing the subject slightly, I ask, "So your serious girlfriend . . . ex-girlfriend . . . before. You don't talk to her anymore?"

"No."

I nod, not sure where to take the conversation from here.

"Her name was Mia." He plays with his coffee stirrer. "I don't think I ever said her name out loud when we talked about her."

"No, you didn't," I say, gently, "but that's okay."

"Yeah. Well, it ended badly, and we wouldn't have had anything to say to each other after the fact."

"Do you mind if I asked why it ended 'badly?'"

"To be honest, I don't really remember. But she had a flair for the dramatic . . . she was Latin," he offers up as justification, "so she was always getting riled up, yelling, sometimes throwing things. And so I ended it, and naturally, that went badly."

He leans back, stretches his arms above his head, and yawns. "Anyway, I think we got off topic," he says. "The point *was*: You can see whoever you want to see. I'm not the boss of you." And then, after a pause, "But I don't think I could be friends with my exes. And I don't think I could be friends with you, because even if you have superhuman self-restraint, I wouldn't be able to keep my hands off you." He leans in and kisses me.

"Ha. Nice salvage, buddy."

* * *

August 4 at 6:59 p.m.

LUKE: WHAT ARE YOU WEARING?

LUKE: SORRY, THAT CAME OUT WRONG. WHAT ARE YOU WEARING TONIGHT? HOT OUT, BUT SUPPOSED TO RAIN.

ALISON: YOU ARE TOO FUNNY - ALWAYS TRYING TO MAKE SURE I DON'T WHIP OUT THE PROM DRESS. BUT SINCE I KNOW WHAT YOU WERE REALLY TRYING TO ASK: WHAT ARE YOU WEARING RIGHT NOW? AND CAN YOU TAKE IT

. . .

ALISON: . . . KIDDING.

After dinner at Upland, we walk over to Wine:30, a nearby wine bar. As Luke waits for his credit card to be returned to him, he asks, "So, do you . . . wanna come home with me tonight?"

"I have to get up early. But, yeah, I think that can be arranged."

He nods, leans in, and kisses me as I remain seated on my bar stool. Whenever I'm with Luke, he somehow manages to get me to abandon all of my previously held misgivings about public displays of affection. When I think about this objectively, even *I'm* grossed out by our PDA.

For reasons not totally clear to me, Luke suggests we relocate to the bar of the W Hotel in Union Square. As we walk there, I rattle off the history of the structure and its prior incarnation as the Germania Life Insurance Building, which I learned about in grad school.

When we finish our round of martinis, Luke asks, "Do you . . . wanna get another one?"

I look at him quizzically. "*Yes*, I can drink another drink; but *also*, I can't help but wonder why you want to stay out drinking since I already said I'd go home with you?"

"Wait. You did? No, inside Wine:30, you said you wouldn't."

"No." I shake my head. "I said, 'I have to get up early, but that can be arranged?'"

"Wait. If you said that, then why are we still here?"

"Beats me." I laugh. He stands up with a start, grabs my hand, and practically yanks me through the revolving doors and into a cab that he immediately hails on Park Avenue South.

We're seated in the cab. "Did you *really* say that?"

"Yes." I nod, giggling. "Not to sound slutty, but we've had lots of sleepovers before. To paraphrase my Jewish peoples, 'Why would this night be different from all other nights?'"

"God, I *am* getting old. I totally heard something different."

"I wondered why we were still paying for drinks at high-end places. . . ."

We're lounging in his bed, our fingers intertwined, our legs overlapping each other's. He kisses me and pulls his head back.

"So, I don't want you to feel pressured, but I just want you to know . . . I'm ready."

"Ready for what?" My stomach forms a knot.

"You know. Ready to . . . become your *lover*."

"You make it sound gross when you say it that way." Then it dawns on me. "Ohhh, *this* is why you thought tonight was different from all other nights. . . ."

"And?" He kisses me. "What do you think of my proposition?"

"I think . . ."

He leans in and kisses me, deeply. "I mean," he kisses me again, "don't you think, we'd have . . ." he rolls on top of me, "just . . . *amazing . . . sex?*"

My heart skips a beat, a sensation all too familiar lately. I kiss him back. "We would. Undoubtedly. . . . Except we can't. Not yet, at least." *I can't relive my James mistakes. If I'm falling ten times harder, won't the fallout be ten times worse?*

"You sure?" He kisses me and grabs my arms and pins them down, gently, on either side of my head.

"I'm sure," I say, willing myself so desperately to keep both my composure and my willpower.

"And why"—kiss —"is that?"—kiss.

"Uhh, because . . . I hope this doesn't ruin the moment but . . . there are some things that need to happen. Before I'm ready to . . ." I trail off.

"Have sex with me?" He kisses me again.

"Yes, that. Thanks."

"And they are . . .?"

"Well, for starters, I know I sound like a junior high sex ed teacher, but . . . I would need you to get tested?" I bite my lip and wince with embarrassment. Not that I've done it so many times, but I've always loathed broaching this subject, especially since I know of only one friend who makes the same request. The impetus is part safety, part self-assessment: If I'm not comfortable enough to ask—and they're not comfortable enough to oblige—I probably shouldn't be sleeping with them anyway, right?

"Okay." He shrugs. "What else?"

"Well, let's start with that and work from there. . . ."

"Oh. No problem," he says, upbeat. "I'll call next week for an appointment."

"Really?"

"Yeah. Obviously." He kisses me again. "I was worried you were going to say something way more dramatic."

* * *

We're talking on the phone the following week, and Nicole's advice is still ringing in my ears. "*Push him to have deeper conversations.*"

While he tells me a story about a deejay class he took years ago, I rack my brain for a way to do this.

"So. Anyway, enough about me and my record-scratching days. Anything new with you?"

I see an entry point here. "No, not really. It's been a bit of an emotional week around the apartment. Cassie got . . . I don't know, not *dumped* because they weren't really dating, but . . . dismissed by a guy she met on Tinder? She's really sad. And I'm sad for her, but it's become one big Leona Lewis concert over here again."

He laughs, then adds quickly, "Oh, sorry. I was laughing at the idea of a private Leona Lewis concert . . . not at Cassie's expense."

"I know. . . . I try to help her, but I can't totally relate, because it was, like, three dates. I feel like you can't let yourself get hung up on three dates. But I need to try to be *sym*pathetic, if not *em*pathetic. . . . What about you?"

"What *about* me?"

"Do you . . . I don't know, ever get the blues? Or . . . get sad?" I add quickly, "Outwardly you're very stoic."

"Yeah, maybe. I don't know. More . . . pensive than sad or blue."

"So what do you do when you get . . . pensive? Do you . . . *talk* to people, or rage, or . . ."

"I don't know. I . . ." Luke has music playing faintly in the background, so his words are hard to hear, and I miss the second half of the sentence.

"Puffy paints?" I repeat. And then before he can reply, I fabricate my own version of what Luke must do when he's "pensive." "So, you, like, stock up on old sweatshirts and canvas bags, and you paint pictures of really sad things. Like wilting flowers . . . and blind three-legged dogs?" I laugh at my own joke.

"No, *huff* paints. I *huff* paints."

"Oh."

"I'm kidding, you know."

"Oh. Yeah, I knew that. Well," I say defensively, "I liked my coping mechanism better. I'm picturing you with your neon puffy paints, decorating sweatshirts you sell on Etsy." And once again, the conversation devolves into giddy laughter and joke one-upmanship.

That Friday, my phone vibrates on my desk in the office.

	August 11 at 3:13 p.m.
LUKE:	TELL ME A JOKE.
ALISON:	TOO MUCH PRESSURE. YOU'RE GIVING ME STAGE FRIGHT.
LUKE:	C'MON. I COULD USE A GOOD LAUGH . . .
ALISON:	OK, HERE GOES. BUT ONLY BECAUSE YOU SEEM REALLY STRESSED ABOUT WORK THIS WEEK, AND BECAUSE I'M REALLY NICE.
ALISON:	CUTE LIL SNAIL ENTERS THE INDY 500. HIRES A DESIGN TEAM TO PAINT & BEDAZZLE HIS CAR WITH S'S ALL OVER. CAR IS MUCH ADMIRED BY ALL. BUT WHAT'S WITH THE S MOTIF?
LUKE:	I'M ON THE EDGE OF MY SEAT HERE . . .
ALISON:	HE CAN'T WAIT TO HEAR THEM ALL SAY, "WOW! LOOK AT THAT S CAR GO!" . . .
ALISON:	UMM. SO. THAT'S WAY BETTER IN PERSON. YOU TRY TELLING A JOKE VIA TEXT. IT'S HARD!
LUKE:	NOT TOO SHABBY, ALSY.
LUKE:	I'VE ACTUALLY HEARD THAT ONE BEFORE. IT'S MY DAD'S FAVORITE. BUT YOU DID WELL UNDER PRESSURE. I NEEDED THAT.
ALISON:	ROUGH DAY?
LUKE:	WILL BE BETTER WHEN I SEE YOU TONIGHT.

I'm lying in his bed flipping through a *Rolling Stone* I took off his nightstand. "Don't get mad, but I think I tracked sand into your bed!" I call out to him.

"I told you riverside drinking can be dangerous!" he calls out from the bathroom.

He takes a running start out of the bathroom and dives across the room onto the bed next to me. "I've got something to tell you."

"Jason was *right*." I stick my nose into his chest. "You *do* smell good."

"Yeah, that was kinda funny, how he kept telling me that all night."

"I thought he might be hitting on you. Uh-oh, are you gonna leave me for Jason?"

"I don't know, he seems like a pret-ty cool guy." He smiles. "But seriously, I'm actually glad you let him tag along. He's cool. I'm glad I met him finally."

"Yeah, he liked you, too."

"Good location choice, too. It was fun to, you know, see you in a different setting. Running around, being all cute, playing volleyball with me and Jason and a bunch of strangers."

"Isn't that bar the *best*?" I marvel. "I just love it there. Highlight of every summer."

"So. I've got something to tell you."

"Oh yeah. What's that?" I prop myself up on an elbow, mirroring his posture.

"I got some test results back this week that you might care about."

"The CFA?" I gasp.

"No. Oh, no I already got those back. I passed." I cock my head, *why didn't you tell me?* "I'm clean. No HIV or gonorrhea . . . or anything else for me."

He smiles, and I smile. And then my nerves tense, and I swallow. "I'm . . . really glad you got tested. So thanks for doing that, but I guess I still need, like, a tiny bit more time to feel . . . ready."

He nods and kisses my forehead. "Okay."

"I'm actually fine talking about it, in fact maybe we *should* talk about it. I just . . . think there needs to be more of a—"

"—No, we don't need to talk about it. Take your time."

"—Okay, but . . . actually, I'd *like* to talk abou—"

"—We can do other things. Let's not talk about it right now," he says, then kisses me deeply.

I melt. These passionate kisses, the grazes, the gropes, the grabs—they're going to be the end of me. "Luke, I just . . ." My heart beats ever faster. "I need to hear—"

"Shhh." He nuzzles into my neck, gently nibbling at the skin. Then he reaches for the corner of the afghan blanket at the foot of his bed, throws it over me, climbs underneath it, and starts kissing my ankles and working his way up my body.

* * *

"You want anything?" I call to Nicole from the fridge.

"Nah. I've got yogurt. Maybe a glass of water though?"

"Sure thing." I fill two glasses and move to join her on the couch. I put the glasses on the table, sigh dramatically, and sink into the couch beside her. "Well, that's it. I'm a goner."

She laughs lightly. "It was just a matter of time. That much was clear weeks ago."

I perk up. "How can I kick this?"

"Sometimes you *can't*," she says, licking her yogurt spoon.

"Is it possible? . . . like, any chance at all, if miniscule? . . . that *he* gets as nervous, or charged, around me as I get around him?"

"It's possible," Nicole concedes, "but not very likely."

"Ugh. I don't know what to *do*," I lament.

"It's not necessarily a bad thing."

"It *is*. At least for me. It's like I have first-day-of-school jitters again. Except every single day. Even when I'm not seeing him that day."

"Do you feel jittery when you're actually *around* him?"

"Sometimes yes. But usually no. I actually feel pretty normal—jubilant and normal—when I'm on the phone with him, or hanging out with him . . . it's just all the time in between that's frickin' miserable." I add, "And because I only *see* him once or maybe twice a week tops, I feel miserable and jittery, like, 95 percent of the week. Ahhhhhhh, this *sucks*," I grumble.

"You do look skinnier."

"I'm not hungry anymore . . . and I *love* food," I grouse.

"Maybe you should talk about it with someone who could help."

"No." I bat the idea away with a wave of my hand. "I don't have the time for that. Or the money."

"I didn't mean it quite that way. I meant, like . . . what about Older Luke?"

* * *

Once it became clear I was gravitating toward Younger Luke, my flurry of correspondence with Older Luke necessarily tapered. However, I recently decided that enough time had elapsed that we might be able to be friends. I suggested as much via email, and he seemed flattered and pleased with the suggestion. So now we're running buddies. One or two afternoons a week, we circle the outer loop of Central Park while chatting about work and news, or gossiping about my friends and their dating lives. But until now, we haven't touched the subject of our own personal lives.

"Would it be . . . weird if I told you about an . . . emotional . . . hiccup . . . I've been having lately?"

"Why would that be weird?"

"Well, because it revolves around my dating life." I keep my eyes focused on the pavement.

"No, that's not weird. Or it shouldn't be. I consider myself a very good listener."

"I know. And you are! And . . . that's why I thought maybe I could run it by you. Like you could . . . shed insight? Or help?"

"Is it anything serious? Or . . . what's up?"

"No, it's not serious. Just . . . I've been really on edge lately. Not, like, angry on edge. Or frightened on edge. More like jittery. I feel like I can't get my heart rate to quit soaring, like I'm always waiting for something to go dramatically wrong."

"If it's anxiety you're experiencing, I could refer you to someone. You know, to talk to professionally. Or to prescribe you something."

"No." I sigh. "I don't think I need to talk to anyone professional. Well, other than you. So long as you're comfortable with this. . . . If you're not, please say so and I will stop talking immediately." I mime turning a key to lock my mouth shut.

"Sure. I can definitely talk to you about it. But if you wanted meds . . . or more regular sessions, there's nothing wrong with that."

"No. It's not like that. Well, it's two things. Hang on, hill."

I wait until we've finished ascending the hill so I can regain my breath. "Okay, sorry. First of all, I'm really only anxious because of *him*. Like, if he vanished, 'poof,'" I mime tossing a puff into the air, "I think my heart rate would just . . . plummet back to normal." I frown at this, knowing it's true. How, or why, can someone I'm so attracted to make me feel like I've become unhinged? "And *second*, I think if you had a Magic 8 Ball, that would serve me better than meds. Maybe make me go back to normal?"

"How do you mean?" He turns his head to look at me, then faces forward again as we keep jogging.

"Is this one of those things where you don't know what a Magic 8 Ball is? Like a Ring Pop? . . . Luke, it's like a crystal ball that gives you *answers*. About the *future*."

He laughs. "Yes, I know what a Magic 8 Ball is, Alison."

"Well . . . I just want to know: Is this going to hit the fan as hard as I'm bracing for? Because if so, I should get out while I can. Before it ends in tears. And if not, maybe I can breathe, and . . . you know, *enjoy* the relationship a little more. Or at least the summer a little more. I've never felt anxious or nervous for no reason."

"Maybe focus on asking yourself, 'What's the worst that can happen here?' I'm not trying to minimize what you're feeling, but if it did, say, 'hit the fan hard,' it wouldn't be the end of the world, would it?"

"No," I admit. "My brain knows that. I just need my *body* to get with the program and understand that, too."

"Have you thought about trying to decompress? Like do yoga or something?"

"Yeah, I took up yoga with Cassie a few weeks ago hoping it would do the trick . . ."

"And?"

"No dice," I sigh.

"Maybe you're doing it wrong."

"I *know* I'm doing it wrong. I'm *that* girl, who sits in the way way back of the room, and the instructor *still* manages to spot me and call out, 'Good. Good, everyone. Hold that pose. Oh, wait! Except you. You there, in the back of the room! You're doing it all wrong!'"

He laughs. "Maybe that's a good metaphor for how you're handling this current relationship. Aren't you supposed to focus on your breathing, your core, your chi, or whatever. There's no such thing as competitive yoga, right?"

"Ugh, you're no help," I say flatly. "Aren't you supposed to say, 'Oh? You've recognized the problem? You've taken up *yoga*? You're on the right track'. . .?" I nod with enthusiasm.

"I don't know, you seemed pretty relaxed and mellow to me when we were . . . dating. Can you get back to that part of yourself? Or try to channel it?"

"I don't know. You're the doctor. Can you tell me how to do that? Please?"

* * *

August 15 at 8:01 p.m.

LUKE: HEY. I COULD USE A NIGHT OFF. WANNA DO SOMETHING THURS-DAY??

I can't help but beam when I read this. Two nights in one week? *PROGRESS*!

ALISON: YES TO THURSDAY. I HAVE BEN'S FRIEND'S CONCERT DOWNTOWN FROM 8-9. WANNA COME WITH OR MEET AFTER?

LUKE: YEAH MIGHT DO THAT. AM GONNA TRY TO GET TO THE GYM NOW. FEELING FLACID - SUCH A GREAT WORD. WILL CALL AFTER.

ALISON: SWOON! I MEAN - LIKE, WHOA - YOU'RE PRACTICALLY A MODERN-DAY CYRANO, THROWING AROUND WORDS LIKE "FLACCID" IN TEXTS TO THE LADIES . . .

LUKE: AND MIS-SPELLING IT, TOO! THANKS FOR THE SLY CORRECTION. YOU'RE FUNNY.

In a glorious turn of events, Luke not only comes to the concert, but he joins me and my girlfriends for drinks beforehand. After, he and I find the nearest restaurant and sit down for a (very) late dinner.

Our martinis arrive at the same time as our food, and I pick mine up first. "I know you're not big on group activities, or staying out late on a school night, so I just want to say thanks for coming out. That was pretty cool of you, and pretty fun for me."

He lifts his glass to meet mine. "Alright, cheers." He smiles, clinking glasses. "Cheers," he says again, to himself. "It's such a funny word."

"Isn't it like . . . 'cheers!'" I raise a fist in the air, cheerleader style.

"Oh. I guess so. I never thought of it that way. But you know that guy at the office I can't stand?"

"The Squeak?"

"Yeah, the Squeak." He laughs. "You're a good listener."

I shrug.

"Anyway, the Squeak always says 'Cheers.' Like, 'Cheers.' 'Cheers!'" Luke says in a girlie voice.

"Is he British? Or Australian?"

"No, he's just really annoying."

"But *I* say cheers."

"Yeah, but when . . . like . . . toasting. Which is normal."

"I also use it in emails all the time."

"I know, and I thought you were lame, too, the first time I got your email."

"Hey!" I scowl.

"But now I know you, and it's cute when you say it. Also, you never say it, you only write it. *He* says it when he hangs up the phone."

"Oh that *is* weird," I say, in mock judgment. "Except now I need to come up with a new e-signature. . . ." I sigh.

Something in our conversation over dinner convinced Luke that he needed to see photos of my work in the Armory. Immediately. So now we're back in his apartment, I am seated on his lap in front of his computer and clicking through the photos of the rooms I've worked on and the murals I've exposed.

He hiccups.

"Was that a hiccup?"

He shakes his head no without saying a word.

"It *totally* was. And now you're holding your breath." I point my finger at him accusatorially. "Luke, this level of drinking *cannot* continue. For either of us!"

"Especially," he hiccups, "if we're now doing it on weeknights." He hiccups again.

* * *

Luke's sister and her family are driving up to visit today, and Luke asked me to spend the day with them. (My heart nearly exploded.) When I get out of the shower and am toweling off my hair in his bedroom, I pause and listen more closely to the music playing on his speakers. He's hunting for clothing in his wardrobe on the opposite side of the room when I ask, "Is this," pointing my forefinger in the air, "you?"

He walks over to me and wraps me in his arms. "You said you wanted to hear my music. Or Nat Rivers's music." He smiles.

"I did. I do." I smile and search his eyes. "Thanks for sharing it with me."

"Here." He walks over to his desk then back to me. "I burned you a CD of it. You know, in case you want to listen to more."

"Of course I will. Luke," I pause, again pointing up to the speakers, "You're really *good*."

Luke's sister is almost as easy to talk to as mine. As I help her unpack the toys and the Pack 'n Play for her twins, she asks me all about my job and tells me about hers.

"These little guys," Luke says from across the room, where he's playing with the twins and their father, "they are nothing if not easy to amuse." Luke's sister and I finish unpacking and walk over to join the play circle.

"It's like they can fixate on *anything*. We should monetize this somehow, like make a new line of video games aimed at babies. Like . . . Wii Door," he says as one of the twins repeatedly opens and shuts the red kitchen cabinet closest to the ground.

"*Or*, Wii Light Switch," I suggest, nodding my head toward the other twin who has been standing on a chair, aided by his father, for the last five minutes flipping the light switch on and off. "*Or* Wii Fan. The possibilities are endless."

The adults all laugh audibly, politely, at my joke. "See?" Luke says, "I told you she was funny." And inexplicably, my stomach knots itself again.

While we're standing on the subway platform waiting for the L train, Brady, the twin who I'm holding, gets his fingers caught in my hair.

"Oh no, I'm so sorry he did that. Braaaady," his mother sings.

"No, it's totally fine. It was my fault for not pulling it back when playing with toddlers."

"Hey, Brady!" Luke commands in a whisper, "I know she has pretty hair. But quit trying to steal my woman."

I blush.

At that moment, Brady's pacifier drops out of his mouth and onto the subway platform. Luke bends down to pick it up. He hands it back to his sister. "Ick. Sorry about that." Commotion ensues as his sister and brother-in-law debate how they can survive a whole day without a pacifier. "What do you need to do to . . . clean it off?" Luke asks.

"I don't know. Find disinfectant, maybe just find a store and buy a *new* pacifier."

Wordlessly, Luke pops the pacifier into his mouth to suck off any residues or germs.

"Oh my goodness." Luke's sister clutches her hand to her heart. "Brady, look! Isn't Uncle Luke the *best* uncle there is? How nice is Uncle Luke??" She and her husband praise Luke for having "saved the day."

Luke turns to me. "See? I *care* about people. Hermit, my ass."

"You are not kissing me ever again," I say, teasing.

* * *

"I'm sorry . . ." I clench my jaw and unclench it, focusing my eyes on the gray laminate conference table before me, trying not to meet Joanne's cutting gaze. ". . . But I'm not sure I entirely understand. What does that mean, 'on notice?'" *Is that, like, being fired? Or being* pre-*fired?*

"You'll have another midyear review this winter. Between now and then, we need to see more dedication, more initiative, more creative thinking—the attributes you and I discussed in my office a few months ago."

"I'm . . . not trying to contradict you, I'm just . . . a little . . ." I breathe in, trying to steady my voice. "Apart from the conversations you and *I* have had, no one at RA has ever given me anything other than positive feedback." I swallow, hard. "You keep saying 'we,' but . . ." I trail off.

Joanne glares at me sharply. "Your annual review is based on the collective assessment of *all* the principals here. We've made that very clear."

"Okay. Sorry. Umm . . ." I swallow again.

"I hope you view these next six months as an *opportunity*," she intones. "We are giving you nearly half a year to turn your performance around. And I think you'll agree that I've adequately laid out the improvements we hope to see in that time."

NOBODY WOULD EVER SAY I'M NOT A CREATIVE THINKER! I silently scream at my desktop computer. *Impatient, hurried*—these are criticisms I would understand. But "not a creative thinker?" It was *my* idea to tint the new, nonmatching Guastavino tiles, *my* idea to reverse the copper-paint corrosion at the Armory with household products like white vinegar and raw potatoes, *my* idea to adjust the pH of tap water and use it to remove overpaints on the murals at Grace Church. I rub my temples and sigh deeply. I'd almost prefer she say I'm not a nice person.

My eyes are fixed on the clock at the lower right hand of my computer screen. How am I going to make it through the remaining three hours of today? How am I going to make it through the next six months?

* * *

"Alsy, that was terrible. I can't believe you made me do that," Luke complains the following weekend.

"What. Run?"

"Yes."

"I'm sure you will find a way to get back at me someday."

"Sweaty kiss!" he cries out and throws his arms around me as we exit Prospect Park.

"Ahhh! Stop!" I turn my cheek and push his face away teasingly.

"Oh, c'mon. You *love* it."

And I do. But I pretend I don't and roll my eyes, feigning aggravation. It's much more fun this way. "Maybe after we're clean. Besides, your hair looks weird and matted. Let me fix it." I run my hand through his sandy-colored hair to lift it up.

"Make. Me. Pretty!" he exclaims, rubbing his head around in circles in my hands. And for some reason, this goofy gesture makes my heart hiccup.

He exits the shower and enters his bedroom with his towel wrapped around his waist. "You know what I was thinking about in the shower?"

"Is this going to be dirty?" I say from the bed, where I'm reading.

"Well, no. But I was thinking about that, too. But, I was thinking that everyone should have an Alison in their life."

"Oh?" And again, that melting sensation overwhelms my heart, my body. I swallow hard as my eyes start to well up. *Pull yourself together, Alison.*

"Yeah. I think everyone should have an Alison in their life," he repeats. Then he pauses, and I'm not sure what he's waiting for, so I say "Awwww" and smile, trying not to cry happy tears.

He lies down on the bed next to me and kisses me. "Do you think everyone should have a Luke in their life?"

"Ohh. Hmm." My eyes search the room as I pretend to ponder this. "That's a tough question . . . I don't think that's necessary, no." I shake my head teasingly. Then I wink and peck him on the lips before sitting up. "Can we go have that ice cream now?" I climb out of bed expecting him to follow me, but instead he reaches out, clutches my wrist, and pulls me back onto the bed.

Laughing, I spring from the bed, making it two steps farther this time, and he reaches out, grabs onto my leg, and pulls me back onto the bed, sideways this time.

I try this one more time, make it even farther, and he launches himself off the bed and tackles me to the floor, both of us in a shared fit of laughter. When he has my arms pinned on the floor beside my head, he asks, "Are you going to give in this time? Or do I have to do it again?"

When I can finally stop laughing, I nod yes.

"Well, good." He kisses me deeply again. And again, this is bliss.

* * *

August 29 at 8:44 p.m.

LUKE: WHY IS IT THAT EVERY TIME YOU COME OVER I PUT THE ICE CREAM IN THE FRIDGE?

ALISON: WEIRDLY, I TOTALLY SAW YOU DO THAT YESTERDAY AND THOUGHT "I GUESS LUKE WANTS HIS 2ND HELPING TO BE SOUPY" AND THOUGHT BETTER OF POINTING IT OUT. THIS IS THE THIRD TIME, YES?

August 31 at 10:58 p.m.

Hey Luke,

Apologies for my word vomit of last night -- as you've learned, I tend not to be super articulate when trying to talk about "feelings." I lose all my words & do this awkward dance thing. But, now that I'm out of the group dinner, in a room where I can find the light switch, and have had some time to let our conversation marinate, I just wanted to say a few things that, in my confusion, I didn't think to say (er, at least I don't think I did? I was flustered). This is not a rant or criticism of you. I'm just sad and confused.

It felt really strange to hear you say we weren't headed where you wanted to be. . . . For these past months I'd been feeling insecure in our relationship, unsure of how much you liked me, or if you even liked me at all. I did my best to ignore that and go with the flow because - well - smart and interesting dudes who make me laugh and laugh and laugh are extremely hard to come by.

Then you started to perk up - calling more, plan-making more, even coming with me to Tim's concert when you weren't sure you should go out that week. In our one previous "relationship" discussion, you asked me to be patient, reassuring me we were moving slowly because you didn't want to blow something that had such good potential, and saying, "Don't worry, babe, we'll get there." And Monday night you were adorably affectionate (maybe more so than ever before) and cuddly. Our conversations felt deep in a comfortable way - and we weren't even drunk. Then you said the most romantic thing of all: "Everyone needs an Alison in their life." Swoon! And then two days later, you cut me out of your life.

I can't quite figure out what happened between Monday and Wednesday. And I don't know what I expect from writing this to you. Perhaps I just wanted to be a little clearer about what I'm feeling since I was caught off guard when we spoke on the phone last night. I feel disappointed and sad -- mainly because I think you're a pretty rad guy, and I'd hoped to see if we could develop a meaningful relationship. Still don't know how to end this since you mock the Squeak for saying "cheers,"

Alison

September 2 at 8:43 p.m.

I know you're hurt, and I'm sorry. Thanks for your thoughts. I've been kicking around our conversation for days, trying to figure out what to say or what to do. Unfortunately, my thoughts haven't cleared. I'll let you know if they do. You're a cool girl and I meant what I said about wanting to be friends. Let me know if you change your mind.

L

nadatsoca: Douchey Dan

The night Luke stomps on my heart, I go home, walk straight into Cassie's bedroom, and cry my eyes out to her and Nicole.

"After we got off the phone," Cassie announces, "I went out and bought something." She leaves the room and comes back with a giant carton of ice cream and three spoons.

I clap my hands with glee. "Edy's Slow Churned Cookies & Cream always makes *every*thing better!" I say in my most commercial voice. Most of the time, it does.

"Hang on." I run into my bedroom and come back donning the EX-BOYFRIEND pajamas. "Never miss an opportunity to show off this hot number," I say, red-eyed but laughing as I sit back down on the bed.

"What can we do to help?" Cassie asks, rubbing my back.

I perk up. "Can we do that Charlie Kaufman memory-erasure thing and pretend that I never met the tattooed banker? You know, *Eternal Sunshine* style?" Once the words have escaped my lips, I realize I've inadvertently reminded myself of Luke and the running joke about his Jedi mind-erasing tricks. The tears stream down my cheeks again.

"I so wish we could do that. We can pretend?"

"No," I gasp, trying to catch my breath. "You're right. I should probably quit living in a fantasy dream world." I dig my spoon into the quart and shovel more Edy's into my mouth.

"So, then, no, you *can't* do that. . . . But you *can* do yoga with me?" Cassie offers.

"Maybe. What else?"

"We could focus on the positives?" Cassie says.

"Like . . .? I can't think of any. You start," I say, reaching for the Edy's again.

"Like . . . I guess on the bright side, you never slept with him," she says, adding quickly, "or did you?"

"No." I sniffle and look around. Nicole hands me a tissue and I wipe my nose. "Thanks. I wanted to. Ugh, I wanted to so badly. That *pheromonal* attraction . . ." I tap my elbow twice like a wrestler, and then I wipe my nose again. ". . . Him and his stupid, stupid pheromones."

"So, can I ask why you didn't? I was wondering for a few months there," Nicole says.

I shrug. "Fear? Since our first date, I felt like I was frantically trying to remain in control and keep my emotions in check at all times. Like I might unwittingly let on how much I liked him and scare him off, or accidentally blurt out, 'I love you!'—not that I loved him, but you know . . ." I wipe away more tears. "Instead of having that 'slow burn' . . . with Luke, it felt more like a nosedive, if I'd give in to it. And I guess, some part of me always knew."

"Knew . . . ?"

"Knew that it wasn't . . . a *relationship*. I mean . . . my heart *ached* to be with him. It still does, but we never . . . *shared* anything. You know? No feelings."

"No future plans . . ." Cassie adds.

"Oh, GOD no. No plans for even, like, two weeks away." I look down at the carton of Cookies & Cream and I gasp. "I can see bottom! Guys," my gasp becomes a wail, "I can see bottom! Take it away from me, this is not going to amount to anything good!" My laughter mixes with tears, and they both hug me from either side.

"Ugh, I'm a mess!"

"No, you really deserve a good cry after this one," Nicole says.

Cassie frowns. "You really deserve several good cries."

"Oh, I think I'm getting those in, don't you worry," I try to say brightly, through gasps for air.

"So back to my original question: What can we do?" Cassie asks.

"Nothing." *Nothing. There is nothing I want right now . . . except to not feel this way.*

She follows up, "Do you want to watch a movie? Go for a walk? We can all get dressed?"

I shake my head slowly. I can't think of anything that will make me feel better.

"You can sleep in my bed tonight? And then we can run together before work?"

I stare at a knot on the floorboard. *Work.* Before, with Luke, the soul-sucking plight of work could be . . . not overlooked, but slightly ignored? My professional dissatisfaction somehow didn't seem quite as pivotal in the scheme of things. The passion of being with him, the thrill of being around him, even the less pleasant jittery nerves, they were a successful distraction from a situation that would normally induce considerable stress. And sadness.

But how can I face work *without* all that? Just the thought of waking up tomorrow feels onerous. Normal-me would spout, "You just need to put one foot in front of the other!" but I don't even feel like trying. I'm not sure I know how to try. I didn't know if Luke was my dream guy or "The One," but I thought I still had time to figure it out. . . . And now I can't imagine ever meeting someone who makes me laugh as incessantly, who makes me feel as euphoric.

In the beginning, in January, this new life, this new dating . . . hobby . . . felt so easy. So easy, fun, and carefree. It never mattered to me if, ten minutes into a date, I discovered there was no romantic potential. Meeting new people in and of itself was an exciting event, and it felt good—revivifying in a way—just to be getting outside and meeting *anyone*. But then I met Luke and that changed. I delighted in being around him, and our dates were heady and fun, but suddenly everything *mattered*. To me, at least. It mattered what we talked about; it mattered what he thought of me; it mattered whether I would hear from him again. For the first time in my life, I actually *tried* to make a guy like me.

Over the past eight months, I've probably corresponded with a hundred men and gone on fifty or sixty dates with three dozen of them. But now I'm back at square one, with nothing to show for it other than emotional bruises and a depleted stash of ice cream. I wish I could turn back the clock and get back to that time when everything was fun and easy and carefree. . . .

Cassie wordlessly collects my used tissues from my hand as Nicole passes me fresh ones.

"Al?" Cassie prods.

"Sorry, what?"

* * *

Later that week, I'm lying on my bed, staring at the ceiling. Nicole cracks open the door. "Hey. I knocked, but I guess you couldn't hear me."

"Oh. Sorry! Come in. Of course, come in."

"Are you okay?" she asks, giving me a sympathetic frown.

I nod slowly.

"Well, I hate to break it to you, but I think you need a new soundtrack."

"I know. But Coldplay has become my Leona Lewis."

"Yes, I can see that. But, *enough* of 'Yellow.' You need to at least pick a new song. Preferably from a new album."

"Can it still be Coldplay?" I look up hopefully.

"Fine."

"I'm going to make it 'Life in Technicolor.'" I climb over to my iPod docking station and click through to find it. "I feel like there's a message in that, and some symmetry. Yellow, now brighter, *Technicolor*. Also, it's a happy song."

"Okay. Well then that's a good choice," Nicole says, as if talking to a child.

I laugh. "So I take it you like it when I'm being histrionic?"

"No. Honestly? I *hate* seeing you this way."

"But. I mean, it *is* kind of funny, right?" I smile. "And I promise, it will be over soon. I just need time to . . . mope."

"Sometimes it helps to feel sorry for yourself. But, only in short bursts. How much longer do you think you have?"

"Oh, I don't feel sorry for myself. I feel *angry* with myself for not being able to rein this in." I gesture to the piles of clothing littering my floor and the wastebasket full of tissues. "But not sorry. As sad as I am for *me*, there are a lot sadder things out there. I know. Normal-people problems put mine to shame. . . ." I continue to stare at the ceiling.

"So, why can't you keep telling yourself that?"

"I am. I will. But first I feel like I need to let it all out. I feel like it's been building inside of me for months, all those jitters, heart palpitations, all the stomach pains . . ." A realization dawns on me so quickly I sit up. "Hey! You know what, though? They're gone! I feel sad and woe-is-me and everything, but I'm not nervous anymore! I'm *not* nervous anymore!"

* * *

Sunday morning, I sit on Ashley's rooftop with Cassie and Nicole.

"I didn't get to hear the story," Ashley says. "If you don't want to talk about it, I won't be offended. But if you *do* want to talk about it, I can be a new captive audience?" I run through the meeting of his family, the "Everyone needs an Alison in their life," the Sunday night wrestling in his room, and the dreaded phone call.

She gets out of her chair, walks across to mine, and hugs me tightly without saying a word. Naturally, I start to cry.

"Oh, no. No! No!" she pleads sweetly, fearful of the waterworks she inspired.

"No, I'll be fine." I wipe my eyes and laugh at myself.

"How'd you get through work this week?" she asks.

"I was so preoccupied, I sliced my finger open with a scalpel when collecting paint samples, and then I nearly gave myself a concussion by navigating my boom lift into the Drill Hall rafters. It was a miracle I survived the week at all." I laugh and then sniffle. And then cry some more.

"You know, hon, you just have to dust yourself off. Get back out there. Go on another date in a few weeks, whenever you're ready."

"Oh, no. I know." I wave at the air. "I actually have one tonight."

"*What?*" Cassie and Nicole say in unison.

"How'd you swing that so fast?" Ashley asks.

"Well, as you all know, I felt like I was constantly waiting for something to go disastrously wrong with Luke. And, I know it sounds crazy, but I thought that if I responded to really good messages when they came in on Match, I wouldn't feel . . . like I was totally giving all of myself over to him." I sniff, trying to clear my sinuses. "I didn't actively search or contact anyone on my own, but . . . I guess I thought of it as a life preserver to keep me from drowning?"

"Did it work?" Cassie asks.

"Are you kidding? Look at me! Of *course* it didn't work. . . ." I laugh and wipe my eyes with the back of my hand. "So tonight's guy . . . Dan . . . contacted me in early August, and, well, you guys know. You can postpone online dates for*ever*. I told him I was busy, traveling, whatever. All true things. And when I got home from work on Thursday, the night after . . . the *phone call* . . . I emailed him and said my schedule had freed up for Sunday."

"Do you think that's a good idea?" Cassie asks gently.

"I mean, clearly if I break down into *this* tonight," I gesture to my eyes and face, "it won't have been a good idea. But . . . I don't know what else to do." I'm a firm believer that you can talk yourself into anything. If I don't start forcing myself to *act* fine, I may never get there. "I feel like summer's my happy time, and now Luke stole it. So I need to break out my favorite suede boots, pretend autumn's arrived a few days early, and declare it a new chapter of life."

* * *

"Nice pick," Dan says as I meet him at the bar of Auction House.

"Thanks. It's kind of my favorite local watering hole."

"Yeah, I like the décor. It's like Renaissance palace meets—"

"—Dive bar?" I laugh. "I always say the same thing. Thanks, by the way, for trekking up here."

"You're pretty hard to pin down, you know. So I thought I should be gentlemanly and make it easy for you."

"Thanks." I smile. "And sorry. August was kind of . . . a crazy time for me."

"No problem. I'm glad our schedules finally aligned."

Dan tells me about how he moved into Manhattan a year ago from New Jersey.

"Why New Jersey?"

"I grew up there, went to college there, my job is there. So when I was living with my then-girlfriend, I bought a house out there to cut down on commute time."

"Did you buy the house together? With your then-girlfriend?"

"No, it's just mine."

"But now you live in Manhattan?"

"Yeah, when we broke up, I didn't want to be a single thirty-year-old in New Jersey. So I rented out the house and took a studio on the West Side, close to Penn Station so I could get out there quickly every morning."

I nod. "What's your house like?"

"It's small. I did a lot of work on it myself."

"Oh, awesome! I wish I had a place of my own that I could spruce up. I restore buildings for a living, so it would be a pretty good use of my skill set. I keep thinking I should quit my job and flip houses full-time."

"You wanna see pictures?"

"Yes, please!"

He pulls out his phone and swipes through photos of his ranch-style home. "Here's the dining room, which I Venetian plastered."

"Shut up. You did *not* Venetian plaster that all by yourself."

"Yeah I did." He nods and turns his head to mine. His deep blue eyes sparkle. He kind of looks like the Irish gypsies I've seen on TV with black hair, pale skin, and bold blue eyes. "You actually know what that is?"

"Of course! I restore, or retouch, Venetian plaster for work all the time. I've never done it from scratch though! So fun!"

"Yeah, it was fun."

"Okay, so promise that if you ever decide to Venetian plaster anything else, you'll call me? So I can come learn/help/watch?"

He laughs. "Okay."

Dan comes back with a second round of martinis, and I thank him and take one off his hands.

"So you were saying . . . that you *are* in business school? Or you just graduated from business school? Or . . . remind me what you said in your emails?"

"Right. So, I spent three years doing a part-time MBA program at Columbia. They call it the 'Executive MBA.'"

"And that means . . ."

"Instead of being full-time, you can keep your job and fulfill your coursework on nights and weekends."

"*That* sounds exhausting. So you work a full day and then go to class after?"

"No. You can, but my schedule was to have class three full weekends a month and alternate Fridays."

"And work was okay with that?"

"Yeah, work wanted me to do it. They paid for the program, so they approved the alternate Fridays off."

"Oh, cool. So, like a free MBA?"

"Yep, that's why I did it . . . well, and because I wanted the MBA."

"So . . . you're done now?"

"I'm about to be done. I'm four finals down, one-point-five to go, and then I'm done. I'll walk at graduation in December."

"That's awesome. Almost-congrats!"

"Thanks."

"So what's your remaining final? Finals?"

"Financial Statement Analysis."

"Ooh, sounds riveting. . . . Why is it considered one-point-five finals? And when is it?"

"It's the most heavily weighted class for me this semester, hence the one-point-five thing. And it's a take-home final, so you have twenty-four hours from when they distribute it before you have to turn it in."

"And when do you get it?" I take a sip from my martini.

"I got it this morning—" I'm so surprised by his answer, my mouth full of gin and vermouth sprays out and soaks his shirt. I freeze in place, my eyes wide and panicked.

"Umm . . . con-tin-ue," I sound out slowly. As he explains that his last final is due the next morning at 8:00 a.m., I maintain eye contact while trying to surreptitiously, carefully, wipe the martini pool from his white button-down shirt with my bare hand.

"Uhhh." I continue subtly patting at his chest and shirtsleeve with my hand. "I. Am. SO. Sorry!" I shut my eyes tightly and try to bury my face in my left, unsullied hand. "I can't believe I just did that. I am *so* sorry! I promise to pay your dry cleaning bill!"

"No, please. This is the most amusing date I've ever been on. Why was my answer so funny?"

"I don't know," I say, biting my lip. "I was just so startled. Like, you have your very last final of a three-year grad program, and it's due *tomorrow*, and you're here, drinking with *me*. For . . . hours! Why are you *here*? Don't you have a final to be slaving over?"

He raises an eyebrow. "You were pretty hard to pin down. Like I said. So I thought it might be a 'now or never' kind of thing. So I chose now." He shrugs.

I am so stunned by my own maladroitness that I can barely muster a word. I nod, repeatedly. "So." I cough. I laugh at myself, then clear my throat and try again. "So, do you have a late night ahead?"

He smiles at my attempt to play it cool and pretend like the last three minutes never happened. "Yeah, probably."

"Okay." I laugh again, and he laughs with me, or at me, or both. "Although I am seriously troubled about ending the date on such a . . . sloppy? note . . . I feel like I should let you go, right? Should we go?"

We walk up 89th Street to my corner. "Well, this is me. Good luck with your final. And thanks for coming out, especially given the circumstances."

"No, I'm really glad I met you. Do you want to do this again sometime? Maybe next week or weekend?"

"Sure. And . . . let me just reiterate how *sorry* I am. I mean, I think you can tell how *embarrassed* I am, but . . ."

"You? Embarrassed? Nope, couldn't tell." He smiles. "I'm kidding, by the way. But you can relax. It was actually cute."

I roll my eyes. "Stop humoring me. But good night! And good luck!"

September 4 at 10:09 a.m.

732-472-0818: THANKS FOR YOUR HELP PROCRASTINATING LAST NIGHT. HOPE WE CAN DO IT AGAIN SOON.

ALISON: GOOD LUCK WITH THE LAST 1.5 FINALS! HOPE YOU KNOW THAT MY SHOWERING YOU WITH DIRTY MARTINI WAS MY WAY OF SAYING "THANKS FOR THESE DRINKS" . . .

September 4 at 12:01 p.m.
Subject: Last night
Well, are you going to tell me about last night? Sorry I went to bed on the early side. I left you a note saying you were welcome to sleep in my bed. Hopefully you got it. It's an open invitation for as long as you'd like.

Love, Cassie

September 4 at 12:33 p.m.

Last night was fun. I did get your note - you are so sweet. I couldn't bear the thought of you losing any more sleep this week on my account, so I decided to give it a try on my own. I slept four hours, which ain't much but is better than three!

OK so all this talk of sleepovers leads me to a big guess what?

I hatched a plan last night during a fit of insomnia. And I actually think (maybe I'm in a worse place than you are, but whatever) it sounds viable: What if we decided to never ever date again? And to have sleepovers together and BYOB dinners with our friends (male and female) and to become rock stars in our fields and really good at yoga and running and then to adopt kiddies (we don't have to share them. You can totally have your own kids, and I can have my own. Or we can be mom partners. Either works for me) and get a bomb-diggity apartment and I'll cook and you clean and we live together in domestic harmony forever and ever? Either in New York or in Italian wine country?

Don't worry, I have weighed the drawbacks of this plan, and I fully agree: We're going to need to get laid by men, it's just that they're all too g-d demented to take seriously in relationships. Sooooo. Be swinger moms who rely on each other for good conversation and companionship and wedding dates and everything else that's important in life except for bedroom stuff?

I know you think I'm kidding.

Guess what?

I'm not.

Love!

Alison

September 4 at 12:42 p.m.

It's me again. Hi!

So wanna know something really weird?

*I literally convinced myself in the last five minutes that
that is the greatest plan of all time. And I even came up with
other people who might want to do the same thing and could
live on the floor(s) above or below us if we bought a townhouse (not that I need other people if you're around). Like
maybe Jason? I'm pretty sure Blaire's determined never to
marry. It would be like Sesame Street where we're all just
happy adult friends.*

* * *

Before our second date, I decided to do a little digging on Dan. Given
that his username is Nadatsoca, it didn't take a cryptologist to determine
that his full name is Dan Acosta. Based on just that keyword search, I
found out that he works for Honeywell's industrial technology, went to
Princeton, posts too many photos of the city skyline on Instagram, and
overuses the hashtag #nofilter. Working backward through his public
profile on Facebook, I can pinpoint the day he and his last girlfriend
broke up and see pictures of her. She looks like she stepped out of a
Pearl Jam-groupie beauty pageant with bleached blonde hair, leather
pants, and leopard-print everything. Maybe she hurt him so badly he's
seeking her polar opposite? Even barring that, the gold cross he wore
around his neck at Auction House, his Facebook profile photo displaying him shirtless, steering a boat, with a bottle of Captain Morgan in
hand . . . something tells me that soul mates we are not.

Over dinner at Maz Mezcal, Dan tells me about his close-knit enor-
mous family and band of thirty cousins. He tells me he's half Puerto
Rican ("Oh, I thought you might be Irish."—"I get that a lot.") and
that he grew up on Latin cuisine.

"Do you want another round?" Dan asks, when the waiter comes
by to check in.

"I will if you will."

I like talking to Dan and his piercing blue eyes. But I'm kind of
over dating people who I have no future with. When our drinks arrive,
I take a sip of liquid courage and begin, "You seem like a fun guy. So,

do you want to play a game? My friend Paige and I have this thing we call the 'three-martini question.'. . . When you've had three martinis, and you're a little more . . . open? . . . you get to throw caution to the wind and ask really probing questions that you might normally save for awkward conversations further down the road. I know we don't have *martinis* per se, but . . . can I tweak that and ask you a three-margarita question?"

"I don't know that I'd say this sounds like a *fun* game necessarily, but I'm up for it if you are. . . . This means I get to ask, too, right?"

I nod.

"Okay. Shoot."

"Okay. So." I take another sip of my margarita. "You wear a cross around your neck."

He nods.

"Which I take to mean that you are religious."

He nods.

"Do you go to church?"

He nods.

"Like, on your own? Or only with family?"

He looks at the ceiling and ponders this. "Honestly? Only with family."

"But it's important to you," I state, and he nods. "So . . . can I ask why you're on a second date with a half-Protestant, half-Jew who, according to her *Match.com* profile, is a self-professed agnostic?" I smile.

He nods, as if to himself. "I'm not gonna lie, you're the first non-Catholic girl I've gone out with."

"Because normally that's a deal breaker?"

He nods a few times, again to himself. Then says, "Yeah."

"So. Are you going to . . . just . . . throw your religious morals out the window here? Or . . . was this just an experiment in crossing over to the dark side?" I smile.

"No. Not that," he says, nodding. "You know, I thought about it. It's not like I ignored that detail or missed it. . . . I just, I guess over the years, I've decided that there are more important things."

"Okay."

"Would it be a deal breaker for you? That I'm Catholic?"

"No." I shake my head. "Keep in mind my parents both diluted their own religious backgrounds through an interfaith marriage. . . ."

"Does it bother you at all, though?"

"No." I shake my head. "I just figured if you were going to turn around and say, 'Ehh, forget it, I can only marry a Catholic,' I'd rather throw in the towel now." I add quickly, "*Not* that I want to marry you. I *don't* want to marry you." I feel my cheeks flushing again. I really need to start speaking more slowly so my brain can keep up with my mouth. I hang my head in embarrassment and sip on my margarita without looking up.

"Don't worry, I wasn't going to ask until at *least* the third date." He smiles. "Okay. So, my turn?"

I nod.

"Why are you on here? Match, I mean."

"Really? That's your question? That's not a three-martini question. That's, like, a sober coffee-date question."

"Well . . ."

"That's easy." I give him a quick summary of my serious relationships, explain my need to branch out beyond the population of my college graduating class, the same unintentional script I've been spewing off since January.

He nods. "Cool, that makes sense."

"I don't know. Doesn't *everyone* use websites or apps or platforms these days? Tinder, Bumble. . . . What about you? Why are you on?"

"I don't have that many friends in New York, so I feel like my circle's kind of small."

"From Princeton? I find that hard to believe . . ."

"Well, right out of college everyone was here. But at this point, most people have left. . . . So when the girlfriend I lived with," I get a mental picture of Nikki with her black choker necklace and fishnet tights, then try to abolish this picture from my mind, "and I broke up . . . I took a while to get over it. And then moved to New York. And then needed a way to meet people."

"Did she go to Princeton, your last girlfriend?" I ask, though I already know the answer.

"No."

"So how did you meet?"

"It started from a random hookup."

"Huh. Really?"

"Yeah, I woke up in the morning and she was gone, but she'd written her number in lipstick on my mirror."

That is one classy chick! "Wait, seriously?"

He nods.

And you are on a date with me because . . .? "How long were you together?"

"About five years."

"And you said you lived together. . . . Why did it end?" He looks taken aback, and although he's right—this question may have been a bit too probing for date number two—I wave my margarita glass in my hand. "Three-margarita question."

He smiles. "Honestly?"

I nod.

"I proposed and she said no."

And suddenly, all the feelings I've been grappling with come back at once, and my heart aches. For Dan this time, though. "I'm so sorry, Dan," I say softly.

"No, it's fine," he says confidently. "But, you know, when you live together for multiple years and propose and get rejected, you've kind of got no choice but to pick up and move on."

I nod. "That's terrible. Did she explain it? Her reasoning?"

"Kind of. Not really. She said she didn't feel ready to settle down."

"But isn't living together kind of settling down anyway? I feel like the marriage license is just the ribbon on the box or something."

"I agree. But that's what she said."

"So I imagine you didn't stay friends?"

"No. But it's kind of a funny story. We both moved out, and two months later, she calls me, asks to come over, and tells me that it was the biggest mistake of her life and she's been . . . I don't know . . . devastated ever since . . . and she asks me to get back together *and* to get married."

"What'd you say?"

"I said no." He shrugs.

"Why'd you say no?"

"I don't know. I think maybe it was a combination of things. I spent so long being angry at her, you can't just shove that aside and get over it. Also, during the time that I *was* angry, I spent a lot of time thinking about all the things that were wrong with her. Or with the relationship."

"No, but mostly with her," I say, half-smiling, and he raises an eyebrow. "Come on, you'd be right to. I'm not judging."

"Well, yeah. Mostly all the things that were wrong with her." He twirls his fork and watches it. "So, this time *I* said no."

"That must have been confusing. And hard." I nod, then he nods. "I'm sorry."

He blinks hard and shakes his head as if clearing it of these thoughts. "Whoa, your three-martini questions can get *deep*."

"Yeah, I've never actually had them be that deep before." I laugh. "Usually it's dumb stuff like, 'I kind of think you're hitting on me. Are you hitting on me?' Or," I add quickly, "that's how Paige always uses it at least."

Dan gets up to go to the bathroom. While he's gone, I check my phone. I have a new text:

September 12 at 10:13 p.m.

GREG: DID YOU JUST EAT MY SLIDERS AT OYSTERFEST?

I type back:

September 12 at 10:47 p.m.

ALISON: HIGHLY LIKELY. THE BLUE POINTS WERE DELICIOUS, SO I WANDERED AROUND PICKING UP THE FLOATERS. . . . SORRY IF I TOOK YOURS! IF YOU SAW ME STANDING NEXT TO YOU, WHY DIDN'T YOU SAY HI?

When Dan sits back down at the table, his demeanor seems to have changed. It's not that he's *not* being nice, or polite; he is, but he seems a little off, a little distracted perhaps? He walks me home after dinner, we hug goodbye, and he asks if I want to get together later in the week. I say yes and head inside. I open up my laptop and go back to Dan's Facebook page to take a closer look at this heartbreaker ex-girlfriend. And there, on his wall, is a new message from her:

September 12 at 9:23 p.m.

Hey Danny. You must be done with school by now. Was thinking about you and just wanted to say congratulations! You deserve it. xx

Posted today at 9:23 p.m. Aha! He must have received this notification on his phone when he got up to go to the bathroom. Which explains his distractedness from that point forward. How completely bizarre that without him ever telling me so much as her name, or his own last name, the Internet has enabled me to tease out Dan's emotional hang-ups. Also, why doesn't the girl use email or text for this kind of thing?

* * *

I meet Dan several days later at Madison Square Park for a dinner date at Shake Shack, a perfect date spot if ever there were one. We sit at a garden table, licking our fingers of dripping cheese, sharing fries, and sipping on peanut butter milkshakes. We talk about sports, specifically our experiences in intramural soccer (we played in different leagues), and this summer's World Cup, and Tim Howard. We talk about public art, specifically the sculptures surrounding us in the park. When we're busing our trays, Dan asks if I want to grab a drink.

We walk over to Vin Sur Vingt wine bar, pleased to discover that their happy hour lasts until midnight tonight. And then, before we know it, happy hour's over and the bar is closing down.

"Where did all that *time* go?" I remark as we exit the bar onto the sidewalk.

Instead of answering, Dan places a hand behind my head and makes out with me. And it's fun.

"So, do you want to . . . come home with me?" he asks.

"Not really," I say. "I mean, I'm having fun and all, but I kind of want to sleep in my own bed tonight. Wake up and run before work. *God*, work is in six and a half hours!" Then I add quickly, "Sorry. Didn't mean to say the . . . 'G' word."

He laughs. "It's okay. You might go to hell, but it's okay." He kisses me again, and I try to critique it while he does. Strong. Leading.

Passionate. I'm pleasantly surprised. "Can I come home with you?" he asks.

"Uhh, I mean, I guess you can? But, you're not getting in my pants tonight. So . . . don't get your hopes up or anything."

"But you're not *wearing* any pants!" he exclaims, slurring slightly.

I look down at my jersey dress. "Touché, but. You know. My *metaphorical* pants."

"Don't you hear it?" Dan scrolls through his phone quickly and then waves it in the air like a lighter as Phil Collins warbles, "I can feel it coming in the air tonight . . ."

"What. You just have that song at the ready for every girl you try to bed?"

"Just the good ones."

"Wow." I nod. "You take 'douchey' to a whole new level. . . . And I *love* Phil Collins!"

September 16 at 11:14 a.m.

732-472-0818: WHAT DID U DO TO ME LAST NIGHT? I FEEL LIKE I'M STILL SEEING DOUBLE.

ALISON: IS THIS DAN? ASSUMING IT IS, DON'T PIN THIS ON ME. BUT IF IT MAKES YOU FEEL BETTER, I THINK THERE'S A JACKHAMMER BEHIND MY EYE SOCKETS.

732-472-0818: DO YOU HAVE MANY 732ERS IN UR PHONE? COME ON ALREADY. ADD MY NUMBER.

732-472-0818: ALSO, WHAT'S SAY WE GET TOGETHER THIS WEEK?

ALISON: NOPE. NOT IN MY PHONE YET. THURSDAY? SORRY, MY ONLY FREE WEEKNIGHT.

732-472-0818: NO CAN DO. WORKING LATE. SATURDAY?

732-472-0818: ALSO. ADD MY NUMBER.

ALISON: OKAY . . . TO SATURDAY. ;)

September 27 at 11:01 a.m.

Subject: I'm so happy . . .

This email is overdue. I meant to send it to you Monday. Where did the week go?

I'm so happy that we finally got to have a one-on-one night out since everything that transpired with he-who-shall-not-be-named. I'm so unhappy that you're struggling, I just didn't want to title my email "I'm so unhappy," because that would only depress you further. If there's anything I can do, let me know. Picnics in the park, BYOB dinners, sleepovers, you name it, and I will be there with bells on.

In case you were curious, I managed to drunk dial Eric from bed after we got home Sunday. He didn't pick up and I didn't leave a message, but come on. What was I thinking? I'm cutting us off at round two next time.

Tell me how I can help.

Nicole

September 27 at 12:54 p.m.

Thank you! You're the best, as always. Goodness, based on your email, I feel like I must be making my silly saga sound much more depressing than it is. Don't worry. After repeating your mantra ad nauseam the last four days ("One day you will wake up and not feel this way"), I feel like I'm one step closer to getting my head back on straight. And though I'm a bit staggered by this weird lack of even keel, I guess life returns, whether you're ready for it or not.

Love!
Alison

P.S. You think that's bad? Did you not see me on the couch the next morning? I wandered out to the Gristedes at God-knows-what hour & picked up a gallon of ice cream, devoured half the carton while watching a marathon of How

*I Met Your Mother, then fell asleep with all my clothes &
makeup on. . . . Let's do it again soon!!!*

Thursday as I'm getting ready for bed, my phone vibrates and a text
message flashes on the screen.

> September 28 at 10:49 p.m.
>
> 732-472-0818: HEY, JUST GETTING HOME FROM WORK. YOU WANT TO COME
> OVER?
>
> ALISON: NO. AM NOT YOUR BOOTY CALL GIRL.
>
> 732-472-0818: CAN'T BLAME A GUY FOR TRYING.
>
> ALISON: EW.

The next night, I happen to walk by Vin Sur Vingt, so I text Dan:

> September 29 at 7:39 p.m.
>
> ALISON: JUSTWALKEDBYVINSURVINGT,ANDITHINKIFELTMYLIVERTREMBLE
> IN FEAR. . . . JUST THOUGHT YOU SHOULD KNOW.
>
> 732-472-0818: YOU'LL BE GLAD TO KNOW MY FINGER IS HEALING NICELY.
>
> ALISON: ???

* * *

The high-profile starchitects for the Armory are flying in from Switzer-
land for a Monday morning meeting to view the progress of our conservation efforts. Because the conservation team has been overworked and
understaffed, a reveal of the original paint scheme in one of the most
prominent public spaces has not been completed . . . or begun.

Throughout the duration of the project, the original murals in the
most famous rooms have been reserved exclusively for the hands of
RA's senior paint conservator, Cyril, who I both adore and revere. In
my opinion (and Bob Vila's, whose show Cyril often appeared on in

the nineties) he is the premier architectural paint conservator in the country. He also happens to be a terrific coworker, sharp-witted and flamboyant, full of fabulous stories that make you forget you've been standing on the scaffold with your syringe poised overhead for eight hours. And perhaps most wonderfully for me, he seems happy to have me as an eager disciple. But because he works in our Washington, DC, office and had weekend commitments, Cyril won't make it up to the Armory before the Swiss architects do.

In his best Princess Leia impersonation, Cyril phoned me at my desk on Friday and pleaded, "Help me, Alison. You're my only hope."

When I stopped by Joanne's office to discuss the task at hand, she said with typical bluntness that "while any work [I could] do over the weekend would be appreciated, [I] would not earn overtime or be otherwise compensated." *What a dream job!*

It's still only Saturday, and already I've spent twelve-plus hours kneeling atop a rolling scaffold, breathing heavily through my respirator, painstakingly removing 135 years of historic paint from the wall, layer by layer.

My phone vibrates on the metal scaffold, and I am relieved to have an excuse to take off my fogged safety goggles and sweaty latex gloves.

	September 30 at 7:25 p.m.
732-472-0818:	PS - U ARE IN MY PHONE AS "LIMITS"
ALISON:	HMM...I AM SOMEHOW INCAPABLE OF COMPREHENDING YOUR TEXT SPEAK TODAY (YOU MAKE ME FEEL SO BLONDE!). COME AGAIN?
732-472-0818:	U CAN PICK IT UP AS WE GO. BE IN TOUCH ESTA NOCHE, WITH LIMITS.

I see the time on my phone and realize I need to pack up if I have any hope of meeting Dan downtown by 9:30 p.m. as planned. I turn back to admire my work on the mural. The nineteenth-century pattern is exquisite: gilded urns flanked by peacocks displaying their full plumage across the cove; a burgundy paisley repeating pattern on the wall field. There hadn't been historic photographs of this room, so we had no idea what lay beneath the current plain yellow paint.

I snap a photo on my phone and text it to Cyril, promising I'll return tomorrow to complete the reveal and varnish the surface to make it picture-perfect for our Swiss colleagues on Monday. My phone vibrates four times, indicating two texts waiting.

September 30 at 7:29 p.m.

CYRIL: YOU ARE A GODDESS.

September 30 at 7:29 p.m.

732-472-0818:   ADD MY NUMBER

I text the same reply to each of them:

ALISON: NOPE. BUT APPRECIATE THE SENTIMENT. :)

"So what was that whole finger-healing-limits thing about?" I sidle up next to Dan at the bar of Death & Co. in the East Village later that night.

"Seriously? You don't remember?"

"I'm *sure* I remember, I just don't know what you're talking about."

"Remember when I sliced my finger open on your 'sculpture' or whatever?"

"Oh my gosh, I *do* remember that! That was . . . awful . . . and hilarious." I laugh. Dan had been admiring the "Dave Chihuly" on my bedroom windowsill when he touched it and instantly began gushing blood.

"Yeah, to you, maybe. I cut my finger pretty badly. I needed, like, five Band-Aids."

"Right! I just . . . out of context, didn't know what you were referring to. So, your finger's good now."

He holds it up, wrapped in a fresh Band-Aid. "Getting there."

"And the limits thing?"

"Oh, I don't know. That's just what I have you in my phone as."

"*Why?* I don't get it."

"Because you put limits on everything. 'Only three drinks tonight,' 'you're not taking off my pants tonight,'" he mimics a high-pitched girlie voice. "You're very . . . restrictive."

"Or . . . under control?" I suggest.

"With limits, under control, same thing."

* * *

October 4 at 4:35 p.m.

732-472-0818:   I'VE GOT A THREE MARTINI QUESTION FOR U.

ALISON: IDON'TTHINKYOUUNDERSTANDTHECONCEPTOFTHETHREE-MARTINI QUESTION, AS I AM SOBER AND AT WORK. BUT YOU CAN ASK ANYWAY, IF YOU LIKE.

732-472-0818:   WHAT R U WEARING RIGHT NOW, AND DO U WANT TO HANG OUT?

October 4 at 5:32 p.m.

ALISON: HA, SORRY-GOTSLAMMEDINTHELASTHOUROFWORK. UMM. CAN WESAY, "LIMITS"? ORATLEAST, "LET'SMAKETHATATRUE3-MARTINI QUESTION" FOR IN PERSON? BEHAVE, DANIEL.

Along with Ashley and Ben, Dan and I climb out the window of some-one's apartment (a friend of a friend of a friend), up their fire escape, over the parapet wall, and onto a huge flat roof that looks out on the Manhattan skyline on one side, the Brooklyn waterfront on the other. A sky full of stars twinkles overhead, and the roof is a mob scene of danc-ing, shouting, laughing men and women in shorts and dresses. There are strobe lights set up and a makeshift deejay booth in the corner with a legitimate sound system. "See? I *told* you this party was gonna be epic," I say. "It's like the last hurrah of summer."

"This might be the best party we've ever been to. Should we hit the bar first?" Ashley asks.

"I spotted a beer pong tournament in the corner near the bar? . . ." Dan suggests.

"Thanks, buuut . . . I'm cool." I shake my head.

"Oh come on, live a little," Dan urges.

"I think I lived through enough beer pong tournaments to last a lifetime . . . in *college*."

"Dance floor then?" Dan pulls me toward the dance floor, and I am surprised by how comfortably he can bust a move.

"So is this," I wave my hand at his body, "your Puerto Rican blood talking?"

"Awww, white girl can't dance?" he says condescendingly.

"Oh, it is *on*. I'll have you know that I was not *only* choreographer of my college dance troupe, I was *also* the president," I say, as I move my hips in time with the music.

"You sound like a Hair Club for Men commercial," he says. "So," he steps toward me, "put your money where your mouth is. It takes two to . . . dance."

"You were going to say 'tango.' You're ridiculous." And we dance. For hours.

The next morning, we wake up under Dan's leopard comforter. I have a suspicion about who picked this out for him. "Look at you, grown man with a leopard comforter. It's like you live in a sex den or something. Don't you think you should change it? Like, get something, I don't know, solid? Or with stripes?"

"Maybe one day. I don't know. It didn't stop *you* from sleeping over," he counters.

"Yeah, but it was late, and I was too tired to leave just on account of your decorating decisions."

"See? So it doesn't matter."

"I didn't say I was coming *back*."

"We'll see. . . ."

"So you think you, like, woo women into your lair and then get them to return because you have a sexy leopard comforter?"

"Look. Even if it *was* part of my larger plan to convert my apartment into a sex den, I'm getting the sense you're not my target demographic. You know, limits and all."

I laugh.

"That said, I have to admit, I never would have pegged you for a girl with hips like Shakira."

"Oh, shut up." I paw his face away.

"What? It's a compliment."

"Fine. I just feel like you act all surprised, like 'Oh, you're so buttoned up, you have so many limits, I thought you'd be this awkward preppy girl who can't dance.' It's . . . offensive." I grimace.

"Well, I mean . . . if the shoe fits . . ." He smiles and rolls toward me. "You wanna get brunch?"

Over brunch at his corner diner, Dan asks, "So, do you *really* not have me in your phone? Or are you just playing?"

"No, I really don't have you in my phone," I say as I cut into my omelet.

"Can I ask *why*?"

I look up at him and put my fork down. "Okay. I don't want you to take this the wrong way at all, because I think you're really great. But, well, let's first start with that: I think you're really great. You're *smart* and *accomplished* and I'm really attracted to you. And I actually think you're a good guy."

"But."

"*But*, you've asked me to sleep with you twice now. And I know that's how you roll, and it's fine. But, to be honest, that's just never going to happen."

"Oh?" He raises an eyebrow.

"I mean, Daniel, you're . . . kind of in a different place than me, I think." He looks at me blankly and says nothing. "You . . . prefer a booty call to an actual date, and when I *do* see you, you want to go out and drink our faces off, and then come home to your leopard-print lair. . . . I . . . well, I hate the term 'serial monogamist,' but I'm way closer to that end of the spectrum than you are." I add, "I mean, I love dancing and all, but . . . I feel like if we were going to make this . . . any kind of a regular thing, we'd be going off in two totally different directions." I make a "V" with my palms.

"So this means you don't want me in your phone because . . ."

"Well, just out of superstition, or not wanting to clog my address book, or something, I don't put guys I'm going on dates with in my phone unless I think it's going to be a *regular* thing. . . ." I pause. "I promise on some level, this makes sense in my head."

"And this isn't a 'regular thing' already?"

I look at the ceiling and try to formulate a response. "No. I don't think so. . . . Look, I'm not going to ask you to be something you're not, or to give me something that you can't. At least not right now, while you're . . . kind of in a fratty phase. I really like you as a person, but I feel like maybe . . . we should call a spade a spade and move on?" I pick up my fork and continue eating, while watching him for a reaction.

"Okay. I mean, I don't think you're totally right, but I get what you're saying."

"Okay. To be clear, I have a lot of fun with you. And you *know* I'm attracted to you. I just think we're not on the same page right now."

* * *

Three weeks later, I'm having drinks with Ashley at Middle Branch when I receive the following text:

October 30 at 10:08 p.m.

732-472-0818:   Hey. Where r u and what r u up to?

Alison: Who is this?

732-472-0818:   Have u met multiple 732ers in my absence?

732-472-0818:   Just got home from work. U want to come over? Where r u?

Alison: This could be . . . interesting. Showing up at some stranger's apartment? Like a Chris Hansen special. . . . I'm at 32nd and third, drinkin', actually.

732-472-0818:   Can I come join? Who r u w/?

Alison: I'm with Ashley. She says it's ok.

Alison: Who is this by the way? :)

732-472-0818:   Give u a hint: I've got a three martini question for u. Which bar?

732-472-0818: Also, did they not teach u about "deductive reasoning" over at Clown College?

Alison: Ah! Douchey Dan! What's up? How are you? Middle Branch.

Alison: P.S. Hey now, be nice. Did I ever mock your alma mater for its profusion of sweater sets, pearls, and tasseled loafers? . . . Oh wait, guess I just did.

Alison: P.P.S. did they not teach you to spell "you" and "your" at Princeton?

732-472-0818: Do not like that nickname. Be there in ten.

"Did I see *Dan* leave our apartment yesterday morning?" Cassie asks as we ride the subway downtown to work Wednesday.

"Yes," I say tentatively, ashamed. "Don't judge me!"

"I'm *not* judging. I'm just . . . confused. Didn't you end it with him?"

"I did. Yes. But then, Monday night I was out with Ashley, and he texted. She was ready to go home, and I was, well—you know I'm still having trouble sleeping—so I figured, if I'm going to be up, I might as well be having fun. . . . Right?"

"Yeah. Why not? So, how was it?"

"It was the same as usual." I shrug. "Good fun. But yesterday morning, I forced myself to regive the 'this clearly isn't working' speech."

"Which said . . ."

"We always have fun together and I'm undoubtedly attracted to him, but outside of those two things, the only other things I know about him are that he's kind of judgmental and extremely inattentive. . . . I said we both know that the other knows how to be in a relationship, and yet we're both exerting extremely minimal, if any, effort in this one."

"That's a good point," Cassie says.

"*I* thought so. So to sum it up I said, 'Let's call a spade a spade, and high-five and part ways.' . . . And then I finally added his phone number to my contacts and made him pinky swear that he'd answer my call sometime in December if I ever actually find a new place and can convince my landlord to let me Venetian plaster it."

"How's the search going?"

"It's going. You know." I sigh.

"You know you don't *have* to move."

"I know." My shoulders sag. "But also, I kind of do."

"Nicole and I have talked about it. A *lot*. We're happy to do whatever you want. You know we're both only living in our tiny walk-up—"

"You mean *palace*," I joke.

She smiles and reaches over to give my arm a squeeze. "Right. Our palace because we love being your roommates. And we are equally happy to strike out on our own right now, too, if the timing works for you. But also, maybe now's *not* the best time for you . . ."

"I know," I say softly. "Thank you." She's still squeezing my arm. My eyes begin to well up. "I just feel like I have to change *something*. Living with you guys is—obviously—the best thing I've got going for me. But I feel like something's gotta give. . . . You know the NYC trifecta: job, relationship, apartment—two of those are so totally sucking for me beyond all possible belief right now. And I can't seem to fix them, no matter how hard I try. But I *need* something in my daily life to change. I can't keep doing . . . *this*."

"So no news from the Landmarks Commission, I take it?"

I shake my head no.

"Or that painting studio?" she asks hopefully.

"I have an interview lined up, but I'm not sure there's really a position there. And even if there is, it's not a perfect fit, since they don't technically practice *conservation*." I groan. "Job openings in conservation come up *so* infrequently. I reached out to pretty much every company and conservator I know. I feel like I'm just going to have to stick it out at RA forever."

"Well, maybe for another few months," Cassie commiserates. "Changing jobs always takes so much more time than it should."

I sigh. "I know it seems stupid, leaving the only good thing I've got. But, I have this idea, this hope, that maybe if I change just one thing, the others will start to change, too? Be in a new neighborhood with a new coffee shop, new faces, a new outlook. . . . I don't know. I need a new perspective . . . even if that just means a new geographic perspective."

Cassie envelops me in a bear hug, and all our fellow straphangers stare as I wipe at my face, doing my best to hold back the tears.

"So if we all *do* move," she says, upbeat, "*why* is Dan interested in your plaster walls?"

"Oh." I stand up straighter. "He's a pro at this, or so he tells me. . . . So back on our first date, I made him promise to teach me one day. Now I'm just holding him to his promise."

"What'd he say to *that*?"

"He said okay, then he proceeded to booty call me last night and text me again this morning. Boys are so strange."

poplockandroll03:
Doppelgänger Greg Returns

Ashley landed free tickets to the US Open from her office and invited me as her plus-one. She's headed to the bar and I'm holding the seats, waiting for Serena Williams's match to recommence. Out of boredom more than anything else, I text Greg:

September 7 at 9:13 p.m.

ALISON: OK, WAIT. IN SERIOUSNESS, I'M AT THE US OPEN. IS THAT YOU DOWN THERE FETCHING BALLS IN YOUR RALPH LAUREN TENNIS STRIPES?

GREG: HEY I TOTALLY JUST WAVED AT YOU, WTF? I GUESS YOU'RE TOO GOOD FOR THE COMMON BALL BOY.

GREG: FYI, THE INTERVIEW PROCESS WASN'T EASY. I PRACTICED RUNNING ACROSS GREENWICH STREET SCOOPING UP RATS ON GARBAGE DAYS TO PREPARE FOR THESE NEXT TWO WEEKS CHASING BALLS.

GREG: CRAP, GOTTA GO. BROOKE SHIELDS NEEDS A REFILL ON HER ARNOLD PALMER AGAIN. I SWEAR SHE EATS BABIES OR SOMETHING TO STILL LOOK THAT GOOD.

Brooke Shields actually *is* here. He must be watching on TV, or at least have turned it on once I texted.

Two days later, I receive the following:

September 9 at 8:31 p.m.

GREG: OK WAIT - NOW I'M AT THE US OPEN. . . . ARE YOU IN A WHITE JUMP-SUIT WIELDING A GIANT ORANGE HAIR-DRYER TO DRY OFF THE COURTS?

ALISON: AS A MATTER OF FACT, YES, THAT'S ME. ON THE ONE HAND, THE BLOW-DRYER'S KINDA HEAVY & AWKWARD; ON THE OTHER, IT'S NICE TO HAVE A MOMENT TO SHINE, PUBLICLY . . .

ALISON: YOU KNOW, MY 15 MINUTES OF FAME.

ALISON: WHY DIDN'T YOU COME DOWN TO SAY HI? HAVE YOU JUST BEEN BREAD-CRUMBING ME THIS WHOLE TIME?

I'm waiting for paint stripper to dry on the third floor of the Armory, and I can feel the reverberations from the sound system of the Proenza Schouler show on the first floor pulsing through the floorboards beneath me. I text Greg:

September 15 at 1:36 p.m.

ALISON: RANDOM, BUT I'M AT FASHION WEEK AT THE PARK AVENUE ARMORY. DID YOU JUST STRUT DOWN THE RUNWAY IN A MESH UNITARD AND CAPE? HOT!

GREG: DID YOU SERIOUSLY NOT KNOW I WAS A MALE MODEL? I MEAN, NOT TO BE BOASTFUL BUT . . . DIDN'T YOU AT LEAST ASSUME?

A few weeks later, he texts again:

October 9 at 4:08 p.m.

GREG: SO FOR SERIOUS, ALISON, WILL YOU BE MY FACEBOOK FRIEND? THOUGHT I'D ASK BEFORE SENDING A REQUEST AND GETTING REJECTED.

ALISON: HMM. . . I DON'T KNOW IF WE'RE READY TO BE FB FRIENDS. WHAT WE'VE GOT GOING ON IS SO GOOD! I DON'T WANT TO RUIN IT WITH UNNECESSARY LEVELS OF COMMUNICATION. . . . I MEAN, RIGHT?

GREG: WORD. IT'LL BE A SANDRA BULLOCK MOVIE IN 2021. PLOT ABOUT HOW I EXILED MYSELF A LA PETERSEN BROS, PERHAPS ON PAROLE BY THE MOVIE'S DENOUEMENT.

ALISON: THERE'S NO FRICKIN' WAY YOU'RE STILL EXILED! REGARDLESS, YOUR MOVIE HAS "BLOCKBUSTER" WRITTEN ALL OVER IT. ANTICIPATION FOR 2021 IS MOUNTING ALREADY!

exexpatMT: Always Mr. Nice Guy (Marc)

"Tell us about the wedding!" Ashley says, pulling a chair out to sit down. "I brought rosé." She extracts a bottle from her handbag and places it on the table.

"Goodness, where to begin? . . . But first, catch up, you're behind." I hand her a glass and the open bottle of Chardonnay. "We haven't ordered yet." I pass her a menu.

"Was it as miserable as we all imagined?" Blaire asks.

"Well, their friends are really nice; there was a bonfire into the wee hours with the singles crowd; and I learned how to swing dance. All good things."

"*But*," Nicole prods.

"*But* I also got a wicked case of poison ivy from having to rake the path down to the wedding site. And then I looked like a rashy icicle with rats-nest hair by the time the reception rolled around because our strapless bridesmaids' dresses were kind of thin, and the bride didn't want us wearing shawls or cardigans during the two-hour-long cere-mony. In forty-degree weather, with twenty mile-per-hour winds."

"Eesh," Ashley says. "Guys, promise me we will never be 'those brides?'"

"Cross my heart," I say at the same time that Nicole and Blaire say, "Promise."

"Wait! What happened to our Sesame Street house? And swearing off marriage forever?" Cassie asks, looking deflated.

"I meant when I marry *you*."

"I don't know," Cassie says disconsolately. "You had a lot of dates this week."

"Taha!" I laugh out loud. "Yes, I'm going to elope with Douchey Dan in lieu of moving into our swingers' townhouse because *he* seems like my Mr. Right. . . . You have nothing to worry about."

"I'm not worried about Douchey Dan. *Marc*," Cassie says.

"Who's Marc?" Blaire asks.

"He's . . . just a guy. Cute. Red hair—"

"—Ooh! Your first ginger!" Ashley exclaims, clapping her hands. "Tell me more."

"He goes to Columbia Business School—"

"Like everyone else she's dating right now," Nicole jumps in.

"Doesn't that get complicated? What if they're friends?" Blaire asks.

"I doubt they know each other. Dan just finished his coursework; Marc just started his second year; Friedrich teaches there. I bet they never cross paths, at least not in a personal sense."

"More about the ginger . . . Marc?" Ashley asks.

"I don't know. He worked in Vienna for several years, just finished a cross-country road trip by himself. . . . Adventurous. Smart. Seems like the nicest person I've ever dated? Just thoroughly, genuinely nice."

"*But*," Nicole says.

"No, stop." I shoot her an admonishing glare. "No 'buts.'"

"But what?" Ashley asks.

"But nothing," I say at the same time that Nicole says, "But she's just not that into him."

"*That*'s not true." I shake my head. "He's basically a prince."

"How so?" Ashley asks.

"So, when I got back from the wedding, I came down with the flu. Probably a combination of freezing rain, poison ivy, whatever."

"Sorry." Ashley frowns.

"No no, it's fine. The *point* was that we didn't even have a date last week, but Marc dropped off chicken soup from Zabar's."

"Prince *indeed*. Where do you *find* people like that?"

"Match.com." I shrug.

"How many dates has it been?" Blaire asks.

"Three."

"That sounds above and beyond for three dates," Ashley says. "Does that mean you've . . . slept over?"

"No no no."

"Have you made out?" Blaire asks.

I shake my head, then self-correct, "Well, actually, he tried. I went in for a hug, he went in for a kiss, and then it was like she hugs-he kisses-she hugs-he kisses," I mime ping-ponging between my hands. "It was actually pretty terrible."

"That's not the terrible part!" Nicole laughs.

I roll my eyes. "Be nice. . . . But yes, he then sent me an email apologizing for the goodbye misfire. Which kind of heightened the awkwardness."

"Awwwww," Ashley says. "He sounds like such a *sweetheart.*"

"He *is.* But . . . it's only been three dates, so . . . not worth talking about. What about you guys?" I glance around the table at each of them in turn.

"Same old, same old."

"Are we wingwomaning after dinner tonight?" Cassie asks.

"What *else* would we be doing?"

"Where to?"

"Have you guys heard of Hotel Delmano? Over in Williamsburg? It sounds kind of trendy, loungy," Ashley suggests.

"Are there men there?"

"Yeah, lots. It's a neat scene, drinks with absinthe and such," I say. "I went there with Luke." Everyone looks at me. "Can we *not* go there tonight? Like, maybe to some other part of Brooklyn instead?" I ask hopefully. "Or stay in Manhattan, since we're *in* Manhattan now?"

"It's fine, we'll go somewhere else." Cassie turns to me. "But why does it matter if he's dead?" she asks with mock sincerity.

I smile weakly.

"You're pretending he's dead?" Blaire asks.

"Not, like, in a murderous, vengeance-filled way. In a happy . . . *not*-injured way—like he just magically . . . ceased to inhabit the same city as me. And the same planet."

"That makes it easier?"

"Slightly."

"So, where should we go?" Nicole asks. "Since *Williamsburg* is officially off the table."

"You're acting like I'm a crazy person." I pout. "You should be happy I'm not suggesting we rent Citi Bikes and cycle around his block for the rest of the night. I'm doing the *opposite,*" I say proudly.

Cassie nods. "It's true. But what if we all promise to verbally assault him if we see him?"

"I could *physically* assault him," Ashley offers.

"Both of those things might actually be more unsettling than seeing him in the first place. . . . How about if you guys pinky swear that if we see him-slash-his ghost, you'll all throw your shoes at him . . . then I *guess* we can go out in Williamsburg." I sigh melodramatically. "But *not* to the Hotel Delmano, please."

"Don't you think you're better off now anyway?" Ashley asks gently. "No more heart palpitations, right?"

I nod weakly.

"And you've got a bevy of eligible bachelors knocking down your door . . ." Ashley continues.

"Well, first, I wouldn't say *that*. And second, it doesn't really work that way, right? Like meeting or dating new people can magically make you forget?"

"If it's the *right* person, they can," Cassie says.

"She hasn't played 'Yellow' in over a week." Nicole raises her glass to toast this accomplishment.

"Actually," I say lifting my glass, "I have . . . but only on my iPod, so you couldn't hear it."

* * *

"So what's new with your Columbia dating triangle? Square?" Blaire asks at a Friday BYOB dinner two weeks later.

"Not much. Though the professor's out of the picture, so it's a triangle now. If you can consider Dan a vertex."

"Have you seen the ginger?" Ashley asks.

"Yeah, we had dinner Wednesday. I'd told him about my thesis research in New Orleans, so he picked this nifty Cajun hole-in-the-wall that's actually near your apartment."

"And?"

"I don't know. He keeps introducing me to cool, off-the-radar bars and eateries—it's fun," I say brightly. "He's just insanely nice. Like, that night, Jason got into a funk. Long story, but this terrible girl he's been seeing broke up with him, and he called me because he was really bummed. . . . When I didn't pick up, he texted. . . . I saw the text, felt bad, asked if I could step outside to call Jason quickly to tell him I'd call him when I got home. . . . Anyway, of course Marc said yes, but then I cut things a bit short after dinner because I felt like I needed to talk to Jason in his . . . time of need or whatever. So then I get this text from Marc the next morning. . . . Hang on, I'll read it to you because I'll botch it otherwise."

I fish my cell phone out of my bag and begin, "'As much as you apologized for getting the phone, picking it up was definitely the best thing to do.' Exclamation point. 'And you were right to peel off early to comfort a friend in need. Absolutely no need to apologize.' Exclamation point. 'It sounded like Jason needed you.' Parenthesis: 'Which was far more important than talking about how disappointing the *Breaking Bad* spin-off was'; end of parenthesis. 'And you were a great friend to him.' Dot dot dot. 'Always a very attractive quality.' Exclamation point. Smiley face."

"Ohhhhh," Cassie and Ashley trill at the same time.

"What did you say back?" Blaire asks.

"You are *too* nice. Stop. Being. So. Nice."

"No, what'd you really say?" she repeats.

"Really, that's what I said."

"I think Nicole's right. I hear undertones of a big 'but,'" Blaire says.

"No buts. He's a prince."

"*But* why are you still seeing Dan then? I mean, I doubt Dan even knows how to *make* a smiley face emoticon," Blaire says pointedly.

I laugh. "I don't know. I have fun with Dan, and I'm really attracted to him. And it's not that I don't have fun with Marc. I do. But . . . I don't want to, like—"

"Jump his bones or anything," Cassie says.

"Exactly."

"Well if he's cute, and so princely, which it sounds like he is . . . why not?"

"I don't know." I take a sip of my wine. "He says things that are kind of . . . turnoffs."

"*Like?* . . ."

"He says 'wee bit' . . . Like, 'I'm feeling a wee bit loopy from the all-nighter I pulled last night.' Or, 'I'm going to take a wee bit of a nap now.'"

"I've heard you say 'wee bit,'" Cassie says.

"I know. But I say it in jest. Like, 'I'm feeling a wee bit squeamish about x, y, z.' Or, 'you, my friend,'" I turn to Cassie, "'seemed a wee bit inebriated after *your* date last night.'"

Nicole snorts.

"I know." I pout. "Isn't that so stupid? I'm being so *stupid*. And *mean*. I know."

"I agree it's kind of a turnoff, but if you liked him, you'd ignore it," Cassie says.

"Not necessarily," I counter.

"James's quirks were *way* worse, and you got past those," Nicole challenges.

"I'm with Nicole," Blaire says. "You don't sound that into him."

"I *am*. He's terrific."

"Look, Al," Nicole says. "Nice is nice . . . but, nice isn't necessarily hot."

* * *

"Cassie," I sing when she walks in the door to our apartment. "Marc brought you a *present*!"

"Is he here?" she asks as she takes off her coat.

"No, he left a while ago. But . . . okay, don't get mad? I'd told him about how you were having a rough week, with Marvin and everything. I didn't go into specifics, don't worry."

"Ohhkay," she says tentatively.

"And so Marc felt bad for you, so he brought over a box of Beard Papa's cream puffs. Apparently it's like a famous Upper West Side thing. . . . Anyway, he said they're for you to share with me and Nicole. But mostly for you."

"Awwwww." Cassie puts her hand to her heart. "Really?"

"Really."

"Can I have one now?" she asks as she sits on the couch to unzip her boots.

"They're there for your taking." I break the tape seal on the box and open them.

"Ooh, so pretty!" She reaches in and plucks out a chocolate-covered cream puff.

"So how *are* you?" I ask.

"I'm okay. Work is a good distracter. But how are *you*? I feel like in all my drama, I keep neglecting to ask about you."

"Don't be silly. But I'm okay."

"So how's Marc?" she asks through a mouth full of cream puff.

"I don't know. Fine. *Princely*." I nod my chin toward the cardboard Beard Papa's box.

"What'd you do tonight?"

"I fought with him about a movie." I bite my lip, ashamed.

"What movie? And why?"

"We watched *Blue Jasmine*. I maintained that it was a takeoff on *A Streetcar Named Desire*, and he pointed out all the reasons it diverged from it, and that made me defend my points even more strongly. . . . But you know what?"

"What?"

"I don't even *care* about the movie, or my theory. And I haven't read *A Streetcar Named Desire* since high school, so I probably got half the facts wrong anyway. Gah!" I run my hands over my head. "Why am I being this way? Why can't I just be nice and . . . I don't know, fawning? Like I was with Luke?"

"Maybe you're in a rebellious phase." Cassie takes another bite of her dessert. "You know, thanks to Luke. Are you picking fights with Dan?"

"No . . . I mean, kind of. We take digs at each other all the time, but it's, like, jousting in good fun. Besides, I don't think he has feelings."

Cassie laughs at this. "Would you argue with Dan about a movie plot?"

"No . . . I can't think of a time I've *argued* about a movie plot with anyone. . . . Debate a plot sure, but . . . not *argue*."

"So why do you think you're picking on Marc?"

"I don't know . . . maybe to get a rise out of him? Have him stop agreeing with everything I say, or inject a little . . . life . . . into the conversation? Banter? I have no idea."

"Maybe Nicole was right? Nice is nice, but . . ."

"How was the black-tie ball last night?" Ben asks over brunch at Hill Country. He and Nicole agreed to keep me company at the five or six most promising open houses I flagged for my apartment hunt this weekend.

"It wasn't a *ball*, but it was fun I guess."

"What'd you wind up wearing?" Nicole asks.

"It had a flapper/roaring twenties theme, so I wore that BCBG feather dress." I pick up a spoonful of grits smothered with barbecue sauce. "Marc actually gave me a pair of earrings to wear with it."

"*That's* really nice. Why didn't you lead with that?" Nicole asks.

I reach for the corn bread. "I keep *telling* you he's really nice, so it's kind of par for the course with him. They're not anything extravagant . . . from a craft market he passed while walking his dog. But yes, a *really* sweet gift. . . . He said the stones match my eyes, or whatever."

"So why was it 'fun I guess?'" Ben asks.

"It was their business school holiday formal, so I didn't know anyone there, and Marc had to network and stuff, but . . . it was fun."

They nod, their eyes glued to the screens broadcasting football over our heads.

"Were his friends cool?" Ben asks, eyes still averted.

"I don't think they're really 'friends,' per se. He's a bit older than his classmates, and he seemed a little ill at ease among them . . . but yeah, everyone was nice." I pause.

"I hear a 'but' coming on," Nicole says, glancing at me as she forks her hash browns.

"Why do you always say that?"

"Well, am I right?"

"No. Just . . . he introduced me to everyone as his *girlfriend*."

"You kind of *are* his girlfriend," Ben says.

"No, I'm not."

"You've been seeing him for, what, three months now?" Ben asks.

"Like, two and a quarter . . . *but!*" I add defensively, "We're *not* exclusive, and we haven't spent a night together."

"And he's still dating you *why*?" Nicole asks.

"I don't know. All our dates are on weeknights, and I always have to get up early for work. He's invited me over, but he hasn't seemed irked by my saying no. . . . I don't know, it doesn't seem weird until you say it out loud."

"Ali, if you know, you know." Ben directs his gaze to me. "Don't string him along."

"I'm *not* stringing him along!" I protest.

"You kind of are," Nicole says.

"I just . . ." I sigh, frustrated because I know they might be right. "He's *so* wonderful. Like, *so* wonderful. How can you walk away from that?"

"But if he's not right for you, let him go be wonderful for someone else," Nicole says.

"It's not that he's *not* right for me, I just . . . can't decide yet."

"He's terrific. You undersold him," Nicole says as she sidles up next to me at the bar of Employees Only in the West Village.

"I said he was a prince! How is that underselling?"

"There were some 'buts' in there."

"*You* threw in those 'buts,' not me!"

She sips on her straw and eyes me suspiciously.

"He's great!" I say emphatically. "He's got the whole package, personality-wise *and* looks-wise, right?"

"You're not the only girl who thinks so." She nods her head sideways toward Marc, who's holding court among a brunette and two blondes, all of whom are laughing riotously at something he said.

"Does that make you jealous? Even the tiniest bit?" Nicole asks.

"No."

"Because . . . you know he's only got eyes for you? Or because . . . you don't care."

"I'm actually kind of happy for him that he has so many people who want to be around him. Is that weird?"

"Well it's weird insofar as every girl here is interested in talking to him. Except you."

"I'm trying really hard. Why can't I *will* myself to fall for him?" I repine.

"How'd it go?" Cassie asks when I open the front door.

"I guess as expected." I put my keys on the living room table.

"How do you feel?"

"Same as before: shitty." I walk into the kitchen and open the freezer. "You want anything?"

"No, thanks. Don't you at least feel a little unburdened?"

"I feel confused." I grab the carton of Edy's Mint Chocolate Chip and two spoons. "We can share." I walk back to the couch and hand Cassie a spoon.

"What'd he say?"

"He said he was afraid this was why I asked him to meet up on relatively short notice. So I guess he saw it coming." I dig my spoon into the carton.

"Anything else?"

I frown. "He said he was sad. And that he thought we had a lot of potential." I suck on my spoon.

"What'd you say to that?"

"I said I feel awful. And that I think he's pretty perfect. But then he asked if there was anything he could have done differently, either in the past or now, to change my feelings. And . . ." I dig my spoon back in, "my heart hurts. For him. *And* for me, because I still don't understand why I couldn't feel about him . . ."

"The way he felt about you?"

"Right. . . . But I didn't have any answers for him. I probably blathered on like an idiot to avoid awkward pauses."

"Huh. . . . I'm sorry." She pauses. "I think you know this, but you did what you had to do."

I nod. "It still just sucks. I feel so bad for him."

"Did he say anything else?

"He asked if we could be friends. If we could get coffee or drinks sometime soon."

"That'd be nice. What'd you say?"

"Of course I said yes, though I kind of doubt hanging out again would be very fun for either of us."

"Why not?"

"It would be . . . imbalanced, right? If he wants to know how to do things differently, seeing him for coffee would just be leading him on all over again. . . ." I shake my head and reach for the Edy's. "I really wish I could have liked him more. I just hope I don't regret this later."

Throwing in the Trowel: Dan

December 5 at 5:30 a.m.

Subject: hello bn3
From: daniel.acosta@gmail.com
hello:

I have good news for you.
*I have Order china 20 Products Apple iPhone X HD 256
GB Unlocked*
I completed bank transfer payments, web: tooaomo.com
*It's amazing! The item has brand new and high quality,
but muc cheaper. I'm pleased to share this good news with
you! I believe you will find what you want and have an good
experience on shopping from them*

Regards!

December 5 at 9:41 p.m.

FW: hello bn3
*What?! You're giving me a free iPhone as a present?
Oh, Daniel, you shouldn't have . . . ;)*

*. . . Thought you'd like the heads-up that you're inadver-
tently spamming everyone. Unless you really did go into the
luxury knock-off goods industry, in which case, congrats on
the new gig! Though you might want to study up on Oxford
English grammar one of these days.*
Hope all's well with you.

Best,
Alison

December 6 at 12:08 p.m.

Alison Have I got deal for you. Box Yale Suck T-shits from nike good quality double stitch. You need buy school spirit now. Real cheep one dollar.

Regards,
Princeton

much better :)

December 6 at 10:17 p.m.

Hey there,

I have to say, some small part of me is really happy that you spammed me. Because just last week I moved downtown into my very own studio (no need to worry about me suffering separation anxiety; Cassie signed a lease on a 1 BR literally on the same block). And to class up the joint, I am eager to Venetian plaster my new digs(!). Don't worry, I DID ask permission of my landlord. I think he sees it as free beautification, which of course it is; I see it as a much-needed change to jump-start the coming year. So I'm making good on my promise to get in touch with you now that I'm ready to learn a new skill, and I'm crossing my fingers that you'll make good on your promise to help me Venetian plaster my apartment?

Nope. Not kidding.

I will take food/booze requests and promise to keep you extremely well fed and well imbibed. I might even let you choose which playlist we listen to.

So. . . . Are you in? I would SUPER appreciate the artistic touch of an expert in the field, and I promise it will not be boring.

Hope all's well on your end,
Alison

December 7 at 11:02 p.m.

Hey Alison,

Congrats on the new place, and on your small achievement of winning your landlord's approval.

So I haven't gotten my hands dirty in a while, but I guess a little manual labor could provide some balance. Assuming I buy into this operation, what are your thoughts on timing? Also, this is just the walls correct? Did you decide whether you want the gloss finish as well?

December 8 at 6:53 a.m.

Hooray! Oh, this makes me so happy. So many questions to respond to:

1. *<<So assuming I buy into this operation, what are your thoughts on timing?>>*

   I recognize the absurdity of my request, so far be it for me to call the shots in terms of scheduling. I will happily work around your calendar. When are you free?

2. *<<Also, this is just the walls correct?>>*

   Umm. What else would one plaster? The floor? The furniture? . . .

3. *<<Did you decide whether you want the gloss finish as well?>>*

   I'm leaning toward yes, but I think I need to pick the color first.

Yay! I promise this will be fun.

Looking forward to catching up,
Alison

My buzzer rings, and Dan is standing before me in a white V-neck undershirt and Adidas warm-up pants. "I come bearing trowels and sandpaper." He holds out his offerings. "I didn't know if you had everything we needed. Better safe than sorry."

"Oh, thanks!" I say brightly. "I do—I borrowed heavily from work—but that's awesome, thanks. Come in, come in!" I usher him into the apartment.

"So is this what you always wear to work? I could . . . get used to this?"

I look down at my paint-splattered white tank top and paint-splattered ripped jeans. "I look like a dirty hippie artist. *No*, I don't wear this to work. Can you imagine seeing clients like this?"

"Might get *more* clients that way," Dan suggests.

"*Okay*, enough, enough. . . . So!" I clap my hands together, "You tell me how to do this. Is there prep work we need to do that requires dry time? Do we just get started? I guess I'm asking if we should eat now or use dinner as a break."

"We need to clean the walls first, and also tape off all your moldings."

I raise an eyebrow. "You know *you're* the master, right? I'm just the apprentice. I did all that grunt work last night *and* moved my furniture into the middle of the room—as you can see—so you could skip to the fun stuff."

"Oh, then yeah. Once you get started, it's probably easiest to keep working straight through since it gets so messy. So, I guess let's eat first?"

"Thai, Mexican, sushi, Chinese . . . you pick."

"Thai."

"Excellent, I'll go get my phone. Do you want anything to drink?"

"What've you got?"

"I stocked the bar just for you. Brand new bottle of Captain Morgan—I still can't believe you like that stuff—and bourbon, gin, and Firefly. Fridge is full of mixers. Help yourself, I'll be right back."

I return with my phone and hand it over to Dan. "You pick. I'll eat anything." I take a look at his glass. "Umm, what did you *make*? That looks gross."

Dan looks at his glass and frowns. "I don't know. Rum and Coke and Firefly with a dash of gin."

"You're like a kid at a Burger King, you know, when they let you fill up your soft drink yourself, so you pull all the levers mixing Coke, root beer, Sprite, Fanta, and Hawaiian Punch."

"I figured you got it all for me, I should try it all."

"You *were* right: you need to work on your limits."

"That's . . . actually the opposite of what I said."

I smile. "I know. But still, it's true."

Over dinner, Dan catches me up on his latest work-travels through Asia, I fill him in on my newest conservation projects, and we talk about *Game of Thrones* and the current football season as one would with an old friend.

We roughly divide the wall surfaces in half: Dan takes the upper walls since he's got nearly an extra foot of reach beyond mine, and I take the middle and lower walls. We start at opposite corners and work our way around the room. As promised, I keep Dan's liquor glass full at all times, and I let him control the music. We've been plastering for several hours when our conversation seems to hit a lull. I break the silence: "So, what's up with your love life these days? . . . You don't have to answer that if you don't want to."

"No, that's fine. Not much."

"'Not much' for Dan Acosta? I find that hard to believe." I smile, and he grunts.

"I don't know why you think I'm such a . . . player?"

"Oh, I don't know. Somewhere between booty call/text number one and nineteen, I started to get that idea." Seated on the floor of the opposite corner, I turn my head to look at him. "But you know I don't think you're a bad person, right? I mean if I thought that I wouldn't—"

"—Invite me over and force me to do all your manual labor?"

"Exactly. Oh, good, I'm glad you understand." I smile again. "So, are you breaking hearts and taking names?"

"Not really."

"Have any funny stories? Anything?" I continue to trowel gray plaster onto the wall and smooth it out.

"I was seeing one girl for a couple months."

"'Was' being past tense?"

"Yeah, she was cool. It was alright, I guess."

"Was it serious?"

"Yeah, I think so. I know *she* thought so."

"Did you meet her on Match?"

"Yeah."

"Why no more?"

"I ended it." He puts his trowel down on the tray and picks up his glass. "I'm empty. You want a refill?"

"Sure."

He comes back from the kitchen area, hands me a rum and Coke, and picks up his trowel again. "So what about you?"

"Hmm?" I rub out the ridges in my applied plaster.

"What's your dating life like these days? Still full of limits and sidewalk speeches, I assume?"

I turn and scowl at him, and he flashes a knowing smile then goes back to plastering.

"Meh. Nothing too exciting."

"Are you seeing anyone right now?"

"No, I actually just ended a . . . mini-relationship, *quasi* . . . thing? I don't know what to call it, but yeah. So, just first dates for me right now."

"Who was the guy?"

"Umm." I dip my trowel back into the bucket. "He was *really* nice. He went to Columbia Business School, just like you, launched his own tech start-up, lives in Washington Heights. . . ."

"But."

"But nothing." I keep troweling, then add, "Okay, but," I sigh, "he's *incredibly* sweet and attentive, but I just didn't," I run my trowel across the upper lip of the baseboard carefully, "feel a spark, you know?"

"That sounds exciting." He strains the word "exciting" as he stretches up to reach the bottom of the crown molding.

I laugh. "Yeah, exactly."

"How long was it?"

"Dunno." I shrug. "Maybe three months?"

"Dude, that's a long time if there's no 'spark,' or whatever."

"I know. It was a mistake. He was just so *nice*, and *smart*, it was kind of scary to walk away from someone who's so good to you and trying so hard."

"Not if there's no spark."

"Well, yeah. There you have it. So . . . what about you? Why did yours end?"

"Seriously?"

"I mean, you just asked me the same question, right?"

"Yeah, I guess." Dan dips his trowel into the bucket of plaster and stands back to look at the wall before answering. "It was good. She was cool. But . . ." he trails off.

"But."

"But when I got your email, I realized I was that much more excited to see you than to see her . . . I figured it meant I needed to cut it off."

I swallow hard and continue troweling my plaster, staring straight at the wall and careful not to make eye contact with Dan. "Oh."

"Look, I know what your feelings were. Are. I'm not trying to make a grand statement or anything. But . . ." He pauses. "I don't know . . . you were the best one." I can hear him scraping his trowel against the wall again.

"Best Match girl?" I laugh, still focusing my eyes on the plaster in front of me.

"Yeah." Dan laughs. "It doesn't have to mean anything, but . . . you were. Are."

And then he's standing over me. "You have plaster on your nose, you know." He bends down, flakes dried plaster off the bridge of my nose, puts his hand under my ponytail, and then we're making out.

"Trowel!" I mumble in between kissing him. "Trowel. Trowel. Trowel." I push him away with my free hand and reach for the plaster bucket and lay my wet trowel on top of it. "Sorry . . . where were we?"

Somehow, when we wake up the next morning, the walls are finished and look perfect.

"I can't believe you made me stay up until 3:00 a.m. plastering," Dan groans.

"I can't believe I *convinced* you to stay up until 3:00 a.m. plastering. *Thank you!*"

"You look . . . different. Something's different," Dan says, squinting. "Oh, I know, it's the new tattoo on your shoulder."

"Gee, I wonder where *that* came from," I say, twisting my head over my left shoulder to see the gray heart with an arrow through it. It says LIM. "I assume you were aiming for 'limits' and ran out of room?"

He smiles and nods proudly. "You want first bathroom or should I?"

"You."

Dan rises from the drop cloth covering my floor, where we slept, and goes to the bathroom.

"My God, woman! What did you *do* to me last night?" he calls out.

I laugh. "Now you know why I wanted you to take first bathroom! Also, aren't you not supposed to say the 'G' word?" I call back.

He comes back out and points to his face. "Really? On my face?"

"It's not like I pranked you while you were sleeping. You *let* me do that. I asked permission before painting." Dan's face looks like a cat.

"I hope your mural-painting . . . inpainting . . . skills are better than your face-painting skills," he says.

"Hey, don't mock my face-painting skills!" I laugh. "So maybe my eagle didn't turn out as well as my snowflake, but *I* thought it was a valiant effort." Dan looks puzzled then runs back to the bathroom to inspect his chest, which he hadn't noticed on first glance in the mirror.

"Why do I not remember any of last night? This stuff comes off, right?"

"You're the master. You tell me."

"Did you roofie me?"

"Yes, Dan." I nod solemnly. "I slipped you a roofie so that I could take advantage of you, *not* sleep with you, and paint animals on your face and chest."

"I thought so. You women are so weird. . . ." He shakes his head. "Why is it that I feel great whenever we hang out, and then I wake up the next morning seeing spots?"

"For the record, I didn't touch that bottle of Captain Morgan. All damage done on that," I point to the half-empty bottle sitting on the windowsill, "you are solely responsible for."

He smiles and kisses my forehead. "You've discovered my Kryptonite. . . . So, do you want me to . . . come back again and help with the sanding and polishing?"

I hesitate, surprised by the offer. "I would *love* it if you did, but you've done more than enough. So, you obviously don't have to."

"I *know* I don't have to. I'm being *nice*." He nods emphatically.

"Then, yes! That would be amazing."

"Cool. Does Sunday work?"

"Okay."

"It's a date," he says.

Sunday comes and goes, and despite a text and an email that I sent Dan to confirm our plaster-polishing plans, I don't hear back from him. Until Monday night.

* * *

A yellow cab slows to the curb on Seventh Avenue. I open the rear door and load the first of three file-storage boxes into the back seat. Deepa hands me the second, and I push it over to the middle seat.

"Forget about Joanne, we'll talk soon." Deepa gives me a quick hug.

"Better get back inside before you get in trouble," I joke. Though, on second thought, that's not a joke. As I lift the last cardboard box from the sidewalk and climb into the taxi, Deepa shuts the door from the outside, waves, then scurries back into the office building.

"Thirty-ninth and third, please." It comes out more strained than I expected. The driver nods.

I try to clear my throat then touch my fingertips to my left cheek: still burning. My mind whirring, I try to replay the last ten minutes, then the last six hours.

"You look like a nice lady," the cab driver calls over his shoulder. "You know what I say?"

"Oh." I'm roused from my contemplation. "What's that?"

"Fuck 'em. Seriously. Fuck 'em all."

Our eyes meet in the rearview mirror and I try to smile kindly. "Thanks."

"No, I mean it. Fuck 'em! You don't need them to succeed. Success comes from within."

I smile again and nod. "Thanks." I look at the haphazardly packed boxes: one even lacks a lid on account of my protruding field microscope. I can see why my midday departure might give the impression I was fired. In fact, Joanne's version of events would support that notion, too.

As we hung up our two o'clock conference call with the Armory architect, I had risen from my chair to leave Joanne's office. *Could you please sit down again?* Joanne had asked.

Earlier this morning I'd gone into Joanne's office to let her know, via a much-rehearsed speech, that I had accepted another job and would be leaving in four weeks. I assured her I would continue to work diligently until my departure. Not surprisingly, Joanne expressed little emotion or interest, apart from asking—multiple times—whom I was going to work for. After initially hesitating, I admitted that I'm going to work for Gilded Artists, a contractor I've interfaced with on several projects. I could see Joanne was not impressed. The view of my RA colleagues (Joanne most especially) is that they are superior to all competing firms along the East Coast. So it's practically sacrilege that I'm not even going to a less prestigious conservation firm, but to a *contractor*. Joanne chastised me for "abandoning [my] responsibilities" and for being "unappreciative of all the resources" they invested in me the past four years.

I wondered what more Joanne had to add to what she'd said this morning?

"I phoned Bill Garland"—the president of Gilded Artists—"and told him you'd be leaving us in the lurch, and I asked him to rescind your offer." I felt the wind knocked out of me, and my eyes began to blur. I wanted to shout, *You put me on notice five months ago! Why do you all of a sudden care that I'm leaving?* But the words didn't come; I was too stunned to speak.

"Since Bill refused to rescind your offer"—I exhaled suddenly, only then realizing that I'd been holding my breath—"we don't see how you could be of any further use to us." Joanne continued, "You can clean out your desk and leave, effective immediately."

As I struggled to process her words, I stumbled through some questions about unfinished exposures at the Armory, about being able to say goodbye to my coworkers. I returned to my cubicle to find three empty cardboard boxes under my desk. Quickly, silently, I threw all my chemistry textbooks, my steel-toe sneakers and site gear, my scalpels and Swiss Army knife into the boxes. Before I was even done, the office manager returned to collect my office ID and company cell phone.

If I needed any further convincing to quit RA, Joanne generously proffered it.

"We have a saying in my country," my cab driver encourages. "A change is as good as a rest."

"Oh. I like that," I say, grateful for this man's compassionate efforts to comfort a stranger. Though Gilded Artists isn't doubling my salary, I did get a 50 percent raise. Now that I can finally afford to quit tutoring, it's fun to dream up what I will *do* with all these reclaimed hours. . . . Rest is at the top of the list. "Change and rest, both reinvigorating," I echo.

"There's another Arabic proverb that my grandfather shared with me when I was nervous, leaving my family to move here. He said, 'Life will show you what you did not know.' Maybe that applies now, too?"

"Oh, I like that one also. Very wise." I nod for emphasis. "Thank you." I'm well aware that there's a *lot* I don't know, and that I still have much to learn. In my newly created position of Supervising Conservator (read: Sole Conservator) for Gilded Artists, my first order of business is to procure a microscope and build out a lab. Though I'll sorely miss having the infrastructure and resources that RA provided, Gilded Artists has entire studios of gilders, decorative painters, and stained-glass artisans; I may not have architectural conservators to bounce ideas off of, but can't I learn equally from the artists who execute the kinds of works we later restore? That's my working theory, at least.

Either way, being surrounded by old-world *art* and *process* on a daily basis, in the eye of such a vortex of creativity and verve . . . surely it trumps walking on eggshells around Joanne.

The driver helps me unload the boxes to the curb in front of my building. "You just made what could have been the worst ride into the best," I say gratefully. We exchange names, a handshake, and I hand him a hefty tip.

"Remember my country's saying, Alison: A change is as good as a rest."

I nod.

"And also, fuck 'em."

* * *

Later that night, I carry the broken-down cardboard boxes to my building's recycling room. On my way back upstairs, I feel unburdened, freer. My phone vibrates in my back pocket just as I reach my front door.

DAN:

December 18 at 8:44 p.m.

HEY. SORRY, YESTERDAY GOT AWAY FROM ME. WAS WATCHING FOOTBALL WITH MY COUSINS OUT IN NEW JERSEY. DO U WANT TO COME OVER?

ALISON:

NO, THANKS. I'VE GOT SOME WALL POLISHING TO DO. :) BUT HAVE HAPPY HOLIDAYS AND MAYBE WE CAN GRAB COFFEE OR SOMETHING IN THE NEW YEAR.

poplockandroll03:
Doppelgänger Greg. Again

When I'm out Saturday night, my phone vibrates and a text flashes on the screen:

December 2 at 11:22 p.m.

GREG: YOUR DANCE ROUTINE TO YOUNG MC'S "BUST A MOVE" WAS SICK. ALL OF ATLANTIC CITY SAYS RESPECT!!

ALISON: I'M SO GLAD YOU NOTICED! I'VE BEEN HITTING UP HIP HOP CLASSES AT THE GYM RELIGIOUSLY AND SPENDING WAY TOO MUCH TIME MEMORIZING VIDEO DANCE STEPS AT THE JOSHUA TREE. YOU MADE MY WEEK BY NOTICING! WHAT'D YOU THINK OF THE BACK HANDSPRING I PULLED OUT OF NOWHERE?

GREG: YOUR DANCE MOVES ARE INSANE. LIKE GANGNAM STYLE MEETS A WHIRLING DERVISH.

GREG: I ALSO HAVE INSANE MOVES. POP LOCKING CLASSES AT ALVIN AILEY NEAR MY APT . . . FIVE SEASONS OF SYTYCD ON MY DVR . . .

GREG: . . . "SO YOU THINK YOU CAN DANCE" (IN CASE YOU'RE NOT A FAN . . . BUT YOU ARE A FAN . . . I HOPE?)

ALISON: YOU TAKE ALVIN AILEY CLASSES? BET WE COULD DO A MEAN PAS DE DEUX TO "ROCKA MY SOUL"!

GREG: I'VE NEVER HEARD OF THAT GAME, BUT IT SOUNDS RIVETING. BFFS . . . FINALLY!

Discovered when I walk in the door to my apartment later that same night:

December 3 at 1:08 a.m.

GREG: STATES ON HE T DANE FLR?

GREG: STATIS ON DAN E FLOOR?

GREG: DAMMIT

ALISON: STATUS? ON THE DANCE FLOOR, YOU MEAN? JUST WHIPPED OUT A MEAN GRAPEVINE FOLLOWED BY A STELLAR RUNNING MAN. HOW DO YOU HAVE A KNACK FOR ALWAYS TEXTING THE MINUTE I GET IN THE DOOR?

His response, early the next morning, reads:

December 3 at 7:57 a.m.

GREG: HOW DO YOU HAVE A KNACK FOR ALWAYS TEXTING JUST AS I HAVE PASSED OUT ON MY COUCH STILL CLUTCHING A HALF-EATEN CHICKEN PARMESAN?

Three days later:

December 6 at 9:24 p.m.

GREG: OK. I'M BEING 100% SERIOUS. ARE YOU AT THE PHISH CONCERT RIGHT NOW? SECTION 114? ROW C? WHEN DID YOU GROW DREADLOCKS, ALISON?

December 6 at 10:11 p.m.

ALISON: OMG SOMEONE'S ALVIN AILEY CLASSES HAVE BEEN PAYING OFF! YOUR SICK MOVES ARE TOTALLY RIGHTEOUS. DIDN'T KNOW YOU'RE A PHISH FAN. MSG'S A GIANT CLAMBAKE RIGHT NOW.

It's Thursday night, and I'm sitting in a beer garden with Cassie and Nicole. My phone buzzes:

December 21 at 10:16 p.m.

GREG: I LIKE RED FISH, BLUE FISH, ONE FISH, AND YOU.

ALISON: ???

GREG: ALISON. ROSES ARE RED, VIOLETS ARE BLUE, YOU'VE BEEN MY TEXT BFF FOR AGES, LET'S BE DRINKING BUDDIES, TOO?

I read this last text aloud, and I hesitate.

"Al, why don't you just meet up with him?" Cassie asks.

"I don't know. I just don't feel like it."

"You can invite him to come join us here," she encourages.

"Thanks. But I just don't really feel like seeing him. You know, in person."

"Then why waste time texting back and forth with him for all these months?"

I have to pause to think about this. "Because he makes me laugh, and usually at odd hours when I don't have anything better to do than text random semistrangers."

"What's the worst that could happen if you two hung out?" she asks.

I look to Nicole for backup, but she raises her eyebrows, silently seconding Cassie's line of questioning.

"Well, if we don't have chemistry—" I interrupt myself, "which I don't think we do—the whole thing could fall apart. And we'd become *ex*–texting buddies."

"Is that really such a terrible outcome? You have *never* hung out with him in all the months of your corresponding. It doesn't sound to me like you've got a whole lot to lose."

I nod.

Ever the optimist, Cassie presses on, "But you *could* stand to gain something."

"Yeah. But I'm just . . ." I search for the right word, then settle on "*tired*, like seriously drained, from all the witty emails, and texts, and telephone conversations. Meaning . . . the witty emails and telephone conversations with everyone *else*. Not Greg because those are one-off no-brainers. But I feel like I have to be funny, and 'on' all the time for everyone else. . . . And three-quarters of the time, you write these thoughtful, hilarious, referential emails that take thirty minutes to draft and revise, and then the correspondence suddenly stops, and you've wasted all this time flirting with someone you've never even met in person. These mystery men could be bots, and I wouldn't know the difference."

"Wait. What?" Nicole laughs heartily at my leap in logic.

"Gah! I don't know," I wail, palming my forehead. "And then here's Greg. And I haven't seen him in . . . ten months? Eleven? And I don't think I'm attracted to him, and we never hang out, and we never will. But I love knowing that he's thinking about me, and I am a more carefree, lighthearted version of myself when we 'talk,' and . . . this is the most functional relationship I've had all year! And I don't want to ruin that."

"That's just plain sad, Al," Cassie says.

"But. I *like* this . . . non-relationship. It's easy, and no-maintenance, and whimsical . . . and I want to freeze it in amber and never have it change."

"So what are you gonna write back?" Nicole tilts her head inquisitively.

ALISON: GREG. I LIKE YOU AND I LIKE BEER, BUT THIS IS THE MOST FUNCTIONAL RELATIONSHIP I'VE HAD ALL YEAR. LET'S CONTINUE AS IS AND HEART-ACHE AVOID, SO WITH EACH OTHER'S EMOTIONS WE WON'T HAVE TOYED.

The following week, an email from *Match.com* lands in my inbox. *Subject: Notification of Account Expiration. Renew Today!*

Has it *truly* been a year already?

I think back to when I first signed up last winter: in many ways, that feels like just yesterday. But on the other hand, when I think of all the men—the personalities I met (Matt, Marc, the Lukes, John, James, Paul . . . when I picture them in that sequence, they sound like the New Testament of bachelors)—who taught me things, or impacted me in ways both small and large, I can't figure out how they all fit into twelve short months.

It's like I told Older Luke: life moves *fast*! . . . And then, sometimes I think it moves slowly. . . . Somehow both seem true?

Well, apparently, it has been a year. I got my six free months and, as with each of these men, it was fun while it lasted. Actually, it was more than fun—in a weird sort of way, I love this past year. I love it madly and deeply and forever for everything it taught me:

I always thought that by the time you became an adult, you were pretty much fully formed, and your actions were, to some extent, predictable. It's now clear to me that this is far from true. Especially when it comes to matters of the heart, you can still surprise yourself.

On a meta-scale, I discovered that everyone has their issues; they just aren't always apparent at first. As a result, everyone perceives things differently. Moments that were brilliant and shiny and glossy to me may have been black-and-white and matte and dull to the person on the other side of the table. And vice versa.

Similarly, different people bring out different things in us. Older Luke elicited my more serious and thoughtful side, Dan my more laid-back and carefree one. For months, I missed Younger Luke and our incessant banter, our fits of laughter. Allowing myself to wallow one night this winter, I fell down the rabbit hole of rereading all our correspondence. But when I scrolled through the hundreds of texts and clicked through the dozens of emails, it dawned on me that he wasn't actually all that funny. Brendan was funnier; Greg was way funnier. With Luke—at least in our e-communication—it was often *me* being funny. Being with him somehow made me funnier. And more fun. And instead of missing Younger Luke quite so desperately, I started to miss that version of myself.

Ideally, I'd like to find someone who can bring out all of my *best* parts, or the parts—like humor and curiosity, and candor—that make my day-to-day life the most satisfying. And the years ahead the most satisfying. I'd like to find someone who makes me the me I'd most want to be around.

Perhaps most importantly, this past year proved to me that there *isn't* one One. There are many Ones who can make you happy—you just need the timing to work out. And timing can be an irritable and erratic thing. I wouldn't have been interested in Paul or Younger Luke if I'd met their younger incarnations. And yet at various points earlier this year I was intensely drawn to Paul and would have given anything to be loved by Younger Luke. If Dan had been in a different point in his life when we met (or if I had been), would our instant ease and chemistry have meant more? Could it have fueled a functional relationship?

Part of the ease and fun of *Match.com* dating was knowing that when one chapter ended, another was waiting to begin with the click of a button. But perhaps I need to admit that, like my relationships with each of these men, my relationship with *Match.com*, too, has run its course. Though I don't know the specifics of how, when, or where, I think it's time again to try my hand at something new. As I explained to Younger Luke with my Pachinko theory, it's all about making the most of where you land. And with a new neighborhood—albeit less than three miles from my old one—and a new job—albeit one with some uncertainties attached, I can't help but wonder if I've pushed my Pachinko marble over to a new set of pegs. I'm eager to see which path it takes next.

My cursor hovers over the DELETE button, and I click.

Acknowledgments

The world is big and I am small. Where to begin?

The genesis of this book began as a list of dating experiences scrawled on the back of a cocktail napkin. At drinks with my sister, Elenna, and the real-life Nicole, rehashing the details of our latest dates, it was their idea to spin our dating lives into Alison's novel. Granted it took a few years, but everything in these pages still derives from that fateful napkin. This novel would be zero pages long were it not for them.

This novel might also still reside on my hard drive were it not for my ever-thoughtful, tireless agent Jennifer Chen Tran, who has championed me and this book from day one, and who helped sculpt Alison and her narrative arc in ways immeasurable. Of course, I feel exceptionally lucky that Jennifer landed Amy Singh as my editor. I couldn't have imagined collaborating with an editor who so thoroughly supported and furthered the threads and themes of this book. Suggestions and edits, both minor and major, always felt carefully considered and expertly instructive. Thanks also to Alex Hess, Chelsey Emmelhainz, and the Skyhorse team for turning this manuscript into a beautiful book and for spearheading its production, and to Michelle Richter of Fuse Literary for shepherding the book through the final phases.

Like Alison, my dating life's been filled with many heady highs and a few relative lows. Heartfelt thanks go to the nonfictional roommates, the Friday BYOB girls, and the real-life Mom, Dad, and Ben—all of whom helped me always find humor in the situations at hand and reminded me that even if you need to sit in your room and play Coldplay on loop for weeks, one day you won't need to anymore. I hope that I am half the friend and familial rock to each of you that you are to me.

I am grateful to Dana Bate, Lauren Miller, Dave White, Sarah Dickman, and Lanie Davis for advising on the trajectory from Word file to book. And I am amazed by the interest level and patience of the many friends who were unflagging in their enthusiasm to talk through plot points and narrative arc: Aleks, Elizabeth, Jane, Ashley, Blaire, Megan, Anna, Emma, Joel, Adam, Jenny, and Justine.

Writing these pages was sheer joy, motivated in a large part by my most avid fan and first reader, who kept asking when he'd get to hear the next chapter. To Jason, *merci encore et encore et encore*. I was similarly propelled forward by the encouragement and eagerness of my first editors, Mom and Elenna. As with my high school newspaper articles, my college thesis, and countless job applications and wedding toasts ever since, your edits have been transformative and invaluable. Also, Mom wants me to clarify that she's slightly less overbearing than Alison's mom.